MAVERICK

IN THE COMPANY OF SNIPERS
Book 9

IRISH WINTERS

COPYRIGHT

MAVERICK; In the Company of Snipers, 9

Copyright ©2015 by Irish Winters
All rights reserved

First Edition

This is a work of fiction. Names, characters, dialogues, places, and incidents either are the product of the author's imagination or are used fictitiously. Any resemblance to actual events, locales, or persons, living or dead, is entirely coincidental. The publisher does not have any control over and does not assume responsibility for author or third-party websites or their content.

No part of this book may be reproduced, scanned, or distributed in any printed or electronic form without permission. Please do not participate in or encourage piracy of copyrighted materials in violation of the author's rights. Purchase only authorized editions.

Cover design and author photo by Kelli Ann Morgan,
http://www.inspirecreativeservices.com

Interior book design by Bob Houston eBook Formatting

Editor: Lauren McKellar, McStellar editing,
http://mcstellarediting.blogspot.com

Editor: Katie Johnson, katiestefan333@gmail.com

ISBN Paperback: 978-1-942895-15-2
ISBN eBook: 978-1-942895-16-9
Library of Congress Number: 2015951242

Irish Winter's author website is http://www.irishwinters.com
or irishwinters.blogspot.com

In the Company of Snipers

You can find Irish Winters on Facebook:
https://www.facebook.com/author.irishwinters

On Twitter: https://twitter.com/irishwinters1

For news on upcoming releases, sign up for Irish Winters' Newsletter at IrishWinters.com.

For more information about all my books, visit IrishWinters.com.

IN THE COMPANY OF SNIPERS

This series revolves around ex-Marine scout sniper, Alex Stewart, and his covert surveillance company, The TEAM, home-based out of Alexandria, Virginia. An obsessive patriot and workaholic, he created the company to give ex-military snipers like him a chance at returning to civilian life with a decent job.

This is not a serial with each book ending at a cliffhanger. I wouldn't do that to you. *In the Company of Snipers* is a collection of passionate love stories involving women and men who are tough enough to take on the world alone. Each is a stand-alone read, where in the course of an active TEAM operation, one agent comes face to face with his or her demons. The men and women I write about are all patriots and warriors, dealing with what they've lived through or the mistakes they've made

Spoiler alert: Every novel contains adult scenes including sexual situations (some explicit), language, and violence. I don't write sweet romance, so be forewarned.

At the end of each story, it's my hope that you, along with my heroes, will come to realize...

Love changes everything.

Chapter One

Pretty girl.

She looked too young to be riding that large horse, but up she went through the new grass, rippling in lime-green waves across the steep mountainside. At least Maverick called it a mountain. Who knew? People in Wyoming called everything a hill. Maybe that was all it was.

He'd heard her before he saw her, which only made him curious. She'd called the animal beneath her Star as she'd charged by, praising him while he dutifully grunted uphill. Already lathered with sweat, her steed sounded more like a pig than a horse. His grunt was why Maverick bothered to look in the first place. A wild pig would've made a few tasty meals. A horse? Not so much.

The warm morning sun warmed his aching shoulders after the cool night sleeping on the—hill. He had just rolled his sleeping bag for another day's travel and stood to stretch the stiffness away before he got back to the work at hand. Walking.

His old guitar rested against the bag, ready to go. The sight of a delicate woman on horseback, her denim-covered legs hugging the animal's massive body as they flew upward and onward, soothed Maverick. It called to his soul of all things wild and free. Of no holds barred. Of hope. Of all the reasons he had walked halfway across the continent in the first place. For a moment, all was right with the world.

Life used to be different. He could've stayed employed and privileged in Virginia. Paid too much. Worked too little. His boss had surely tried to talk him out of leaving.

"You'll always have a job here, son," Alex Stewart had said at their final handshake.

Maverick respected Alex and his TEAM like few others, but the need to leave the past behind called. Sick and tired, his heart ached as deeply as his life sucked. He had returned the hard man's grip, sublet his apartment and didn't look back.

Two good pairs of work boots got him a long way from the Potomac River of Northern Virginia. It would have helped if he knew where he meant to end up when he first put the soles of those boots to the asphalt, but truth was? He didn't. Didn't even think. Just walked.

He learned the rules of the road the hard way. Most big-rig truckers could be trusted. Not all. Kansas sucked in the dead of winter. Big time. The interstates meant Highway Patrol. While most troopers went out of their way to be helpful, some thought they owned the road and the people on it. The back roads meant common folks who looked out for each other. Not always, but most of the time.

Nebraska resembled his home state of Ohio in a lot of ways. The standing fields of corn, for one. The football mania didn't hurt, either. Huskers Red, the color of the University of Nebraska's intercollegiate football team, blossomed everywhere. Like a plague. Almost as bad as the blazing red of their nemesis and their better, Maverick's home team, the Ohio State Buckeyes, *God bless 'em.*

A splash of the morning breeze in his face drew Maverick back to the hillside with its unexpected view. He didn't know much about horses, but it seemed this reddish-brown fellow wasn't the usual breed for running. The big guy would've been better suited for a plow or wagon, harnessed up and pulling beer. He made a magnificent but massive sight, maybe because the rider on his back was so small.

She rode bareback. Her legs spread wide to accommodate the girth of the horse, her fingers buried in the black ruffles of his mane. They moved as one, her head tucked into his neck, her long, black hair blending with his mane in the wind. Damned magical.

What man wouldn't stop to watch? Peace instilled into Maverick's whole being at the sight of those two creatures in sync with each other and nature. It didn't take much to imagine Star as a unicorn with a lovely fairy on his back. Looked like she had wings. Looked like she and that horse were flying.

Yeah, right. He turned away. The horse had no glittery horn sticking out of that big head. The girl had no wings. Magic was for little kids. If there ever were such a thing, it lay dead and buried on another grassy hillside called Arlington National Cemetery. His path lay elsewhere, somewhere along the highway below, not in the morning light on the hill.

Until Star screamed.

Maverick jolted around in time to catch sight of the horse rearing up, front hooves flailing and the ground collapsing beneath him. Another blood-curdling scream rent the morning peace and over the edge of the hill he slid, taking his elfin rider down with him in a cloud of red dust.

And God, Maverick couldn't run fast enough to the edge of the rift, his heart thundering while rocks and earth settled below. A clean, half-moon cut of the hill he thought was solid rock had dropped into the ravine below.

Billowing dust obscured the sight, but not the screams of what had to be a dying horse. As terrifying as it sounded, Star's squeal amongst the rattle of sliding stones and dirt meant he and the girl might still be alive.

Maverick doubted it. Life was an unfair gift, ripped away without warning. He stepped off the edge anyway, his boots scraping yard-long steps while he half-stumbled, half-slid on his butt the rest of the way. Panic hurried him, panic that he would arrive too late. That he couldn't help once he got there. That God had played another damned, cruel joke.

He kept going, at last able to distinguish a toss of dark mane through the dust-laden air. It took seconds to get to Star. A screaming, snorting demon had replaced the magical unicorn. No sign of the girl.

"Steady boy." Maverick soothed the animal as he approached from above. *Well, that makes two of us.* How could he soothe a horse scared out of its wits when his own heart was jackhammering?

The way Star had slid downhill had worked to his benefit. He had lain into the slide instead of fighting it and ended up buried on his left side more than his right. It had also prevented him from tumbling end-over-end. Nonetheless, his legs and belly and left side were encased in red sandy dirt. Only his head and neck and the barest part of his broad back cleared the rubble.

No sign of the girl. Damn. This was no rescue. Only a body recovery. Maverick's stomach pitched at the thought. He forced a swallow. *Not again.*

Still standing above the horse, he crouched and placed his hand on the horse's neck. Star tossed his head, bared his teeth and—growled? That was a first, but then what animal wouldn't growl when confronted by the scumbag who just might have yanked the earth out from beneath him?

"Take it easy, big fella. Just here to help." Maverick stretched a hand to that big, whiskered nose, half-afraid the gnashing, grunting animal with flared, wide nostrils might bite his fingers off.

Star didn't. He nickered, stretched his nose and bumped Maverick's palm as if he wanted another touch. Good enough. Maverick slid alongside the horse's head, searching for signs of cuts or blood. "It's okay to be scared. That was a helluva ride you just took, big guy."

As if in answer, Star bowed his head. A shudder raced over him. An unexpected communication passed from horse to man. This horse was in better shape than Maverick expected. Scared maybe, but damned spunky. Both good signs. Maybe the rider had fared as well?

Hope flickered to life again.

God, I hope so.

He stepped away from Star and slid farther down the ravine, studying the loose ground for signs of a body as he descended. An arm. An exposed hand. A boot. Anything.

She has to be here.

A noise caught his ear. Maverick cocked his head to listen better. Star still wheezed and snorted, but this voice was more human. Softer. Feminine. He climbed back above the horse, planted his boots and stilled, needing with every last particle of his weary soul to find a living, breathing woman instead of a broken body.

The murmur again. A patch of dirt shifted a few yards up from Star. *There she is.* Maverick ran to her, so damned glad for small blessings. With careful fingers, he brushed the dirt from her head. A web of thick, black hair, now mingled with plenty of dirt, encased her face. He tugged it clear of her eyes, nose and mouth, his poor damned heart hammering against his ribs at her good fortune.

"You're going to be okay," he lied because that was what first responders were supposed to do. Offer encouragement no matter how bad the injuries. Make the victim believe they were going to make it. "Hold still. Let me get you out of here."

He scraped more dirt. Uncovered her button-up blouse. Cut-off jeans. One cowboy boot. One bare foot. Her limbs seemed intact. A bloody scrape marked her forehead over her left eye, but no other injuries were obvious.

A groan lifted from her throat.

"Tell me what hurts, ma'am." He tried to get her to speak, mentally diagnosing the possible internal injuries she might have sustained. He didn't want to move her if he didn't have to. Broken backs or necks were invisible death sentences for trauma victims. Helping her might kill her. He needn't have worried.

"Star!" She snapped upright so quickly that he damned near knocked heads with her.

"Now hold on." He grabbed her forearms and leveled her back to the ground. "You need to stay still."

She planted her elbows behind her and pushed him off. "Who the hell are you?"

"You're hurt. You can't just jump up and—"

The prettiest dark blues glared up at him. "The hell I can't."

Maverick didn't argue. No sense in it. He stabbed his Oakleys tight to his nose and sat back on the hill, not sure why he cared if she was hurt or not. She obviously didn't.

The woman rolled to her side, shook her head to free the dirt in her hair, and didn't stop moving until she crouched at her horse's head, smoothing her fingers over his big, long face. "My poor baby."

Damned if he didn't nicker some kind of horse-speak back at her. She pressed her forehead to his, her hands cupped around his big ears. "Don't worry. I'll get you out of here."

Oh yeah? You and what man's army?

The big guy calmed. Who wouldn't, the way she cooed all over his face?

Great. Guess I'm the army.

Maverick slid his butt down to the next job of the day, unearthing a very large equine with big, white teeth and doing it quickly. He had other places to be. This wasn't one of them.

The woman glanced up at him from her love affair with her horse. "What are you doing?"

He pushed a mound of loose dirt over Star's back and down the hill. The big guy peered at him while the disaster turned into a simple excavation. Hopefully.

"I asked what you think you're doing?" She swiped more dirt from the corner of her eyes, waiting for an answer.

"Digging."

"I can see that."

Then why'd you ask?

She scrambled below Star. It didn't seem to bother her that she'd lost one boot. "Do you think we can move all this dirt? Just the two us?"

Another obvious question. He let his actions speak for themselves and pushed another load of dirt over Star. The woman scooped it away with both hands clasped together to form a decent-sized human shovel. He pushed. She pulled. It worked. Enough said.

After Star's back and most of his topside were cleared, she took a breather, pushing that mop of hair over her shoulder. "Howdy, stranger. I'm China Wolf."

"Maverick Carson." He offered a half-salute and decided right then and there it had to go. No more salutes. No more *yes sir, no sir*, either. Didn't know why the automatic response even surfaced after all these months on the road.

She stuck her hand out. "Nice to meet you, Maverick Carson. You related to Kit?"

He reached across Star to return the handshake. "No, ma'am."

China Wolf had a firm grip, something most woman didn't. She stayed sprawled across Star's belly, catching her breath and fiddling with his mane. Her gaze strayed to the wide-open spaces around them. "Mind if I ask what you're doing out here in the middle of nowhere?"

"Walking." He brushed a hand through his hair, surprised at the amount of dirt on his head and wondering where on this damned hill he had lost his ball cap. A guy could get a helluva sunburn without decent cover.

Besides, the reason for this damned long walk lay tucked inside that simple baseball cap. A photo of him and his baby brother in some godforsaken desert a long way from home. Both in cammies. Both with big, shit-eating grins. One half-memory. One half-ghost. Maverick hadn't figured out which one he was yet. At least he hadn't lost his Oakleys, his first line of self-defense against the world that had crapped all over him.

China eyed him. "You one of those crazy guys who decides to hitchhike across the country for no damned reason?"

He doffed his leather jacket. "Something like that."

She resumed her task, too. Star stilled. For a while, Maverick and China were nothing but a sweaty, human backhoes, the morning sun a relentless taskmaster and climbing higher in the sky.

She brushed one hand over her forehead. "Whew. I don't know if we can do this. It's a lot of dirt." She scrambled back to Star's long face again. "How's my pretty boy doing?"

Maverick couldn't stand to watch the mugging and kissing. He looked away. This woman really liked her horse, but damn it to hell. They were miles from anywhere and trapped in a ravine where cell coverage couldn't reach. He grabbed his jacket and half-slid, half-walked down the hill to the stand of aspen below. All those green trees and shrubbery wouldn't be thriving without water.

"Hey. Where are you going?" she called after him.

He didn't answer. No sense leading her on if this harebrained idea proved fruitless. Fortunately, a stream gurgled at the crook of the ravine just as he had hoped.

Maverick zipped his jacket, tied the sleeves together as tightly as he could, and improvised a water jug of sorts. Laying the leather bag into the stream, he let it fill. It leaked like a sieve until he cinched the collar and rolled it tight. Tried again. Damn thing worked. Well, mostly. In minutes, he was uphill again with a leaking leather jug that turned his ragged jeans to muddy streaks. It cooled him, along with the breeze on his sweaty back.

The big horse twitched his nose at the scent of water. Star wasted no time ducking his snout into the improvised bucket. "How much should I let him drink?" Maverick asked.

A pretty smile tweaked China's lips. "I don't think you've got enough water in there to hurt him. He's a big horse. Let him have all he wants."

Star slurped and sucked. Between his thirst and the water leaking between Maverick's fingers, it didn't take long before the water was gone. Star pulled his face up from the leather and snorted. The animal seemed to understand Maverick was there to help, but time was ticking. He tossed his soggy jacket aside and resumed excavation.

By then China had wandered down to the trees. *Probably needs to pee.*

Maverick concentrated on the dirt impacted at Star's front legs, hoping that once he got them loose, he would know for sure if there were injuries to be dealt with. Some horses needed to be put down when they broke a leg. Of course, he didn't know much about that kind of stuff. Never really wanted to until now.

He scratched behind his big buddy's ears. Star lifted his nose and nickered softly. "You like that, don't you? Sure hope you're okay, big fella. You've been buried too long."

"You haven't been around horses much, have you?"

Great. Caught talking to her horse. I'm as bad as she is.

Maverick glanced over his shoulder. "Nope."

China handed him a short but sturdy branch and a baseball-sized rock. "I don't know if this will work, but if we pound these sticks into the dirt, we could loosen the impacted dirt quicker."

Made sense. He took the stick she offered and complied with her wishes. She seemed a very practical woman. That said a lot about China Wolf in his book. The primitive tools worked.

China labored along Star's rear quarters until Maverick uncovered a bloody gash dead center of Star's broad chest. Damn it. Bleeding, too. "You'd better come see at this. He's hurt. Looks bad."

Maverick edged away from Star to make room for China. Star had dozed off, the crazy animal. He kept on with his nap while China examined him. Briefly. With a quiet grunt, she wiped her bloodied fingers on her jeans, scooted back to the horse's hindquarters and continued digging.

"Well?"

"Well, what?"

"Don't you want to clean it or something? I can haul more water."

She pounded the pointed end of her stick into the hard earth and twisted it. "No. He's okay."

"It's deep and it's bleeding."

"I know. I saw it. He's fine."

Maverick shook his head. "Whatever. He's your horse."

China stopped digging. She leaned onto her butt and pushed her hair out of her eyes for the umpteenth time. Sweat glistened on her face and ran down her neck. Ringlets of frizzy hair spiraled at all angles. The bright sunshine overhead didn't help. Her ruddy cheeks didn't fit with the fairytale mystique he had imagined earlier.

She blew out a big breath and licked her lips. If anything, she resembled a lizard, parched and on the verge of sunstroke. Not an elfin fairy at all. The last thing he would call her was good looking. Tolerable, maybe. At a distance. After a few tequila shooters.

She sighed. "This is the deal, Maverick. You're right. Star is a horse. He's not human. Horses are tougher than us, especially this guy. His hide's thicker. His bones are harder and stronger. He's got a higher pain threshold than we do. That cut you found isn't that bad. He'll be fine. Trust me."

Maverick let the argument go. *Not my problem.*

"I'll clean the scratch when we get home. You'll see. He'll be okay."

No, I won't see. I'll be gone. Maverick smoothed his palm over the mane hanging over Star's face. Damned if a rumbling sound didn't lift up from the horse's throat. Sounded as if he purred. The simple vibration soothed Maverick, too. He scratched more dirt from behind Star's ears, wishing he could do more for this gentle-tempered beast, especially since his owner didn't seem to care.

China took a deep breath and rested, her hands stuck in the dirt behind her like a tripod. "Never thought the hill would cave in like this. Must've been all the spring rains we had."

Maverick had no idea why the hillside had shifted. It just did. No sense talking about it.

It was a beautiful place to sit for a spell, though. Remote. Secluded. Even the slide had brought a splash of color to this wild country called Wyoming. The red gash that capricious Mother Nature had deemed necessary in her morning gardening, contrasted beautifully against the ocean of green grass.

The only problem was the lazy horse napping in the middle of it. Said horse seemed able to read Maverick's mind.

With one of those pig-like grunts, he nudged his nose onto Maverick's thigh. Before Maverick knew it, he had a lap full of horse head, twitchy ears, and whiskers.

"What brings you to Wyoming?" China asked.

He shrugged at her gentle inquisition and cast his gaze to the mountains to the west even while he scratched behind Star's ears. There was no good answer. It was simply what bums like him did. They walked until they had a reason to stop. Why Wyoming? It was as good a place as any.

"You need a job?" she asked when he didn't answer.

"No, ma'am. I don't." That much he knew for sure. He already had a job. Walking. Leaving. Getting as far as possible—away. He would be content to be on his way when this random act of kindness was done. Getting Star back on his feet was work enough.

"Just thought I'd ask." China pushed to her knees. "We don't get many good men just passing through, and you look like you could use a hand up. Are you lost, or do you know where you're going?"

Good question—one he hadn't figured out the answer to yet. He was lost when he started walking. Damned lost. And sometimes the quiet beat of steady footfalls on concrete highways and byways convinced him he might have found himself again. But all he had to do was draw too close to civilization to know better. He wasn't lost, but neither was he found. Whatever he was looking for was still *that a way*. Farther west. Any place else but here.

"At least let me offer you a warm meal and a shower when we're done." She dusted her palms against her jeans. "It's not much, but you look like you can use both."

Right on cue, Star bumped Maverick's hand with his nose. The animal seemed to be waiting on an answer.

China seemed earnest enough. "Come on, Mr. Carson. Take a chance on me. I'm not too bad a cook. I promise I'll wash my hands first."

"I can't stay." Maverick tossed a glance at her without really seeing her. Eye contact with a woman could be fatal. *Any guy knows that.*

"Who said anything about staying? I'm just asking you to eat one meal." She climbed down from the high ground above Star. "Let's see if he'll get off his lazy butt, shall we?"

Maverick pushed to his feet and stepped out of her way. *This oughta be good.*

She grasped the horse's halter, shook the dirt off, and with a tender caress to Star's wide cheek, China tugged. "Come on, baby boy. Break's over. We've got a long walk home."

He grunted, pulled those two massive front hooves from the loose dirt, and damned if he didn't scramble up with a snort. He shook like a dog. A really big dog. Dirt shuddered off his flanks. It rolled off his mane. He staggered a moment before he caught sure footing.

Maverick took another full step back. *Holy hell.* The breadth and height of this horse was nothing short of tremendous. Star towered over his mistress, his chest at least four times as wide as she was. Maybe more. Hell, he towered over Maverick, too.

Maverick brushed more dirt off Star's wide rump, revealing another jagged wound. "You probably don't care, but he's got a cut on his rear end, too."

Both China and Star turned to look at him. Damned if those two semi-interested faces didn't almost crack a smile on Maverick's mouth. Almost.

China investigated. "That's nothing. His big butt has already snagged every nail, splinter, or barbed wire in the county. We'll just get out the old *Preparation H* when we get home, huh, big fella?" she said as she stroked Star's long nose.

"Preparation H?"

A mischievous smile lit China's face. "Sure. It tightens more than just assholes."

Maverick had no answer to that interesting info byte. *Preparation H? For horses? Who would have thought?*

She pinned him with an appraising stare, her hand stuck out for another handshake. "Now, are you going to join me for dinner or is this goodbye?"

He raked a hand through his hair and looked west. The song of the lonesome road called up to him from the ravine. *You have other places to be. You're not done walking. Not by a long shot. And yet...*

"A home-cooked meal would be nice," he admitted as he accepted her hand. The words were no more than out of his mouth when Star swished his lengthy tail, catching Maverick in its wake. He spit and brushed the strands of horsehair off his lips.

China laughed, a pleasant sound under the hot afternoon sun. "Told you he likes you."

Chapter Two

I like him.

Who wouldn't like the handsome stranger who'd just saved her horse's life? But the man didn't talk unless he was spoken to. When she asked questions, most times she didn't get an answer. Just a grunt. China liked that, too, crazy as it sounded. Some men just didn't have much to say.

She had always respected the trait in her father. Jefferson Wolf never needed much in the way of words to communicate, either. Even when he'd died of cancer, their last words were nothing more than, *'Bye. See you around.'*

He had built the Wild Wolf Horse Ranch from the ground up and ran it like the business he meant it to be. The finest Percherons in the west were born and bred there. Ask anyone. She could trace their bloodlines all the way back to *Diligence* himself, the first imported Percheron stallion successfully bred in the country.

Instrumental in preserving the breed, the Wild Wolf was more than just a horse ranch and a business to China. It was her life and pure joy. She lived the Wild Wolf. Breathed it. Intended on dying for it if the good Lord asked.

It took most of the day to free Star and walk home. It hadn't helped that she'd lost one of her boots in the fall and had to walk home barefoot. The sun was low in the west by the time they strolled beneath the Wild Wolf sign hung over the end of her long gravel drive. It branched off the highway, Devil's Tower to the east, Yellowstone to the west. Stuck between heaven and hell, her father used to say. No place better.

Maverick hadn't said two words while he'd trailed behind Star's big caboose. Even his dirty baseball cap gave nothing away. Black with a gold logo on it: The TEAM. *Boring.* He had slung his backpack and guitar over his shoulder, pulled the brim of his cap low over his eyes, always gazing west as if he had other places to be.

China suspected he didn't. When he wasn't holed up behind his dark glasses, the man had a far-off stare. It didn't take a genius to put that stare and the Marine Corps jacket he had so willingly transformed into a water jug, together. She had seen the same look on her father's face the few times he had talked about the war in Vietnam. The veteran's stare—not so much seeing anything as reliving long past tragedies, remembering ghosts, regretting things that couldn't be changed and trying to find a way to move on.

Maverick was all tomcat straggly. Scruffy. Maybe homeless, too. His clothes were shabby, and the soles of his boots worn thin. Like him. No doubt he would gulp his dinner and bolt for the road the first chance he got.

"You're welcome to use the shower in the bunkhouse." She nodded toward the log cabin-style building across the yard. "The guys went into town for supplies, so it's empty.

You'll find clean towels on the bathroom shelf. It's got a washer and dryer, too. Help yourself."

"Thanks." He ambled past her and Star, and darn it anyway, she had to look twice. The man beneath those dirty denims walked like a gunslinger. A little bowlegged. Lazy. As if no one could make him do what he didn't want to do. *Don't ask. Don't even try.*

A funny feeling caught at the back of her throat watching his dusty butt. Trim. Tight. Not baggy and saggy like most guys' backsides. She swallowed hard and walked Star into the barn, needing to get her mind off the ass of that moody man on his way to what might be his first shower in a few days.

Star, she understood. All he needed was a good brushing, a rubdown, and maybe a handful of grain. But Maverick? Another animal all together. He might benefit from a good meal and a hot shower, but the look in his eyes when she had offered a simple handshake declared there would be no rubdown. No camaraderie, either. This guy radiated *'leave me alone'* in bright, radioactive neon.

It didn't take long to get Star settled and cared for. By the time China finished cleaning his minor wounds and doctoring him, Maverick returned.

Holy smokes. He cleaned up damned good.

She looked twice again. Dark hair, wet, but nicely parted and combed. Rugged good looks. Intense dark eyes with no hint of a smile. He looked more like a roughneck from the oil fields when she'd first opened her eyes to him on the hillside, but showered and dressed in what was probably his last clean shirt, he was worth looking at. Clean-shaven chin. His sunglasses folded and stowed in his shirt pocket for a change.

Her nostrils flared. It didn't hurt that he smelled like soap.

Coffee brown eyes hit her with—what? Insolence? Hostility? Dislike?

An odd mix of emotions shifted in those dark depths. He would've scared her with that ornery lift of his upper lip if she hadn't experienced kindness at his hand.

"Tell me what you need done around here," he said by way of greeting, his thumb tucked inside his belt buckle.

"Me? Nothing right now." She floated a stable blanket over Star's back. Her motherly side allowed a little wriggle room to coddle her one-ton, baby boy just this once with a covering for the night. He didn't need it as much as she needed to do it for him. "How about you? What do you need?"

"I can clean stalls, pitch hay, anything you need, ma'am." Maverick seemed so earnestly intent on working for his supper.

"No. You've done enough for one day." She placed her hand on his forearm in a friendly gesture, but even that didn't breach the barrier erected around him. He was a tough one, this Maverick Carson who wasn't related to Kit. He stiffened, so she pulled back and gave him his space. "Besides, it's dinnertime. You don't need to get dirty the first minute you're clean. Do you like chicken?"

"Yes, ma'am." He closed the barn door while she led the way to the ranch house.

"Good. You grill while I shower. You do know how to grill, don't you?"

"Yeah. I cook," he muttered.

She'd glanced sideways at him and honestly, her breath caught. This guy was hands-down the handsomest man she had laid eyes on in ages. His hair needed a trim the way it curled under his ears and at the nape of his neck. But those unsmiling eyes, fixed on the horizon, already looking ahead and beyond? Yeah. He was sullen from the ground up. But damned beautiful.

She knew good bloodlines, and this guy had them in aces. He carried himself with pride and strength; his shoulders squared but tense, as if he trusted no one. He looked ready to fight, like he could take on the world at the drop of a hat.

The thick fringe of lashes bracketing his eyes would've made them seem bigger and brighter if he relaxed enough to smile. Instead, he scowled. The gentle arch of his brows softened the hard line of his jaw, though.

Oddly, that was another thing she liked about him. He was a deadly serious man, nothing like the braggarts and know-it-alls from town.

And polite. He took the porch steps two at a time and opened the squeaky screen door for her. A shiver raced up her spine. A true gentleman lay beneath this brooding exterior. His parents had taught him well.

She nodded once, accepting yet another act of kindness from a man who barely spoke, and whom she didn't know well enough to have invited home for dinner. But there he was. Six-foot-plus, hands washed and hungry.

Once in the kitchen, she pulled the container of marinating chicken from the refrigerator. Handing him the chicken and a platter, she pointed to the back door. "Grill's on the patio. Utensils and lighter, too. I'll be finished showering by the time you're done. Don't burn the wings."

He accepted the assignment without a word or eye contact and headed for the patio with a quick, "Yes, ma'am."

Hurrying to her upstairs bathroom, she locked herself in, not scared so much as cautious. Still, she couldn't resist parting the curtains to steal a peek at the man on the patio.

Grilling fit this Good Samaritan to a T. He attended to it like a sentry on duty and never once looked at the back door. An opportunist could've robbed her blind while she showered. Maybe taken other liberties as well. Not this guy. She knew horseflesh. People flesh, too. Maverick might be a puzzle, but he was not *most men*.

Her shower steamed behind her, but China stalled, the view on her patio more tantalizing than she had expected. Maverick turned the chicken pieces with the tongs. One by one. Carefully. Deliberately. Short bursts of fire flashed up from the grill. He paid attention, moving the thicker pieces to the center, the smaller to the outside where they wouldn't burn.

The man seemed stuck in a military mindset. In between turning and basting, he returned to the same position, his hands clenched behind his back, his feet spread maybe a foot or two apart.

Argh. She tore herself away from the view and pulled the glass shower door open. Reality hit her the second the water poured over her face. She had been so worried about Star that she hadn't given a thought to herself. She did now.

I could've died on that hillside. No one would've known where I was.

Warm water or not, she shivered. If not for that quiet man on her patio right this very minute, she would still be buried, still suffocating while Star languished nearby. He would've died a terrible death.

Oh, Daddy. What have I done?

Her knees turned to jelly. She braced her palms and forehead to the shower tiles as the tears came. *Maverick saved my life today. He didn't have to, but he did. My God, I owe this stranger everything.*

Chapter Three

By the time Maverick delivered the chicken, charred in all the right places, China looked more like a woman again. Her damp hair was pulled into a ponytail snug against the back of her neck. She exuded maturity in everything she did, from the simple clean jeans she wore to the dusty cowboy boots on her feet.

"You want a beer?" she asked at the open refrigerator.

"No, thank you, ma'am."

"Water then?" She snagged a tall-necked bottle for herself and twisted the top off. "I've got milk, too. Juice?"

"Water's fine. I'll get it myself."

He lingered at the kitchen doorway, not sure how much hospitality he dared accept. A woman's world was dangerous territory, not unlike the minefields he had traversed overseas. One wrong step and he could be in a world of hurt.

"You're welcome to have a beer. Don't be shy. Help yourself." She nudged the door shut with her hip and turned back to the stove. "Water glasses are in the cupboard to the left of the sink. Could you hand me that hot pad on the table? I tend to leave 'em everywhere but where I need 'em."

He brought it to her at the stove and filled himself a glass of water. Still at the sink, he downed the whole thing in a few gulps. He had taken his fill in the bunkhouse shower, too. A man never knew how long a dry spell might last.

"Thanks." She grasped the handles on the boiling pan with the hot pads and emptied the steaming contents into a colander in the sink. "Carrots are done. Let's eat."

He held her chair for her. When she finally settled, he took the opposite chair, wishing he were back on the road. Small talk sucked and he had never been good at it.

China passed a plate of thick-sliced bread. "Like I said before, I don't get many visitors. Hope you don't mind simple food. It's not much, but it'll stick to your bones."

He filled his plate, sampling each entrée. Simple? Grilled chicken that tasted like garlic and crushed pepper with a hint of sage? Baked potatoes slathered in butter, sour cream, and chives? Parsley carrots, still crisp and crunchy? A cucumber salad doused with onions, vinegar, salt, and pepper? Nothing simple about it. More like heaven to a man who'd spent the last two months traipsing across western Nebraska to get to Nowhere, Wyoming.

He dug in. Life on the road was tough, with good meals few and far between. Something about China's brand of simple soothed him all the way to his soul. Her house reflected the same. Clean. Orderly. Not decorated for show as much as utility.

An antlered deer head hung over the stone fireplace in her living room, no doubt killed for the venison it provided instead of sport. Looked like a twelve-point buck from where he sat.

A lever-action Henry rifle stood in the corner behind the kitchen door, another sign of the practical nature of this woman. She meant to protect herself. Good on her.

The wooden cabinet in the dining room held fishing poles and a wicker creel. A stack of books covered an end table next to a couch beneath a collection of portraits. The wood floors were polished and clean.

Even her yard was neat and tidy. A small vegetable garden told him exactly where the carrots he was eating had come from. Red-and-black speckled chickens roamed free. And that black metal birdbath with the prancing black horse statue just off her front porch? Had to be copper. One of a kind. *Like China.*

No men's boots lingered near the back door. He hoped that meant an angry husband or boyfriend wouldn't show up and challenge him before he had finished eating. She was right. He was hungry, and he didn't want to be disturbed. Home-cooked beat fast food and spit-roasted rabbit any day.

Maverick wiped his mouth with his napkin and tried to show an interest in something besides stuffing his face and leaving. "How long have you lived here?"

"All my life." She sliced the chicken breast on her plate with a steak knife. Her fingers were delicate—not what he had expected. Her nails were clean and trimmed and—natural. Dainty. "How about you? Where's home?"

"Virginia, last year." He stabbed another drumstick from the platter. *Damned if I know where tomorrow.*

"You're a Marine," she said with certainty.

"Yes, ma'am." He filled his mouth, hoping to forestall the inevitable question. It didn't.

"Where?"

He took a long minute to swallow before he answered, shrugging for nonchalance and hoping for an end to the gentle interview. "Afghanistan. Iraq. South America. The usual."

"Kandahar?"

He nodded with a quick blink. Yeah. Kandahar. Camp Leatherneck. Helmand Province. Lashkar Gah. That rat bastard, Mullah Mamood. Just the thought of the psychotic Taliban commander pitched acid up his throat, spoiling the quiet pleasure of eating at a kind woman's kitchen table. Maverick took a long drink of water, wishing it washed the last two years away. Every last damned memory.

They ate the rest of dinner in silence. The food was good, but the lack of a television or radio made China's house uncomfortably quiet. He shifted his boots beneath the table. Restless. Time to be gone.

"Thank you."

He looked up from his empty plate. Her quiet comment surprised him. He shrugged. "No big deal. Couldn't let you and the horse just—"

"No. I meant for your military service, Maverick." She lifted her bottle in a toast. "I know it wasn't easy. You've seen and done things the rest of us haven't. Thanks for everything you've sacrificed."

God, not that. His eyes brimmed as quickly as his heart. She meant well, but she had no idea what he had sacrificed. The loss. The sonofabitchin' grief.

He bowed his head, blocking the nausea that always assailed him when good-meaning people thought they needed to say something. His throat clamped shut. Civilians just didn't get it. The decent ones tried, but not a damned one understood how much his country had asked. How much he had freely given. And how much that other nation took.

His kid brother's cocky, know-it-all smirk flashed to mind, and Maverick was done eating. When he didn't join her in the toast, she lowered her hand as if nothing uncomfortable had happened. As if he hadn't just dropped off the face of the Earth like he wished he could have. He gripped his fork and breathed slowly.

China changed the subject. "Star is a Percheron, a draft horse. The British army used horses like him in both World Wars, poor things."

Maverick followed her lead, needing to get his head back to Wyoming and out of Hell. "I've seen pictures. They pulled artillery."

"Yes. They pulled whatever the army needed: artillery, hospital wagons, supplies, just about anything an intelligent, agile animal could handle. Glad those days are done."

"He's a big horse."

Her eyes sparkled. "He is. Almost eighteen hands and a tad over a ton. He's one of my larger geldings on the ranch."

"There's more?"

"Oh, yes." Now her eyes really sparkled. "Ebony is the biggest. He's my pure black stud and comes in at twenty hands. Do you want to meet them after dinner?"

She had used an interesting choice of words. *Meet them* instead of *look at them*, as if they were more than livestock.

"No, thanks. I really shouldn't—"

"Oh, I know. Now you're going to tell me you need to leave, that you shouldn't take advantage of me, or some lame excuse like that. Am I right?"

He clamped his lips tight on his version of that very same, lame excuse. She seemed able to read him like a book. "Just not going to overstay my welcome, ma'am. That's all."

She set her fork down and looked him in the eye. "Good. Then it's settled. We'll take a walk around the ranch before you leave. By then the guys will be back, and I can introduce you."

He stalled accepting her lengthy agenda for the rest of the day. "I need to be on the road before dark."

"And I need you to meet my ranch hands, Zeke and Xavier. Course I just call them Z and X. They're a little on the eccentric side, but they'll give you a lift into town if you're headed west."

He pursed his lips. This woman might just be as stubborn as he was. "Okay."

She smiled as if they'd just struck a deal. "Great! Besides, I want to show off my kids. You'll like them."

He doubted that, but oh well. If that was what she wanted to do, let it begin and be done. He helped her clear the table and stored the leftover chicken in the refrigerator, while she filled the sink with hot soapy water and left the dishes to soak.

China escorted him across her yard to the rear of her weathered, gray barn and right out the back door into a metal-railed corral. Split-rail fencing lined the field beyond for miles in either direction. Shadows stretched from the windrow of cottonwoods west of her house, casting columns of shade over the yard.

Again, peace wound across his shoulders and down his back. This place felt isolated, pleasantly removed from the rest of the world, and once again, he felt at ease.

She secured the corral gate behind them. The opposite gate stood wide open to the field. "Listen. They're on their way. Can you hear them?"

He cocked his head. The distant *clomp-clomp* of heavy feet and the quiet nickering of different equine voices drifted closer. "They know to come home every night?"

She climbed to the top rung of the metal fence. "Every once in a while one of them decides to take the long way home, but most times they're right on schedule. Come on. Hop up here with me. Let's see what they do when they meet you."

There was that word again. *Meet.* Not *see.*

Maverick hooked one boot on the lower rail and joined her while Star whinnied from the barn.

"Did you hear that? Star wants to be out here with us." China peered behind her. "Horses like people. Least, mine do." Another long drawn out nicker coaxed from within the barn. "Ha! He's so spoiled. Thinks if he keeps chatting me up, I'll let him come out and play."

The big guy did seem to be asking. The more he whinnied, the more she smiled. Maverick averted his gaze, not falling for that again. "Why can't he come out?"

"It's not that he can't. I just want him to take it easy after what he's been through. He's a big boy, but that slide was a big deal. I'm treating it like whiplash. Sometimes a person doesn't know they're hurt until a couple days after a car accident. I want to be sure he's okay before I let him run with the herd."

"How many?"

"Twenty-two at the moment, more on the way."

"You keep all of them in the barn?"

"Only at night. The world's a mixed up place anymore. Some creeps spray painted filthy words on one of the mares two ranches west of here. Guess they thought it was funny. Another guy's Arabian stallion had its tail and mane hacked off. So, yeah, my kids come home every night."

"The barn's that large?"

She nodded at the weathered building. "Could be bigger. It's crowded right now, but it'll do."

"How are you feeling?" He could've bit his tongue off for blurting that question out like he—cared. He didn't. Not really. If nothing else, China Wolf exuded strength and confidence. Still, the place was big. What'd she do? Work it all by herself?

China brushed his concern aside. "Me? I'm fine. How about you?"

"Good." Wasn't that what guys were supposed to say? Besides, he had a feeling he and China were both too tough to admit when they were hurt. She still hadn't admitted to the scuffmark on her forehead, though she had spread some salve on it.

The sound of hooves on hard-packed dirt drew nearer. In seconds, galloping draft horses, their heads held high with manes tossing in the breeze, zeroed in on the gate. Most were the same reddish-brown with black manes as Star, but one was nearly pearlescent with a white mane, the dappling on its hide nearly imperceptible. A glossy, coal black fellow with a coat that glistened in the early evening light galloped in. It had to be China's boy, Ebony.

Once they reached the open livestock gate, they bumped and jockeyed until all entered in a fairly reasonable order. That many large animals milling inside the smaller corral made Maverick nervous, but not China. She dropped over the rail and walked straight into the mass of horseflesh.

Crossing the corral, she secured the outside gate with a chain. She had no more than turned around when the white horse bumped her shoulders, nickering in greeting and nudging her forward.

China turned into the animal's big face with a happy smile. "Hey, you. Come here, Gorgeous. There's someone I want you to meet."

The horse followed without China latching onto its halter. The minute it saw Maverick, it planted its feet, tossed its considerably long mane and blew out a loud snort. Its long tail swished over its back. Another unicorn if ever he had seen one. All it needed was a glittery horn. Or wings.

"Oh, knock it off." China hooked her fingers through the horse's halter and pulled it closer to Maverick. She nodded toward another big fellow that could've passed for Star's twin. "You might want to get down from there and join me. Joker likes to butt folks off the fence."

Maverick stayed put. Somehow being knocked off a fence didn't seem as bad as mixing it up with this herd of burly *kids* that could easily stomp him to death. Every one of these animals was well-muscled with big rumps, thick necks, and broad chests. They reminded him of rowdy Navy SEALs on shore leave. Just needed the dapper shemaghs and Raybans to make 'em look cool.

An evil smile blossomed on China's face. "You aren't scared, are you?"

He slid off the fence.

Grinning, she introduced him to the white horse. "This is Gorgeous, my favorite brood mare. Gorgeous, meet Maverick Carson, and no, he's not related to Kit, so don't ask."

He scowled at this ridiculous conversation, but just as he did, Gorgeous put one hoof forward and lowered her nose to her knee. Her bow complete, she tossed her head and nickered at him.

China stroked the animal's powerful neck, nodding at him. "Go on. Be a good girl. Tell him you like him."

Gorgeous walked toward Maverick, her head bobbing until she came to a stop directly in front of him. He reached for her halter, thinking it might be a good idea to keep her at arm's length. She didn't seem to notice his blocking maneuver. She stepped right up to him and leaned her long horse face into his chest, as if she had a right to be there. Maverick adjusted his stance to accommodate her pushy hug.

And once again he felt the same link he had felt with Star. Peace flooded him right down to his boots. He scratched behind her ears. She nickered. Maverick swallowed hard at the gentleness of the beast beneath his fingertips. This Percheron mare literally towered over him, outweighed him and could just plain stomp him into the ground without any effort, yet there she stood, meek as a lamb and offering—what? Companionship? Welcome? Sure felt like it.

"She likes you, too. I can tell."

Maverick looked up from his quiet communion with the mare. For once, he actually looked China in the eye. The woman grinned, but there was something in the air. Something golden. The low sunlight made her eyes sparkle.

Maverick damned the flood of forgotten feelings her smile brought to mind. He dropped his gaze, searching for something to say that didn't sound too friendly. "Are they all this gentle?"

"Yes, they are, ah... Excuse me?" Another long face leaned over her shoulder, like a kid who wanted his share of attention. This guy's snout was darker than Star's, though, with a thin sliver of white running down the middle of his nose.

"Maverick, meet Sixes, my friendliest boy." China stroked the gentle intruder's nose with both hands. "He aced socialization. That's part of what I do when I break them. All my kids have to be able to stand John Q. Public before I'll let them go. You understand."

Maverick continued to pat the beautiful white creature beneath his hands. Yeah, he understood John Q, the lowest common denominator in the human equation. Basically self-centered. Privileged. Entitled to the freedom he hadn't spilled one drop of blood to defend.

"She bothering you?" China watched with that same sappy look on her face.

"No." He answered too quickly, but he didn't want this horse to move yet. Gorgeous was, well, gorgeous. Handling her seemed a good way to end a day. His tension drained away; his breathing eased. She was living proof there was goodness left in the world, even if it was just in the animal world.

"I'll keep her in the barn from now on. She's not usually this big. Come here. Feel this." Without so much as a by your leave, China grabbed him by the crook of his arm and hauled him back to the horse's rear quarters. She snagged his right hand and shoved it under the mare's big belly, all the way to—

He jerked his hand away. He had just touched the horse's udder. Teats. Wet teats. *Damn it.*

China giggled. "You should see the look on your face."

"Ah, yeah." He wiped the surprise on his pant leg. *Not funny. That was damned rude.*

"Oh, c'mon. It's just horse milk. You're so uptight. Don't you ever smile?" Her eyes glowed at her practical joke, and for the first time since he'd caught sight of China this morning, Maverick did just that. He smiled. Least he meant to. It kind of hurt.

"She's bagging up. It's a good sign. A mare won't leak milk unless her time's real close. Okay now, let's give a listen." China seemed energized around these *kids* of hers. She laid her head against the mare's side, her eyes bright, and—damn it. Everything about her pulled Maverick in. She might not be covered with glitter, but she may as well have been.

He placed both palms to the horse's ribs, not willing to lay his ear against a creature so large. Gorgeous twisted her neck around to watch him.

"Here's a better spot." China moved his hands to where she had just been listening. She grinned up at him, and then he felt it. Something inside the mare moved. He spread his fingers wider. It bumped him again. Wow. A baby horse. A colt. Okay. That was kind of cool.

China made it worse. She laced her fingers with his, pulling them down to the mare's underbelly. The colt moved again, but Maverick felt something else. China's fingers. Small and delicate. Soft and strong. Feminine.

His breath hitched at the innocent contact. She stood way too close to him. Her delicate body too warm. Too full of other things, too. Enthusiasm. Excitement. Life.

His nostrils flared, pulling in the perfume in her hair, the detergent scent of her clean clothes, her breath. He could hear her breathing. Heat filled his body. Heat and blood and a shot of desire, odd sensations for a man as dead as he was. Yet there it was, fire in his veins whether he wanted it or not.

"She's ready to throw her fifth foal. I'll have a new baby by morning." China grinned up deliciously, and, damn, it had to stop.

He untangled his fingers from hers and stepped back. This kind of excitement was the last thing he needed. It was what got a man into trouble, what made him believe in fairy tales and happily ever after. All that crap. Time to leave. The sooner the better.

Crunch, and damn it. Joker's hoof landed on the tip of his boot, nailing Maverick to the ground. He grimaced and pulled at his leg, but Joker didn't move. Not an inch. Didn't even look as if he cared.

"Oh no! Joker. Get off, you big oaf." China attempted to lift Joker's very impressive hoof while Maverick shoved the guy's impressive chest. He had two big handfuls of the horse's pecs or whatever they were called, but it didn't work. When they pushed, Joker leaned forward. When they pulled, he leaned backward. Just enough to keep his hoof in place.

It would've been aggravating if the big guy didn't look away, as if he knew exactly what he was doing. China knew her kids all right. *Joker, huh? Good name.*

Maverick winced at the pressure of this one-ton clown on his toes. To make things worse, the damned horse shifted his weight back and forth. Rocking. This guy thought he was funny.

China burst out laughing, catching Maverick's heart in his throat again. God, her voice tinkled with unabashed joy, like church bells on an early Sunday morning, clear and crisp. Damned if another shockwave of lust didn't ripple up his legs to his groin, filling him to the hilt where no lust should be. He couldn't allow it. He had to leave. Soon. Right damned now.

Get the hell off my foot.

China clapped her hands. "I don't know what it is about you, Maverick Carson, but all of my horses like you."

He gave Joker another heave-ho, but the big horse's body took up all the space, leaving Maverick off balance and with no way to gain leverage.

And there it was, that same sensation of rightness with the world. He gave up and hunkered into Joker's wide chest. When the big oaf hung his head over Maverick's shoulder, he did what any guy would do. He whispered, "I give up. You win."

Just that fast, Joker swished his tail and moseyed over to stand nose-to-butt with Gorgeous.

Maverick wriggled his toes to make sure they weren't broken. They should've been, but now that the pressure was off, they were fine.

"Holy smokes." China stood with her hands on her hips. "I've never seen the likes of this. My kids don't like X and Z as much as they like you. You're a natural." She had an odd look in her eye. Not so much sparkle as—

Time. To. Leave. Move it. Now!

He brushed his hands one last time over Gorgeous's big gentle head, scratched her ears and stepped away. "Thanks for the hospitality, ma'am."

"You're very welcome." She swatted a few extra-large equine backsides on their way out of the corral and back to her porch. "Wait. Before you go—" China stepped inside her front door. When she returned, she handed him a leather jacket very similar to his. "I'm sorry about your jacket. Take this."

He shouldered his pack and replaced his cap. The guitar went over his back, but not the jacket. "No, thanks. I'll be fine. A little water never hurt good leather."

"But it's not dry *now*, is it?" That determined glint snapped to life in her eye. The color drew him in like an F5 tornado out of a thunder-blue sky. *Hmmm, China has the deepest blue eyes.* It took strength to turn away. "For heaven's sake, Maverick. You saved my life. Star's, too. Please take it. It will keep you warm tonight."

"No, ma'am. I'm fine. Really."

"You are one stubborn man, you know that? Nights are still cold this time of year in Wyoming. Take it." She stood there with her arm outstretched, the jacket offered and the demand unanswered, but not withdrawn. This woman expected to be obeyed.

He bit his lip. Handouts were against his rules. Somehow accepting this jacket felt bigger than just accepting hospitality. But obeying her? Yeah. Not going to happen.

"Are you refusing my thank you?" She cocked her head in challenge, probably the same look she gave her horses. Even her voice carried a definite tone of *'how-dare-you?'*

He took the damned jacket. It could be mailed back to her. "Thanks for dinner, ma'am."

"It's been a pleasure." She stood at the front door, one boot headed inside, the other waiting on him. "Will you be okay?"

He slung his pack over his shoulder before he turned to face her one last time. It had been a helluva day and night was coming on, but he saw the real question in her eyes. She was one hundred percent woman, and women liked to talk. They liked to dig a man's heart apart and analyze feelings he didn't understand himself. Right about now, she would bat those eyes and start asking leading questions, and then she—

"Goodbye, Maverick. Take care of yourself, ya hear?"

That was different. Surprised at her quick dismissal, he nodded once, put his cap on his head and faced the road. He had nothing else to say.

He headed out and retraced the winding road they'd walked earlier. In a couple of miles, it would join with the highway, and he would be back to where he'd started before life had thrown that curveball at him this morning.

Star nickered loudly from the barn. Maverick gave it a backward glance. *Horses. Who'd have thought they had personalities?*

Once out of sight, he set his bag and guitar to the road to really take a good look at the jacket. It wasn't just a jacket. Hell, no. It was USMC right down to the eagle, globe, and anchor embossed across the back, the bulldog emblem on the chest.

He shook it out. By the wear on the collar and cuffs, it was old, but well-cared for. The yellow and red patch on the shoulder declared *Third Battalion, Ninth Marines*. He'd heard plenty about their hard-fought battles in another thankless war in Vietnam. He slung it over his shoulders and found it a comfortable old thing, the leather soft, the fit just right.

Somewhere along the line, that lady had had a Marine in her life.

The road called to him. Maverick shouldered his gear and kept walking. He could make another ten to fifteen miles. Might be dark when he stopped. Just as well. Darkness was an old friend.

The peaceful evening filled with the raucous roar of a string of bikers headed back to China's ranch. The leader sneered on his way by and flipped Maverick off. They disappeared in a billow of dust and racket.

A ripple of uneasiness irked his shoulders. He turned to face the road he'd just walked.

It's none of my business.

China seemed a strong woman. Capable of taking care of herself. Maybe she did dig Harleys. Bad boys. All that crap. It could happen. Some women did.

It's really none of my business.

She might be strong, but China didn't seem the biker type. No tattoos. No piercings. And the deepest blue eyes.

Not China. Horses, yes. Bikers, no.

He stood on the only road into the Wild Wolf, debating if he had good enough reason to return. The longer he stared, the worse he felt. A dozen or so riders rode in that biker gang, yet China was alone. What the hell did they want with her?

Am I going to regret this in the morning?

Gunshots from the ranch cinched the deal.

Like hell.

Chapter Four

What's that woman thinking?

China stood on her porch with the Henry in her hand. The roar of the cycles drowned out any attempt to reason or argue with the gang tearing around her yard, although judging by the way her jaw worked, it didn't stop her from trying.

Maverick only paused at the end of her driveway long enough to stow his sunglasses and pull his pistol from his pack. A man needed to look a man in the eye before he kicked his ass, not that this pack of bikers knew one damned thing about being real men. Dirt bags, maybe.

Several roared around her yard in a wide circle, digging up her vegetable garden. They had snagged her clothesline and pulled it behind them, knocking over the birdbath and dragging the horse sculpture through the dirt. Two wielded handguns, popping off shots over their heads. Assholes. With howls of laughter, they fired at the few chickens squawking around the yard. The whole gang circled again, and by hell. Enough was enough.

Maverick lifted his weapon and let it do his talking for him. It only spoke once, but when a .357 Magnum has something to say, once is generally enough.

The bastards all rolled to a stop and stared.

That's right. Take a good look, boys. It's time to man up or run home to Mommy.

China didn't deserve the crap these guys dished out. No woman did. But one biker must've felt braver than the rest. He booted his kickstand down and climbed off his ride. Spitting to the side, he swaggered across the yard, all macho and sure of himself, as if he had a dog in this fight.

His ugly face was pockmarked and scarred, his hair gray and straggly under a dirty blue bandana. His mouth seemed twisted in a permanent scowl, the kind of guy who led with his chin.

Maverick clenched his left hand. *Stick it out here, tough guy. Let's see how brave you are.*

"You think you're pretty big with that pop gun, do ya?"

Maverick didn't answer. Didn't need to. He had already caught sight of the knives and guns in some of the biker's hands. This little showdown could get real ugly real fast, and he was outnumbered. Like that meant squat to a Marine from Kilo Company. Guess again. He'd been outnumbered before. When it counted.

Tough Guy kept threatening. "Why don't you put that toy back in your cute little purse and walk away? This don't concern you, asshole."

Maverick steadied the pistol, the barrel pointed down where he meant it to be. For now. Usually, just the sight of a .357 Magnum cooled over-inflated hotheads and opinions. Maverick didn't want to offer more than a warning shot, but if he needed to...

China still seemed intent on conversation. At least she had the good sense to stay on her porch. "Troy Reardon! Get your ass off my land and you do it now."

She knew how to use that rifle, but hell. Once a weapon was drawn, the time for discussion was gone. Maverick never appreciated small talk anyway.

Every last biker rolled his ride into a circle around Tough Guy and Maverick. Maverick took a half step back to steady his stance. The weight of his pistol felt sure and right. Ready. If things went south, more than just Tough Guy would go to Hell tonight.

He spat a clot of slimy tobacco chew onto Maverick's boot. Simple rules for a simple game. *Poke until the big dog bites your head off.*

Maverick didn't blink while Troy Reardon, wanna-be tough guy and major-league dick, sized him up. No worries. Maverick had seen this type of guy plenty of times before. He had faced off with men more dangerous. Lots of them. All mouth and no action, unless his gang of twenty got the chance to beat a single adversary to death. Terrorists were pretty much the same the world over. Cowards. Every last one of them.

Tough Guy swiped his nose with his knuckles. Like the degenerate scumbag he was, he wiped his hand up his pant leg and jerked his head at his gang, not breaking eye contact with Maverick. "Mount up, boys."

Yeah, boys. Drop dead while you're at it.

Dumbass really should've looked around, though. Not one of his chicken-shit buddies had set a boot to the ground.

They didn't need to mount up because they didn't seem too eager to dance.

Tough Guy hawked up another mouthful of crap and spat. He retreated to his ride, threw one leg over his hog and kicked it free. He revved its engine long and hard, grinning like that should've been intimidating or something. It wasn't. Just more hot air.

Go for it. Try to run me over. Let's see how hot that hog burns with a round in its tank.

The bastard didn't have the balls for a real fight. Most cowards didn't. He and his minions roared another full circle around China's yard, ending at her porch steps.

Maverick couldn't hear what Tough Guy said, but the way she jerked that Henry into her shoulder and aimed at his head talked plenty loud.

Troy What's-His-Name laughed. Flipped her off. Made another leisurely tour of the trashed yard before he and his club raced away in a cloud of ugly.

Maverick felt bad for her. A woman alone and this far from town lived a dangerous life. As much as she loved her horses, she had her hands full and she was seriously outnumbered. A guy wouldn't know it to look at her, though. She did cut an impressive profile the way she had faced Reardon. She leaned the rifle by her front door and stalked off the porch.

Maverick stowed his revolver in his bag, snug inside the jacket she had just given him.

She marched straight for him, her chin forward and her fists clenched. Not what he'd expected. Worse were the words out of her mouth.

"Why the hell did you come back?"

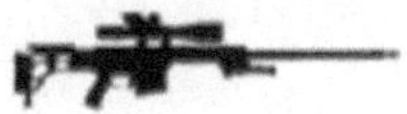

An old Ford pickup rolled into the yard while the rumble of motorcycles receded.

"You need ta clear out here." The older guy in the driver's seat jerked his thumb at the bikers as he cussed Maverick. "Now. Move it, buddy. Git with the rest a yer boy band."

"No." China waved to the men. She ran a hand through her hair as she turned slowly to survey the damage. "It's okay, Z. He's... okay. I guess. Damn it."

Maverick stayed put. Those two old duffers must be her hired hands. They poured out of the truck and ran to China. "You hurt?" The guy she'd called Z took hold of her forearms and squinted into her face, his nose scrunched up as if that helped him see better. "They touch you at all, Miss China?"

"No. They didn't get a chance." She nodded toward Maverick. "Zeke Knudsen. Xavier Albright. Meet Maverick Carson. He chased Troy and his club off. Maverick, meet the best hired hands in the county."

"Hey there." Xavier stuck out a hand, his child-like smile missing a front top tooth. "Ya related to Kit Carson?"

Maverick shook X's hand without answering. Always the same old question once he hit the Wyoming border, but from this guy, it seemed totally innocent. Dressed in worn, brown Carhartt bib overalls, X stood a foot taller than his buddy. The crown of his baldhead was nicely covered with the gray strands of a comb-over whereas a scroungy ball cap covered Zeke's graying head. X appeared to be in his fifties, younger than Zeke, whose face was lined with wrinkles.

China still held a hand to her forehead, her hair undone. Maverick blinked. She had changed since dinner. He couldn't stop looking. Damn. Angry eyes. Flushed cheeks. Her lips pinched together. *Kissable...*

She glanced apologetically at him, then back to the rutted vegetable garden. "Sorry I yelled at you before. Now I have to shop at the grocer. I hate canned vegetables. And look at the mess."

Maverick didn't take a step forward or backward. He had no reason to stay, but couldn't bring himself to leave. Common sense told him to get moving. He had done what he meant to do. China wasn't alone. Zeke and Xavier were there now. She proved she could take care of herself. She didn't need him.

"Oh no!" X dropped to his knees beside the birdbath, one piece of the copper horse statue in each hand. "They busted it, Miss China. They busted it all ta pieces. Look it here."

Something wasn't quite right in X's head. The tears dripping off his chin over a broken statue proved it.

China crouched alongside him, her hand gentle on his shoulder. "I'm sorry. Do you think you can fix it for me?"

The man looked up with a somber nod, his brows furrowed. "I kin fix anything fer you if'n you want me to."

"But can you make it like new again?" She sounded very much as if she were talking with a child, emphasizing how much she depended on him. "Can you polish it up so it will shine like it's brand new again?"

His lips pursed. X hugged both pieces to his chest. "You betcha, Miss China. I kin make it jes' like new again. Jes' fer you."

"Well, good. Let's find all the pieces then." She helped him to his feet.

X had regained his composure. "There's only two. I got 'em and I'm gonna fix 'em, good as new. Jes' you wait. You'll see."

"Thanks, X. I knew you could do it."

A frission of insight skated over Maverick's shoulders and clipped the back of his head, as if he needed to remember this. China Wolf knew how to handle more than horses. She had just given X a hand-up without him even knowing it. Smart woman.

"Damned bikers." Z dragged the tangled clothesline and clothes off the ground. "We'd a been here sooner, but we run into yer little sister."

China stopped in her tracks. "She have Kyrie with her?"

Both men nodded, their attitude somber. Z handed the jumbled mass of laundry and line to her before he returned to the truck. "Sorry I brought it up. Just thought you oughta know. Leezel said to tell ya she'd be by ta pay a visit."

"Well, that figures. It doesn't rain but it pours. She say when?"

"Yes, ma'am. Tonight."

"Thanks, Z."

"Bye-bye," X called out the truck window. "I'll be real busy fixing yer horse fer ya."

"Thanks guys." She waved and turned to face Maverick, her hands on her hips. "You sure attract trouble. That's Troy Reardon you squared off with. He runs the local bikers' club—at least, that's what he calls it. *Kings and Kreepers*, with a capital K. They're nothing but a pack of lowlifes and losers if you ask me."

"Looks like you've got enough help around here." Maverick nodded toward X and Z. They'd rolled to a stop at the bunkhouse door and climbed out of the truck, two eccentric ranch hands if he had ever seen any.

"Yes, I do. They're good guys. X and Z help me as much as they can." A shadow shifted through China's eyes. Weariness pegged her tone. "You probably didn't notice, but they've been drinking. Most likely they spent the afternoon at Shorty's Saloon. I'll bet that's where they ran into my sister."

"What do they do when they're not at Shorty's?" What he meant was how could two old farts like them be any help?

"They handle the heavy work, plowing, planting, and haying. X is a little shy on social skills. Z's got a touch of arthritis coming on, but they're good guys, just a little dog-eared like the rest of us."

"Reardon come around here often?"

"He does now. Leezel used to run with the *Kings*. My sister..." China raked a hand through her hair, lifting a mass of curls to the top of her head and exposing an elegant neck in the process. "Let's just say she's got a different outlook on life than I do."

Damn, he didn't want to look. But he did. With the setting sun behind her and her hair a mass of soft, black tangles, the golden glow cascading over her knocked the breath out of him. Other body parts noticed her, too, and not just her hair. The two buttons of her shirt had come undone in the hubbub, exposing the lacy top of a white bra that accentuated the swell of two fine, plump breasts.

Of all the times not to be wearing his Oakleys.

With every heaving breath she took, those pleasant girls swelled against the lace and enticed him. He debated telling her that her blouse was open, like a gentleman should have, but decided to keep his mouth shut and enjoy this very feminine side of a bossy woman. A smile tugged the corners of his mouth. She might be embarrassed later when she discovered her wardrobe malfunction. *Let her be.*

China took another look at her yard. She blew out a deep sigh. "Well, damn. No sense in crying over spilled milk. I'll clean this in the morning. So. You come back for dessert?"

Umm, yeah. Maybe.

"No, ma'am." Maverick shook his head to clear his stray thoughts. He looked China dead in the eye instead of at her cleavage. "Came back for that job."

"I don't need pity."

The hard tone in her voice told him plenty. She knew how to use that Henry rifle and he had better watch his step. He countered with, "Neither do I."

Approval softened her features. Her chin jutted out enough for him to know she meant business. She lifted her head and turned into a damned boss. "Summer's hard in these parts. You think you're tough enough?"

He shouldered his pack and guitar and headed to the bunkhouse. "Guess we'll find out."

Chapter Five

China watched him go. The man had guts, she had to give him that, but watching Maverick walk away gave her a whole new perspective. Squared-off shoulders, head held high and a lazy kind of arrogance to his gait. His hips rolled with every step, as if he had nowhere to go and all day to get there. *If* he wanted to go.

He presented a strong profile no matter which way she looked at him. Right now, the rear view was pretty nice. A man in denim with long legs always worked magic on her insides. Yeah. The guy was F. I. N. E.

Why he changed his mind and decided to stay was another thing all together. He might not stay long, but having an ex-military guy around for a day or two gave her an immediate sense of security. If he was anything like her father, and she was pretty sure he was, Maverick had nothing but honorable intentions. That was why he came back.

She had the feeling that he had been to war, done his duty, and maybe gotten a little lost once he'd come home. The horses liked him. That alone spoke volumes about the drifter she had just hired. *Well, good. I can use a lost but honorable man.*

It didn't hurt that he looked good, too. Handsome and honorable. The perfect combination.

She headed inside and upstairs to make up the extra bedroom for Leezel and her daughter, Kyrie. China caught a glimpse of herself in the dresser mirror. She hurried to button her blouse, her face flushed with the knowledge that he had to have seen more of her than she wanted.

Darn it anyway. No wonder he decided to hang around.

She traced the edge of her bra, her fingertips dipping between her breasts. It had been a long time since any man had seen her in anything but denim and button-up western shirts. Now this moody stranger might have gotten an eyeful. Somehow, that didn't seem all too bad.

Her heartbeat picked up an extra beat or two. Maverick Carson, huh?

It wasn't ten minutes later that Leezel pulled up the drive, her 1999 beater piece of crap rattling all the way to the front step. Two car doors slammed, but only one pair of pounding feet hit the porch. The screen door squeaked open and slammed shut.

"Andy China?" a young girl's voice called. "Is you here?"

A smile split China's face. For the next few days, she would be Andy China instead of Auntie China. "Up here. I'm in your room, baby girl."

More pounding feet hit the staircase. In no time at all, a grimy five-year-old bundle of excitement named Kyrie hit China.

"Andy China!" Shenestled into China's arms, breathless, her head pressed hard into her aunt's shirt. "I missed you so-o-o much."

"I missed you too, angel." China ran her fingers through the child's tangled black hair and looked past the dirt and dry, scabby skin on her sweet face. She kissed her niece's forehead and Kyrie sighed. For a moment, they just held each other tight, but China could've cried.

Kyrie's ragged clothes smelled as if they hadn't been changed in days. Her tiny T-shirt barely covered her tummy, and her pants were so short she looked as if she had dressed for a flood. Kyrie had grown taller and thinner—again.

The screen door slammed. Great. The only downside to Kyrie's visit. Her mother. Leezel was back.

"I'm here too, ya know," she yelled up the stairs. Of course, Leezel wouldn't think of wasting her energy by climbing the flight of twelve steps to greet China, even though her older sister was in the middle of making up the guest bedroom for her. Not Leezel. No way. No how. She would never change.

"We'll be right down." China set Kyrie's feet back on the floor.

"Kin I hewp?" The little girl moved to the other side of the bed, smoothing the wrinkles out of the fitted sheet as she went. "Mommy showed me how. I kin make my own bed. Honest."

"Well, of course you can help. Here you go." China lifted the flat sheet high in the air. For a moment Kyrie was visible between the sheet and the bed. China cringed. The little girl standing there with dark circles under her eyes needed to eat.

Thank heavens Maverick had grilled all the chicken. Kyrie never had the option of becoming a picky-eater, not with her mother's transient lifestyle. And Kyrie desperately needed professional help with her speech, another symptom of Leezel's lax attitude toward parenting.

"Did you make cookies?" she asked, fixing China with the same wide blue gaze.

"I always have cookies for you, darling." China tucked the bottom edge of the sheet under the mattress and tossed a light cotton blanket over the bed. "Did you remember your blankie?"

Kyrie shook her head, her lip stuck out in a sad pout. "Uh uh."

"What happened? Did you lose it?"

Kyrie barreled into her aunt's embrace. "Mommy threw it away. I gotta be a big girl now."

That news ruffled China's feathers. *A five-year-old doesn't have to be a big girl. Your mother ought to try being one for a change.* "Well, let's go have dinner and a couple cookies for dessert. I'll see if I can find another blanket for you while you're here. Would you like that?"

"I missed you so much," Kyrie whispered fervently. "I reawy, reawy did."

The love of that child stabbed China to the core. She snagged Kyrie's hand before she started to bawl. "After you eat, you can take a bath before bedtime."

"A bubba baff?"

Kyrie was so easy to please. It warmed China's heart.

"An extra-bubbly *bubba baff*."

"Oh, goodie!"

China all but skipped down the steps with Kyrie. The kitchen light was on. Leezel sat in their father's chair with her long tanned legs stretched across the floor and crossed at the ankles. Good grief. Glittery red stilettos, a tinier than tiny tee and short shorts. Brassy red hair. A diamond studded belly button ring. Why not? Everything else was pierced, inked or dyed.

She had fixed herself a plate of cold chicken and a handful of cookies. It amazed China that Leezel could fix something to eat for herself but forget her child might be hungry, too.

"Long drive?" China leveled the sarcasm out of her voice and made a chicken sandwich for Kyrie.

"No more 'n usual." Leezel picked the meat off her piece of chicken with her fake fingernails. She might not be able to afford proper food for her daughter, but she never missed a manicure. The polish matched her hair color. "Heard you had company tonight, Sis."

"How did you hear that?" *Not like it was hard to tell, with the yard torn up.*

Leezel shrugged. "Just did. A person hears things when they're out and about. You oughta try it sometime."

"Guess I've been a little busy defending my property. Never mind. We'll talk about that business with your ex later." China bit her lip. Now wasn't the time to discuss

Reardon and his biker club, not in front of Kyrie. "Where have you been staying?"

"Around. You got anything to drink?"

"You know where the beer is. Are you back with Reardon?"

"That all you got? Just beer? Hell. You're as bad as the old man was. Too cheap to buy something folks might actually wanna drink."

"I buy what I need. Tell me where you're living. With Reardon? You are, aren't you?"

"You oughta keep decent booze on hand for company. Maybe something stronger."

"Company can bring their own, Leezel. If you're living with him again—"

Leezel's light blue eyes pierced China's.

Funny. We used to look so much alike, but now...

Leezel licked her fingers, sticking each into her mouth and sucking, smacking her lips and still avoiding the question. The way she wrinkled her insolent nose always made China want to pop her, just once, but as usual, she didn't. Their sisterly relationship balanced on a boatload of patience and just as much restraint on China's part for Kyrie's sake. Once Leezel returned home pregnant and homeless there had been no other choice.

Troy Reardon. The bane of China's existence. Unfortunately, Kyrie's biological father. If Leezel had shacked up with him and his *Kreeps* again, China meant to enforce her threat and call the sheriff and Child Protective

Services. Kyrie didn't need to grow up in the middle of that crap.

"I'm only going to ask you one—"

"Oh, for hell's sake, shut up. I'm staying at Vivian's. She good enough for you? She goes to church."

China bit her lip. A church turned into a community center with free room and board for the janitor didn't qualify as a church for worship, but it was safer than *Hog Heaven*, or whatever Reardon called his dive. Should've named it *Krud* in keeping with the whole K thing he seemed stuck on.

China turned her attention to Kyrie, the irony of her name yet another slap in the face of propriety and decency. Reardon had chosen her name. Of course. Why wouldn't he? It started with a K.

The moron had no idea of its Greek origin or its reverent message. Coupled with its ancient partner, it became *Kyrie Eleison. Lord, have mercy.* The perfect name for a child with parents the likes of Leezel and Reardon. *Lord, have mercy indeed.*

Kyrie had already devoured the first sandwich. She sat watching her mother and aunt's conversation, her gaze bobbing back and forth.

"Would you like another sandwich?" China asked.

Kyrie nodded and rubbed her stomach. "Uh huh. I yike samiches. They yummy."

"See. Ain't she the polite little lady? Told you I know how to raise a good kid."

China couldn't answer. She had nothing nice to say as she fixed another sandwich and cut a slice of melon for the hungry child, who probably hadn't eaten since breakfast. The way Kyrie gulped her food pained China. More than anything, she ached to throw Leezel out the door and run away with this baby. No child should have to live the kind of life Leezel lived, but then, no child should have a mother the likes of Leezel to begin with.

"Are you still seeing your PO?"

"Yes, *mother*, I'm still seeing my pro-ba-tion of-fic-er." Sarcasm fit her. "Hell. I'm barely in the door and you're giving me the third-degree. What the shit's wrong with you?"

Y.O.U. China bit her lip. Any question Leezel didn't want to answer was third-degree.

"And yes. I got her vaccinated. Damn. Don't even ask. I told you I would. God, you're as big a bitch as ever. You oughta try hanging around with a guy now and then instead of all those damned horses. Now, can I please be excused like the good girl I am or should I stay here and put up with you?"

You can go to hell for all I care.

"Andy China?" Kyrie asked. "Kin I have—"

"Kyrie! Don't you dare—" Leezel's hand whipped across the table, but China was quicker. She grabbed her sister's wrist before she made contact with Kyrie's frightened little face. That the child cowered spiked China's anger from high simmer to flaming.

It was clear this baby had been hit before. *Never again.*

Kyrie's eyes filled with tears, her voice quavering. "I… I sowwy, Mommy. I forgot."

China had made up her mind long ago that her home would be filled with peace, quiet, and children if the opportunity ever presented itself. Physical discipline wasn't something she visited upon her horses, and she wouldn't allow it on an innocent little girl.

She steeled her temper. "You might have forgotten since you've been gone a while, Leezel, but Auntie China's got a rule. We don't hit anyone. Ever."

Leezel jerked her hand out of China's, her upper lip lifted on one side, her teeth bared. She wouldn't stay long, only enough to eat decently for a change, and to steal any loose change she could get her hands on, or worse, something that belonged to their father. She needed a place to crash and something to pawn. That was the only reason she had driven the fifteen miles from town.When she left, poor little Kyrie would be at her mercy again, so China walked the tightrope every damned time.

Leezel arched a wicked eye at her daughter. "I'll talk to you later."

Kyrie's face hit the floor. Her lower lip, too.

China couldn't take it. She picked Kyrie up from her chair and swung her around in a circle before she hugged her tight. "It's bath time, little miss."

Kyrie cuddled into her aunt's arms with an extra quiet, "'Kay."

China shielded her from Leezel's view while they walked down the hall and into the bathroom. "And I've got pink *bubba baff*, just for you. And a pink frog that blows bubbles out of the top of his head, like a fountain. Just you wait and see. He's wearing a gold crown."

Kyrie had turned into a very serious and obedient child. As soon as the bathroom door was shut, she turned to China, her lip quivering and her eyes full of tears. "I vewy sowwy, Andy China. Mommy says I—"

"You shush now. You have nothing to be sorry about in Auntie China's house. Never in a million years. You're the most beautiful girl in the whole world and I'll make you as many chicken sandwiches as you want." China's heart broke. She held her niece tight, her face in Kyrie's dirty, tangled hair so the child wouldn't see her cry.

"I is boo-ti-foo?" Kyrie's sniffed. "Reawy? I is?"

China pressed Kyrie to her chest while she turned the bath water on. Nothing filled her heart like this child. She kissed Kyrie's grubby forehead again and again. If there were any way to hold her niece forever, she would do it. Oh yes. She would give up everything to keep this baby safe and make her happy. "You're so perfect that the angels in heaven cried for happiness the day you were born because they'd never seen such a beautiful little girl like you."

Kyrie scrunched her shoulders. "I yike angels."

China scrunched her shoulders just like Kyrie. "Me too, baby. Me, too. And you are definitely my favorite."

"Can I pour bubba baff? Pwease?" Kyrie asked very quietly.

Her hesitance stabbed China all over again. She handed the bottle of to Kyrie. "Sure. Do you know how to open it?"

"Uh huh." Kyrie nodded, her tongue sticking out as she unscrewed the cap and tipped the bottle slowly. Too slowly.

The teeniest drip plopped out under the running faucet. She glanced over her shoulder at China. "Is that okay?"

China sat on the edge of the tub. "Go on. Pour some more. You need lots of bubbles."

Kyrie poured another teensy bit, again watching for her aunt's reaction.

"Tip it upside down. Pour it all in if you want. That's why I bought it."

Kyrie handed the bottle back with a serious shake of her head. "Mommy might not—"

China snagged the bottle and tipped it upside down. A stream of pink liquid hit the flowing water and suds commenced to billow. Kyrie's eyes lit up and her cute angel lips made the sweetest, silent *wow.*

"Mommy can't get mad at Auntie China, can she? Now let's get your clothes off so you can play with all those bubbles."

"Oh goodie!" In a minute, Kyrie was in the tub and just another naked little girl with suds in her hair and a happy, clean face.

China shampooed and bathed her niece to her heart's content. Everything about this darling child made her exquisitely happy. They mounded bubbles into mountains just to blow them apart. She styled Kyrie's shampoo-laden hair into licorice-colored swirls until they had a spike twisted around the top of her head. China took a handful of bubbles and blew them high into the air so they'd fall all over Kyrie. The little girl squealed with delight. No better music in the world.

At last she stood naked and pleasantly pink on the bath mat while China dried her and rubbed lotion all over her body. The lotion moisturized the little girl's skin from top to bottom, but it also gave China a chance to check for bruises, ringworm, and eczema. Kyrie had had problem skin all of her life. Tonight was no different.

China didn't see any bruises, but too many dried, scabby patches on the girl's face, arms, and along the back of her neck needed attention. That she sighed when the soothing lotion touched her skin told China everything she needed to know. This baby needed a real mother, damn it. How could Leezel not see that?

China braided her niece's hair into two long pigtails. She held out clean underwear and pajama bottoms for Kyrie to step into. She had made up her mind long ago and shopped accordingly. Kyrie always went home with plenty of new underwear, clothes and shoes when she came for a visit to Auntie China's.

"Hmm, you smell good."

"I kinda smew yike a faiwy pwincess, huh?" Kyrie's nose wrinkled with happiness.

"You do." China tugged the pajama top over the little girl's head. "You smell like a heavenly fairy princess, my favorite kind."

Kyrie giggled. She was firmly seated inside China's arms when the two left the steam of the bathroom behind and headed back to the kitchen. Good. No Leezel in sight. No doubt she needed a smoke and a beer. At least, Kyrie would have a bedtime snack and a story in peace.

"Are you ready for milk and cookies, little one?"

"Uh huh." Kyrie settled back into her chair at the kitchen table with a big smile.

The sound of voices drifted through the screen door along with the rancid stink of cigarette smoke, Leezel's gravelly voice unmistakable, and the other too low to make out. It had better not be Reardon. Not after what he did today. That would be just like Leezel, to be kissing all over the jerk who ransacked her sister's yard. The girl had no loyalty to family. No common sense, either. If she did, she would've left Reardon in the dust years ago.

China poured a glass of milk for Kyrie and settled next to her most favorite person in the world. Kyrie ate with gusto, but with her tummy full, and after the nice warm bath, it only took one cookie and a half-glass of milk before her eyes drooped. She rubbed her nose with a big yawn. "I tired."

China lifted her out of the chair and into her arms. "You can sleep in my bed tonight, okay?"

Kyrie mumbled 'okay' and laid her sleepy head on China's shoulder. Within seconds, China had the baby snuggled under the sheet in her bedroom. While Leezel's raucous laughter rose up from the porch, China searched for one of the extra baby blankets she had bought when Kyrie was born.

Who on earth was Leezel talking to? Couldn't be X or Z. They might have an occasional beer with her in town, most likely when Leezel invited herself to their table and ordered a round she never intended to pay for. That was Leezel through and through. Content to be a party girl on everyone else's dime.

China located the spare blanket in. She'd bought extras, simply because she knew her sister. Leezel tended to forget important things like little girl's blankets and teddy bears. This blanket wasn't much, but it was exactly what Kyrie needed. She tucked it under her niece's chin, turned on the pink princess nightlight she only used when Kyrie visited and quietly shut the door.

The satisfaction of having her niece safe and sound for the night filled China with peace even as the very real knowledge of what needed to be done filled her with foreboding. She had to find a way to help Kyrie and Leezel too, hopefully without further damaging their already strained relationship. Leezel needed to understand the importance of raising her only child in a decent environment. Rented rooms over bars and over-nighters on friends' couches weren't the same as a good, stable home. Kyrie deserved more.

China went quietly downstairs to clear the dishes and straighten the kitchen. Leezel's flirty laugh drifted through the front door again. How her sister could turn a laugh into a seductive come-on always amazed China, but Leezel had always had a way with men. From little on up, boys had climbed all over her. China climbed all over horses.

She glanced out the screen door, ready to send Reardon packing.

Damn.

It was Maverick.

Chapter Six

"Can I get you two a beer? Or a room?"

Maverick jumped to his feet. His glasses were out of sight and his baseball cap was on backwards, which spiked China's irritation even more. The minute he saw her, he yanked it off his head. She didn't know if that meant he was polite or apologetic or just another dumb-assed male caught in Leezel's snare. Right then she didn't care.

"Oh, come on now, Mav honey. You just sit yourself back down and I'll tell you about my daddy." Leezel patted the porch step beside her and rolled her eyes at China. "And yeah, Sis. A couple beers would be nice, especially since that's all you got to offer anyway."

Maverick's gaze fixed on China. "Just came by to see what you needed done first thing in the morning, ma'am."

Leezel trailed a finger along a crack in the weathered porch boards. "Well, I can think of a couple things I might need done first thing in the morning if you're up to it, cowboy." She cast an exaggerated shy look at him, which China caught and he didn't.

China's fins clenched to knock her on her ass, but Maverick just looked exceedingly uncomfortable. *Well, good.*

If he meant to fall for the likes of Leezel, China wanted him gone. *Might as well get the hell out of here tonight.* She let him have it. "Stalls need mucking. Chickens need feeding. In the morning. Before the sun's up. Can you handle that?"

"Yes, ma'am. No problem."

"I've got forty acres of grass hay to cut. Another fifteen to plow. Tomorrow. By sunset."

"Yes, ma'am." His head kept bobbing. He was suddenly so formal she had a feeling he might salute next. He folded the brim of his cap in his hands and refolded it, worried it. Good. She had made him nervous. Damned good.

China bit her tongue before she said anything else. She was far too ready with a snarky comeback, and after the kind of day she had just had, she wasn't up for one more waste-of-time confrontation. Or maybe she was.

"I need help with Gorgeous tonight if you're not *too busy.* You do remember her, don't you?" China winced at the very snarky tone to her voice. "The white horse? The one that *liked* you?" *The dumb one, like me, you ass?*

He gulped, his Adam's apple hard at work in his throat. "I already settled her in the big stall in your barn, ma'am. She's sweating a lot and she's pacing all over the place, but I figured that's where you wanted her."

You did? China blinked at that profound insight. For a man of few words, he had just said a mouthful. The guy was no dummy. He hadn't backed down one bit, either. Just stood there and took what she had thrown at him. *Good. I think.*

"Oh, come on, Sis." Leezel cocked her head to one side and resorted to her coquettish, southern belle drawl. "Let Mav take a load off. That old nag isn't going foal for hours. You know that. We got all kinds of time. Let's all have a beer or two. Then we'll worry about—"

"Beer's in the fridge. Get it yourself." China slammed the screen door and stormed down the front steps and past the pair. If Maverick was smart, he would know which sister to follow. If he wasn't, it didn't much matter what he did next. China didn't need the trouble. If this guy was dumber than dirt—*good riddance!*

Footsteps followed close behind her. Sounded like work boots. Not glittery stilettos.

Excellent choice, Maverick.

She paused at the barn door and took a deep breath to clear the ugly thoughts out of her head. The first time she stepped foot into a barn as a little girl, she had felt its magical powers. Barns were sanctuaries for pigeons in the rafters, cows in the manger and newborn babies in the storm.

The natural odors of beast and hay, combined with the musty wood smell of any well-built barn became her happy place. She had played there, worked there, and brought enough foals into the world to rival any other rancher in the state. But tonight—nothing. No magic and no happy place.

She clenched her fingers into fists. A pack of thugs had ruined her yard and garden. She had nearly lost Star to a bizarre act of Mother Nature. Leezel didn't give a flying rat's ass about her own flesh-and-blood daughter. The planets and stars were all out of alignment, every last one of them. Nothing in the universe felt right, damn it! Could this day get any worse?

China opened the door and stepped inside, silently biting her lip, and trying to decide between swearing or crying or kicking the shit out of the nearest bale of hay. Days like this made her realize how much work there was to running a ranch, and how understaffed she had always been. X and Z were a great help, but they were only two. She didn't dare trust just anyone with her horses. Never Leezel.

Maverick took a silent position at her elbow. Well, good. Let him stand there.

She stilled the rant in her head and finally noticed that all of her kids were at rest in their stalls. Star nickered in greeting. Gorgeous, too.

China swallowed her temper tantrum. Maverick had been busy. She flipped on the switch for the overhead lights and took in a view of the foaling stall. For a greenhorn, he had done good. He had put down a clean cover of straw for Gorgeous, but that wasn't what pleased China all the way to her toes. His backpack lay propped against the outside rail of the stall. His guitar leaned against the wall. It looked like he planned to spend the night with a gorgeous female, and God bless him, it was the right one.

China took a deep breath and ceased being the alpha bitch. "Thanks," she said quietly.

"Yes, ma'am." He sounded subdued, his voice baritone deep and rich like single barrel whiskey. It damned near curled her toes in her boots, despite the fact that he had been caught red-handed talking and laughing with Leezel. Well, Leezel had been laughing. Come to think of it, China had only heard her sister's raucous voice. Not Maverick's. *Hmm.*

"Thought I'd sleep in here tonight if it's okay with you. Your hired hands, umm, snore when they've been drinking."

China drew in a deep, slow breath of humility. Maverick might not have deserved her wrath. He'd had a hard day, too. Embarrassment heated her cheeks at the way she had blasted him. She bit her lip, but instead of apologizing...

"I see that. Sure. Sleep here. It's fine with me." She crossed the barn to the stall and slid the gate aside. "Let's see how Gorgeous is doing. Hold her halter."

The oddest thing happened. He had only to reach for Gorgeous's halter and the gentle lady pushed her face into his chest again, like a long, lost friend. Whatever or whoever this guy was, her favorite brood mare had made up her mind about Maverick Carson.

China stilled her hostile feelings for her sister and strove for calmness. She examined the mare to determine how close she was to dropping her foal. Gorgeous was sweating plenty. All that tail swishing was a good sign, too. China ended the visual double-check with a soothing hand over her horse's rump. "I could teach you how to examine a mare in labor if you're interested."

He shook his head. "No, thanks."

"Are you sure? It's really quite fascinating."

"I'll pass."

"Okay then. Looks like tonight's the night. It won't be long."

Gorgeous still leaned into Maverick. The sight of that big animal's face in this handsome man's hands had a quieting effect on China as well. He dipped his forehead into the horse's long nose, but she couldn't miss the tender glint in his eye.

Had he looked at Star like this when they were up on the hill? She'd been so busy with excavation and worry she hadn't noticed. His eyes. The color of black coffee. Clear. Hot. Sexy as hell.

He lifted his chin and caught her looking. "What's next?"

"I, umm, I need to wrap her tail." China stuttered and attempted a more professional train of thought. Yes, he had sexy eyes. Yes, he was built, but this was business. *He's a hired hand like X and Z. That's all.* "Then we wait. The foal might take all night to get here, or it could show in the next hour."

"How do we wrap her tail? It's really long."

"Like this." China steeled her heart and retrieved a bag designed specifically for mares in labor. "You hold the bag. I'll tuck it inside. It's important we get all of it."

He shook the bag open and stepped behind Gorgeous.

China lifted the course strands of the elegant and very long tail. Flowing manes and tails added to the beauty of her horses. The longer and fuller, the more handsome the animal. Gorgeous was one of the most beautiful horses she had ever owned. Wrapping it during foaling would keep it as clean as possible, if she could make her fingers stop trembling enough to get the job done right.

She twisted the strands into a loose knot and folded it up around the stump of the tail. Maverick angled the bag into position. While she made sure no strands escaped, he lifted the bag around her hands and arms.

"Wow. It's a lot easier with help. Thanks." She pulled her hands out of the bag while he pulled the drawstring tight.

"Well, ain't that sweet?" Leezel's sarcastic voice at the barn door squelched the peaceful feeling. She stepped daintily through the barn door in her six-inch, red glittery heels, two bottles of beer lifted high and her tiny T-shirt exposing her belly button ring.

"Did you check on Kyrie? She's in my bed."

"No, Sis. Thought I'd bring some refreshments to our handsome guest here first. Then I'll take care of my *motherly* chores."

China caught the outright disrespect in her sister's voice. What she had really meant to say was more like *'Mind your own business, bitch. I'm looking for a little action, and you're in my way.'* Only with a few X-rated expletives thrown into the mix.

"Thought I'd check on my favorite pony." Leezel sauntered up to the stall and peered at Gorgeous, dangling the bottles over the top rail. "She in the first or second stage, huh, Sis? Do you know yet?"

China bit her tongue and busied herself with finishing the wrapping. Maverick stood nearby, bless his heart. "Could you hold her halter while I tie this off?" China asked, striving to hold onto the peace Leezel seemed intent on driving out.

"You bet." He shifted to take Gorgeous's halter.

The lady bowed her head to him again and China's heart thumped. This horse knew something about Maverick.

"Hey, China. Sis. Boss lady, or whatever it is they call you around here." Leezel clinked the bottles. "I asked you what stage is she in. Do ya know or not? You checked her yet?"

"Heard you. Stage one." China finished securing Gorgeous's tail before she turned to Maverick. "How is she?"

He shrugged. "Okay, I guess." The puzzled look on his face was somehow endearing. This man so did not have a clue what he was in for. "She keeps blowing air at me."

"She's huffing. That's normal. Labor hurts."

Leezel pointed a bottle at Maverick. "Did you know most mares deliver their babies on their feet?"

He raised a brow at that detail, but shook his head at her offer of beer. He pulled the baseball cap low on his forehead, like a wall. He ducked, the brim cutting his line of sight.

China relaxed even more. The tension across her shoulders lifted. She took in a deep breath. Maverick had just erected his trusty barrier, this time to keep Leezel at bay.

"Course my darling Gorgeous likes to lay down like a good mama should, don't you, pretty baby?" Leezel emptied one of the bottles in a long chug, tossed it onto a nearby bale of hay and entered the birthing stall. "Here. Hold this." She shoved the last beer bottle into Maverick's chest and snatched the halter out of his hand.

Gorgeous reared her head back, but Leezel kept tugging the halter until the heavily panting mare was eye to eye with her. "Come on. Walk. It's good for you."

"Let her be," China warned.

"Why should I? In case you forgot, I know as much about horses as you do." Leezel pulled until Gorgeous was forced to follow. The horse took one halting step after another. It didn't hurt her to walk, but Leezel's antics could prolong stage one. Gorgeous needed to feel safe and secure at this critical time, not be harassed by some wanna-be horsewoman who showed up once in a blue moon and thought she could take over. Any breeder worth her salt knew a mare would put off foaling until no one was watching, much less bugging her.

Maverick watched with his arms folded over his chest, his eyes hooded.

Good. Let Leezel make up your mind for you.

Leezel continued demonstrating her vast equine knowledge. "You see, Mav? The foal has to turn inside its mama's belly before it can be born. It's been on its back this whole time, but now, if my big sister is as smart as she thinks she is, this little guy is ready to come out. That's what stage two is about. His front feet should be pushing up the birth canal this very minute if he's ready to be borned, the little darlin'."

"You need to be careful," China warned again. *And stop acting so stupid.* She had caught the silly southern accent Leezel reverted to at her leisure. Real men didn't fall for that crap.

A contraction rippled through the horse. China soothed her hands over the mare's quivering belly. "She's ready to—"

Gorgeous dropped onto the hay with a noisy grunt. She rolled to her side and pushed her legs straight in front of her.

"Oh, my." Leezel released the halter and squealed like a delighted little girl. "See, Mav? See how smart this little mama is? She knows it's better to lie down to have her baby.

That's why she's my favorite mare in the *whole* world. She's such a good mama."

Maverick hunkered down behind Gorgeous, his brows furrowed. China grunted along with *her* favorite mare. It was that or throw up. "We need to back off now and let her alone."

The horse strained, all four legs extended and her neck stretched out straight. At this rate, it wouldn't be long.

Of course, Leezel dropped alongside Maverick, her arm draped casually over his shoulders. She had already retrieved and opened the other bottle of beer. "You got enough room for little ol' me? Want some?" she offered suggestively.

Maverick held up a palm to block the offer and adjusted his position. He didn't act as if he appreciated her company, not with his elbows planted on his knees and his chin to his clenched fists.

No problem. Leezel tipped the bottle back and drained it.

China looked away. Bile thickened at the back of her throat, and she seriously needed to spit. A mare's labor and delivery she could stand, not the cat-in-heat her sister turned into whenever a man came into view. "Umm, listen, guys. I'll go check on Kyrie. Take good care of Gorgeous. Be right back."

She bolted from the barn. She had to. The sight of Leezel putting the moves on a decent guy like Maverick turned her stomach. She stopped just outside the door, thankful for the cool night air in her face.

Leezel brought out the worst in her. Not once in her life had she taken responsibility seriously, not even when she had gotten pregnant. That Kyrie wasn't born with fetal alcohol syndrome spoke more to the divine hand of providence than the prenatal care of her thoughtless mother.

And it wasn't as if she'd gotten pregnant as an innocent teenager, either. No. Leezel had been smarter than most girls back then. She had found a way to get birth control when others couldn't or weren't brave enough to. Jefferson Wolf never knew she had gone to Planned Parenthood. Of course, she had also achieved quite the reputation by then, but that was why she'd needed protection. Like any good father, he never believed those salacious rumors, either. Not about his daughter. Not perfect little Leezel.

The knowledge that Reardon was Kyrie's father sickened China. God, what a pig of a man. How could that perfect little angel be the product of two such disgusting adults? The unwanted pregnancy didn't happen until Leezel took up with Reardon, and Kyrie was born the week before Jefferson died. Leezel never let him see the baby, though. Said it didn't make any difference. He wouldn't be around much longer.

Leezel had been right. Brain cancer had destroyed Jefferson quickly and ruthlessly. Still... China bit the inside of her lip hard. She would've made damned sure her father met his only grandchild if it had been up to her. Damn sure.

She drew in another deep breath of air, her rampaging thoughts so loud in her head she didn't hear anything until Maverick politely tapped her shoulder.

"Oh, my!" She nearly turned into his arms; he stood so close. A whiff of manly scent struck her nostrils—and her libido. "You... you startled me." *And God, I like it.*

"Sorry, ma'am." He took a precise step backward and nodded toward the barn, his dark eyes sweeping over her from head to foot. "Should I give her a drink?"

Oh, hell no.

"Who? Leezel? God, no. She's already half lit and—" China stuck a hand in her hair, forking her unruly locks back over her shoulder. Damn, he smelled good, but why the hell would he think Leezel needed another beer? What? Had she downed the other one already?

"I meant the horse." He answered so politely it all but stopped her heart. How could four words sound that good?

China rubbed three fingertips across her forehead, hiding her embarrassment with her palm. Of course he didn't mean Leezel. "Ah," *shit I'm stupid,* "is Gorgeous on her feet again?"

He nodded.

I am so, SO stupid.

"She probably won't stay up for long. If she'll drink, that's fine, but watch out she doesn't kick you. She doesn't know what she wants right now, and she's in pain." China licked her lips, needing a drink of water as much as Gorgeous probably did.

His eyes zeroed in on her mouth with that little action. She didn't know if he did it on purpose or not, but the tip of his tongue at his bottom lip certainly caught her attention. The man had perfect lips. Full. Probably soft. That bottom lip might be damned tasty.

"Thanks, ma'am." He tipped the brim of his baseball cap to her and turned back to the barn.

A surge of warmth filled her chest. She didn't want him to leave. "Ah, Maverick?"

He stopped at the door and turned sideways, his body half in, half out of the barn, his eyes locked on her.

"You've helped me a lot today. I couldn't do this without you. Thanks." *Well, I could, but I don't want to.*

"No problem." He stood waiting, a bemused twinkle in his eye.

Her fingers went to the top buttons of her blouse, checking. He didn't crack a smile, which only flustered her more because—she really wanted him to smile at what he had seen earlier. Not only that, but she wanted him to like what he'd seen, too. She wanted him to know there were other sides to her, that she wasn't just his boss. That she was a woman, too. A flesh-and-blood woman with pretty damned perky boobs.

She waved toward the house, not able to make her eyes move off of him. "I'll, umm, just be a couple minutes."

He nodded respectfully.

"I just, umm, need to check on the baby. Kyrie. My sister's little girl. She's five. Kyrie." She combed her hand through her hair again, disgusted at her inability to think straight or sound intelligent around this guy. *Why am I telling him something he already knows?*

"And I'll check on Gorgeous, ma'am." He had used the horse's name. Intentionally. He wanted her to know exactly where his loyalty stood. *With Gorgeous. He's just going back in the barn to check on—Gorgeous. Not Leezel. Gorgeous. Oh, good, good, good.*

A boatload of butterflies assaulted China's stomach. She pointed to the house again. "I'll... I'll be right back."

He tipped two fingers to the brim of his cap one last time, stepped inside the barn and closed the door.

Oh my heck, China. Knock it off. You're making a fool of yourself.

She strode back to the house with determined steps, her mind awhirl and confused at the depth of feelings Maverick sparked. *He doesn't care about you. He wants to be left alone. He's nothing but a drifter on his way to who knows where. In a couple days, he'll walk away, and... You, China Wolf, are as dumb as your sister!*

She opened the screen door very quietly so it wouldn't squeak, climbed the stairs and made her way to her bedroom. The second she laid her eyes on the child of her heart, China's confusion fled. A surge of love filled her soul for the little girl asleep in her bed with her thumb in her mouth, her new baby blanket tucked tightly against her nose.

God didn't make 'em any sweeter.

Once stringy with grime, Kyrie's hair had come undone from the braids. It laid clean and shiny black on the pillow, crimped and beautiful. Tendrils of black silk nestled in wispy curls around her face. Like a fairy princess.

China sat on the edge of the bed and studied the sleeping child. She took in a deep breath and slowly exhaled. This was who mattered most in the world. Not Maverick. Not Leezel. Not Reardon. Not even all of her beautiful horses. Only Kyrie.

With all her heart, China wanted this little girl to grow up safe, happy, and loved. Somehow, that would happen. She placed a kiss on Kyrie's cheek before she left.

All might not be perfect with the world, but for tonight, God really was in his heaven.

Chapter Seven

What is taking China so long?

Panic spiked in Maverick's gut. Gorgeous groaned in obvious pain while he crouched alongside the suffering beast, not a clue how to ease her discomfort. A thick sheen of sweat coated her neck and sides. She couldn't hold still and nothing he did helped, not talking to her, not petting or scratching behind her ears. She had gotten to her feet a couple times, but kept lying back down.

He worried. This poor mare suffered, and watching her suffer didn't make for a fun evening. China needed to get her butt back in the barn, and she needed to do it now. Leezel was no damned help. She spent more time admiring her fingernails than paying attention to Gorgeous. What was it about women and fake nails? *Shit.*

"Here ya go, Mav. You might need these." She draped a long pair of gloves over his shoulder, her nails trailing a line across his shoulders as she strolled behind him. "Especially if this little guy comes breach."

More acid poured into his stomach. Breach didn't sound like a good thing. Neither did that name she kept throwing at him as if they'd known each other before. As if he cared one iota about her. Kimmie used to call him *Mav. Mav honey.*

Mav darling. Right before she'd kicked his sorry ass to the curb and married someone else.

He dragged the arm-length rubber gloves off his shoulder. Leezel continued spouting rhetoric that sounded right. "You might have to reach inside her butt and pull that foal out."

He seriously doubted that. Leezel leaned toward pessimism. Anyone knew that babies, even horse babies, didn't develop up their mother's butts. Still. Reach into a mare's nether regions? Pull a baby horse out after all the pain this poor mother was going through? He folded the fingers of the glove into the palm and rolled them up. *Not me. No way.*

Leezel examined her nails again. Her lips pulled to the side of her face as if she had discovered a flaw in all that stupid acrylic. "Course sometimes it's already dead. That'd be too bad, but a mare's still gotta drop a dead foal, you know. The umbilical cord can strangle these little guys just like it does with human babies. Course they're not really whatcha might call little. You want to know how much one of these horses weighs when they're born?"

He smoothed his hands over Gorgeous's tight belly while she shuddered through another contraction. If Leezel would shut up and leave, this mother would feel a lot better. So would he.

"You can bet it'll be around one hundred and fifty pounds, if it's alive. How much you weigh, Mav? One-eighty? Two hundred? Hell, if it's deformed and diseased, it might be bigger than you."

"The foal's not dead." China dimmed the lights at the stable door as she strode back into the stall. Star nickered.

She raised a brow at Maverick, a black bag clutched in her left hand. "You felt it move earlier, remember? Out in the corral?"

Oh, yeah. That's right. It moved a couple hours ago.

He relaxed. She had wrapped her hair up on the top of her head with a big toothy clip. It lent her a regal air. Like a queen. A few wisps and chunks of it still twirled down her neck, but the confidence she brought with her settled him, too.

Leezel leaned back into the stall bars. Poor Gorgeous grunted and huffed through another contraction.

"Is there something you can give her?" he asked quietly, hoping Leezel wouldn't hear the question because he didn't want to have to listen to her answer. He handed China the gloves. "You really need these?"

The tender light in her eyes touched him. China took the gloves and stuffed them in her back pocket. "No. I don't use gloves. We do this naturally for as long as we can. Remember, she's got a higher pain threshold than we do," she said firmly. "If there's trouble, I know what to do."

"But it's a big baby." *A really big baby.*

"I'm not worried. Her body's built for carrying babies and giving birth, just like a woman's. The worst I've had to do is reposition a foal before its mother could deliver it." China was at the mare's rear quarters, one hand on the horse's rump while she examined her again. "We haven't lost one yet, have we girl?"

Gorgeous shuddered. China jumped out of the way as a flood of water gushed from the mare's backside.

"Ha!" Leezel gloated. "She almost got you."

Maverick stepped back in case there was more where that ten gallons came from. Holy, umm, crap. The stall was a mess.

"Excellent. Her water's broken. Maverick. Come here." China ignored her sister and waved Maverick to join her. "It's time. You don't want to miss this little guy being born. It's really awesome."

I don't? It is? He sucked up a good case of nerves and crouched behind China, but not too close to Gorgeous. He wasn't taking chances.

Leezel sauntered over and stood behind him, her legs snug against his back and her shoes tucked under his butt. God, she had gotten more and more annoying, and he plain didn't have the patience for it. These two girls couldn't possibly be blood sisters.

"Yeah, Mav. It isn't every day you get to see a derriere this big, huh?" She chuckled, but once again, he chose not to reply. Leezel treated this whole thing as if it were a joke. She resembled an annoying horse fly. One he wanted to bat away—or squash.

The mare groaned again and sure as hell, something happened. A balloon protruded beneath her tail. Had to be— what's it called—the amniotic sack? He brushed a hand over his sweaty face, hoping he didn't look as worried as he felt. *Poor damned Gorgeous. That's got to hurt.*

"Good. It's white," China murmured to herself. She glanced at him. "Sorry. A white sac is good. Red means trouble. We're doing great."

If you say so.

"You seeing two hooves, Sis? One?" Leezel leaned over Maverick's back to watch, damned near tipping him over yet again.

He stuck four fingers to the floor to keep her from pushing him over and rolled the pain in his neck away.

The gal just didn't leave, damn it. Her fingers clamped alongside his neck, her pointy knees under his shoulder blades. He shrugged her off, more important things on his mind than a pushy woman who didn't understand limits. He had never been so nervous in his life, even during battle. Tonight was different.

Gorgeous tossed her head back with an edgy neigh, looked over her shoulder and stared at him. She sounded just like Star out there on that broken hillside. Scared of dying. He smoothed a hand over the poor mare's hindquarter. "You can do this," he offered quietly. *I sure as hell hope.*

One hoof appeared. Then the other.

"Come on, Gorgeous." China's eyes glimmered. She checked the hooves. Another big sigh. "Good. It's okay, mama. Your baby's coming out right."

"Yeah, mama. You're almost there," Leezel added. "Step on it."

Maverick had never seen anything more painful looking. A pair of stilts protruded out of Gorgeous's ass. He held his breath because she held hers. His butt cheeks clenched with sympathy with every flex of her backside. The baby's legs just kept coming. *Ouch, damn it. That has got to hurt.*

She stiffened. Another long, drawn-out groan rumbled up her throat. Every part of her poor body quivered.

"Good girl," China said calmly. "Keep pushing. I'll catch your baby for you."

"Oh, for hell's sake. Get it over with." Leezel kneed Maverick extra-hard. "You've done this four times already, you dumbass. It ain't no big deal." She bumped Maverick as if they were best friends. "Git it? I called the horse an ass. Ha."

Holy shit, he wanted to smack her.

"Shhhhh." China glanced sharply at her sister and then turned right back to Gorgeous. "Take it easy. I'm here."

Maverick pushed off the floor. Between Leezel's roaming hands and mean spirit, he needed away from her. The girl just didn't take a hint.

Gorgeous arched her head back and—*whoosh*. The baby horse's head appeared, quickly followed by its shoulders. Gorgeous blew out a big huff. Relief flooded his body. Goosebumps, too.

Leezel peered at the half-delivered foal sprawled on the hay. "He even alive? Man, he don't look like he's breathing in that sack, does he?"

Maverick's heart pitched into high gear. He looked to Gorgeous. *No. Not a dead baby. Not after all this work.*

"Stop with the doom and gloom, Leezel. The hardest part is over. He's fine." China crouched at the foal's head, took a pair of scissors from the medical bag near her side and clipped through the membrane that covered its face. She suctioned its nostrils until the baby coughed and sputtered, its front hooves already seeking traction on the barn floor even though its rear legs were still inside Gorgeous.

Maverick watched in awe. There was nothing tiny about this baby, but *holy mother of God. What a rush.*

China ducked her head into her shoulders, the brightest smile on her face. "We've got us a brand new foal." Her eyes locked with his. Or something. The instant connection with this very capable and determined woman jolted him. Damn. Her smile was worth walking halfway across country for.

His fingers lifted of their own accord as if they wanted to feel the silky softness of her cheek. As if they had the right to that exquisite pleasure. He dropped them into a fist instead. Minded his business. Someone should've told his eyes to stop looking. They caught the shadow drift through her smile, and he wished he wasn't responsible for it.

"You gonna cut the cord, Sis?" Leezel's annoying voice interrupted the reverent moment. "Or are you gonna keep making goo-goo eyes with the hired help?"

China gulped hard and recovered her smile. Maverick, too. An impulse to gather her and her big baby into his arms rushed him. God, she needed a kiss on that happy face. It was a nice thought. A tremendously tempting thought. But just a thought.

Damned if Leezel didn't spoil that, too. "Shit. Cut the damn cord. I got better things to do than watch this crap all night."

"Not unless I have to. It's better if it happens naturally. You know that. Let him finish coming into the world on his own."

"Whatever. Come on, Mav. Show's over. Let's go."

He lowered his damned eyes, but didn't make a move. The foal did. The rest of him slid onto the hay with another gentle grunt from the mare. She tossed her head and clambered to her feet, breaking the umbilical cord in the process.

China smiled up at Gorgeous. "Look at your pretty baby girl, Mama."

"It's a girl?" Maverick asked.

China nodded, stars in her eyes. "Uh huh. She's thrown a beautiful baby."

Gorgeous plodded over to the bundle of long legs, her nose and tongue snuffling all over the wet body.

Maverick crouched beside China. If his hands had been clean, he would've scrubbed the smile off his face, because he knew he looked ten kinds of silly. Damn it anyway, this gangly creature's birth was the coolest thing he had witnessed in—ever. For a change, his face hurt in a really good way.

China's eyes couldn't have been more radiant, and Maverick had to agree. Gorgeous had thrown a beauty. The foal at her feet was as white as she was. Like mother, like daughter. Both absolutely—gorgeous.

"She threw a filly?" Leezel asked sharply. "Shit. That ain't no good."

China kept grinning. "I don't know why you'd say that. She's perfect, Leezel. Look at her. Not a dark spot on her that I can see."

Leezel stretched and yawned loudly. "So what you wanna do, Mav honey? You gonna stay here and watch nothing, or you wanna celebrate over a bottle of cheap beer, since that's all Sis buys? Course we could always do something else if you're interested in a really good time."

China didn't give him a chance to answer the suggestive invitation. "Look at her. Isn't she beautiful, Leezel?"

"Yeah. Yeah. You seen one horse, you seen 'em all." She took a step toward the door instead of looking at the foal. "I'm real tired after all this drama. It's just a horse. Big deal."

He couldn't believe his ears. Just another horse? No way. This little gal was special. She was Gorgeous's daughter. Maverick made the mistake of glancing up. Leezel had stopped at the barn door, her hands smoothing suggestively down her waist and over her backside. She stuck her bottom lip out like a petulant child that always got her way. Not tonight.

He stifled the urge to throw up in his mouth. He had seen a lot of crap on his overseas tours, but she had the market on *skanky* locked up good and tight.

"Well?" Leezel pouted. "You ready or what?"

He shook his head, hiding his disgust at her continual bawdy lines of bullshit. Yeah, he was ready all right—for her to be gone.

"What's next?" he asked China.

She hadn't moved out of the hay. The foal still lay draped over her lap and the smile of a thousand suns brightened her face. "Third stage. Gorgeous needs to drop the placenta. You can go. I'll stay. I don't mind."

Maverick hunkered down to wait. "How long does that take?"

"Aw, come on. You don't want to wait for that, Mav. It's disgusting. Could be a couple minutes or it could be hours." For some reason, Leezel hadn't left. "It's just twenty pounds of—"

Whoosh. The placenta dropped into the hay behind Gorgeous. Maverick didn't even want to look. It sounded bad enough. He didn't need to see it.

Leezel giggled. "What'd I say? Didn't I just tell you it could take a couple minutes? Do I know this horse, or what?"

He didn't respond. No reason to. The woman was hard angles and brass tacks. Depressing as hell. The sound of her voice assaulted his nerves like nails scratching a chalkboard. Like a toothache on Sunday when dentist offices were closed.

Gorgeous nipped his cap off and tugged his hair as if she needed a snack after all her hard work.

"Hey." He smoothed his hand over the horse's friendly face, and pushed her prehensile lips away. "I get it. You did a good job, but go look at your pretty baby girl and stop eating my hair."

He caught the look on China's face. A wave of heat flushed his face. Yeah. Gorgeous liked him. Maybe China, too.

And maybe he didn't mind.

Chapter Eight

China stayed with Gorgeous and her newborn for the next hour. Mostly she wanted to be there when the foal took her first step. This was the golden hour. The world seemed perfect. One angel slept in her bed and another in the barn. Could another night be so grand? So legendary? Hardly. Miracles like tonight's didn't happen often enough.

Besides, Maverick had already cleaned the stall and settled cross-legged beside her, his elbows on his knees, keeping silent vigil at her side. Another miracle. He had turned from the leaving kind of guy into the very attentive family kind of guy, and she liked it. A lot. His willingness to stay and help lent her a kind of quiet strength she hadn't known since her father passed away. Magic filled the barn again, right up to the rafters. It seemed full of peace, the way a good barn should be.

Unfortunately, Leezel stayed, too. She had commandeered Maverick's bedroll as if she had a right to it. She sprawled across it like a stray cat, her long legs tanned, shaved and ready for action, and her red heels on display. That was Leezel through and through. Up for anything.

"The baby horse isn't eating, yet," Maverick said, still in the middle of his crash course on equine basics. "Shouldn't he be—"

"She's not a baby horse, Mav honey," Leezel said. "She's a foal. If she'd been male like she was supposed to be, she would be a colt. When she gets older she'll be called a filly. Anyway, most foals don't nurse right away. You've been watching too much *Discovery Channel*."

His left brow spiked. Something flittered through his dark eyes. China stifled a smile. He might not say much with his mouth, but those sexy eyes were easy to read. For whatever reason, she and he were on the same wavelength. Another miracle of the barn?

Leezel rambled on, impressing no one but herself. "Sometimes they don't eat at all. Then you gotta take over for their mama and wet nurse 'em."

Maverick looked down between his knees and outright grinned. China pursed her lips before they blossomed into a smile. Apparently, he and she watched a different *Discovery Channel* than Leezel.

China glanced over her shoulder at her sister, still flat on her back on Maverick's bedroll and admiring her nails. "Umm, are you sure you meant wet nurse? Don't you mean—?"

"What did I just say? Wet. Nurse. With gallon-sized baby bottles, smelly formula and all that crap. Don't you remember? Shit. You even milked a mare that time."

China kept her voice as steady as possible. "I remember, but a wet nurse is a woman who breastfeeds another woman's child. You probably meant—"

"Shit! I know what I meant!" Leezel bolted upright. "What's the matter with you? Can't you hear with all those goo-goo eyes you been making at the hired help? Why don't you listen for once?"

China stopped talking. It didn't matter what she said or did. This was just another in a long line of stupid arguments with her sister. She gathered the foal into her arms and wished her sister far, far away.

Leezel jumped to her feet. Hostility radiated off of her. The red polish on her nails flashed under the overhead lights as if sparks might fly from her fingers next. Or her dancing shoes. "You always think you're so smart, don't you? Wet nursing is what you hafta do when you're stuck with a foal whose mother can't stand to look at her!"

Maverick kept his head down, but China couldn't. Leezel's revealing outburst shocked her. They stared at each other, and China didn't like what she saw. Leezel stood there with her high-heeled feet spread and her hands fisted at her side. She had gotten agitated beyond anything this ridiculous argument merited, but that chilly declaration—stuck with a foal whose mother couldn't stand to look at her?

My God. She means Kyrie.

China offered her a way out. "You can stay here for as long as you need to, Leezel. You know that. I'll gladly help you raise Kyrie. Please. It would be like old times again, and we could—"

"Why the hell would I ever stay here? You're such a stupid bitch. Always have been. God, I hate you almost as much as I hate this place." She stomped out the barn door and slammed it behind her.

The gentleman beside her kept looking at the straw, more interested in the floor than the girl fight, but he had heard it all, and now he knew how things truly stood at the Wild Wolf.

China closed her eyes to contain the threatening torrent. She had tried for years to pull Leezel back to the ranch, and every time it ended the same. Screaming at each other. Name calling. Lies and insinuations on Leezel's part. Missing change and small items from the house. The screen door slamming. Then months of silence.

Kyrie deserves so much better. Hell. We all do.

"You milked a mare?"

She gulped, needing to switch gears and let the hurt go. Again. "Yes, umm, my black mare, Minnie, rejected her first foal. It happens. A baby needs its mother's colostrum in the first twelve hours, so I did what I had to do. That's all."

"The foal live?"

She stroked the innocent in her arms, wishing human beings were as easy to get along with as horses. "It's no big deal. New mares get scared sometimes, just like human mothers. I gave Minnie a shot to help her milk drop. She was fine after that."

"You ever lose one?"

She glanced at the door, aching for the tender child sound asleep in her bed. "Not yet."

"Where's the girl?"

"You mean Kyrie?" His probing question startled her. China hoped with all her heart she hadn't triggered Leezel's vindictive side. It didn't take much. "She's sleeping in my room tonight, unless my sister decides to pay me back and makes her move. I'd better go check. Sorry you had to hear that."

He didn't answer, not like she expected him to. She would've left right then and there to check on Kyrie, but Gorgeous whinnied, and up the foal scrambled on shaky, uncertain legs.

China scooted out of her way before the little thing could stumble over her boots.

The foal kissed the floor with her nose once, trembling while she figured out the logistics of four extra-long legs and a heavy head. With one more hopping, little bounce, she planted all four hooves. She still bobbed and weaved back and forth, but this little girl got the hang of standing in record time.

The night was complete. Not perfect anymore, not with Leezel's ugly declaration, but good enough. China couldn't expect more than a healthy foal, a happy mare and her darling niece in her bed for the night. Hopefully, Leezel would go after the rest of the beer and leave Kyrie alone.

China scrambled to her feet, dusting the butt of her jeans as she sighed a deep breath of relief. The foal stalked through the hay to Gorgeous and nuzzled under her mother's belly. And Maverick smiled, another pleasant way to end a long day. There might just be hope for him after all.

"Looks like she knows her way around." Maverick pushed up from the floor and stretched, arching his back, his hands to his hips.

Oh. My. Gosh. Her heart thumped extra hard, and then faltered. Skipped a beat. Or three.

How had she not noticed this man up on the hillside the way she noticed him now? Wide, broad shoulders that led to a narrow waist, his plaid shirt neatly tucked into denims and a belt, slender hips that led to long legs. Work boots. He had cleaned up good.

"What's her name?"

China paused. She had already chosen a very proper name for registration. If a female, *Gypsy Riot*. For a male, *Diligence Dream*. But now she hesitated. The night begged further consideration from this gentleman of very few words. "I'm not sure. What sounds good to you?"

Dark eyes struck her with their intensity. "I've learned a lot today," he admitted quietly. "If she were mine, I'd name her China Love."

She stared at his mouth. How could something so sweet come from a man so taciturn and moody? The crazy thing in her chest accelerated in the quiet hush of the barn. She could've thrown her arms around him and kissed him on the spot, but then he spoiled it. "She's your horse. Name her whatever you want."

He slapped his ball cap against his thigh, pinched the brim and latched it over his forehead as if he had locked himself up for the night. He dropped to his butt on his bedroll and pulled the brim over his face.

Her heart stuttered, threw a rod and puttered back to slower-than-dirt school zone speed. He puzzled the heck out of her, smiling one moment, but barricading himself behind the brim of that darn cap the next.

China latched the stall gate and turned the light off. Despite his indifference, she liked his words. Maverick Carson wasn't the gruff guy she had met on the hillside. Not anymore. He might want to be, but he had blown his stone-cold cover to kingdom come right there in her magical barn. He'd changed the instant he decided to stay and see this thing through.

The trick was on him. China Love it was.

Put that in your pipe and smoke it, Mr. Crabby Carson.

Chapter Nine

Maverick couldn't sleep.

The barn was filled with too much peace. And joy.

After China left, he rolled to his side on his bedroll, propped his head on his elbow and flipped on his penlight. The miracle he had just witnessed had him pumped too full of adrenaline to go to sleep, only this adrenaline rush felt good. His head didn't pound with it like it did after those get-the-hell-out-of-there jolts before overseas battles and firefights. The barn seemed full of energy, a pleasant buzz that kept his brain working overtime.

Life. That's what it was. A squeaky, clean life had just come to be right here in this very barn. Purity and perfection, the ultimate gift of the universe. To him of all people. Damned if he didn't think of his kid brother. Darrell would've loved something like this. Crazy kid.

Gorgeous stood over her foal, the perfect picture of motherhood. The mare seemed to have recovered from the trauma of the whole 'giving birth' experience. The foal mastered those stilt-like legs as quickly as her mother forgot the pains of labor. Curiosity got the best of the baby. She approached him slowly, testing the air in his direction.

He rolled to his butt, cross-legged, his elbows on his knees, and let the foal get acquainted.

Gorgeous didn't seem to care what her offspring did. She dozed while the still damp baby headed toward him.

"Come on, China Love. You can do it," he murmured quietly. China might not use the name, but he intended to. At least, for the night.

With another long-necked step, she allowed his hands on her nose. Then her face. While he smoothed his fingers up her snout and behind her ears, she nuzzled a path over his head, down his neck and into his shirt collar, huffing moist breaths all the way. She had the softest touch. Gentle. Furry. Warm. He shivered. Goosebumps lifted across his shoulders and up his neck. He had never been kissed or tasted by a horse before.

By then she stood over him with her tent-pole legs, her velvet ears twitching as much as her nose and lips. Without a warning, her legs buckled. Down she went with a thump and there he was, sitting in a big old barn with a lapful of one tired, brand-new baby horse.

It didn't seem to bother her where she'd landed, but it humbled him. A tear trickled down his cheek. He had thought himself a failure for so long, the man who'd let his brother die, then left his body behind in the ultimate betrayal. Now there he was, somehow good enough to be blessed with the trust of a tiny creature fresh from Heaven. Pure and innocent and damned near perfect.

The grace of her choosing him lightened the remorse in his heart. Just a little. Just enough that he reached for the guitar by his bedroll.

Maverick pulled it clear of its sturdy case and hugged it against the baby already in his lap. An old cowboy song came to mind. China Love didn't seem upset by the racket, so he strummed a few bars and plunked a few chords just to warm it up in case. It never hurt to find out what a lady liked before a guy let rip a lightning charge of Jimmy Hendrix or the drinking songs of George Jones.

An easier song rolled out of his heart, a simple thing about little baby ducks, old pickup trucks and rain. Should've been about baby horses, but he didn't have one in his repertoire. God, the music matched the mood of the barn. It was good to sing again.

He plunked a few more chords, trying to finish the song he had started miles ago for his brother. It didn't gel. The harmonics didn't feel quite right. He gave it another shot, hoping for inspiration.

They say a man is not supposed to cry.
He's s'posed to tough it out, man up, always show a clear, dry
eye.
They say buck up, that's life, sure sorry, son, and lots of other
crap.
There's just one problem.
You're still gone.
I'm still here...

They say a man is made to do hard tasks.
Go to war. Put down dogs. Do whatever your country asks.
They say be brave, be strong, be all that you can be.
There's just one problem.
You're still gone.
I'm still here...

I watched you fall. I saw you leave.
And I'm left standing here where I don't want to be.
I ain't no hero. I ain't no man.
I'm next to nothing without you
And like hell I understand...

The last word whined out of him. God, no matter how much he worked this piece of shit song, he couldn't make it work. He hit the face of his guitar, angry all over again.

Damned song! Damned broken, messed-up world!

The foal bolted out of his lap, nearly taking the instrument with her.

Maverick reached after her but only caught the brush of her stubby tail as she scampered back to the safety of her mama. He repented instantly. "I didn't mean to scare you. I've just been working out some, umm, things. Damn it, baby. I'm sure sorry."

Here I am telling a horse what's wrong in my head, like I even know. I suck. That's all. I just plain suck.

Swallowing hard, he strummed a sweeter lullaby. Mellow chords filled the barn with peace again. He closed his eyes and let the rage in his heart ease back to simmer with the childhood tune.

It didn't work. His sweet China Love stayed her distance, but he kept trying. When Gorgeous nudged his head with her nose, he took the hint. He had spoiled the concert and the mood, the last thing he wanted to do. The barn had deflated. Or something. All the glow vanished. There he was. Sitting in the dark again.

Pfftt.

The truth was he had been running on empty, going on two years. He could even remember the day it began—the day his guys brought Darrell's body back to camp.

He had already known, but seeing the body bag made it real. Killed the last shred of hope. The whole damned world stopped revolving right then and there. The fight to live and enjoy life, too. It poured out of him onto the tarmac the second the chopper's skids touched down.

His buddy Taylor Armstrong had looked as hard and mean as Maverick had ever seen him that day when he stepped boots to the concrete. He jockeyed to be first off, while Maverick ran straight for him. Got straight away in Maverick's face. Pushed him back. Shoved him. Bellowed some shit about, "You need to back off and let him go, Corporal."

Like any brother could do that.

Taylor made Maverick mad as hell. Didn't let him even touch the bag. Kept him away from Darrell. What was left of Darrell. Hugged him so gawddamned hard it hurt to breathe, not like he could have caught a breath anyway.

That sonofabitchin' medic, Eric *What's-His-Name,* called to Taylor to back off. Angry black eyes full of tears. Red smears on his latex gloves that had to have come from handling what was left of Darrell. "It's okay, man. Let him help. He knows. He knows."

"Knows what? That I let him fucking die?" With that unanswered shriek at heaven, Maverick had dropped to his knees and fell into outer darkness because that was *exactly* what he had done. Let his little brother die when he should've been watching out for him. That's what big brothers were supposed to do. That was what he had promised his mother he would do.

A vortex of suffocating black quicksand had opened beneath his feet and anchored him to shithole Afghanistan to rot for time and eternity. Maybe longer.

And there he had stayed. Stuck in time. Stuck in Hell. His soul couldn't seem to exist inside his mortal frame anymore. It dissolved that day out there in the desert. Like ice. Bit by bit and drop by drop. It didn't even linger long enough to puddle at his feet, just evaporated into—nothing.

The fearsome duo was gone.

Batman failed Robin.

The Caped Crusaders, otherwise known as the Carson brothers, died that day.

Only one brother remained. The wrong one.

Hell sucks.

Maverick had never realized until that telling moment how much Darrell filled his soul. How much an integral part of him a brother could be. Hell, he was a pain in the ass, but baby brothers were made that way. They whined to tag along everywhere their big brother went. They teased until their big brother elbowed or punched them a good one to shut them up. They squealed that their big brother hurt them, then grinned because they got big brother in trouble when they tattled.

Spoiled brats. Every last one of them.

God, I miss him.

Baby Darrell was so damned small the first time his mother put him in Maverick's arms. He had smelled like powder, but his breath smelled sweet, like milk. His hair had been combed into a curl on his rosy forehead. His lips were perfect, pinched together like an old man's into a funny smile. The kid had long, straight fingers, all stiff under his chin, as if he needed to be ready to twiddle them or something.

"Be careful you don't hold him too tight. He's just a baby, you know."

Older brother Maverick had nodded to his mother, and a damned smile had nearly cracked his face. He felt the connection on the spot. *A brother. I've got a brother. And he's all mine.*

Hell, he had never been prouder. *I'd give anything to have him back.*

Recrimination sneaked up on Maverick sometimes, even months after the funeral. The chaplain said it took time to process grief. Hell. There wasn't enough time in all of eternity to process this kind of empty. This barren, hollow hole where a reason to get up in the morning had once existed. A reason to feel. A reason to live. To laugh.

All he'd gotten stuck with was a reason to cry.

The Corps taught *keeping on* no matter what, but Maverick had walked away from the Corps and all their high, patriotic ideals. The TEAM, too. Walking helped, but it didn't change what had happened. The medical field hadn't come up with prosthetic hearts yet. Doctors still couldn't heal the empty, *brotherless* feeling.

Maverick put the guitar back in its case, zipped it shut and leaned against his bedroll. The busy day caught up with him. He'd rescued a horse and its owner from a little landslide, then walked what felt like twenty miles, but was more likely five, to said owner's ranch. He helped with a few domestic chores. Ran a biker club off China's property. Witnessed a blessed miracle. Not bad for a guy who hadn't had a clue where he was headed when the sun came up.

Well, he knew now. Tomorrow would be busy. He had stalls to muck. Chickens to feed. Fields to plow. He'd already done a quick load of laundry in the bunkhouse while he had showered, then dried his jeans and raggedy shirts in the dryer and repacked everything in his backpack.

The scent of alfalfa and straw filled his nostrils. He didn't want much, and he sure as hell didn't expect much, but the comfort of the barn lulled him into a more peaceful frame of mind. The last thing he felt was the foal's hard head against his chest again. A pointed knee in his ribs. The sweet, milky breath of a newborn in his face.

Friendly, old Star nickered from another stall. The big guy didn't seem fazed in the least that he had a new roommate. Stall mate. Stable mate? Whatever. Maverick let the farm terminology go. A couple of cats roamed the stacks of baled hay in the corner. Life seemed simple again.

She couldn't sleep.

It honestly felt like Christmas morning, only the best gift had been stashed out in the barn. China eased out of her bed. Kyrie was still fast asleep, so China kept her movements quiet. She wrapped her robe around her tank top and flannel shorts. Silently, she padded down her stairs and opened her screen door as slowly as possible to avoid the squeak. *So far, so good.*

The quarter moon cast shadows across the empty lawn from the west. A spring moon, it would be over the horizon by sunrise. Just as carefully, she closed the screen door behind her and tiptoed down the steps and across the yard. The bunkhouse lights were off. X and Z were no doubt sleeping off their liquid lunch from Shorty's. The Milky Way glittered overhead in the dark sky. What a night. It seemed somehow reverent and holy.

She smiled with each step. With one hand pressed against the doorjamb and the other on the handle, China pulled it slowly open so as not to disturb her new baby.

Gorgeous nickered. A soft glow glimmered at the edge of the stall.

China's heart melted to a puddle at her feet. Her eyes went misty, her knees weak.

Oh my.

There lay Maverick, on his back, fully dressed. The most beautiful, long-legged foal in the world was snuggled sound asleep in his arms. She lay with her back even with his side, her long legs spread out on the barn floor next to him, her head on his shoulder like a faithful puppy.

Gorgeous nickered again, as if scolding China. *'Shouldn't you be in bed, too?'*

She pressed her fist to her mouth to keep from voicing the song alive in her heart, *Joy to the World*.

He looked like a kid, his hair mussed and his handsome face relaxed. Not one defensive line etched his forehead. His brows didn't flex into that perpetual, pesky *V*. Both hat and dark glasses were somewhere else instead of hiding those beautiful eyes, now closed in slumber. The man looked like he hadn't a care in the world.

She took a few steps into the barn, not wanting to disturb him or the foal, but needing to see more. What a perfect picture. Warmth flooded her chest, rising high in her throat. The thickest dark lashes curled against his cheek. All the grumpiness he projected during the day had been replaced with innocent boyish charm. She wanted to kneel beside him and smooth a hand over that manly face. Hell, she wanted to wake him up and kiss him.

Instead, she kept her hands to herself and retreated, her heart full of emotion she had to wipe the excess of it off her face. In the middle of her torn-up yard with its broken clothesline and ruined garden, she paused to gaze heavenward. The Milky Way glittered across the top of her world. Her father was up there somewhere, maybe smiling down. Only he could understand.

She sniffed one more time and wiped her eyes.

Oh, Daddy. Isn't it cool? Our barn is full of magic again.

Chapter Ten

"Aww! She so cute!" Kyrie stood on the lowest rail of the stall, pointing in excitement.

The foal turned into a bouncing livewire one minute and a sleeping baby the next. The innocent similarities between all newborn animals, including those of the human variety, made China smile. Nothing sweeter than babies in spring.

She had come early to the barn, last night's tender picture still on her mind. Kyrie had tagged along. Maverick was nowhere in sight, but he had packed his bedroll in the corner outside the stall.

"Kin I give her a name?"

China tested the name Maverick had chosen. She liked it even more this morning, especially, after what she had seen last night. "She's already got a name. China Love."

"China what?" Leezel was already awake and hung-over. Crabby. No surprise there.

China shot her a quick glance, not sure where her sister slept last night. Her bed was still made when she had walked by earlier. "I'm going to register her as China Love."

"Figures you'd name 'em all after you." Leezel huffed.

"I didn't. Maverick chose it, and I happen to like it. Besides, it fits. She's pure-white like a piece of fine china, and she's a love."

Leezel came to the stall gate, her hand extended through it, snapping her fingers to coax Gorgeous closer. Oddly, her hair was washed, her makeup already applied too thickly for the day, and her eyes darkened with extra liner.

China looked twice. Leezel wore a tinier pair of shorts than yesterday, if that was even possible. Those stupid red heels. The skimpy T-shirt she'd chosen resembled a corset of all things. She was on the prowl, but not for horses.

When Gorgeous didn't move a hoof in her direction, Leezel flicked her fingernails at the mare in dismissal. She turned and planted her backside against the stall gate. "Not like it would stop me, but you got something going on with that cowboy you just hired? That Maverick fella?"

China glanced at Kyrie to make sure she wouldn't overhear. It was uncanny that Leezel had picked up on that lone gunslinger, cowboy quality Maverick hid beneath that unsmiling face, but then, Leezel knew men.

"Come on, Sis. How long's he been hanging around? A week? A month? Spit it out."

"He showed up yesterday. Maverick helped me rescue Star from a slide just past Kotter's cabin. That's all. I was out riding and—"

"I don't care what you were doing. You're always riding or racing. What I want to know is, is he fun? Does he drink? Smoke? Pop pills? Anything?"

"No. He's a good man." He had a knack for showing up at the right place at the right time. Her horses liked him. What else was there? *Heck, I like him. He's a gentle man who honestly cares about others. Maybe even—me.*

"He's a hunk." Leezel bit the edge of a manicured nail. "Kinda uptight, but I'm working on that."

"You are, huh?" Anything in pants and breathing made Leezel's list. If she had her sights set on Maverick, well, China didn't care. He seemed the kind who could take care of himself.

"Come on." China reached for Kyrie's hand and pulled her off the ground and into her arms, in case the girl might say something Leezel wouldn't like. It was too early in the day for another confrontation. "I'll bet you're hungry. Let's go make breakfast."

"Kin you make pamcakes?" Kyrie whispered, her hand cupped against China's ear.

"I can make *pamcakes* that look like horses," China whispered back.

Kyrie scrunched her shoulders. "Kin you make 'em wook wike puppies and kitties?"

China chuckled. She would make pancakes fly if it made her niece smile. The rumble of an approaching motorcycle brought her to a halt. She shielded her eyes from the early morning sun. Damn it. Not Reardon again.

"Sounds like you got company, Sis." Leezel walked a few steps behind China and Kyrie.

Reardon gunned his Harley into the yard. He rode alone.

China planted her feet and glared. Troy had a lot of nerve showing up. Bike trails and ruts still circled her yard and the ruined vegetable garden. She hadn't had the time to clean anything.

Then she looked twice. The clothesline posts stood straight in their holes, the lines re-strung. Her ruined vegetable garden didn't look so bad, either. Although wilted and bedraggled, the pepper and tomato plants were upright, some staked. A circle of dark soil around each plant declared all had been watered. Carefully.

The spinach, cucumbers, and carrots resembled plants again instead of the roadkill they looked like yesterday. Even the birdbath had been restored to its proper place, its basin filled with water. No copper statue rose up from the center of the dish yet, but everything else looked—damned good.

Had Maverick already fed the chickens? Mucked the stalls? She hadn't noticed earlier if those chores were done, but she wondered now. Her eyes sought the chicken coop. The hens scratching near the entrance seemed content. Darn. He would be hard to replace when the time came that he up and left.

Leezel already stood with Reardon at his bike, their knees interlocked and her hands under his leather vest. He had removed his helmet, and silenced his bike. Judging by the salacious smirk on his ugly face, Leezel must've been saying all the right things.

China couldn't tell which was worse. He kept coming back for more crap and Leezel kept dishing it out. Kyrie snuggled deeper into her arms and buried her face in her neck. Her little body trembled. China's hackles lifted. This baby was scared. *Why?*

China squared her shoulders and prepared for another standoff. "What are you doing here, Reardon? You need to leave."

He stuck his insolent chin at her. "Came to see my woman. What else?"

Leezel glanced back. "Do you mind? We're talking here."

"I don't care if you're baking a cake. Get off my land. Now."

"This ain't just your land." Leezel turned on China. "It's half mine too, and my man can stay if he wants."

"Your man? Now he's *your* man? Who do you think did all this damage to *your* land?" China waved her hand around the yard. "He and his club tore this place up yesterday. He threatened me with a gun, Leezel. Don't you get it? He's trouble, and I've had enough of him coming around here whenever he wants. It stops now. Take your game somewhere else, Reardon."

He shot an arc of brown spit between his two front teeth and grinned. "Why? You think you can hurt me with that little pea shooter you keep behind your back door?"

"You bet your ass." She meant to sound tough, but her heart thudded. How did he know where she kept her father's rifle? He had never been in her home, unless—Leezel let him in. China pressed Kyrie to her breast, scared for the first time in a long time. Leezel wouldn't do that, would she? *Oh, my God. She would.*

China sensed him behind her before she turned around and saw him. *Maverick.* He hadn't said a word, just appeared like he had some sixth sense for trouble.

Reardon noticed him. So did Leezel. She untangled her arms and legs from Reardon's and turned, her eyes gleaming and her hips twitching. "Morning, cowboy. You're up kinda late this morning, aren't you?"

He didn't respond. Didn't even grunt in acknowledgement that he had heard her. He had set his jaw in a hard line, locked in a stare behind those dark glasses and the brim of his ball cap. There was nothing threatening in his stance, but China saw what Leezel and Reardon couldn't possibly understand. This man had backbone. He might not talk much, but he stood for something.

Leezel sauntered flirtatiously toward Maverick, straight through his and Reardon's line of sight. She always had to be the center of attention, causing trouble with every step.

"Git yer ass back here," Reardon ordered, his index finger stabbed toward the dirt at his boots.

Leezel paid her ex-boyfriend no more attention than she paid Kyrie.

Reardon bellowed again. "I didn't come all the way out here to watch your fat ass walking away from me, woman."

That did it. Leezel spun around and the war was on. She would've made it more believable if she hadn't bent forward while she shook her finger at Reardon. Then China knew. This wasn't an argument. It was a show for Maverick's benefit. Want to or not, he was getting an eyeful of her sister's ass in those tiny shorts.

"I know what you came for and I got news for you, Mr. Troy Reardon. You can't have her."

China's heart stalled. *Her?*

Reardon took a step away from his bike, his lip lifted in a sneer. "I can if I want. I'll take her. Wanna watch? Court says she's mine, too."

His pockmarked chin defined his whole face. He stuck it out like no one could make him leave. Like he would take Kyrie when he did.

China clutched the child tighter. Her mouth went dry. *My God, Leezel. What have you done this time? You wouldn't. Not to Kyrie.*

"You don't really want her. You and me both know that. All you want is to make trouble and the answer is no. No. No!" By the time Leezel ended her dramatic rant, she was red-faced and screaming, her backside shaking plenty. "You can't have my baby girl. Now git the hell out of here like my big sister said."

She almost sounded convincing, but fear flooded China's stomach. She knew her sister. Kyrie was a helpless pawn in a nasty power play between two selfish punks. Or—Leezel thought she could manipulate Maverick into coming to her rescue. All that *'poor me'* bullshit was nothing but a show for his sake. She had said he was uptight. Was this part of her plan to loosen him up? Get him to fight Reardon to save her child, when in the end, Leezel would cast both men aside the minute she tired of the game.

China couldn't swallow. Leezel was capable of both scenarios. China turned her niece's face into her shoulder and marched to the porch. Bile lifted up the back of her throat just thinking of this precious child with the likes of a scumbag like Reardon. Leezel was bad enough, but Reardon?

Hell no. You can't have her. I'll fight you to the death this time. Both of you. Or I'll run and I'll take Kyrie with me. You'll never see me again.

"Hey, c'mon now. Mellow out, babe. Why don't you and me go grab us a bite of breakfast and talk about it?" Reardon's voice softened. He had his helmet back on and the kickstand up. "You know you like an early morning ride."

He knew Leezel to a T as well. Just like clockwork, she strutted straight back to his side and sidled onto the seat behind him. He lifted his chin and tossed a final sneer toward Maverick. Leezel refused the helmet he offered, but ran her fingers through her hair as if putting on a show.

The bike rumbled. She stretched both arms wide and blew Maverick a kiss behind Reardon's back as they roared away.

China bit her lip. Reardon had no more business with a child than a pig had with wings. There had to be a way to keep her niece safe. Her brain pinged over solutions. Maybe it was time to have that custody fight. Better yet, sell the ranch and move someplace where Leezel and Reardon couldn't find her. Non-custodial parents did it all the time. They kidnapped their children to give them a better life. Not all countries allowed extradition. She would change her name. Kyrie's, too. It could work.

"You is squishin' me, Andy China," Kyrie complained.

"Oh. Sorry." China loosened her desperate grip. "I'm sorry. I just... I just..." *I'm just scared to death what could happen to you.*

"You okay, ma'am?" Maverick asked.

She jumped, startled at his hand on her forearm. "No, I mean, I'm, umm, yes. I'm fine. I'm just..." *Scared.*

The odd mix of emotions she read in his eyes took her breath. His sunglasses were up high on the brim of his cap. This morning his pupils were darker and dangerous, yet full of concern at the same time. And fire. Fire that could bring warmth as easily as pain.

She opened her mouth to tell him how scared she was, how bad Leezel could make Kyrie's life, but snapped it closed again. Bosses didn't do stuff like that. They kept the line between them and their employees. Besides, he was a short-timer. Here today. Gone tomorrow.

He tipped two fingers to the brim, replaced his dark glasses and turned to leave.

"Umm, breakfast?" China couldn't believe the stupid words she had just blurted out. What made her an idiot when Maverick was around? She cleared her throat and tried again. "What I meant to say is that I'm going inside to make breakfast. Are you hungry? You're welcome to join me and Kyrie." She blew a loose twirl of hair out of her eyes while she composed herself and waited.

Maverick pivoted on his heel to face her. "No thanks, ma'am. I'm in the middle of something right now."

Darn, why did I give him all those chores?

"Bacon?" And now she wanted to smack herself. *Yes, men like bacon, but he's not a dog.* "I'm going to fix bacon and eggs, and you need a good breakfast to start your day. Please join us."

"And pamcakes," Kyrie declared proudly. Her body relaxed the second her mother and Reardon rode away. "Andy China is makin' me puppy pamcakes. Want some?"

"Yes. Pancakes, too." China grimaced. By now, he probably thought she was as big a flirt as Leezel. At least she hadn't wiggled her ass yet. Or had she? She wasn't so sure.

His shaded face beneath the brim of his cap remained as expressionless as before. No hint of a smile or a frown. Just— nothing. Once again, his lack of conversational skills struck her. This man didn't have a clue about small talk, and she could sure use some.

She got the point and waved him away. "That's okay. Never mind. You're busy."

"Yes, ma'am. I am." He stood there, as if waiting for her to finish.

Her brain kicked into I-own-this-ranch gear. "I'll leave some food on the table. Come and eat when you're ready."

"Thanks. I will." He turned and walked toward the tractor shed, and it was her turn to look twice. This man had shoulders. He walked with purpose, as if he knew where he was going even though he didn't. This was her place, yet somehow he had walked into it as if he had work to do here, and one way or the other, it would get done.

Damn. He's growing on me whether I like it or not.

China smoothed Kyrie's hair out of her eyes and pulled the screen door open. She closed it and opened it again, looking the piano hinge up and down. It hadn't squeaked. Not once. Someone oiled it. The door fit smoothly into the frame, too. The hydraulic hinge actually worked. The door didn't even slam. Instead, it closed silently and slowly for the first time since she installed it.

She cast another glance at Maverick's retreating backside. He had been busy, but damn. He had nice pockets.

Chapter Eleven

"She's a purdy little thing."

Old man Foster glowed with pride as he studied China Love with her mother.

Maverick had just cleaned their stall and stood watching. He missed breakfast, but that was nothing new. He went without most days.

The old codger rubbed a hand over his whiskered chin. China must've called him, and Maverick suspected the reason why. Foster tipped his dusty old cowboy hat back on his forehead when he talked with China, but he couldn't take his eyes off his prize. He already owned the foal, damn him.

"Whatcha gonna name her, Miss China?"

"I'm registering her as China Love. Course, it is up to you, Mr. Foster. Name her whatever you want."

So, she had taken his suggestion for a name for the foal to heart, just not enough to keep the baby that went with it. Maverick growled under his breath. The feeling they'd shared last night, that feeling of tenderness or whatever it was, changed to a stone in his gut. This newborn meant nothing to her but another buck in the bank. The ranch was a moneymaking business. A place where horses were bred, raised, and sold. That was all. *Kids, my ass. Damn her.*

He steeled his heart again. *Should've known better, Carson. You never learn.*

"I was thinking something like Opal or Pearl cuz she's so purdy and so white." Foster grinned, a funny sight amidst all the wrinkles and lines on his old face. The man had to be eighty if he were a day. "Yer daddy would sure be proud of you, little girl."

China beamed. "I'll wean her in six months. She'll be ready to go a month or so after that if you want to handle the socializing yourself. Are you okay with that timeframe?"

Foster stepped away from the corral. "Sure glad you're letting me have her."

"She comes from good stock, Henry. Her sire is Hex, and you already know her dam. China Love will do a good job pulling for you when she's old enough. I'm sure of it."

"Can't go wrong with bloodlines like that." The old man grinned and took China's hand. "Thanks again for the call. Wish I'd been here when she was foaled, but..." he chuckled. "Ladies always seem to be on their own time schedules, don't they? If I'd a been here, we'd probably still be waiting."

China shook his hand. "You come see her anytime you want. You're always welcome."

"I will. Thanks again." Mr. Foster waved once more before he climbed into his rattletrap of a pick-up truck and drove away.

Pearl? Opal? Hell no. They'd fit an old woman, not a spritely young foal that danced on air.

"What's he need her for?" Even Maverick heard the accusation in his voice.

"Foster?" China turned with a gentle smile on her lips. "Henry runs the street trolley over in Cody. He lost one of his Clydesdales, Whiskers, last winter. China Love will pull the trolley once she's old enough."

"Sounds like hard work for a young horse."

"It's a small trolley."

"He won't work her until she's ready?"

China's face softened. "Foster's a decent man. He'll take good care of her. I don't sell my kids to just anyone."

Maverick stood with one boot on the lowest rail, unhappy with this turn of events, and damned if he knew why. It wasn't like he intended to buy her. The minute he placed his arms on the top of the fence, the foal bounced over to him and stuck her head through the rails. He scratched her ears, and in turn, she wiggled them as if she was half-rabbit instead of all horse. *Foster better take damned good care of you or I'll kick that old man's ass.*

"You like her, don't you?" China had that light in her eyes again, as if she could see right into his head and might know exactly what was going on in there. *Good luck with that.*

"She's okay." Maverick stepped away from the corral. Truth was, China Love was more than okay. The danged little thing had wormed her way into his heart the minute he laid eyes on her, and sleeping in her stall had only made her friendlier. He guessed the foal thought he was another horse or something. And sometimes the way Gorgeous acted, he wasn't sure who was the pet—him or her. They nibbled at him as much as he had handled them. Damn. It had only taken one night to get his heart wrapped around the axle again. *I should've kept on walking.*

"I've got six more mares ready to deliver, you know."

Maverick looked up at that comment, not sure how to respond. Was that supposed to soften the loss of China Love? Did China mean for him to hang around and help with those births, too?

He tucked both hands in his pockets and waited her out.

"You didn't think Gorgeous was my only brood mare, did you?"

He shrugged. It didn't matter what he thought. He didn't plan to hang around.

"Gorgeous foaled early this year. Most of the mares won't drop for another month. If you're still around, maybe you can help out with Misty, Sunshine, Cookie, Frost, Minnie, and Sugar."

He raised a brow when she spouted off the names of her mares like a mother runs through the names of her children.

"You selling them, too?" He meant to soften his tone, but ended up sounding as snarky as before.

"Well, of course, but right now, I've got a fence line to check. My neighbor, Rich Williams, thinks I might have a hole up along the south line of the east forty. You interested in a ride? I promise the hill won't move this time." China stood waiting, like a boss who'd just made a request that was really an order.

He scanned her straw hat, her western shirt and on down to her dusty boots. His Oakleys provided an instant barrier when he needed one, and right now they allowed him to look and not be seen doing it.

She wore denim. The red-checkered western shirt tied off at her midriff gave her a carefree look, not what Maverick expected in a calculating horse breeder. Her boots were scuffed. She didn't indulge in those stupid fake nails like her sister did. China's hands looked sturdy, as if they could help a man dig a half-buried horse out of the hillside when needed. That racked up another couple more points in her favor. If he cared, which he didn't. Not really.

"How you getting there?"

"We'll be riding Star and Ebony. I'm taking Kyrie along, too."

Maverick shrugged. He suspected she would bring the girl since Leezel hadn't returned from her morning *ride* yet. "Tell me when."

"Now."

Now? Great. He had other self-appointed work to do. The ranch house rain gutter sagged off the east end of the house. The roof was missing a few shingles out back. Two windows on the barn were cracked and the birdbath needed a concrete base to make it more stable.

Once those two hired hands in the bunkhouse stopped snoring, he had a field of grass hay to cut and another to plow. He would've taken care of that already if he had found the tractor. Apparently, the equipment shed wasn't meant for vehicles. The thing was full of tractor and truck parts, but nothing that worked. If he hadn't been so pigheaded, he would've asked China where she kept the tractor, but hell. A man doesn't ask his boss where she keeps her tools. He just finds 'em and takes care of business.

China headed into the barn so he followed her straight out the back door where Star and Ebony were saddled and ready to go. Damned if she hadn't anticipated his answer before she asked. That was kind of sneaky. Or smart.

China busied herself with the horses. "Would you find Kyrie for me? She was playing with some kittens earlier, so she's got to be in the barn somewhere."

Great. Now I'm a babysitter. He did as he was told anyway. After all, she was the boss lady. He was just the help. Like a dumbass, he hadn't even negotiated a salary when he accepted this twenty-four-seven job. Not like he needed the money, but still. He should've played that hand a little smarter.

The girl wasn't hard to locate. She lay tucked between two bales of hay, sound asleep with a couple orange tabby kittens snuggled in her arms. The mother and a black kitten were nestled between her boots.

Damned if that little girl, her black hair glistening beneath her head, didn't touch him in a way he didn't expect. The mother cat yowled a low warning, but he had already stopped moving. It was one of those picture-perfect moments that took a man's breath away.

A glimmering shaft of sunlight streaked across Kyrie's face like a beam from heaven. He looked down on her in her cowboy boots and jeans, wondering how he was supposed to pick up an angel in the first place, and wishing he didn't have to in the second. She looked—breakable. Too damned sweet for the likes of him.

China came up beside him. "Aw. She looks cute, doesn't she?"

He nodded. Cute was a good word for this tiny little gal, the spitting image of her aunt.

She dropped to her knees beside Kyrie. Very gently, she reached past the snippy mother cat and stroked her niece's cheek. "Hey there. Time to wake up."

Maverick took a step back and folded his arms. China seemed different this morning and that shirt she wore was killing him. He liked it. Funny thing was her top button was fastened up good and proper. No cleavage showed, just a couple inches of bare skin around her back and stomach.

Plus, she handled Kyrie as if she had all the time in the world. As if Kyrie was the most important thing in her life. He liked that, too. After a couple more stokes on her cheek, Kyrie's nose twitched. She looked up at her aunt through sleepy, dazed eyes.

"Do you want to go for a ride with me and Maverick?" China asked. Very carefully, she pulled one limp kitten after another out of Kyrie's arms and set them out of the way, then scooped Kyrie up and dusted the hay off. "You can help me fix the fence, okay?"

"Uh huh." Kyrie snuggled into her aunt's shoulder and went right back to sleep.

China nodded toward Star. "You mount Star and I'll hand Kyrie up to you," she told Maverick.

"Me?" *Why the hell me?*

"Sure. You're a big guy. You'll be okay."

Maverick grunted and did as he was told, not sure how he would handle holding onto a little kid and a horse the size of Star at the same time. He hadn't ridden since his eighth birthday party, and that Shetland pony didn't count. Still, how hard could it be?

Star didn't flinch or shift when he grabbed the saddle horn.

"Come around to this side," China said. "You always mount from the left."

He shifted to the other side of the horse and began again. Clutching the saddle horn where the reins were loosely wrapped, he put one boot in the stirrup and swung his leg over the horse's broad back. Star didn't move that time, either. For a draft horse, he was a comfortable fit.

"I already check the girth and stirrups," China said, lifting Kyrie up high for him to take. "You look to be about X's height, but tell me if they're uncomfortable. I don't want you falling off."

"Feels about right." He leaned over and scooped Kyrie out of China's arms. The little girl accepted the handoff without so much as a sigh.

China mounted Ebony. "You two doing okay?"

"We're good." Maverick reined Star to the right until the horses were neck to neck.

"Then let's go." China urged the black stallion through the barn and out the open front doors.

Maverick tapped Star's sides with the inside of his boots and followed. He didn't have to do much other than hold onto the girl and the reins. The horses seemed to know where they were going. Before long, they turned off the gravel road and travelled up the gently swelling hills that circled the ranch.

China pivoted in her saddle. "How is she?"

"Sleeping." The sun was out in full force again. Maverick had already covered Kyrie's head with his cap so she wouldn't get burned. The little girl had turned into a sweaty little ragdoll in his arm, but holding her created a surge of feelings he wasn't prepared for. Kyrie reminded him of the newborn foal, only much more delicate.

The dichotomy between what he used his hands for in the past and what he held now made him thoughtful. Holding reins in one hand and life in the other felt so much better than squeezing off triggers and ramming ammo.

"Spring is her favorite time of year. She loves all the new babies here at the ranch."

"Yep."

The horses plodded steadily uphill. It wasn't a steep climb. The higher they went, the more the panoramic view expanded into sheer, breathtaking beauty.

Rolling hills covered in grass and sagebrush, along with quaking aspen tucked into the valleys and ravines, made for a beautiful sight, one a man couldn't see from the road below. Purple mountains to the west stood snowcapped under a clear blue sky that boasted circling hawks overhead and a light, fragrant breeze in his face.

The air felt cleaner in Wyoming, or maybe it was just the altitude. He took a deep breath. Star's ambling gait added to the peaceful morning. Between the warmth of the child snuggled into his side and the scenery, the troubles he had carried from sea-to-shining-sea dropped away.

"This is where the eastern property line of the Wild Wolf begins." China nodded at the fence line as she edged Ebony closer to Star. "You want me to take her for a while?"

"She's fine." Maverick looked down at the little girl's face. His cap had slid over her forehead so he tipped it back with his finger. Thinking of Leezel and Reardon's argument over child custody sparked a protective instinct, but then, Reardon sparked a lot of other instincts. None of them pleasant.

It wasn't his business, but it was surprising Leezel didn't have a passel of illegitimate kids given her slutty behavior. Still—holding this little one in his arm, Maverick knew he would do what he could for Kyrie despite her mother. He was dumb like that.

China had *that look* on her face again, the one she had worn since the foal's birth. He stiffened his back and slapped the reins, glad for his dark glasses. Whatever she was thinking about him needed to stop.

"Hey. Slow down. We're here." She reined Ebony to a halt. The barbed wire fence they'd been following turned at an obtuse angle and continued up and over the next hill before it dipped into the neighboring ravine.

Maverick turned Star around. "The horses come up this high?"

"No, but the cattle do."

"You raise cattle?" That was news.

"Yeah. We turned them out a couple weeks ago for summer grazing. They're around here somewhere."

"How many head?"

"Should be ninety Black Angus in this field, give or take a few; another hundred and fifty head of red in the next field yonder. I'm hoping for twice that number by fall if all goes well." She seemed so sure of herself.

"They'll all calve?"

"No, but most of them will." China urged Ebony slowly forward as they patrolled the fence. "I keep the horses closer to the barn. Beef might be pricey, but my kids are priceless." She straightened in her saddle and turned halfway around, pointing to a grove of scraggly pines not far from the fence. "See? There's part of the herd."

All he saw was the tanned, bare skin at her waist and the swell of her ass against the leather saddle when she tilted forward. A spark sprang to life in his belly.

"Maverick. Don't you see them? They're right over there."

Damn. Busted. Well, almost. His Oakleys saved his sorry butt. He averted his gaze from her backside to the direction she pointed. Sure enough, a couple dozen black cows stared back at him, their tails switching. A group of calves lay curled on the ground while another nursed from its mother.

"One, two, eight, nine." She nodded as if she agreed with herself. "Yeah. Double or nothing by October. That's the plan."

"What makes you so sure?" He had to ask.

She nodded. "Because of bulls like my buddy over there, Sir T-Bone."

Maverick followed the direction of her nod. A black bull sauntered out of the trees, his ears pitched forward, definitely on guard duty.

"What happens in October?" Maverick's arm had gone to sleep, but as much as he needed to readjust Kyrie, he didn't want to. The privilege of her trust resonated with him, and frankly, he liked her sleeping there.

"My neighbors help me with round up. The yearlings go to the auction and the rest will winter in the lower pastures. I might put one or two in the freezer, but most pay the bills."

"Then you start all over again next year?" He kicked Star's belly lightly to keep up with Ebony while China continued checking the fence. The big fella seemed to think he should nibble on every daisy within range of his prehensile lips.

"That or I sell 'em and move to Alaska."

"You what?"

China giggled. "Just kidding. I could never leave this place. This is my home."

The fragrant breeze rippling uphill tossed her hair. She grabbed her hat before it blew away. She seemed as much a part of this wide-open country as the wind and sky. "It smells good up here. Don't you think?"

He barely twitched his nose and shrugged. "Smells like horseshit to me."

Her mouth dropped opened. "Why, Mr. Carson. Did you just make a joke?"

Maybe. Even a city boy like him could tell the pleasant scent on the breeze today didn't have anything to do with horses. Or beef cattle.

"It's Russian Olive. It only blooms in spring. It makes me want to take a bite out of the air or just breathe it all in. Every last morsel." China seemed especially talkative this morning. She leaned over her saddle horn, as if she was trying to figure him out. "Don't you ever take your glasses off? It would be easier to know when you were teasing if I could see your eyes."

Thankfully, Kyrie stirred in his arms, and he didn't have to answer. He peered down into the face of a worried but smiling angel with apple-red cheeks. The resemblance to China startled him. Kyrie stared up at him with serious dark eyes lined with the longest lashes. Her lips turned into a pout, and her bottom lip stuck out. She didn't struggle or cry, but she was concerned.

"Hey, sleepyhead." He adjusted her so she could see her aunt. "Who's that?"

"Andy China," Kyrie whispered somberly. She scratched her nose and yawned.

China reined Ebony around so she faced Maverick and Kyrie. "You want to ride with me a while?"

"Nope." She wiggled her butt tighter into the crook of Maverick's arm. "I is ridin' my favwit horsey."

"Yes, you and Maverick are riding Star. Are you sure you don't want to ride with me?"

"Uh huh." Kyrie squinted in the bright sunshine as she leaned back to see Maverick better. "You is Mavwick?"

He tapped his dark glasses down his nose and peered over the rims. "Yes, ma'am. At your service."

"Does you yike me?"

The question irked him, not because she had asked it, but because of the worry in her pretty blue eyes. He couldn't help himself. "I like you a lot, Kyrie."

Two little arms circled his neck, and once again he was glad for his Oakleys. He stabbed them back into place. This baby girl had just touched a part of him he had long thought dead. Turned out it wasn't.

He hoped he wasn't out of line, hugging a little girl, but darn it anyway, Kyrie was an angel, and he needed a hug with no strings attached.

"I yikes you, too, Mavwick," she whispered as if it was their secret.

God, she was breaking his heart. He closed his eyes and let the warmth of her gentleness in. *How the hell do little kids do this? Reach into the darkest cave and splash sunshine all over the place like it's no big deal?*

"Damn it anyway." China slid off Ebony and stood with her hands on her hips. "I hate it when Rich is right. He said he saw a couple of my strays roaming his land. I was hoping he mistook a couple deer for my beef, but look at this."

Three strands of the barbed-wire fence were busted through, one post down. Maverick urged Star alongside it for a better view. The wire hadn't been broken. It had been cut. Definite chain marks circled the middle of the fence post.

China shielded her eyes with her palm while she surveyed the hills around her. "Who would drive all the way up here in the middle of nowhere just to vandalize my fence?"

Maverick looked the nearby ground over. A single set of tire tracks was evident alongside the fence, but he saw things China wouldn't have known to look for. Sniper hides. Ambushes. Buried explosive devices and mayhem. Those kinds of things.

The perfect concealment for an enemy combatant in a stand of quakies about twenty fence posts ahead. The rocky outcrop of red rock two clicks away on the opposite hill where a good sniper could lie in wait all day, make a kill shot, and slip away without being noticed.

This place wasn't safe. Not by a long shot. The pleasant hill morphed into another hill in a very different country far away. Minarets and prayer towers sprung up everywhere. Darkness thundered in his head, paralyzing his sense of direction. It took all of his resolve to not dive off Star's back with Kyrie and run for cover.

"You okay?" China peered up at him, her face wrinkled with worry.

"Fine," he lied, his fingers trembling on the reins. The scenery shimmered, then transformed back into grass and quakies. He took a deep breath and forced the panic down. Striving for control, he changed the subject. "You bring anything to fix the fence?"

"Yes." China didn't say anything more. She walked the fence line, straight toward that dangerous stand of quakies and the sniper that wasn't really there. She stopped, removed a loop of coiled wire from a post about ten posts down and started back to him. To safety.

His heart pounded like a mother. Every inch of him roared, '*Run, damn it. Get your ass back here.*'

Out of the blue, a meadowlark burst forth with a joyful peal, jolting him back to the hills of Wyoming. The breeze cooled his worried brow, and the countryside was once again full of nothing more than the determination of a very stubborn woman. He wasn't in the middle of a kill-zone. This wasn't even Afghanistan. She hadn't seen what he had seen because snipers and Taliban soldiers weren't there to be seen. They were in his hard head, damn it.

The annoying troll, hypervigilance skulking up the back of his neck slacked off. He sucked in a big breath of relief and let it fill his gut. *Okay, yeah. I'm not there. I'm here. In Wyoming.*

The view of her walking back to him eased the last of his irrational fear away. She looked angry, but man, it was a beautiful kind of anger. China wasn't made of fluff and hair products. Certainly not acrylic nails. No. She was denim and boots, a cowboy hat for shade instead of show, and the mother of all creatures great and small on her ranch. She was more than a businesswoman handling a serious horse-breeding ranch, though. With the blush of the sun on her face and the wind playing with her hat and hair, she was—damned beautiful. Sexier than hell, especially in that shirt. One of them sights for sore eyes. And hearts.

He looked away. She was the last thing he needed.

"I yikes Andy China," Kyrie said from the crook of his arm.

Me, too, kid. Damn it. Me, too.

China stopped at Ebony's side. She dropped the coiled wire to the ground and lifted a collapsible shovel with a narrow blade and a pair of well-worn work gloves from her saddlebag.

Maverick slid off Star with Kyrie. He held her at arm's length for China to take. "Here. Hold the girl."

"'S okay. I've got it." China didn't even look up. She braced a boot to the back edge of the shovel and forced the blade into the rocky soil. "This won't take but a minute. Maybe two."

"No, ma'am." He set Kyrie on the ground between them and reached for the handle. "Let me do that."

China lifted a shovelful of soil and tossed it aside. Her boot hit the shovel again. "I said I've got this."

Before she could kick the shovel back into the hole, he wrapped his fingers around the handle. "And I said I'll do it. You take care of your niece. You can't be doing man's work dressed like you are, anyway. I'll dig."

She glanced down at her shirt. Her brows furrowed. "What's wrong with my shirt?"

Not one damned thing. Nothing's wrong with those perky breasts snuggled beneath it, either. Shit. What the hell am I thinking? He was just the hired hand. Nothing more. This boss lady could tell him to get the hell off her land as easy as not.

China raised her head and stared him down, right damned through the dark lenses of his Oakleys. Damn it to hell. A spark lit in the deepest depths of those blue eyes. A flash of defiance. Everything about this fierce woman, squared-off and ready to fight like she was, assaulted his better senses. A physical jolt to his groin opened his eyes. Wide.

She blew a loose strand of hair off her nose. Her chin jutted out. It didn't take a genius to read the vibes coming off of her. China didn't like being bossed around, either.

Like the fragrance on the breeze, he wanted to take a bite out of her. A big bite. His fingers itched to delve into her hair, to twist it into a knot so he could steer her mouth and her lips toward his. He licked his lips thinking what she would taste like. Minty toothpaste? Strawberries? Coffee? All tantalizing flavors on a woman's tongue. On China's tongue.

"It's just a posthole. It's not like I'm digging a well or anything," she threw at him.

Maverick held his ground. Every part of his body just plain ached for relief. *Like that was going to happen.* But there was no damned way he would stand around and let her do a man's job. Not as long as he was breathing.

He eased the shovel out of her grip, not wanting to piss her off any worse. "Understand that, ma'am. You dig the wells. I'll just dig postholes. Now, if you don't mind—"

She stepped back, the look on her face gentle again. He tore his gaze from her and concentrated on digging the perfect hole instead of her lips. He didn't need to fall into those stormy pools of blue. No way in hell.

One foot down that slippery slope and all bets were off. He wouldn't be able to stop himself, and he plain wasn't going there. Only a dumbass kept making the same mistakes over and over. He had learned the hard way, damn it. He, Maverick Carson, was no dumbass.

China watched him work for a moment before she turned to her niece. "Come on, Kyrie. Let's cut some wire and patch the fence."

She and Kyrie walked back to the coiled fencing. He hadn't noticed until then that every dozen posts held a similar coil of barbed wire. Good thinking. She cut three lengths of wire with a pair of pliers she retrieved from the saddlebag, something not every woman knew how to use. Damned if she didn't splice the strands of wire together as if she knew what she was doing.

With a few deft turns of the tool, she and Kyrie were waiting on him to finish tamping the post into place. China handed the pliers to Kyrie. "Don't pinch your fingers."

"I be carefo," Kyrie promised.

Before China could do it, Maverick finger tightened the spliced wire until it snapped against the post. "You got a hammer? Some tacks?"

China frowned and pulled a small hammer out of her belt. "Of course I've got a hammer."

He held his hand out, palm up.

She deliberated, her brows furrowed. Something shifted through those pretty eyes, but whatever it was, it kept on going. Looked a lot like stubbornness for a second there. This woman didn't have a passive bone in her body, but she handed the hammer over, handle first. "You'll need these, too." She gave him several fencing staples.

He took the staples out of her palm, careful not to touch her skin any more than he had to. It took a few hammer swings to set the tacks and finish the job.

Kyrie clapped her hands. "Mavwick! You did reawwy good!"

He couldn't help but smile at her boisterous praise over a simple job. China and Kyrie could've passed for mother and daughter, right down to the way they tossed their hair and sniffed the wind. The only difference between them was the over-sized baseball cap on Kyrie's head, and the dusty cowboy hat on China's.

Oh yeah, and that pretty checkered shirt.

Prettiest damned sight in all of Wyoming.

Chapter Twelve

"I've got barbequed pork chops for dinner." China looked to Maverick as they unsaddled the horses back at the barn. Kyrie had scampered off to find her kittens the moment she landed. "You're welcome to join us."

As usual, Maverick didn't answer. Not even a grunt.

The ride back had been uneventful, except for the very disturbing knowledge that someone had cut her fence. This kind of nonsense had only happened one other time, when a group of teenage boys decided they wanted to ride Sir T-Bone. Of course, they were drunker than skunks. Sheriff Hammer had visited her in the middle of the night because one of the boys got hurt on her property.

The kid was lucky the bull didn't trounce him and stomp him to death.

None of the tough guys even got on the bull. The young man fell through the barbed wire after he had cut the fence. He'd sliced his leg and hand enough that he needed quite a few stitches. It seemed a fitting reward for vandalizing a rancher's property, but his parents thought otherwise. A couple of transplants from New Jersey, they'd threatened to sue her for damages their foolish son caused. They'd thought wrong.

Wyoming law protected the rancher and the bull instead of the idiot looking for a thrill ride. Last she had heard, the kid and his folks had moved back east where they belonged. Whoever had cut her fence this time had to be local. She planned to call the Sheriff as soon as she hit the barn.

The task of rounding up her strays had gone smoothly with Maverick's help. Everything seemed easier with him around. He stepped up every time, although somewhat begrudgingly when she had first asked him to hold Kyrie. China smiled. She had gotten the same grumble from him when she'd asked for her niece back.

Kyrie had solved the problem with her very direct observation. "Uh uh. Me 'n Mavwick is ridin' Tar. We goin' home."

China had acquiesced. The man had a way with animals and children. Only a good heart could communicate without saying a word the way this guy did.

Whether he knew it or not, *Mavwick* had a way with women, too. He'd let Kyrie hold *Tar's* reins, as if she were in charge. The sight of that little girl chucking the reins and ordering Star to: "Giddy-up," warmed China like nothing else. Kyrie had no positive male role models in her life and being treated special always made her happy. She chattered like a magpie all the way home, telling him about her kittens and how she liked the orange ones best, and on and on.

Surprisingly, once or twice he had offered an actual comment instead of a grunt.

China sighed. The handsome guy had plans to leave the Wild Wolf, but while he was there, she meant to do what she could to see that elusive smile one more time.

He loosened the cinch and removed Star's saddle. A woman had to be blind to miss the biceps straining beneath his sleeve and the ease with which he handled the weight of the bulky saddle. He made it look easy. Light. Slinging it over the stall rail, he lifted Ebony's saddle out of her grip before she could stop him.

"It's not heavy," she insisted. "I can handle my own tack."

No answer, other than him hanging the saddle blankets next.

China let his male chauvinistic tendencies slide. She removed the bridles. Both horses tossed their heads as they waited patiently to be released to the outside corral. It was late afternoon and the herd was on its way back. Even Gorgeous nickered in excitement from the outside corral where she and China Love were penned for now.

China always erred on the side of caution when it came to her newborns. She kept mother and baby in a separate enclosure until she knew the foal nursed properly. Once the foal had properly bonded with its mother, she released them to the big pasture for a few months.

As far as weaning went, that was entirely up to the foal. This youngster might start nibbling grass and grain as soon as she noticed them, but removing China Love from her mother meant an entirely different thing. China would do that as gently as possible. Fortunately, she had plenty of acreage to fence off a portion of the pasture for the foals. That enabled them to graze alongside their mothers without being able to nurse. It made for less trauma to the foals and China was all about happy babies.

Maverick nodded to Ebony. "Isn't he your stud?"

China nodded. "I have three stallions. Hex is my white and Aces Wild is my bay. Why?"

Kyrie still wore Maverick's baseball cap, but he raised an automatic hand to his forehead, as if it were still there. All he touched were his sunglasses perched on his head. At least he didn't push them down. "Maybe I'm wrong, but don't stallions fight with other horses?"

"They fight with other stallions, but I don't let Ebony have free run of this place, if that's what you're thinking. He shares a separate corral with Hex and Aces Wild. He's not allowed to breed unless I say so."

He's not allowed to breed. Ha. To a greenhorn, that probably sounded like she turned into some weird dominatrix with leather pants, stiletto heels and a whip come breeding time. She chuckled quietly to herself. It sounded like something Leezel would've said.

Maverick didn't even crack a smile at that salacious comment.

She tossed a brush to him and busied herself with grooming Ebony's sleek flank so she wouldn't have to look Maverick in the eye. The whole idea of horse breeding was a risky conversation with a good-looking guy, but she continued if only to tease. This guy needed to relax. "Some breeders think artificial insemination is the only way, but it's too much trouble if you ask me. I like the good old-fashioned method myself."

Maverick stood diligently at Star's side, brushing long strokes down the horse's neck and chest while he took in the latest chapter of Horses 101. For a fleeting second, she thought of those strong, capable hands smoothing over her shoulders and rubbing her back. Maybe other parts, too.

"So you lock 'em up in the same corral or something when it's, ah, *time*?" His question snatched her mind back to the business of horse breeding. *Kind of.*

"Umm, yeah." She forced herself to focus, thankful Ebony hadn't picked up on her nervousness. Brushing her horses usually soothed and relaxed her, but right now her heart thumped like a jackrabbit's hind leg in a patch of spring clover. "The mares are only receptive at certain times of the year. A stallion knows when it's their time better than me. I let them figure it out for themselves. The boys have free run of the pasture when it's time, and so far, so good."

Maverick sniffed at that comment.

She looked up to see what he thought, but he ignored her, intent on brushing Star, one sure stroke after another.

"How about Gorgeous?" he asked without turning around. "You gonna let her and the foal loose tonight?"

"You mean China Love?" China leaned around Ebony's big chest to peer at Maverick. He nodded, not taking the bait she'd just tossed his way. "Are you upset that I sold her?"

He shrugged as if he didn't care, but she knew better. She had caught the disappointment in his voice when he questioned earlier if she was going to sell all the foals.

"Well, are you or not?"

"Don't matter to me one way or the other."

Bet me. It matters. You just won't let it show.

He faced away from her, his back toward her as he worked, but she liked the view. He had moved to Star's hindquarters, still taking long even strokes that had quite the calming effect on the big Percheron. Star stood with his eyes closed, one hoof pointed into the ground like a tiptoe.

But China noticed something else again. Maverick's firm ass and long legs. He didn't wear cowboy boots, more like work boots with worn heels and scuffed toes. His jeans were threadbare on the butt, as if he had about worn them out. The hems were frayed. But those shoulders. Damned if he didn't make that worn-out shirt look good.

She swallowed hard. A dark tan colored the skin showing between his hair and collar. Her mind went wandering to the rest of his body. Farmer's tan or not, watching the ripple of his back muscles while he brushed lazy Star created a wave of heat up her legs and into her stomach.

"Well?"

"I'm sorry." Her cheeks flushed with embarrassment. For the life of her, China couldn't remember what he had asked. "Umm, what?"

"You're going to keep Gorgeous and the foal separate from the rest of the horses for a couple more weeks, aren't you?" He raised a stern brow as he repeated his concern.

"Yes. Of course. I do that with all my foals. Besides, China Love is special." She had to smile. This was the longest conversation she and Maverick had had.

After a couple of moments of quiet brushing, she voiced a tempting thought. "Hmm. Maybe I could persuade Mr. Foster to let me keep her. I'm sure he would be just as happy with another one of my kids. Maybe Star. He would be ready to pull the trolley this summer."

She let that comment hang until Maverick cleared his throat. When she turned to see what he wanted, her hands were suddenly flat on his chest, the brush included.

China gulped, startled she hadn't heard him approach. He didn't make any attempt to step back and give her more space. She lifted her hands from his very muscular pecs. He took a step closer. She pressed her back against Ebony's side, pleased that Maverick had taken a first move. If that was what this was. Sure felt like it.

She fisted her fingers between them instead of touching him again like she wanted. That chest was solid. Hard. Darn, but he filled her line of sight. Two very formidable Percherons were out there. Somewhere. She couldn't see either of them. Just him. Just the plaid and the coffee-brown windows to this man's soul.

She had to crane her neck to look up at him. Z would call him a tall drink of water. She licked her bottom lip, thirsty for a sip of some of that water.

Her heart stalled. Looking all the way up at him while he looked all the way down at her sent a surge of quivering heat up through the floorboards, through the soles of her boots and into her legs. She was no tiny little dewdrop of a girl. She smelled like horse twenty-four-seven. What the hell was that man looking at?

His gaze fell to her mouth. He blinked. The corners of his lips didn't offer the hint of a smile breaking out. She held her breath, frozen as he scanned her every feature. Her brows. The line of her nose. Her lips. His eyes flickered down her neck to her top button. Damn him. He knew what lay beneath that top button and she was glad he did.

Her fingers itched to trace the hard edges of his face, so many angles and corners. The dark line of his furrowed brows. The scruffy shadow that graced his chin and jaw.

He gave not a hint of emotion away. His eyes moved back to hers and suddenly, there wasn't enough air in the whole damned barn. She might as well have been looking at a rock. On a mountain. Mount Everest. Where the air was really, really thin. Where oxygen didn't exist. Only—him.

One of them should step back, and it probably should be her. Bosses should do those kinds of things. They should be smart.

She didn't.

She couldn't.

She had been caught in a tantalizing trap of do or dare, the one she had started by needling him about keeping the foal. Only now—

Oh. My. Hell. He's glorious.

Indecision darkened his face. His brows crinkled just a titch. Very slowly, he leaned toward her.

China forgot how to breathe. She couldn't, not with her heart pounding up her throat. It was happening right then and there, and she wanted it with every tingling nerve in her body. She wanted this man. This incredible now.

He circled the back of her neck with a very gentle hand, but paused, his breath already on her chin, and his eyes searching hers for an eternity. His other hand slid down to her side. His thumb smoothed circles on her bare stomach.

"What?" she asked in an unusually hoarse voice. *Kiss me, damn you. Don't stop. Not now. Not when you've come this close.*

"May I?" he asked, his voice as gravelly as hers.

She grabbed him by his damned collar and closed the gap. White-hot heat melted their lips together. She shut her eyes as the taste of Maverick's mouth and tongue erased every last misgiving. Her lungs pulled in the breath he breathed, needing more. The delicious taste of him. Wintergreen. The smell of him. A hint of manly sweat mingled with the great outdoors.

Yes!

The thunderstorm racing through China's veins burned any apprehension clean clear away. Kyrie might see them. *Let her look. She's seen worse.*

He murmured deep in his chest and lifted China off the floor and into his arms, boots and all. She wrapped her legs around his waist, surprised when he didn't shift to catch her. Just clutched the cheeks of her ass in a firm, masculine grip.

A rumbling groan ground out of him. The barn rafters faded from view. Nothing else existed, only the feel of his iron bands wrapped around her, and the taste of his tongue making intimate love with hers. His fingers traced the seam up the crack of her ass as he pressed her against his zipper.

Deep, cleansing fire rippled up through her core in a tantalizing wave that played every taut nerve in her body like a harp. She moaned, surprised at the response his fingers sparked in her deepest depths of her damned near virgin body. Heat pooled at her core. The sensible woman she thought she was changed into an insatiable creature, a predator starved for the male body pressed against hers. Ready to devour him.

He eased his lips from hers and gently tucked her head under his chin, one hand still cupping her bottom. This man was handling her, and she liked it. A lot.

Oh. My. God. His heart's pounding, too. The intensity of the moment must have surprised him as much as her. She stilled to gather her wits, listening to the runaway racehorse inside his ribcage. When her feet finally touched the earth, he held her tight. She couldn't have stood on her own two feet if she wanted to. Not yet.

She cringed. It had been so long since any man had dared approach her, much less taken her by storm like Maverick did. Had she just made a total fool of herself? *Holy smokes.* She had never felt this delicate or treasured before. He had simply, wonderfully, *oh my goodness—kissed the living hell out of me.*

His manly strength overpowered her. She leaned into the depth of his arms, surprised how much she liked the smell and feel of him.

"You okay?" he asked quietly, his breathing heavy at the top of her head.

She stayed where she was, content to know he couldn't catch his breath, either. He was warm and strong and she couldn't imagine a better place to be than encircled by him.

Ebony nickered. China came back to her senses. There was still work to be done. This tender, magical moment was nearly over. She needed to get the stallion back into his corral before the mares showed up. In season or not, she didn't need him getting frisky. But she didn't want to move, not if it took her out of Maverick's firm hold.

He stoked one hand down the center of her back. It slid over her bare skin, coming to rest at her waist while he held her tight with the other arm. Two fingers slid under her belt, then beneath her panties, pointing down to her tailbone. And there he stopped.

She squeezed her eyes tight as desire coursed strong and hot. Every muscle in her body clenched in agreement with those two wayward fingers. Thrumming with need, she wanted his fingers to keep going. She ached. It was all she could do to not give into the moment. Kyrie was close by with her kittens and... and...

Oh, yes. I have to tend to my stallion. My, um, other stallion. All her talk about horse breeding had backfired on her. Ebony might not be frisky, but she sure as hell was.

"I really should take Ebony back to his corral," she muttered as her fingers wandered over Maverick's hard chest muscles again. The feel of his nipples beneath the plaid pockets brought another wiggling surge of lust through her body. This man was an addiction she wanted very much to feed for a long and satisfying time. Every last inch of him. With her tongue. Her lips. Her mouth.

Instead, she asked, "Can you, umm, take Kyrie up to the house for me? I'll be right there."

He didn't release her. Didn't even hint that he might. Instead he tipped her chin up with those same two fingers that had just been in her pants. He peered into her eyes. The man didn't smile.

All of her lust-filled thoughts crashed to a halt. *Have I made a fool of myself? No. Don't spoil this, too. Don't say goodbye. Don't tell me you're leaving. Not yet.*

"I happen to like the old-fashioned method myself," he said quietly. He kissed her lightly on her forehead, and— *ahhhhh!* He was killing her!

He set her back a half step, his hands still comfortable on her hips. She shivered. Yes. He wanted her, too. She could read it in his eyes, and she felt it in the strong fingers still latched onto her. Pinpoint welding. That was what bound them together for now. Each of his fingertips had somehow melted her to him.

Ebony snorted. He had gotten a whiff of the mares. *Well, hold your horses, Ebony old buddy, because it's my turn. I've just gotten a good whiff of Maverick.*

Common sense prevailed. Ebony came first.

"I really have to go," she whispered. "The mares. The stallions..."

Tendrils of molten desire lingered between them. "That whole breeding thing, huh?"

She nodded because she couldn't speak. *Yeah, that whole wild, wonderful breeding thing. Wow.*

He stepped back into polite mode. "I'll find Kyrie. She's around here somewhere."

"Uh huh." China couldn't break his gaze. She didn't want to look away, but Ebony's hoof striking the wooden floor broke the spell. He'd picked up the mare's scent like she had picked up Maverick's. Slightly sweaty. Definitely masculine. Delightfully carnal. Her idea of heaven.

She stepped away from Maverick and latched onto Ebony's halter. With one last look, she led the horse away and left Maverick to search for Kyrie. She wasn't worried. This man was a rock of safety. He'd find Kyrie.

No sooner thought than done. Her niece darted out of nowhere and ran full bore into Maverick's arms. He crouched to catch her, then swung her high over his head, and China was a goner. What a sight to see that baby enamored with a real man instead of manipulated by her biological creep of a father.

China tugged Ebony across the yard behind the barn and into his enclosed pasture with Aces Wild, and Hex. With every step away from Maverick, reality settled in. Bottom line, she had never given her heart to anyone, not with the responsibilities of the ranch and her equine kids. Until now, they had been enough. A woman who worked from sunup to sundown, then dealt with a wagon full of Leezel's family problems, didn't take time for foolish things like romance or boyfriends. Life didn't work that way. Either you played the field or the game went on without you. She had made her choice long ago and the ranch had won.

China glanced behind her to see her niece sitting on Maverick's shoulder, his cap on her head while he took the porch steps two at a time. Kyrie had already fallen for him. Star and Gorgeous, too. China Love for sure. Damn. The day he up and left, he would break all of their hearts.

Mine, too.

Chapter Thirteen

Why the hell did I do that?

Maverick knocked on the ranch house door while Kyrie peered down at him from her lofty perch. Kissing China hadn't been on his agenda. It wasn't smart. Not as a ranch hand or as a drifter. Or whatever the hell he was. Yet he had done it. Like a lovesick fool, he'd done it, damn it to hell. Hadn't been able to help himself was more like it. Didn't want to try when she turned into his arms like she had.

One touch of that silken skin on her back and he lost it. One whiff of her breath, the fragrance of her shampoo, one taste of the honey of her lips, and—shit. All the more reason to pack up and leave now, before things got crazy. This damned woman had gotten under his skin.

He scrolled his gaze over the wide yard between the barn and the bunkhouse. This place. So quiet. Too peaceful. Everything he wanted, but everything he was running away from, too.

Damn it. I'm not staying.

Maverick swung Kyrie to her feet. Leezel might not be back yet, so he knocked again, irritated at himself for jumping the gun and damned near jumping China, too. She just seemed so—genuine. And those damned blue eyes of hers were charged with two-twenty-volts of pure zest for life. Honesty, too. She had a way of looking through him. Of seeing behind his mask, and damn it, being with her felt like he was suddenly standing on quicksand. Sliding into what, he didn't know. Didn't want to even think about.

She seemed to love everything in her life, and why shouldn't she? She had centered her soul in what mattered, even if it was in the backwoods of Wyoming. Hell, even the color of her eyes seemed part of the wild land she called home. The Wild Wolf resonated China Wolf right on down to the dust on the porch railing.

"Is you mad?" Kyrie asked.

He glanced down at the little girl squeezing the little finger of his left hand. "Me? No. Why would I be mad?" *Frustrated as hell, yes. Mad, no.*

Her lower lip stuck out. The little tyke was a miniature China right down to her cowboy boots. "Cuz your eyes wook kinda scary to me."

He lifted one brow in a scary tease. "How about now? Do I look scarier?"

"Yes!" she shrieked and giggled. "Do it again."

"How about if we sit on the porch swing and wait for your Aunt China? It looks like your mother's not home yet."

"Okay." Kyrie scrambled up on the swing and patted the slats on the bench. "Come on. Les swing."

He took his place next to her, stretched his legs and drew them in to work the swing. Kyrie leaned forward and backward, pumping for more lift. "Did you have fun today?"

"Uh huh, and I got five kitties, only don't tell Mommy," she whispered, her index finger to her lips. "'Kay?"

"Mommy doesn't like cats?"

Kyrie's demeanor dropped. "Mommy says they stinky, but I yike 'em. I yike 'em a yot. They so cute."

He filed Leezel's comment in his mental *Bitch* folder, with What's-Her-Name. Oh, yeah. Kimberly. Kimmie. Whatever. His ex. The liar and the cheat. "Which kitten is your favorite?"

"Da tiger ones!" Kyrie beamed.

"Whatcha going to name it?"

"Yousee." She pumped harder.

"You see?" he asked to be sure he had heard right.

"No. You-see. Yike you se-e-e-e." Kyrie enunciated carefully while she bounced on the bench. "You-see. You-see. You-see."

Hmm. He took a long second to puzzle that one out. Did she mean UC like it sounded? Goosey? Juicy? Or—

"Oh. Lucy?"

Her face brightened into a big smile. "Yeah. Yike Yousee and Charwie Brown."

He grinned. Lucy and Charlie Brown. Perfect names for a couple of cats.

"You could've gone inside and waited for me. The door isn't locked," China said from the porch step, that sappy look back on her face.

Maverick lifted off the swing to his feet, determined to set this thing between them straight before it got any more out of control. "No, ma'am. I've still got plowing to do."

"It can wait. You have a dinner date with me and Kyrie." China hadn't moved from the step. She wanted an answer, one he didn't want to have to say. "Six o'clock. Be here or be square."

A date? He didn't like the sound of that. He had better things to do. Ranch-hand things. Minding-his-own-business things. Not-getting-involved-with-the-boss kinds of things. Damn. He hesitated a second too long. His big mouth spoke right up. "See you at six."

Damn it. I'm staying.

Maverick didn't mean to overhear the catfight, but it was hard to miss with the screen door the only thing between him and the Wolf sisters.

"Why don't you mind your business for once in your life, Sis?" Leezel's nasty tone was hard to miss. "Hell. You act like you own the whole world. Well, I got news for you. You don't! And you got no right talking to Troy like you did today neither. Mind your damned business!"

"But Leezel, Kyrie needs a decent home for once in her life." China didn't scream like her sister, but her sensible argument stood a snowball's chance in hell of being heard over Leezel's on-going rant.

"Bitch, bitch, bitch. That's all you do. I come home to pay you a visit and all I get is chewed out and bitched at."

He paused at the front door, unwilling to knock and intrude. He had washed for dinner, but this was family trouble, and he didn't want to get involved.

"And what did he mean about getting joint custody? That's the first I heard of that lie."

"It ain't a lie. He's her father. He's got rights."

Her denial ignited China. "Why do you defend him? He's cruel to you, and he couldn't care less about Kyrie."

"Why do you hate every guy I hang with?"

"That's the problem. You hang with a lot of guys. How do you know he's her father? Has he taken a paternity test? How can you be sure?"

"Cuz I'm not stupid. That's how!"

"But you've been with so many guys and—"

"Shut up! Damn it! You're just scared I'm gonna take your cowboy friend away from you, too. That's what your problem is. You been screwing horses for so long, you don't have a clue what a real man feels like between your legs."

Maverick took another step away from the screen door, but the argument only got louder. One of the sisters threw something, judging by the glass shattering. Probably Leezel.

"Stop talking nonsense. I just want what's best for—"

"Bullshit! You want him. It's all over your face. Well, I got news for you, big-shot boss lady. I can have any man I want, and that goes for your cowboy friend, too. If I want him, he's mine."

"I don't want him." That was China, painfully loud and adamantly sure of herself. "I want what's best for Kyrie. That's all I've ever wanted."

Ouch. Damn. He cringed, not quite what he had expected after their encounter in the barn. No man could blame her, though. Leezel had backed China into a corner and she'd come out fighting for that little girl she loved. Maverick turned to leave. At least he knew where he stood now. His problem was solved. The sooner he got the hell off the Wild Wolf, the better.

"Bullshit! *I want what's best for Kyrie. I want what's best for Kyrie.*" Leezel's singsong voice sounded all the way out to the yard. "That's all you think about, *Kyrie this* and *Kyrie that*. Damn. I wish I'd never had that brat. I should've had an abortion like I wanted! I never should've listened to you and kept her!!"

Thump. Thump. Thump.

Maverick glanced over his shoulder. Kyrie was making her way carefully down the inside staircase in China's too-large cowboy boots, a yellow blanket dragging behind her. She grabbed to the banister with both hands when the footwear nearly got away from her.

He couldn't just walk away and leave her. Not like this. Kyrie was concentrating on her feet. She didn't need to hear her mother and aunt going after each other like they were, and she sure didn't need to hear the ugly things coming out of her mother's foul mouth.

Maverick retraced his steps and knocked politely at the door.

The argument ceased.

Kyrie shot him a big smile. "Hi, Mavwick. Whatcha doin'?"

He winked at her.

China came to the screen door. She waved him in. "Umm, hi. Dinner's ready."

He shook his head and stayed on the porch. "I'm guessing now isn't a good time?"

"No, it's fine. We're just..." China glanced over her shoulder to the kitchen where her sister stood with a bottle of beer to her lips.

"Well, howdy, Mav." Leezel had recovered quickly from her screaming fit, her voice as syrupy as molasses. "It's nice there's at least one friendly face around here."

"We're just—talking," China explained awkwardly.

Kyrie clomped over to her and grabbed hold of her aunt's index finger, her eyes wide with worry.

"Yeah, Mav," Leezel said. "We was just having us a little sisterly disagreement. You know how it is. Hell, you probably fight with your brother all the time, don't you? You've got one, don't you? Come on in and I'll fix you a plate. It's dinnertime. Join us. You're always welcome in my half of my daddy's house." Leezel could've purred she sounded so nice all of a sudden. And dead, damned wrong. It would be a cold day in hell that he told her one word about his brother.

"No thanks." Maverick nodded down to Kyrie. "I came for her."

"Me?" Kyrie's eyes lit up.

"Yeah. You. Thought I'd take my new girlfriend for a walk while you ladies are having your *discussion*." He looked at China to gauge her reaction. He would've understood if she had said no, but all he read in her eyes was sadness and regret.

"Oh, goodie!" Kyrie clapped her hands and looked up at her aunt. "Kin I go, Andy China? Pwease? Kin I?" Her little body turned into one big wiggle of excitement. "Kin I, huh?"

Leezel clicked her six-inch heels over to the screen door, one long manicured fingernail pointed directly at Maverick's chest. "In case you didn't know, Mav honey, Kyrie is *my* daughter, not China's. You oughta be asking me for permission, not my *older* sister."

Kyrie's face fell. China stiffened. Her sister seemed to know how to hurt everyone who loved her.

Maverick met Leezel in the eye. "May Kyrie come for a short walk with me? We won't be long." He fully expected she would assume that invitation meant her, too, but hell. If it got her out of the house maybe China could settle down.

"Why, sure! You take extra good care of my baby, you hear?" She elbowed China out of her way and pushed the door open. The second it opened, Kyrie scrambled toward Maverick's hands. He lifted her against him and sat her on his forearm. The little girl clung to him as China's boots fell off of her feet to the porch boards.

"Thanks," China said softly as she took a step back.

Maverick caught the look in her eye. She wanted to say more. So did he, damn it. Smart or not, she needed him and he didn't want to leave. Not yet.

"Yeah, thanks Mav," Leezel gushed. "That's real gentlemanly of you. Dinner's almost ready, so don't be gone too long, ya hear? My little girl needs her proper nutrition, you know."

"Yes, ma'am." He hoisted said little girl high onto his shoulder. "Come on, Missy Kyrie. We've got wild tiger kittens to tame."

Chapter Fourteen

Wake up. Kyrie is crying.

China grunted in her sleep. One minute the little girl was snuggled in her arms, but the next she stood at the window, her thumb stuck in her mouth and her blanket against her cheek. "My kitties," she whined.

"They're in the barn," China mumbled. "Come back to bed. It's still night."

"But my kitties is in the barn." Kyrie kept whining, but China was nearly too exhausted to care. Cats lived in the barn, not the house. She peeled one eyelid open. The crazy princess nightlight cast eerie shadows across the wall instead of the dim pink light it was supposed to provide. Someone yelled outside from the yard, and—

China bolted upright in her bed. She blinked the sleep out of her eyes. She'd had less than two hours of sleep. The fight with Leezel had spoiled the whole evening. Then her sister, the skank, took off with Reardon, and—

What the hell's going on?

How could a seven-watt bulb fill the room with so much ugly, orange light? *My hell, it looks like—Fire! Oh, my God! The barn's on fire!*

China jumped out of bed. She grabbed Kyrie away from the window and sat her in the middle of her bed. "Stay here! Be a good girl for Auntie China and stay right here. Don't move. Don't leave this bedroom. Okay?"

She didn't wait for an answer. She grabbed the phone off her nightstand and dialed 911, screaming her name and address at the dispatcher on the way out the door. By the time China blasted onto the scene below, her nightshirt was stuffed in her pants and her zipper was up, but her heart was stuck in her throat. *My barn's on fire!*

Zeke and Xavier already had the irrigation hoses hooked to the tank, spraying thick streams of water high to the rafters of the barn roof. Fires were a normal threat during hot summer months, so all ranches maintained fire suppression deterrents. Industrial-sized pumps. Sturdy fire hoses in case the nightmare happened. Like now.

"Get 'em out! Get my horses out of there!" she screamed, racing toward the barn.

Z hollered something back at her, but the noise from the fire was too loud. Flames licked through the open hayloft doors and God, this was the worst possible disaster for a rancher. All that grass hay left over from winter made for instant fuel. It had been a dry winter. Too many bales were left inside—with the horses.

But worse—the lack of any noises coming from inside the barn. No frightened neighs. No frantic squeals. No enraged screams.

"My horses! Gorgeous! Star! God damn it, guys! Get them out of there! Save 'em!" She couldn't breathe in enough air to scream any louder. Ash fell from the sky in thick, sooty chunks. Smoke suffocated her, but fear clutched her throat. *Ebony! Joker! They're all in there. My babies!*

Tremendous heat forced the two hired hands backward into the yard and away from the barn. As much water as they sprayed, the more useless their efforts. The flames devoured the streams of water like ravenous burning beasts that gulped everything in their path and wanting more. An eerie whirlwind of flame swirled lazily upward, its message clear. The god of fire and flame ruled the night and all the sky. Stay away!

"Z!" she screamed, pointing at the fire devil. "More water! There!"

A tiny hand at her knee jolted her back to sanity. China looked down into Kyrie's frightened, teary face. She pulled the little girl off the ground and smothered her into her chest. "What are you doing out here?" China didn't mean to bark at the child.

"I sorry," Kyrie whimpered. "I scared."

"Oh, baby. It's not your fault. I'm sorry." China choked, her emotions so raw she could barely comfort the child. She wanted to be strong, but all she could do was hold Kyrie and cry while her barn burned. *My horses. God! My horses!*

Kyrie pointed at the barn sobbing. "My kitties is on fire, Andy China!"

China clasped the child to her chest as the fire-beast snatched a piece of Kyrie's heart, too. God! How much more could she take? And then it dawned on her. Had Maverick gone to sleep in the foaling stall again? *God. Not Maverick, too.*

China ran Kyrie back to the front porch. "You've got to stay here baby, okay? Please stay here for me. Don't move."

Kyrie clutched the porch railing and nodded, her eyes wide with fright at the tremendous blaze and her aunt's severity. Without a thought, China raced straight for the front door, but X caught her around the waist when she barreled past him.

"What in tarnation are you thinkin'? You ain't going in there!" Her feet flew out from beneath her. He dropped her butt to the ground.

"I have to. Maverick's in there! Have you seen him?"

X looked away. "Not anymore he ain't. Sorry, Miss China."

Z shook his head. She saw the somber look in his eye. She lifted her fist to her teeth and bit her knuckles. The heat roiling off the building was so great, she would've passed out within a couple more steps anyway. No one could get into the barn

The fire devil had won. Both of her hired hands battled it with a continual torrent from the hose, but there she stayed, frozen in shock as her world turned to glowing embers in front of her eyes. The Devil took everything. Maverick. Her horses. Her heart. Her soul.

Z dropped his useless hose. He lifted her to her feet and forced her back to the porch steps. "You gotta stay clear, Miss China. Please. Keep close to Miss Kyrie. It's gonna come down any minute now and I don't want you hurt."

"No," she whined. "It can't. It's all I have."

"No, it ain't. You got that cute little baby girl and she needs you. Take care of Miss Kyrie."

Kyrie coughed and China came to her senses. She climbed up the steps to where Kyrie stood in tears. The distraught child buried herself into her aunt's arms and wailed. "I want my kitties!"

"I know, baby. I know. Shush, shush. It's... it's..." China couldn't finish the lie. She smothered her sobbing niece against her and stifled her own anguish. It would never be okay, and worse, it was too late for Maverick.

I want my babies, too, Kyrie. And Maverick. I want Maverick! A wretched hiccup lurched up from her throat. *God. Yes. I want Maverick. Why'd you have to take him, too?*

The barn's main timbers groaned mightily. The burning wood hissed and growled under the weight of the water. With a crackling whoosh, the loft collapsed to ground level. A cloud of sparks and cinders filled the night sky, forced upward by the tremendous heat.

The rafters followed suit, dropping one by one. The fire devil sucked everything into the night in a whirling vortex of ash and death. It wanted every last piece of the barn and it took it. Everything.

"I sorry. I sorry," Kyrie muttered over and over until China had no choice but to take her inside and close the door behind them to block the terror of the fire. There was nothing to be done. Every last bit of her dreams lay burned to death and buried in muddy ash and smoking timbers inside that barn.

She choked. *Even Maverick.* Her back against the closed door, she collapsed to the floor with Kyrie tight in her arms. X and Z would attend to the hoses. They would do what they could, which was nothing more than stand and watch at this point. The volunteer fire department and every available man and woman within miles would arrive soon, but the damage was done.

The Wild Wolf was lost. Her kids. Her dreams. The poor man who had done nothing more than stop to help a foolish woman who thought she could fight the world alone. China sobbed into Kyrie's sweaty head as they clung to each other in total misery, their hair undone in one comingled shroud to hide their tears.

The bright eyes of her horses blinked back at her from flames.

Gorgeous and her brand new baby.

Aces Wild. Ebony. God! All my stallions.

Poor, poor Maverick.

The thought was too much to bear. His dark eyes. The way he hardly ever spoke. His gentle words when he finally did. *I happen to like the old-fashioned method myself.* The sweet look on his face the night China Love was born.

A cry crawled up her throat. "God, don't let Maverick or my horses suffer anymore. If they're still alive, take 'em." She smothered Kyrie under her chin, her eyes squeezed tight against the crushing hurt in her chest. "Please, please don't let them suffer."

Even Kyrie's kitties, she thought, unable to voice that prayer for Kyrie's sake. *God, let them all die in peace. Not agony. Please, please help me. Help Kyrie. Help everyone.*

A siren sounded outside. Red and blue lights flashed over the front room walls, signaling help had come. By the sounds of it, the county fire engine had rolled into the yard with its troupe of volunteer firemen all ready to run to her aid. They had a hook and ladder truck. They'd have foam. They would have access to the hydrant at the corner of her yard. The fire would finally be forced to relinquish its stranglehold.

Too late.

Too damned late.

China buried her face in the child's curly hair, ashamed she wasn't the stronger one. Anguish filled her with nausea. The sickest tendrils of despair strangled her. She clung to Kyrie, so damned thankful the fire hadn't claimed her niece, too.

"Too much, Lord. You've taken too much this time," she sobbed.

"Up! I wan' up." The little girl lifted her arms, pushing out of China's grasp.

"No, baby. Stay here."

"But I wan' up."

Someone lifted Kyrie out of China's arms. He pulled her off the floor at the same time. She stabbed a hand in her hair and pushed the thick curtain out of her eyes, prepared to face Fire Marshall Garth Burton's kindly face. He had been fire marshal for years. Gray-haired and kindhearted, he had seen it all and knew it all, from whose boys ditched school regularly to whose daughters ran around with the wrong boys.

Only the man tugging her into his arms wasn't him.

"Oh, my God! Maverick!" She hit the solid wall of his chest with all she had, needing to feel him in her arms right damned now. "I thought you were dead. You're not. You're alive!"

He buried his sooty face in her neck while he gathered her under his arm. "Thank God, you're safe," he ground out, shuddering, his voice raw and gruff. "I was so damned scared when I didn't see you outside with X and Z."

China eased back enough to run her fingers over his dirty, sweat-covered cheeks. His signature cap and glasses were gone. He smelled strongly of smoke and ash, but she didn't care. He and Kyrie were safe.

She burrowed into his arms and wept. Nothing had ever hurt like this before, not even when her father died. That was natural. This was murder.

Kyrie cried along with her. So far Leezel had yet to make an appearance, but China didn't care. Not one bit. But wait. She pushed back from Maverick again. "Where's my sister? Have you seen her?"

He shook his head, but his eyes held a terrible secret. Her heart lurched. Had Leezel gone to the barn for a smoke? Did she start the fire with one of her damned cigarettes? Was she the cause of the flames, or worse, was she lost in them? Was that the secret?

China writhed to get out of his arms, but he wouldn't let her go, and she didn't have the strength to resist. "But I've got to find her," she whined as he held her tight.

"You stay with Kyrie." He nodded upstairs. "Which room?"

China blinked at that very real possibility. Could Leezel have slept through this whole thing? "First door on the right."

Maverick shifted Kyrie into China's arms and cleared the staircase three steps at a time. He didn't knock, but he was only in Leezel's room for a second before he emerged, nodding, his face grim. "She's in bed. Drunk. Passed out."

China sagged against him at that good, ugly news. Her sister might be a drunk, but at least she was a live drunk. Someone pounded on China's door. Maverick eased her and Kyrie to the couch and answered it.

Fire Marshall Garth Burton nodded somberly from the doorway. "Miss China home?"

"Yes, sir." Maverick gestured for him to enter.

He came in and crouched beside her at the couch. "I'm sure sorry, China. The fire is out now. Do you know how it started?"

His sympathy stabbed her. She couldn't meet his kind eye. *Poor Gorgeous. Poor, poor baby China Love.* "We were sleeping and—"

"Your ranch hands said you had trouble with Reardon's boys last night. You think they're behind this?"

She ran a tired hand through her hair, not sure what she thought at the moment. "I... I don't know. I didn't hear anything."

He cocked his head suspiciously. "Your sister around?"

"Yes. She's upstairs, sleeping."

Garth rolled his eyes. "What? She drunk again?"

China nodded. There was no need to explain. Garth knew what little Leezel contributed to the operation of the ranch, and the Wolf family, for that matter. He reached out and patted Kyrie's curly head, a somber glint in his eye. "Your barn's a total loss. Sure you already knew that. I'm sorry."

She choked, pulling Kyrie in closer. Sorry was such a worthless word.

"At least you got your horses out."

China blinked hard and fast. It hurt to correct Garth's false notion that she had saved any of her kids. "But... I didn't."

"You don't know?" Garth looked at Maverick. "You need to tell her, son." With that, he replaced his fire helmet and walked out the door.

Maverick's grip stiffened on her arms. China turned to him as she wiped the sudden onslaught of tears away. "Tell me what?"

He shook his head even as he looked to the floor. "I got all of them out, but—"

All out? Her heart nearly leapt for joy, but she saw that terrible secret flit through his eyes again. She couldn't be happy. Not yet. She held her breath. He had more to tell.

Had he saved them only to have them turn in panic and roar back into the fire? Were they badly burned? Were they smoldering corpses? She eased Kyrie out of her arms and lifted to her feet to face what could only be more bad news. She clutched his biceps. "But what?"

He choked back a growl. "I couldn't get to her, China. I tried. But Gorgeous and..."

She blinked. "Gorgeous? Why not?"

He stepped away from her and Kyrie. "I didn't save them."

Why not? Of all her kids, had he just told her only two were lost? Had he just said that Star, Joker, and Ebony were safe, but not Gorgeous and China Love? Had he let Gorgeous die? Her mind couldn't process the information fast enough.

He turned toward the door. "I'm sorry. I... I never should've come. I never should've stayed. I need to go." But instead of leaving he sank to the floor, his elbows to his knees and his face buried in his hands.

Kyrie wiggled off the couch and went to him. She laid her head on his broad back, her arms stretched wide as she tried to hug him. "I reawy sowwy. I here. I sowwy."

Those strong shoulders shuddered, and China couldn't bear it anymore. She crumbled to his side. She cupped his chin and made him look at her. She had to hear the words. "Where's Star? Where's Joker? Please tell me. Are they all—"

"Safe. Only Gorgeous and her foal... God," he ground out. "I couldn't get to them."

She blinked as that terrible truth hit home. She hadn't lost them all. Only Gorgeous and China Love. Only the best brood mare on the ranch. Only the pretty baby Maverick had helped into the world. Only—

God! She closed her eyes to stop the storm of anguish in her head. *Most* of her kids were safe. Only two were lost. She gulped. Not all. Only two, yes, but those two—

But Maverick and Kyrie are alive. I didn't lose them.

She clutched his head to her shoulder. "God, Maverick. I'm sorry."

He pushed her away, but China refused to let him go. Now she understood. He must've been in the barn when the fire broke out. He had done all he could, and he had done it alone. It had to have been a frightening nightmare, him against the inferno and all those panicked horses.

She burrowed into him until he had no choice but to hold her. Unbearable pain surged up through her chest for the two she had lost, but God, it could've been so much worse. It could've been him in that fire. Or X and Z.

Kyrie shoved her little backside into his arms, and together they sat in a sad heap on the floor and cried.

"How?" China finally thought of a word she could actually speak.

"I... I heard something... someone behind the barn." Maverick rubbed the back of his head. When he looked at his hand, China finally saw the blood on his fingers. And the burns.

"You're hurt." That did it. Her common sense kicked in. She pulled him off the floor and dragged him and Kyrie into the kitchen and made them sit at her table. Cookies and milk. That's what Kyrie liked so that's what China did. She poured two tall glasses of cold milk and placed the rest of the chocolate chip cookies on two plates on the table. One for

Maverick. One for Kyrie. The simple, routine act seemed surreal, but China was running on automatic.

Once the treat was served, she turned her attention to the gash at the back of his head. Without asking if she could touch him, she gently fingered the swollen, bloody bump. He flinched. "Someone hit you. Hard. You need stitches."

Ice. He needs ice on that bump. Within minutes, she had a cold compress on his poor head.

His shoulders slumped.

She leaned around him to peer into his face. "Am I hurting you? Are you okay? Do you feel dizzy or anything?"

He stared at the cookies and milk in front of him. "I heard someone laughing. It sounded like—"

"What did they hit you with?" China interrupted, only half-listening as she dabbed at his head. The size of the bruised bump and the gash concerned her. Stitches were one thing. A concussion was something else. He might need to be seen by a doctor.

He shrugged. "I don't know. I stepped out the back door and everything went black."

"Did you tell Garth this?"

"The fire chief? Yeah." Maverick nodded. "I told him everything. By the time I came to, the north end of the barn roof was on fire, and the horses were frantic. I ran in."

He huffed out a big sigh. "I opened every stall and yelled my guts out, but I couldn't get... I couldn't get..." A tremor jerked through him. Maverick covered his eyes with one hand. "I should've gone to them first. I couldn't... God, I didn't save them, either."

China wiped her eyes, her jaw clenched tight against the pain she would have to learn to live with. *Them.* Gorgeous and China Love. He had saved all of her kids, but—*them.*

She brushed her tears away as her only way forward crystallized. What happened wasn't Maverick's fault. Heck, she could've lost all of her horses if it hadn't been for him. But she'd heard the telling word, too. *Either.*

Somehow, this loss was connected to another loss, one that still tortured him. This poor man was so damned broken. The last thing he needed was another regret in his life, and she refused to let him have it.

She leaned against his bicep and parted his hair while she carefully cleansed the wound. Damn it, she needed to see what she was doing. The light was better if she leaned in close, and, oh hell. This man needed a lifeline, and she meant to toss him one. Better yet, she meant make damned sure the stubborn fool grabbed hold of it whether he wanted to or not.

Bad things happened in life. That's just the way it was. She would survive this godawful tragedy and so would he. She blew out a breath and gave him what he needed to hear. "Well, you're still alive. Kyrie, too. That's all that matters to me. I can replace my horses, but I could never replace you two."

He trembled. For a moment, she thought she had been too rough with her cleaning, that she had hurt him—until his arm circled her waist. He pulled her in close, his face pressed against her stomach. He sucked up a deep breath, and groaned into her nightshirt.

She stopped worrying about his head. His heart needed something more. "I'm so sorry," she whispered into the top of his sweaty hair. "I know you loved that baby as much as I did. I'm sorry I wasn't there to help you save her and her mother."

He choked.

"But loosing you would've hurt me so much worse." She kissed the crown of his head and rested her cheek there. "I can rebuild my barn, but you've come to mean a lot to me these last few days. I hope you understand that."

She meant it with every beat of her heart. This moody, somber man had saved her life and now most of her kids. China clutched Maverick to her, her fingers gentle in his hair and her own tears uncontainable.

Kyrie slid off her chair and clung to China's leg, whimpering. China could absorb her heartbreak for kittens lost, but the pain grinding out of Maverick seemed so much darker. So much deeper.

His shoulders shuddered. He mashed his face farther into her nightshirt. She wrapped her body around him as his torment eked out. It wasn't the wailing whine of a woman. No. The misery that wretched out of Maverick growled. It shuddered like a terrible beast kept caged and deprived too long. Finally let loose, it struggled out of him in ragged spasms.

All she could do was cry with him while he fell apart.

Chapter Fifteen

I hate everything.

Maverick sat by himself on China's porch step and stared at the smoking carcass of the barn. He thought he had escaped misery when he left Afghanistan behind, but here it was again, stalking him like a fire-breathing dragon. It didn't matter where he went or how far he walked, the beast still lashed out and burned every shred of his soul away with one belching breath. It could reach him and it always smelled the same. Smoke. Ash. Charred bodies. Death.

X and Z hadn't even known he had slept in the barn with the horses, much less that he had safely rescued them. Well, almost all of them. The white one and her baby weren't so lucky. He couldn't even think their names, much less say them out loud.

At least China hadn't been there to hear their death screams. He groaned, shaking with restraint as he tried to maintain his thin hold on composure. The horrible loss of that beautiful mare and her brand new baby was one more ugly thing to live with. With his baseball cap on his head, the brim pulled low, and his Oakleys firmly in place, he had a fairly solid wall erected, at least until Zeke Knudsen strolled to the porch and sat down beside him.

Damned friendly old man.

Z placed a gnarled hand on Maverick's knee. "You doin' okay, son?"

He seemed to be a nice enough older guy, but Maverick didn't want company or friendship. They got a guy into trouble. The second a man started to care about others, shit happened. He turned away. The road called his name, loud and clear. He never should've come back to the Wild Wolf, much less stayed this long. All he had brought was pain and death. It followed him everywhere. China deserved better. Kyrie, too.

I need to leave.

"That was a mighty fine thing you did for Miss China last night, saving her horses like you did. You're dang lucky you didn't get yerself killed."

Maverick steeled his heart against the old codger's attempt to forgive. China had bandaged his burned hands last night, but he'd torn the bandages off the moment he left the ranch house. She wanted him to get stitches, but he refused that, too. He had been hurt a helluva lot worse and in more disgusting ways than she would ever know. No. There would be no forgiving today.

An old yellow dog appeared out of nowhere. It trotted along China's gravel driveway toward the ranch.

That's me. A stray. A mutt. Smart enough to stay alive for whatever that's worth, but not smart enough to know when to leave. Kick me. Beat me. Throw me a bone now and then. Just don't get too close. I'm not worth the trouble.

"Sure gonna be a big job rebuilding."

Maverick heard the clever hint loud and clear, but he ignored the veiled invitation to stay on and help. The thought smacked of permanence, and he wasn't looking for that. Not now. Maybe never. *Give it up, old man.*

He grunted his usual noncommittal answer to life in general and watched the stupid dog. It had its nose in a gopher hole alongside the road. Or something just as useless. Any minute now, the dumb dog would take off and never be seen again like the mongrel it was. He wished it luck and planned to follow its lead. Anywhere else was better than there.

"The fire marshal thinks it was arson."

No shit. Maverick tensed. Of course it was arson, but knowing someone had deliberately set this fire only created more problems, because now he wanted to strike out. He wanted to hurt that someone for hurting China and Kyrie. He wanted that someone to suffer like... like Gorgeous had suffered. He wanted them to scream like poor China Love.

God. He could still hear that sweet baby's panicked squeals. She had cried! God damn it! She cried. Maverick put two fingers to the temple that hurt the worst because he couldn't reach his heart. Nothing could. Never again. It hurt too damned bad!

Worse, he knew what he had heard. The whine of a Harley. Leezel laughing just before he got knocked unconscious. The *Kings and Kreepers* on the loose. He told Fire Chief Burton—he just couldn't bring himself to tell China. Not yet.

And damned if he knew how Reardon got Leezel to help commit such a godawful crime against her sister. But he had, the pig. And then she must've taken something to make her sleep, sealing her alibi. Making her look innocent. Yes, Leezel had been sound asleep in her room when Maverick checked on her whereabouts, but he knew what he'd heard.

Z sighed heavily. "Reardon done this. He's been trying to get back at Miss China ever since Leezel left him. That boy's ten kinds a mean with a fifth of ugly rolled into one worthless SOB."

Maverick clenched his jaw. Yeah. Reardon was the bastard behind the fire. Worthless didn't begin to describe a guy who could hurt innocent animals. But Leezel had been there, too.

"Coffee's ready." China stood at the screen door.

Maverick didn't bother to acknowledge her presence. He heard the question and plea behind her simple statement. *Will you stay? Please don't go.* He didn't accept and he didn't refuse. For now he just sat and watched the dumb dog. Its stupid tail wagged as if it was ready to make friends with that gopher in the hole.

Damned stupid dog. Beat it. Take off. Get the hell out of here.

The door opened and closed behind Maverick. Z pushed to his feet and shuffled off toward the bunkhouse. At least it survived. For the most part, only the barn had burned. Damn thing probably didn't even need an accelerant. Just a match and an asshole to strike it.

Maverick jumped at China's gentle hand on his arm. She didn't say anything as she sat at his side, and he was glad for that. Words were only good for a couple times in life, and this wasn't one of them. She didn't sigh like most women did, either, and he was glad of that, too. A sigh was a hint. It was meant to invite conversation, like a leading question or statement. It was a ploy. A fishhook. A trap.

The stupid dog faced him now, both ears alert, probably waiting for a handout, as if he had anything decent to offer. *Sorry, dog. You're barking up the wrong tree. I got nothing and I wouldn't feed you if I did.*

The dog wasn't much of a mutt though. Maverick detected a yellow Lab's intelligent face and squared off ears. The way it sat at attention reminded Maverick of the explosive ordnance dogs overseas. Maybe this fellow wasn't so much a stray as he was—lost.

Yeah. Me, too. One lost, sorry sonofabitch. Beat it, dog.

"Andy China." Kyrie stood at the screen. "Mommy's sweepin'."

"Then come out here and sit with me." China opened her arms and immediately Kyrie pushed the screen door aside and scampered to her aunt's lap.

Maverick felt the child's eyes on him. He didn't look her way—it wasn't like she could see through the Oakleys, but still. She might smile and that would wreck him for sure.

They sat in silence, the stray dog waiting to be invited onto the porch, and Maverick wishing the damn mutt would leave. It kept its distance. Maybe it could read minds.

Read this, Fido. Get the hell out of here and don't come back.

"Oh, yook. A puppy." Kyrie pointed her index finger at it. Of course, her finger was firmly attached to her blankie, so she ended up pointing the whole thing at the dog.

Fido noticed the flag she had raised. Both ears perked up. He came to his feet in rapt attention, his dumb tail wagging, like he had half a chance of a handout or staying. Maverick shrugged any kindness he might have felt for the homeless beast out of his heart. *Not today. You better leave before you get hurt, too. Before you die.*

Thundering hooves announced a runaway Percheron. Of all the horses it could have been, it had to be Star. X followed close on the big guy's heels with a lead and a broken halter. Once Star rounded the burned shell of the barn, he stopped and reared back on his haunches, both front hooves flailing. He snorted, the whites of his eyes wild.

Poor Star's whole world had changed, and he didn't understand. It smelled bad enough with the fire and ash, but Maverick suspected the big fellow could smell death, too. He certainly could.

Maverick rolled his weary butt off the porch step. He raised both palms toward Star and walked toward the horse. "Whoa now, big guy. Settle down. You're okay."

Star fell to all fours, snorting as he tossed his mane in what sure looked like disagreement.

"It's okay, Star. It's gonna be okay, buddy."

"He won't let me touch him," X said softly. "I's jes tryin' ta help."

"'S okay. "I've got this." Maverick kept walking. Star kept snorting and tossing his head, but Maverick didn't hesitate. He took one final step before he pressed a calming hand to the middle of Star's forehead, the other to his neck under his ear.

Star blew out one final snort before he lowered his forehead against Maverick's shoulder.

"There, now. Whoa. You're going to be okay, boy."

Star shuddered and Maverick shuddered with him. The horse was just scared. His life had been brutally changed, and no doubt, he had heard the final screams of the two animals that died in the fire. Maverick felt a kinship with the beast. Star's fear became his. He was there, too. He had heard the pain of a brother dying—alone. Without his big brother to hold his hand.

"It ain't easy, is it?" He asked the right question.

Star huffed, but closed his eyes. His long tail swished and he stomped one rear hoof as if saying, *'You're damned right. It's hell, and I'm still scared.'*

"Me too, boy. Me, too." Somehow the touch of Maverick's hand sent strength to this frightened animal. They knew what the other felt. Star nickered soft and low. He sent enough strength to *hold on for one more minute* right back. Maverick knotted his fingers into Star's black mane and bowed his forehead to what seemed like his only friend in the world.

The memory of what they'd lost was too much to endure alone. The smell and feel of the mighty horse at his fingertips pulled the grief right out of Maverick. He couldn't stop the tears. Didn't even try. Just held on for dear life as the anguish poured out. He had seen so much ugliness and suffering in his life, and now it had followed him to the beautiful wilds of Wyoming, a place so rare with skies as blue as the heaven in China's blue eyes. Even now, she sat on the porch waiting and trusting. God, was the woman out of her mind to trust him the way she did? Did she have a clue what kind of a man he was?

"I let my brother die," he confided in the horse. "I couldn't get to him. He fell. I ran, but Gabe knocked me down trying to save me. Me! Me! Then Gabe got shot, and Taylor tried to save him and me, but... God. They outnumbered us. We were taking heavy fire. None of us stood a chance. We had to haul ass out of there just to save... ourselves."

And there it was, the truth, finally spoken out loud. To a horse. *I saved myself. Not Darrell. Not my baby brother.*

Star nickered low and soft.

"They say it just takes time," Maverick whispered, "but I've been walking a damned long time and it never gets better. Never."

The morning sun warmed his shoulders, but Star's gentle presence warmed him more. Maverick coughed and wiped his face. He had been walking a long time, but he'd brought Darrell with him every step of the way. The kid's brown eyes were in the setting of every sun, the rising of every moon. He heard Darrell's voice in the hoot owls' lonely call at night and the cooing of doves at morning. And he didn't want it any other way, because he would never—never—leave his brother behind again.

He leaned away from the horse and gave the big fellow one more scratch behind his ears. "You going to be okay now?"

Star didn't answer, but he purred just like he had done up there on the hillside. Damned if that wasn't the perfect answer for a man packing a shitload of guilt. Darrell would've gotten a kick out of this horse.

Maverick took a deep breath and let it release slowly. He had walked all the way to Wyoming, and just maybe—maybe—he'd finally found what he needed to heal.

He stepped away from Star, immediately worried if China had seen. He shot a quick glance over his shoulder. Of course she'd seen. She hadn't moved an inch, just sat there on the top step rocking Kyrie, her eyes on him and Star.

Maverick swallowed his pride and reached down for the broken halter and lead. He looped the lead around Star's neck and fastened the snap. "Let's go see China."

"Come on, sweetheart," China called out.

Maverick didn't want to know which of them she meant that word for, him or the horse clomping along behind him. He kept his head down and his feet walking. Thank God for Oakleys.

"Come on, my handsome guy," she crooned.

Had to be talking to the horse.

Finally, Star stretched his nose to her outstretched fingers, and Maverick sat beside her, blinking the moisture out of his eyes and forever wishing he were tougher. Meaner. Hard enough not to break.

"Are you okay?" she asked, and Maverick had to look at her again to see if she meant him or Star. Things had taken too personal of a turn last night after the fire. He wasn't sure where he stood with China anymore, but he didn't want to take any chances. It was easier to assume the worst and be pleasantly surprised if things turned out better than they usually did.

Her hand was stretched out to the horse. Not him. Good enough. Star's ears pitched forward, but he didn't approach China. Instead, he spotted Fido and stood with nostrils flared.

The stupid dog wagged its tail. Fido took one step forward. The dog crept on its belly until it was nearly to the horse's mammoth hooves.

Star tossed his head and watched.

"Look, Andy China." Kyrie wiggled in excitement. "The puppy wants ta play."

"He does, huh?"

Maverick heard the sadness in her voice. China was bone-weary and empty inside, too. She had nothing left to give, and he knew exactly where that hollow feeling came from. He had been there. Heck, he was still there.

Fido didn't give up. He barked once and the horse tossed his head. Other than that, the two seemed content to size each other up and stare each other down at a safe distance.

The miracle happened slowly. Star stretched his nose toward the dog, his ears forward and his eyes alert while Fido stretched up to the horse. It looked like an old-fashioned slow motion picture, frame by frame, happening cautiously until the animals' noses touched.

Star sniffed noisily. His lips reached out to sample the dog's snout. Fido shied back a step, but no more than that. In a second, he was back at the horse's muzzle, sniffing and wagging his tail. Star bumped the dog's head with his nose, and just like that, friends were made. Fido wagged his tail and sniffed Star's very impressive front hooves, then returned to the horse's nose for another tail waggling round of meet and greet.

There was no wild neighing or flying hooves. No frantic barking or biting. No nipping. Only a very unhappy horse who needed a true friend in the worst way. What was God thinking? He had sent a stupid mongrel dog to be that friend. A mutt and a registered Percheron? Fido and Star? Who would've thought?

Maverick summoned his inner Marine and turned to face a very sad China. She bit her lip and he wiped his eyes beneath his dark glasses. They were Fido and Star all over again. He the mutt. She the purebred. And a world of hurt between them.

"You gave me cookies and milk."

China looked at him as if he were daft. "I what?"

He repeated himself. "Cookies and milk. Last night. You gave me cookies and milk like I was a little kid."

A tear eked out of the corner of her eye. She wiped it away. "Guess I thought chocolate chip cookies cure everything."

"I'm sorry I couldn't save them all," he whispered as he reached for her hand.

China nodded sadly at Star. "But you saved him and everyone else. Thank you. You could have died, then I would feel so much worse."

She leaned her head into his shoulder and that was all it took. Tears fell onto his shirt. He wrapped an arm around her and Kyrie, and prepared for the meltdown of his heart. Again.

"I couldn't get them to move." Even he heard the angst in his voice. He had pushed and slapped enough horse butts last night that they all should've run from him. He'd changed into the devil incarnate, screaming to be heard over the roar of the flames, waving his arms and beating the horses to get them to move. The only one who ran out the first time like a good boy and didn't come back was Joker.

China interlocked her fingers with his and nodded against his shoulder. "Horses lose their heads in a fire."

"But I thought once I opened the barn doors, they would get out of there."

"You saved twenty-one. I'll never be able to thank you enough." She wiped her eyes and faced him. "Let's focus on the good you did, not the miracle no one could've worked. Twenty-one is better than two. It could've been a lot worse."

He gulped. Not a hint of recrimination lingered on her face. If anything, she looked grateful. At peace. He turned away, his feelings too raw. Twenty-one wasn't good enough. He had lost two very precious friends. He choked as the memory of the mare's big face in his chest came back to him. She had liked him instantly, but now she was gone.

Maverick knew it right then and there. He'd worn out his welcome. Pain followed him everywhere and China deserved better, but her touch anchored him. He looked down at her fingers still interlocked with his. She didn't clutch or rub up against him like Leezel had. China was just there, breathing the same air and letting him breathe, too. Letting him decide to leave or to stay.

He removed the Oakleys, folded them and stuck them in his shirt pocket. His eyes were red, probably puffy, too. Well, so be it. She might as well get used to it.

"Morning," he said sincerely.

"Good morning, Maverick," she answered with a sad smile.

He nodded to Fido. "Looks like you got yourself a new dog."

"Oh, goodie." Kyrie clapped both hands and scrunched her shoulders. "Kin I keep him? Huh, Andy China? Pwease?"

China smiled down at the happy child, but then turned to Maverick with a pointed brow. "You do know that's not fair, don't you?"

He studied the stupid dog. "But he looks lost."

China tightened her hold on his fingers. Damn, she had tiny fingers. How the hell could she manage the ranch? He honestly didn't understand her will or her heart. It seemed a damned big challenge for one woman.

"Do you think he's smart enough to stay?"

Maverick shrugged. He knew what she was really asking. Hell. He knew what he was really answering. He squeezed her fingers. "Maybe."

Chapter Sixteen

The neighbors showed up in droves.

Fire Marshall Garth got the word out, and by noon, an army of good people descended on the Wild Wolf Ranch. Oscar Higgins from two ranches over brought a flatbed trailer with twenty-foot eight-by-eight beams for the skeleton of a new barn while Lon Denton from town showed up with his caterpillar and backhoe. The local vet, Betsy Connelly, arrived to give all the horses a thorough examination, and the local diner promised refreshments for everyone for as long as the rebuild took. All China had to do was stand and watch while the kindness of neighbors stepped into the tragedy and lifted her burden.

Before long, the smoking debris was fully extinguished and bulldozed from the burn site to the acre behind the barn. Leezel showed her puffy, hung-over face around one in the afternoon, angry no one had thought to wake her up from her stupor so she could've watched the barn burn. She had no comment on the tragedy that had occurred, only petulance that she had missed it.

Fire Marshall Garth cornered Maverick, and together the two men constructed a nighttime holding pen for the horses until the new barn was completed. They barely spoke as they worked. The serious expression on Maverick's face made China smile. She remembered with a bittersweet tear the practical joke she'd played on him. He had been disgusted to feel a horse's teats, but then he had stayed steadfast beside her through the delivery of that beautiful foal. She wiped her eyes. Her heart would hurt for a long time.

"Ya know, little girl." Rich Williams stood at her elbow with a sizeable wad of chew in his cheek. He was one of the good ol' boys in town. He still owned the tract of grazing land that bordered hers, but had given up ranching, content with just a few head of cattle and a couple of horses. He said arthritis took too much of his strength, and that ranching was meant for younger guys. "I'd be glad to loan you my Savannah Joy if'n you want to try your luck at breeding a white again."

China clasped his proffered hand. Savannah Joy was a beautiful animal, too, but there'd be no replacing a mare like Gorgeous. Not yet.

"That's very kind, Rich. I just might take you up on your offer one of these days."

"Well, she's yours for the asking." Rich had a habit of working his jaw from side to side as he talked and chewed. Right now it sat to the right of his normal jaw line. "You know what I mean?"

"The whites are special, aren't they?"

Rich nodded wisely. "Yep. They kinda glow in the dark, especially that Gorgeous—well, she was just like you named her. Never seen such a handsome mare in my life."

China blinked fast and looked away. It was too soon to chat about the treasure she had just lost.

Rich put a kind hand on her arm. "I'm right sorry, Miss China." He placed a whiskered kiss to her cheek. "They's kinda like our kids, ain't they?"

She bit her lip and nodded.

"I'll let you alone, young 'un, but you ever need anything, anything at all, you come see me." He tipped her forehead to his. "Lots of us folks think the world of you, little girl. You done your daddy proud the way you took over this place."

China could only nod. Good ol' Rich Williams had better turn around and leave before she burst into tears. A warm hand wrapped her waist. She looked up into Maverick's dark eyes.

"Sorry, Mr. Williams, but I need to steal Miss Wolf for a minute, if that's okay with you."

Rich nodded and winked at China. "You steal her for as long as you'd like, young man."

Maverick guided China to the porch steps where he had an icy glass of lemonade waiting for her. He sat next to her. They watched the neighbors scurry back and forth, chatting and helping each other.

China composed herself while she waited for Maverick to tell her what he needed, but it took so long. Honestly, the man seemed content to sit and say nothing. Her curiosity got the best of her. "What did you need?"

"Nothing." He stretched his long legs down the porch steps, leaned back on one elbow, and made himself more comfortable, which only added to her confusion.

"Excuse me?"

"You're excused."

"No. I mean, what did you want to talk to me about?"

He turned to face her, the sunglasses perched on his nose again and creating the wall he so easily maintained. "Already told you. Nothing."

"Okay then." She sighed a deep breath. For now Leezel was actually helpful as she worked with the lady from the diner, distributing bottles of water to the men at work and cookies to the little ones. Kyrie played with her new dog, Puppy. The temporary corral was finished, but for now, twenty-one four-legged kids grazed on the hillside.

China leaned back onto her elbows. Life was damn hard sometimes, but the good will of neighbors and friends had come to her rescue. She turned and stared at Maverick until he grew uncomfortable under her gaze.

"What?" he asked.

She gave him a small smile and a wink. "Nothing."

The barn raising took seven days, and then they rested, which seemed appropriate because it was Sunday. The upright beams had been planted, the electrical lines were installed, and the concrete flooring needed time to cure. The neighbors promised they'd return in a week to finish the job, but for now the barnyard had fallen peacefully silent.

China toured the new facility before anyone else woke. By the time the barn was finished, it would be larger and better constructed than her old one. An indoor horse-washing station with a built-in hot water heater was in the plans. The feed store had already promised a free week's worth of premium horse pellets. Even with all the generosity of her neighbors and the insurance settlement, she would still owe a hefty bank loan, but she would be okay. Loans were a way of life for farmers and ranchers.

She continued her solitary tour to the back of the barn. The corral that had once stood there was temporarily converted to a debris field. Bits and pieces of construction material had been tossed into a burn pile. An industrial-sized garbage can looked as if it needed to be emptied of soda pop cans and fast food garbage. She walked past it to the edge of the temporary corral, intending to release the horses to the pasture, but someone had already done that. The corral stood empty, its gate flung open.

She gazed up at the stand of aspen in the pasture. That's where the horses liked to congregate on a hot day, in amongst the shady grove that stretched from the barn and up the hill. It was always a peaceful picture, all those noble creatures resting amidst the trees.

That was where X and Z had kindly dug a grave with Denton's backhoe, large enough for a favored brood mare and her foal under the trees where the rest of her horses stood now.

It had been one helluva tough week, but China wasn't about to sink into the depths of depression. X and Z had taken care of the burial the day after the fire, and done it without her knowledge. Z told her later she didn't need to remember her beautiful girl in any other way than as the gorgeous animal she was when she was alive. China knew without a doubt that he was right. Still, she needed to see where Gorgeous lay in peace with her perfect foal.

Ebony saw her first. The black stallion neighed from his pasture, along with Hex, and Aces Wild. The stallions' friendly voices drew the others' attention. Before long, the herd descended to the lower field. China climbed the fence to be with them. This was her way of healing, her therapy. After all was said and done, her horses renewed her strength and energy. She relied on them now.

After a round of pats and caresses, she continued uphill to the grave. It wasn't far, just a grassy landing notched into the hillside where the earth had been disturbed and a good friend laid to rest. The higher she climbed, the more she felt like a teacher on a fieldtrip with a class full of big kids tagging along.

At last she stood over her favorite brood mare. She couldn't help it. She cried. X and Z had done well. Gorgeous and China Love were laid down to rest together. A hefty flat stone was pressed into the center of the freshly mounded earth. The instant she saw the words etched into the stone, she knew the artist.

Bye and bye we's all go home to Him who gived us wings to fly and horses to love.

Xavier, bless his heart, the man who most folks disregarded as a halfwit, had provided a very eloquent and fitting eulogy. China wiped her face. Somehow the words on that plain old piece of granite jerked the sorrow straight out of her. He had etched a pair of wings above the words and the date beneath. She had always thought of Gorgeous with wings. Now she was sure.

The first time she'd seen the mare online, China had been smitten. She had travelled all the way to Vermont to inspect the year-old filly before she bought her. While she fully expected an exceptional animal, what she got was something else.

The horse was not only an unblemished, spotless white, but she was intelligent, too. Gorgeous was the horse of China's dreams, and she'd known right then and there, she would be taking the mare home to Wyoming, no matter the cost. It was a friendship made in heaven—and the bank.

China lowered herself to the ground and sat cross-legged by the stone. Of course, that only invited a few curious horses' noses in her face, and since the last thing she needed was a horse in her lap, she didn't stay there for too long.

Right on cue, Joker nudged her butt with his nose, pushing her forward a couple of feet as he made his presence known. Rascal or not, he came for a scratch behind his ears, and she obliged. For a moment, it was just China and her kids remembering their fallen companions together. She paused with one hand on Joker's strong neck, the other on his velvet-soft nose. Her kids always calmed her and today was no different.

Spring mornings were peaceful in Wyoming. The sky seemed extra blue and she didn't want to leave the shady grove. Buds covered the trees and the few straggly pines in the grove showed lime green tips on all their branches where new growth sprouted. One of the horses nickered as they grazed nearby.

Her mares Sunshine, Sugar, and Frost were wide and ready to foal any day now. That would be a challenge with the barn unfinished, but China would find a way. The thought of new foals brought a smile to her lips. Rich Williams' offer to lend his Savannah Joy was an enticing idea. She would need another white mare, not so much to replace Gorgeous, but just to get on with the business of living.

That was why she had come up the hill in the first place. As hard as it was, she needed to close this sad chapter and get on with life. She had learned that lesson long ago from her father.

Get up. Get back to work. Keep living.

Movement below caught her eyes. Someone else was up. Maverick. She watched as he rounded the bunkhouse and walked purposefully toward the back of the barn. He wore his baseball cap and dark glasses as usual, and even at this distance, he was easy on the eyes. Several horses turned his way, but none of them seemed too interested until Star looked up. With a friendly nicker, the nosey horse trotted downhill.

Star stopped at the lower fence. At first, Maverick only glanced at him, but then he walked over and scratched his ears. Maverick liked Star; she just didn't expect him to climb the fence and slide off the top rail of the fence and onto the horse's broad back. Neither did she expect to see him lean into Star's neck and hug him like he did.

She blinked. Maverick stayed there for another couple minutes before he righted himself and slid to the ground. Even then, he stayed alongside Star, as if he was talking to the animal. They looked like compadres, their heads together in secret guy-talk.

China watched the pleasant scene. It touched her. Maverick and Star had a bond. They stood there for a moment longer until Maverick climbed the fence and walked away. Star followed along the fence as if keeping track of his friend. Maverick paused at the burn pile, pulled a few two-by-four scraps from the heap and disappeared around the bunkhouse.

China turned back to the grave for one last word with Gorgeous.

"See you around."

Beer bottles clinked together. Had to be Leezel.

Maverick glanced over his shoulder up at her and immediately looked back down to the two-by-fours on the sawhorse, damned glad for his dark glasses. He figured she would come looking for him. She needed to know what he remembered from the night of the fire. Two could play that game. He needed something, too. The truth.

She came up behind him and stood damned near at his back pocket and in imminent danger of his backstroke. "Whatcha doing, cowboy?"

He rolled his neck at the unwelcome interruption. "You need to move."

"I do, huh?" For whatever reason, that request sparked a smile on her face. She made it difficult for a guy not to notice her. Today's get-up consisted of extra-short shorts and a sheer top tied off at her waist. The black bra beneath the see-through top screamed her usual message. *I'm easy.*

She had been extra liberal with her eye makeup again. Soap and a breath mint wouldn't hurt her none, either. Beer never made an attractive mouthwash.

She had a wiggly way of walking, as if every part of her was ready and available for exploitation. The shimmy in her shoulders shook the rest of her. She took another mincing step toward him in those same ridiculous, red heels she always seemed to wear. The dame was dressed to party at oh-six-hundred hours. On a ranch. A horse ranch.

"Where's X and Z?"

"They went into town."

"They gonna be back soon?"

He shrugged. "Didn't ask."

"That was real decent of you to take my daughter for another walk last night. She said you found where that mama cat hid her kittens after the fire."

"Yep."

"Kyrie likes baby kitties."

Maverick ignored her baby talk, another distinctly feminine trait he didn't understand. Not all women employed it. Thank God, China didn't.

"I brought you a drink." She stuck a bottle under his nose where he couldn't miss it.

He leaned away from her and resumed sawing. "No thanks."

"Whatcha making?" She didn't move far.

Although he was plenty busy and sweaty to boot, she traced a fingernail across the back of his neck and accompanied that with a soft murmur, as if that simple touch should've gotten him worked up. It didn't come close. He shrugged it off and re-focused. The saw went up. The saw went down. Simple work for a Sunday morning.

The problem with confronting Leezel about her part in the barn burning had everything to do with Kyrie. Leezel clearly didn't want her child, so Maverick needed to be careful how he went about it. He'd seen her at work. He didn't want retaliation for what he might say or ask misdirected back at her daughter.

"The sheriff is questioning my old boyfriend, you know."

He should. Maverick wanted to question Reardon himself, only not at the police station.

He lined up another length of two-by-fours according to the rough plan in his head. His project required four longs and eight shorts. Puppy size.

"Sheriff Hammer thinks Troy's an ars-on-ist." Leezel was a fountain of useless trivia this morning and still trying to sound like a southern belle while she dispensed it. It wasn't working for her. It made her sound stupid, something Maverick doubted she was. "I don't hang out with him anymore, just so y'all know."

He shrugged, his usual non-answer when someone lied to his face. Who was she trying to kid? All Reardon had to do was show back up and threaten to take Kyrie, and Leezel would be all over him again. She was a follower, and he was the stupid brain that told her when to jump.

"I used to think he was the only man in the whole world for me." She sighed deeply. "I mean, he was exciting and a little crazy. I like that in my guys. We used to go riding on his Harley, just take off for Yellowstone or the West Coast. One time we drove all the way to Malibu before we stopped for the night."

Another sigh.

The way she sighed told Maverick there was more to the story whether he wanted to hear it or not. He stacked the long lengths he had just cut aside and measured the scrap two-by-fours for the shorter ones. He needed a sheet of CDX plywood to complete the project, and maybe a couple more two-by-fours. If the lumber store was open, this project would be done by dusk and Kyrie would be one happy little girl.

He let Leezel keep talking, let her keep thinking she had a reason to stay.

"I really loved him, ya know?" The wistful saga continued. "We were crazy. Couldn't keep our hands off each other." She hiccupped at that last comment, as if it were too delightful to forget.

Not for Maverick. He forgot it instantly.

"We made love on the beach under a full moon one time."

Shit damn! Poke my eyes out with a sharp stick. That was the last image he needed in his head—a gnarly old dude bumping uglies with a trashy younger woman who looked like a hooker.

He didn't have to look up to know she was staring off into space, batting her eyes and waiting for him to ask what happened next. He didn't. The saw went up. The saw went down.

"Wanna know why we broke up the first time?"

No. Hell. No.

"I kinda got pregnant." She actually whispered, as if the whole world didn't know Kyrie had been born out of wedlock.

He stifled a grunt while the saw chewed away at the black mark on the wood in quick measured bites. He enjoyed physical labor. A man could accomplish something.

Leezel put her hand on his shoulder, and once again he had to stop the saw. She moved in close. He clenched his jaw as the endurance test continued.

"You're a v-e-r-y strong man." She ran her fingernails up his neck and into his hairline, tipping his cap over his forehead and knocking his glasses off.

Time to dance. He jerked his cap off and tucked the brim of it into his back pocket. The Oakleys went onto his shirt collar. "You always start your day with a beer?"

She lifted the bottle to her lips and ran her tongue around the rim. "When I can get it."

He softened his tone and glanced at the bottle in her other hand. "It's going to be another hot day. Maybe I'll take you up on that offer."

She handed the already opened bottle over. The corners of her mouth lifted into a wide smile that showed her perfectly straight and white teeth. Dental work. Acrylic nails. Dancing shoes. Yet her daughter wore rags. Yeah. This woman was selfish from the ground up.

He parked his rear on the sawhorse, which forced her to keep standing. Raising the bottle to his lips, he took a swallow. Good on her. China knew a good beer.

He ran the back of his other hand over his brow and looked toward the new construction. "You know what I don't understand?"

"What's that, Mav?"

Inwardly he cringed. *Mav* had died a long time ago, but explaining it to Leezel would only mislead her into thinking he cared.

"I don't understand how you could've slept through all the noise that night." He took another sip and kept his eyes on the barn.

"I use a sleep-aid," she confided, sidling closer. "It's real hard being a single mom. It's a twenty-four-hour-a-day job, and sometimes I just can't fall asleep."

Twenty-four-hour a job, nothing. But her lie did explain her grogginess the day after.

"Funny thing about that night." He kept looking at the barn. "I'm almost sure I heard someone behind the barn. Thought it was you."

"You tell Sheriff Hammer?" she asked, her eyes a titch brighter and sharper as she took another swig.

"Nothing to tell. I couldn't say for sure. Could've been my imagination."

"Probably just cats fighting. Maybe raccoons. There's plenty of varmints around these parts."

"Maybe." He took another sip, determined to draw her out. "See, here's the thing. I thought I heard a Harley, too. I thought there might be trouble with your ex, but then I got clobbered."

Leezel took a step toward him, a seductive smile blossoming on her overly painted lips.

He crossed his ankles to block her brazen attempt to stand between his legs. *No. Way. In. Hell.*

"Me and Reardon took us a midnight swim up at Minter's Creek," she drawled. "That's when we broke up again. He's been cheating on me. I could see it all over his face. The man's a real prick."

And you, my dear, are full of bullshit. But you do have all your bases covered.

"I told him I don't never want to see him again, then I come home and took my pills and went to sleep." She pinched her lips together at the rim of her bottle. "You do believe me, don't you, Mav?"

He shrugged. "Don't matter if I do or not. I'm out of here once the barn's done." He polished off the beer in one long pull. Let her believe what she wanted. He knew better. Leezel was as full of shit as Reardon.

Chapter Seventeen

He didn't watch her backside while she strutted away because that was exactly what she wanted. Instead he wiped his brow and got back to work. He'd seen enough dumbasses in his life, he didn't need to watch this one. This little job was supposed to be a day project, not a weeklong chore.

His stomach gurgled. Maverick finished cutting the boards to size and stacked them by the sawhorse. He couldn't do anymore work on the project until he went to town, so he headed into the ranch house. Breakfast would be good, surprising China better.

A man can't surprise a woman if he has to knock, so he didn't. He opened the front door and peered inside. Thankfully, Leezel was nowhere to be seen. Someone was moving around upstairs, but he took his chances. Nothing got a person up early in the morning like breakfast cooking. Hopefully that person would be China.

He went quietly into the kitchen and scrubbed his hands at the sink. It took a minute to figure out the coffeemaker, but he managed to set a twelve-cup pot to drip. The smells of bacon and coffee filled the house in no time at all, just as he had intended.

He was flipping French toast on the griddle when a chair scraped behind him. Maverick turned to the littlest lady of the house. Her light blue pajamas only enhanced the color in her teary blue eyes. He set the spatula aside and knelt to her level. "Hey, there. Are you okay?"

She nodded, but her lip stuck out so far that he knew better. He pulled a kitchen chair out from the table and Kyrie scrambled up. "You want something to drink? Orange juice?" *Kids don't drink coffee, do they?*

"Miwk, pwease." Worry shifted over her face. She scrunched her nose. "Is that okay?"

"You bet." He poured her a big glass of milk and watched her take a good, long swallow. "What can I fix you for breakfast, ma'am?"

She wiped her milk moustache off and scrunched her shoulders. "I not a ma'am."

"Sure you are. You're a lady, aren't you? That makes you a ma'am."

"No." A shy giggle replaced the pout. "I a widdle girl."

"Then why is a little girl sad on a nice morning like this?"

She glanced furtively toward the staircase. "Cuz I hafta be a big girl now."

Her lip quivered and Maverick turned to mush.

Kyrie squeezed her eyes tight, but tears eked out beneath her lashes anyway. "I don't wanna be a big girl."

Maverick made himself comfortable on the floor beside her chair, needing her to cheer up. He never could stand to see a woman cry, especially a tiny one. "Hey, there. How hard can it be? Look at me. I'm a big boy, ain't I?"

"Uh huh." She nodded emphatically. "You is bigger 'n me and Andy China and evwyone."

"There isn't anything to it. You just eat your breakfast every day, and it happens." His mind pinged for anything to make this unhappy child smile.

"But I miss bwankie." Again her lip turned to the cutest pout. "And I don't wanna be a big boy."

His heart stuttered. Maverick placed a hand on her back, intending to pat her once or twice, just enough to get her past this little fit. It didn't work that way. She slid off the chair and into his lap.

"And Mommy says I can't keep Puppy." Kyrie tipped her curly head back and wailed. "I hafta give him aw-a-a-a-a-a-y."

Maverick couldn't think of anything more to say so he just rocked her in his arms in the middle of China's kitchen floor. What the hell made Leezel so damned mean to this little tyke? Kyrie was all of thirty pounds and most of that had to be hair.

"I want bwankie and," she hiccupped, "and I... I want Puppy, to-o-o-o-o."

"There, there. How about if I keep him for you?" Maverick hugged her tight. "I'll feed him. You play with him. Sound like a deal?"

She lifted her sad face and sniffed. With her hair all fuzzy and tangled, she looked like an angel. "Ah huh. I be reawwy nice to him," she said somberly. "I pwomise."

He couldn't resist. He kissed her forehead. "I know you will. You're a good girl, Kyrie. You want to eat breakfast outside with me?"

That changed the subject as he hoped. In a minute, he and Kyrie were off the floor and on the front porch swing with a tray of breakfast. Kyrie blinked up at him as she chewed her French toast very daintily. "Is you a cowboy?"

"Nah." He took a swallow of coffee and stared across the yard. "I'm not smart enough to be a cowboy."

China hadn't made her appearance for the day yet, but he doubted she was still asleep. The woman should've been a Marine with that crack-of-dawn, internal alarm clock of hers.

"Hmm." Kyrie seemed extra thoughtful. "Mommy says you is."

"Yeah, well..." Leezel probably said a lot of things. He changed the subject. "So where is your friend Puppy this morning? Where'd he run off to?"

Her brows furrowed. "I don't know. Where is he, Unca Mavwick?"

He damned near spit his coffee. *Unca Mavwick? When the hell had that happened?* "He's, umm, got to be around here somewhere. How about we look for him after breakfast?"

"Okay." She nodded while she chewed. "Unca Mavwick?"

"Yes?" He rested his arm along the back of the bench and took another sip of his coffee. Uncle Maverick wasn't so bad. It could've been Daddy.

Little Kyrie's innocence smiled up at him. "Is you gonna be my daddy?"

Maverick looked into those honest little blue eyes. Half of him wanted to choke Leezel for shooting her big mouth off, but the other half wanted to say, 'You bet.' He dropped his hand to Kyrie's shoulder.

"Hey, you two." China saved the day when she rounded the corner of the house. "Save some breakfast for me?"

"Andy China!" Kyrie squealed. "Unca Mavwick made Fwench toast an' it's reawwy good."

"He did, did he?" China winked at him as she came up the stairs. "Uncle Maverick cooks, too?"

He looked past her to the barn. "Reckon it could be worse."

China scooped Kyrie onto her lap, running her fingers through the child's tangled locks. "How?"

He deadpanned. "Could be Uncle *Mav*."

China laughed. Kyrie giggled too, but Maverick just kept sipping his coffee. There weren't many things better than the company of two happy women, especially since he was the guy who'd put the smiles on their faces. It was one of those small things in life.

China's smile faded too quickly. She gazed up the hill to the shady spot beneath the trees. "I went up to the grave."

"Wondered where you were."

"X and Z did a real good job. You should take a walk up there. It's peaceful."

He didn't respond. This whole place was peaceful—now.

"I looked for you on my way back. You're building a dog house?"

He lifted a brow. "It was supposed to be a surprise."

"I don't think she heard me." China glanced at Kyrie, who was still busy chewing her toast. "Thank you. So what's next?"

He shrugged. "Guess you're gonna eat breakfast."

Her smile lit up her whole face. It didn't hurt his heart none, either. They'd crossed a line during the last week. Now when he looked at her, the connection was already made. Her smile pulled him in, and he knew exactly where they were headed. What scared him was that he'd been burned before, his heart tossed out like yesterday's trash. Yet with China...

His best defenses had been breached and he'd let his guard down. Truth was, he didn't feel the need to guard against her. She had a way of restoring light in his dark world. Sunshine and the scent of Russian Olive, too. She made him want to play his guitar and sing again. She made him want to be a better man. To live.

"Can I talk you into another horseback ride?" she asked. "I'd like to double check that fence line."

"That depends."

"On what?"

He set his coffee cup on the porch floor and stood to stretch. China didn't bat her eyes or play games. She said what she meant and she meant what she said. He liked that in a woman.

"Can Kyrie come with us?"

Kyrie went with them.

Leezel had gone back to bed with a migraine, or at least that was what she had said when China checked to tell her they were leaving. But China knew the way Leezel worked. She might be able to take off at a moment's notice with Reardon, but when it came to the real, no-kidding work of caring for her only child, Leezel always had better things to do. It didn't matter. China loved Kyrie's company on a twenty-four seven basis, not just when she felt like it. Besides, Leezel already smelled of beer.

For now, Kyrie sat on Star in front of Maverick. The sight made China happy. He seemed protective of the little girl and maybe a little over-attentive, too. She knew he had found the mama cat and kittens again, and thank goodness for that.

Then there was the stray dog. Puppy followed behind the horses as if he already knew his place—with Kyrie. China didn't need the old stray hanging around anymore than she needed the kittens, but what the heck. The hapless mutt made Kyrie happy. Puppy could stay.

Whether he knew it or not, Maverick had a natural way with horses. The tender scene China had witnessed earlier with Star endeared him to her all the more. He fit the saddle well, but he had an authority thing going on, too. She had seen it before when he'd confronted the bikers.

He didn't talk much, just acted and let the pieces fall. And he helped himself to things around the ranch too, but instead of beer and loose change, Maverick was more inclined to help with squeaky doors and rain gutters. He mucked stalls and built doghouses. Not a bad work ethic for a drifter.

China urged Ebony forward until she rode alongside Maverick and Kyrie. He automatically tipped the brim of his baseball cap to her while Kyrie waved and smiled her cute little munchkin grin. This morning she wore a small cowboy hat to protect her from the sun. She looked like a very happy cowgirl riding with a very handsome cowboy. All Maverick needed was the right kind of a hat. Not a baseball cap. No. He needed a Stetson.

China had to look away. Just the sight of him sent her heart into a backward somersault that ended in free fall off the high dive. She had to get a grip, but on what? Even barricaded behind those darn dark glasses of his, he was irresistible.

Despite the tragedy they'd just suffered, he offered more of those rare half-smiles every day. Maybe he did it to get her to smile, but it worked. She focused on the fence line, only the barbs knotted on the wire resembled little hearts, and little hearts brought her back to Maverick again. He had touched her heart without even trying to, or wanting to, if she remembered correctly. The tough exterior he had once presented had somehow faded into heart and soul.

"My fence!" China scrambled off Ebony. Not only was it cut again, but also several posts were pulled out of the ground. "What the hell?"

Maverick slid off Star with Kyrie in his arm. "Tire tracks. Here." He pointed to one side of the fence line. "Over there, too. Whoever did this circled around and went back down the hill the same way they came."

"Damn it." China looked both directions of the fence. Sure enough, two different sets of tracks were visible, but they were irregular, not the evenly spaced tracks a four-wheeled vehicle might have made. "Those are motorcycle tracks. Damn it. Reardon did this. Do I need to post a rider on my fence line from now on?"

BLAM!

Lightning hot pain dug into her hip. The impact sent her flying. "Kyrie!"

Bullets kicked up splatters of dirt beside her, but Maverick had already snatched the girl like a quarterback with a football. He dived for China and sprawled over them both. She barely had time to roll to her back before he flattened her to the ground. He dropped Kyrie beside her and maintained a push-up position, his knees at her thighs.

Adrenaline rushed her in a shuddering wave. Kyrie whimpered. Somewhere out there, Ebony squealed. Horse hooves thrummed the hard ground. China lifted her head, needing to see where Ebony and Star had gone.

"Stay down," Maverick ordered, his voice harsh.

"But I'm... I'm shot." She clutched Kyrie shaking with the violation of the bullet in her body. "God, Maverick. Someone shot me," she repeated because it didn't seem real. It couldn't be. "They tried to kill me. My… my horses."

"Your horses are fine. Now be still." Anger radiated off of him. The ball cap and glasses were missing. Maverick's pupils were black and feral, his body taut as iron. Gone was the indifferent man with the far-off gaze. Someone deadly had just stepped up to the plate.

His gaze scrolled over her, settling on her hip and the swelling patch of burning fire that had to be there. Stinging sparks raced outward, igniting the rest of her body. His hand slid down her stomach to the wound, his gaze along with it.

Another shot rang out. It echoed long and far.

"They're going to kill us," China whined, pulling Kyrie tighter.

"No, they're not," he muttered, barely lifting his head above the grass. "Not on my watch, damn 'em."

"God, my horses. They might shoot... Ebony. Star."

"China, stop it. Settle down. They won't shoot your horses and they sure as hell won't kill you or Kyrie." He growled another curse and eased off of her. For a quick moment, he laid on his stomach beside her, the length of his leg touching hers from hip to boot.

A pistol appeared in his right hand.Her brain overloaded. Where had that weapon come from? He wasn't carrying it while he held Kyrie, was he? She honestly didn't know anything at the moment, not why she was lying in the grass or who Maverick really was.

"I scared," Kyrie whimpered into her neck.

"Shush. Uncle Maverick is here. We're going to be okay." Her own heart calmed. Maverick *was* there. He seemed to know what to do.

He faced the opposite hill, his knees cocked to move, aiming toward the granite face on the other side of the ravine.

She felt the power of a predator beside her, coiled and ready to strike back.

He shoved up from the grass, his right hand extended and the pistol aimed. She'd barely had time to cover Kyrie's ear with her hand when his weapon roared once. Twice. And a third time. Adrenaline thundered inside her skull. Her ears rang.

He jumped up and all she could do was press Kyrie to her and pray he was as good a shot as he seemed to think he was. The outcropping had to be a good thousand yards away, if that was where the shooter had hidden. No one could make a shot that long with just a handgun.

Chapter Eighteen

"They're gone." Maverick crouched beside her once more. The hard look in his eye had softened. He stuck his pistol in a side holster that seemed to have appeared out of nowhere, too. Who was this guy? A magician? "You're shot. I need to see it."

Panic climbed up her throat. She grabbed hold of his shirt. "Reardon did this. He shot me, didn't he?"

Maverick clamped onto her shoulders, his fingers gently kneading her tight muscles. "Settle down, China. It wasn't Reardon. It was some other guy on a dirt bike. I hit the bastard."

"You kill him?" Damn. She wanted the guy dead.

"No. He got away. Lie still."

"How can you... How can you..." The shakes hit hard. She forgot what she wanted to ask. "Where'd you get the gun?"

His eyes narrowed. "My saddlebag. Figured if you can keep a shovel, pliers, and gloves in yours, I could keep my piece in mine."

"Okay. Okay." She nodded more than she needed to. "Good idea. Good. Okay. Yeah. That works."

"China. Settle down, honey. You're going to be okay. I promise, but I need to look at your wound." He drilled her with those deep browns, still asking permission and massaging her shoulder and collarbone. "Now."

"Okay. Okay." She couldn't stop shaking or talking. She had been shot. Not killed. Not hurt enough to miss the fact that he had called her *honey* instead of *ma'am*. She nodded again, trembling from the top of her head to the toes of her boots. *So look, already.*

His fingers flew to her belt. He loosened the buckle and undid the snap to her jeans in two seconds flat before her common sense caught up with her. She clutched his hand to make him stop. "No. Wait. Don't. Kyrie. Puppy."

Okay, so maybe Puppy didn't care if Maverick stripped her bare right there under God and heaven, but Kyrie didn't need to see anything more, especially if it meant blood. The girl just didn't need any more crap in her life. She snuggled under China's arm, holding on tight.

"Kyrie will help me take care of Auntie China, won't you, honey?"

"Uh huh. I kin hewp." She scrambled to her knees at Maverick's side, as if she couldn't wait to help him. Her cute little smile turned upside-down. "Oh, no. Andy China. You hurted."

"'S okay, Kyrie. You be a good girl and help Uncle Maverick. Listen to him, ok-k-a-yyyy?" Damn, China shook so hard her teeth chattered. She wanted to press her palm into that burning hole on her hip, but wouldn't chance frightening Kyrie with any more blood. Or screaming.

"I kin be a good hewper." The pain shadowing her sweet face cut China to the bone.

"K-k-keep her safe, damn you," she chattered to Maverick.

"You know I will." He peered across the grassy landscape one more time, his fingers frozen at China's hips. Not helpful when a woman was flat on her back with what felt like a red-hot poker in her hip.

She writhed against the clenching pain. "Is… is someone still out there?"

"No," he said, but he didn't sound convinced, and neither was she. "Kyrie, stay with your aunt. Don't let her go anywhere, okay?"

China still clutched his hand. "Maverick, wait. I can't... You can't..."

"Yes. You can. And yes. I will. I'll be right back. Stay put."

She squeezed her eyes closed as he pushed off the ground. "Please stay safe," China whispered to the breeze weaving through the tall grass. "Don't take chances. Not with Reardon."

Kyrie dropped to her butt beside her. "Andy China. You is okay. I here. You wanna sing a song?"

China closed her eyes, fighting for the patience to endure. "Sure. How about *You Are My Sunshine*? Remember the words?" she asked, trying desperately to act normal for Kyrie's sake. They'd barely made it through a nervous rendition of the first verse when the steady clomp of heavy horses sounded nearby. Two long handsome faces peered down at her, their reins trailing.

"Can you make them lie down?" Maverick asked from Star's side.

China winced. The pain in her hip had evolved into a biting, gnawing beast that wouldn't let go. Every little movement hurt, even breathing. "Just tell them *down*, but back them off a few steps first. They're big."

He did as she directed, then crouched at her side again once Star and Ebony settled to the ground between her and the ravine. "Just thought you'd feel better with them nearby."

"Liar," she whispered. "They're nothing but a wall to protect me, aren't they? You think someone's still out there."

"It doesn't matter what I think. I'm not taking chances."

Tears filled her eyes. God, she hated the thought of anything happening to Ebony or Star, but Kyrie's safety came first. China stretched one hand toward her four-legged kids, needing to touch them. Ebony came through, his lips warm and softly nibbling her fingers. Star nickered.

"Okay, good," she whispered, panting hard from the simple exertion. "Good. Good."

Maverick knelt beside her again and took her hand in his. "Hey. Everything is going to be okay. Trust me."

Clutching his hand made her aware of two things: She wasn't strong enough to stop him from doing what needed to be done, and Maverick had big hands. Big, warm, gentle hands that encompassed hers with rock-solid strength.

He turned to Kyrie. "Sweetheart, I need you to be real brave for Auntie China. Can you do that?"

Kyrie nodded. The fear in her eyes stabbed China almost as bad as the hole in her hip. But then Maverick made it worse. With one long reach over his head, he peeled his shirt up and off and, *holy shit*. China bit her lip. Not in her wildest dreams...

He wasn't sporting a six-pack. No. There had to be eight well-defined stomach muscles there, all drawn downward into a *V* that just kept going. Every speck of him was lightly dusted with dark hairs. The trail from his naval to below, well, she couldn't begin to imagine.

Her core tightened, something else on its mind for sure. *Sex. Now? Yeah. Okay. I'm in.*

She jerked her eyes up from his belt to his chest, squared off into two carved blocks of granite with the same tight definition. Dusky man-sized nipples. Dark hair dusted, well, everything, right up to his tanned neckline. This man was damned glorious.

He leaned over her, but this couldn't be real. No way. She stuck her palms flat against his chest.

"N-no," she croaked as her palms and fingers contacted one damned solid, male body. She had to touch him to make sure she wasn't seeing things. The body she touched was warm. Sweaty. Too damn close. Not close enough.

Her blood filled with fire. She gasped at the sparks blazing up her arms, but he mistook that for pain. He balanced his forearm on the ground as he leaned into her face. "Trust me. I won't hurt you."

Fine. Whatever. Her hip hurt like heck, but her eyes felt damned good. So did her fingertips. Her palms. His lips were so close that hers lifted automatically. Hopefully.

That small movement caught his attention. A smile tugged at the corner of his eye. He leaned in closer. His breath whispered over her cheek. "I promise. Once you're home safe and sound, I'll most definitely kiss you again, and more."

Kiss me? And more? Her foolish heart knocked off a set of flying cartwheels. Her fear fled. Of all the idiotic times to be thinking of sex. Embarrassment groaned out of her, but that incentive he had just offered went a long way toward easing the pain. Well, almost.

"Are you ready?" He peered so tenderly into her soul.

Oh, my hell. Is there anything this guy can't do?

She let go of any resistance she might have offered, any bull-headedness she might have used to pretend she was tougher than he was. A very submissive feeling entered her spirit for the first time in her life. She wanted his hands on her in every way possible. Protectively. Honorably. Savagely.

China nodded because she couldn't trust her tongue. This man was going to undress her. Okay, so it wasn't the most romantic setting, but it had been a really long time since a man had uncovered any part of her. In fact, the last guy, Doc Wilson, didn't really count. Besides, she had undressed herself that day. Closed her eyes and endured her yearly physical—but this?

Maverick was going to do more than undress her now, and she very much wanted him to.

"This is how it will work, ladies. Kyrie is going to hold my shirt up nice and high." He raised the shirt in front of Kyrie's face so she couldn't see the unveiling. "And then she's going to lower it like it's her blankie and cover you when I tell her. Okay, Kyrie? Are you ready?"

"Uh huh," she answered quickly. "I is a good hewper, huh?"

"Yes, you are, sweetheart." Maverick winked at her. "You're the best helper ever."

Kyrie beamed under his praise, and China relaxed. At least, her niece wouldn't see more of her aunt than necessary.

Maverick leaned into her face, his lips so close she could scarcely breathe. "Do you trust me, China Wolf?"

Yes! Her foolish heart danced with delight. *I trust you. I want you. Undress me. I'm yours and only yours.* But she simply nodded again, her very savvy, practical side turned into a silly bobble-headed doll. The adrenaline made her loopy. That was all.

Quicker than any guy before him, Maverick pulled her jeans down over her hips to her thighs. Her ass was nearly naked, and he could see everything. She caught the admiring look on his face when he glanced over her body, but ruined the moment when she wondered what underwear she had on. *Please not the ones with little pink hearts.*

The fleeting look of reverence on his handsome face didn't go unnoticed, neither did the heated glance of honest appraisal. He liked what he saw, and damned if that didn't make her happy.

He eased Kyrie's hands down, the shirt along with it. China sighed in relief. The awkward moment was done. She was covered again and Kyrie wouldn't grow up with deep emotional scars.

"Can you sit here with Auntie China for a minute?" he asked the little girl.

"Uh huh." Kyrie immediately snuggled into China's side again while Maverick retrieved his bag from Star's saddle. China hadn't even noticed he had removed the saddles until that moment. The man seemed to have everything under control. Even her.

He pulled a small plastic case from his bag and turned to Kyrie. "Are you ready to be my helper again?"

The little girl nodded quickly.

"Great. Would you pick a big handful of flowers for her then? She's got an ow-eee and she needs something to cheer her up. Can you do that?"

Kyrie nodded with a big smile. "I yike fwowers, too."

"But you have to stay right between me and Star, okay? Don't go any farther."

And off she went as happy as a lark in spring.

Maverick turned his attention back to China. He knelt at her side and opened the plastic case full of medical supplies. "This is going to be quick."

China barely had time to respond when he lifted his shirt off of her. Another tender smirk lit his face. He glanced back to where Kyrie was crouched in the grass, before his eyes hit China's and winked. "You look good in purple."

A heat wave flushed every last inch of her. *Thank goodness. Not pink hearts. Now I remember.*

Without another word, he sliced through the side of her panties with a knife she didn't know he had, either. His eyes darkened as he peeled the satin fabric away from her bloody hip.

It stung. Hell, it hurt like a sonofabitch. She squeezed her eyes shut, fighting tears, then opened them again, not wanting to miss anything he might say or do.

His lips pursed as he zeroed in on the gunshot wound. Very gently, he dipped his head lower and probed the skin around it with his fingertips. Yeah, it hurt plenty, but his intense scrutiny only added to her confusion. How could her libido be doing handstands when she was in this much pain? How could he look so damned tender and angry at the same time? He pinched a little too hard. Pulled something out of the wound.

"Ow."

"Sorry. Some denim threads were stuck. No bullet inside. The shot grazed you. Went right through your jeans. You're lucky it didn't hit your hipbone. Three inches to the left would've struck your femoral artery." He leaned back and grabbed a small foil pouch from his bag. "This may hurt. Hang in there."

The words were no more than out of his mouth when he doused the hole in her hip with a powdery substance that hurt like—

Arghhh! Hell. She gritted her teeth to keep from groaning or screaming. He made it worse when he opened another foil package and pressed a thick layer of medical gauze against her hip.

She screwed her eyes tight. "You're... hurting... me." The words growled out of her instead of what she meant, which was more like '*get the hell away from me.*'

"Hey." He brushed a finger against her cheek. "I know this hurts, but I have to do it. It's a combination antiseptic and clotting agent. It's filled with anesthetic, too. It will sting for a couple minutes. Hang on."

Clenching her teeth didn't help. Tears trickled down the sides of her face anyway. Anesthetic nothing. It hurt!

"Almost done, baby. I'm only doing this to stop the bleeding. I'd never hurt you."

Baby? That sweet endearment surprised her. She certainly felt like a big baby, but no one—NO ONE—had ever called her that.

He reached for her hand. "Hey, there. Take a big breath. I'm done. You did real good."

Done what good? Get shot? Cry? But the sensation of his lips, moist and tender on her hand, jolted another part of her body. She opened her eyes to him kissing her knuckles one by one while he kept the pressure on her hip with his other hand. She didn't feel the pain so much anymore. Well, okay, maybe a little bit.

A wave of relief ebbed out from the gentle pressure of his hand. "Are you... a doctor?"

"No. Why would you think that?"

"Are you sure? You're not one of those doctors without borders or something like that?"

"No." He had a roll of tape in his hands now. "Here." He positioned two of her fingers on the gauze over her wound. "Hold this in place while I tape it."

She did as he asked. "But, you're so good at..." *Everything.*

When he finished taping her wound with great care, he leaned back on his legs. "I already told you. I'm a Marine, China. I know a few things most folks don't. I've been places. That's all."

"But you knew exactly what to do."

"I've had practice." A shadow extinguished the light in his eyes. He resituated the makeshift covering of his shirt and pressed two fingers to her neck. "How are you feeling?"

"Fine. Can, umm, you help me get my pants up?" She struggled to her elbows.

"I doubt you're feeling fine, and no, you stay put for now." With a shake of his head, he stopped checking her pulse and pushed her gently back to the ground. "We'll worry about your pants when it comes time to move."

"But I'm kind of naked under this shirt of yours." *And I sound like a damn fool telling you something you already know.*

"But you're feeling better, aren't you?"

"Umm. Yeah. I guess. It doesn't hurt like it did at first."

He sunk to her side, resting his head on the heel of his hand while he placed his other very warm and gentle hand right over her navel. The pain in her hip faded as the heat in her belly intensified.

He glanced over to where Kyrie crouched picking flowers by Star before he leaned into China, his eyes soft and tender. He framed her face with one big, warm hand.

Her lungs failed. Her eyes fluttered shut when he closed the distance and placed a warm, moist kiss on her lips. Her mouth remembered the taste of him. She brought her hand to the nape of his neck and pulled him close. *More. More. More!*

A rumbling groan vibrated up from his chest, sparking every damned feminine nerve cell in her body. Her toes curled. She would've turned into him if his hand on her stomach hadn't pressed her to the earth.

He eased away from her mouth. "Are you all done?" he asked Kyrie nonchalantly.

She traipsed into view with a smile and a big handful of bluebells mixed with wild phlox. "I is," she announced proudly. "Here, Andy China. I picked fwowers jes' for you."

China took the bouquet, trying to squelch the raging fire in her blood by pulling Kyrie into her side. She couldn't focus. All she wanted to do was close her eyes and wake up in her own bed, especially if Maverick were in it with her. China stroked the baby's tresses. "You picked beautiful flowers. You helped me a lot. You're a very big girl."

Star enjoyed the rest so much he had rolled to his side while Ebony dozed on the hoof.

China couldn't take her eyes off Maverick. Lying with him had given her yet another perspective of this half-naked man, from his long legs all the way down to his worn out boots. He had cocked one knee, but kept that incredibly warm hand flat to her stomach.

He might not know a lot about horses or Wyoming, but she had never felt safer—or more feminine. This unfortunate event made her wonder what this man had really seen in his life. She knew he was a Marine, but now she wanted to know more. What he looked like in the shower. Waking up first thing in the morning with sleep in his eyes. Everything. She wanted him to tell her his dreams, pains, joys, and sorrows. What made him laugh? What made him cry? His favorite color. His hometown. She wanted to know what food he liked besides grilled chicken and her homemade bread.

"We'll need help getting you out of here."

China shook her head. "No. Really. I'll be okay. I can ride. Just give me a minute. Let me get dressed and catch my... breath."

"Is that all?" he asked with a twinge of sarcasm. He looked down the hill, and honestly, she could've watched him forever. Her fingers ached to trace the cord in his neck. To caress his Adam's apple. To smooth her fingers over his chin. To pull him back to her mouth for another kiss.

"You girls rest. I'm going to repair the fence while we wait, but first." He reached behind him and pulled a cell phone from his bag.

China watched his stomach muscles wrinkle and ripple at that simple movement, and she was a lost cause. It had to be the extreme circumstances, but all she wanted to do was lie with him here in the grass, feel his hands on her body, and let the rest of the world take care of itself for a change. Instead, she snuggled Kyrie while he rested on his elbow and checked his phone. He thumbed the keypad.

He stilled as he listened. "Yes. It's me. I know. It's been a while. No, I'm fine, but a friend of mine needs help. Can you track my signal? Yes. I finally put the battery in my cell. Good. We need a sheriff and a medic. A helicopter would be nice, too. Can you contact them for me?" He quieted and listened. "Thanks, Mother."

China cocked her head. She couldn't believe it. "You called your mom?"

Chapter Nineteen

"You say there were three of them?"

"Yes, sir." Maverick stood patiently repeating everything he had already told Sheriff Hammer. "I saw three men on that rock ledge across the ravine. Pretty sure I hit one of them."

Hammer wasn't happy he had driven up the hill to investigate a crime scene while the medic flew in by helicopter. By the time he arrived, the medics had China bundled onto a gurney. They'd already given her something for the pain, and the chopper rotors were spinning. The medics seated Kyrie on the front seat of the helicopter, letting her play a child's video game on one of their Ipad. They hadn't taken off yet because she insisted on speaking with the sheriff.

Hammer peered at the ledge. "You mean that granite outcrop all the way over there?"

"Yes, sir." If he'd send someone to confirm his story, Maverick could signal the pilot to take off.

Hammer eyed him with suspicion. "That's quite a ways for an accurate shot. Don't seem like most folks coulda hit Miss China from there even if they wanted to."

"They could if they used a high-powered scope and a tripod. Did you find any slugs yet?" *Are you even looking for them?*

"Guess it wouldn't hurt to look. Dusty, come on over here and see what you can find."

Deputy Clark sauntered over, holding out a single bullet. "Already did. Found this."

The sheriff scowled. "Thirty-thirty? That's all? Nah. It could've come from any one of a hundred deer hunts around these parts. That what you think hit Miss China?"

Maverick looked the man square in the eye. "You won't know for sure until you locate the gun that fired it, will you? Whoever shot her fired three shots in quick succession. The first knocked her down. They weren't just out hunting deer. Someone meant to kill her."

Maverick's frustration level with the local law enforcement escalated. Deputy Clark seemed more concerned than his boss. "I think whoever cut her fence set her up. They knew she would be checking it again. All they had to do was wait for her to check it."

"Guess if you hit 'em like you think you did, they would've gone to the hospital." The Sheriff put a hand to Maverick's shoulder. "Hey. Aren't you the kid who saved her horses from the fire last week?"

Maverick nodded. That seemed to make the difference in Sheriff Hammer's attitude. He turned back to his deputy. "I know it's late, but you're gonna have to go all the way over there and check that granite ledge. See if you can find blood or anything while you're at it. Mr. Carson here says he shot one of 'em. Check for brass. They mighta left something behind once they got hit."

Finally!

Deputy Clark nodded and stepped away.

"Damn. This is the last thing I need," Hammer muttered. "I got a guy in town who's been cut up real bad and now this."

"Anyone I know?" Maverick asked, not exactly sure where Sheriff Hammer was going with this news, but trying to be neighborly.

"Probably not. This guy hangs with the *Kreepers*. Least he used to. Doctors aren't sure he'll make it."

"Do you know who did it?"

"Not yet. Had to be someone who's just plain mean with a knife." He raised a suspicious eyebrow at Maverick. "Bastards cut his privates off. Carved out his eyes. You don't know anyone who would do a thing like that, do you?"

"Only in Afghanistan," Maverick muttered, not wanting to remember. The only other knife expert he knew lived in Virginia, but Taylor Armstrong didn't have a mean bone in his body. Junior Agent Izza Maher might though. Connor's feisty wife was a different case all together.

Hammer stared off into the distance. "Whoever did it stuck him more than eight times. Looked like torture. I've been on the phone with the folks in Cody all morning. Guess the same thing happened over there last week. Only telling you because of Miss China. Folks around here know you're working for her. They like *her*."

Maverick got the message loud and clear. Folks liked China. Not him. He waited for the other shoe to drop. He had met most of the folks from town the day of the barn raising, but what was the sheriff getting at?

"You take care of her, ya hear?" Sheriff Hammer finally got to the point.

Maverick relaxed. "Yes, sir." *Don't worry. She's safe with me.*

Hammer walked over to her and peered into her drowsy face. "You okay, Miss China?"

She blinked at him with a dazed expression. "Yes-s-s," she hissed.

Maverick smirked. Damn, but she was one stubborn woman. If he had his way, she would've been in the hospital hours ago.

"I called your sister, Hammer said. "She's waiting for you at the emergency room. She sounded real worried." He turned back to Maverick. "You'll see to it her horses get back home safe and sound?"

"Yes, sir. I will." Maverick glanced at Star and Ebony. They'd reacted well under gunfire. He was proud of them.

"I'll take the little girl with us. I imagine her mama will be glad to see her."

Maverick grimaced. Leezel could care less about Kyrie. He would rather have kept the little girl with him where she was safe.

"Mav-er-rick." China reached for his hand. She clutched the sleeve of his shirt, blinking up through heavily lidded eyes.

"I'm right here." He leaned in close to keep their conversation private.

"I just want to... say..." She sighed heavily. "You got a ver-r-ry nice... bo-dy."

With that mission accomplished, she blew out a deep breath, closed her eyes, and relaxed back into the pillow. He placed a kiss on her forehead.

One of the medics wheeled her into the helicopter and secured the gurney. The other closed the door. Within seconds, it lifted off with Kyrie waving at him through the bubble glass. The chopper hovered briefly before it disappeared down the hillside.

Maverick watched it leave, concerned for China and Kyra, but also concerned he had set off another maelstrom of worry. After all, he had called Mother. Now Alex knew everything.

"Sure hope Miss China won't have ta stay in the hospital tonight." Z ran a hand over his thinning buzz cut. He and X sat in wooden lawn chairs outside the bunkhouse while Puppy lounged in another chair, as if he were just one of the guys. A scruffy cat with a crooked tail lingered under X's chair. One or two of the strays seemed to follow him wherever he went.

Maverick had already brushed Ebony and Star down after their ride home. They'd been fed and settled in their respective corrals for the night. Z had put together a raft of turkey sandwiches, and X brought a twenty-four pack of beer to the picnic. It hit the spot.

The roaring fire in the fire pit didn't hurt. Neither did X strumming on his old guitar, another surprise Maverick hadn't seen coming. The man was a gentle genius with his hands. The sounds coming from X's fingertips off the battered and worn acoustic seemed the perfect end to the harrowing day. Maverick had dragged his guitar from beneath his bunk, but he had yet to unzip it out of its case.

"Any word from Leezel or the hospital yet?"

X looked up from his playing and shook his head. "Not likely she woulda called us anyway." He glanced furtively at Z.

"Yeah." Z took a big bite of his sandwich. "That's fer sure. She don't like us much."

That surprised Maverick. "But I thought you guys shared the same watering hole?"

"We do," Z answered through another gulp of his beer, "but she's still Jefferson Wolf's daughter."

He said that like it meant something, but Maverick didn't understand. "So?"

"Used to be ol' man Wolf would run off any kid who come courting his girls." Z stared into the dark. "He was a mean ol' cuss. Used ta slap his girls around once in a while. Course he never hit his horses. Nosirree Bob. They was his pride and joy."

The Wolf family story unraveled. Xavier and Zeke had no doubt seen a lot. The way Z's face darkened as he talked gave Maverick a new insight into China. Leezel, too.

"He caught 'em playing doctor once. They was just little tykes and curious about how things worked, you know how kids are, but he hauled them inside and all we heard was crying and screaming." Z stopped strumming and wiped his eye.

"Was there a boy involved?" Maverick couldn't believe his ears.

"Nope. Jes' Missy China and Missy Leezel."

"How old were they?"

"I think Miss China was eight?" Z turned to X with that question. "Never mind. You didn't work here back then."

X nodded somberly. "You shoulda gone to the po-lice right then and there."

"That's easy for you to say, but them were different days." Z patted his friend's arm. "Police wouldn't a done a thing."

Maverick set his sandwich back on the plate, his appetite gone.

"The next time I saw 'em, Miss China was black 'n blue, but Miss Leezel didn't seem none too worse for wear." Z ran his hand over his face, as if he was tired of remembering. "Course I never knew what really happened. Jefferson said she fell down the steps. Whose ta say? Maybe she did."

"That's jes' like Miss China," X interjected, "takin' the blame so's her little sister wouldn't get beat none."

Maverick's mouth went dry. What kind of a man would hit little girls?

"Miss China's a real nice lady," X murmured. "She was always doing stuff like that, taking Leezel's lickin' for her and doing her chores."

"Yep. Them were different days." Z gave Puppy a gentle smack on the rump.

"Where was their mother when all this happened?" Maverick couldn't believe a woman would've allowed the beating of her daughters. His mother would've killed anyone who touched him or his brother, including his dad. But then, his parents had never hit their sons in the first place, even though they'd probably deserved a good spanking every now and then.

X stilled his guitar strings and pointed a finger toward the gravel road. "Cemetery down yonder. Celeste died giving birth ta China and Leezel's little sister. Golly, what'd you tell me that little gal's name was?"

"Martha. She didn't live but a couple hours." Z pursed his lips, his gaze fixed to the flames in the fire pit. "That's when life got bad 'round here, least 'til China turned old enough to handle a horse good enough to suit her daddy. Helluva horseman, but once Celeste died, he couldn't seem to tolerate the sight of his own flesh and blood some days."

"Ah, he weren't that bad," X muttered. "He just missed Celeste. That's all."

"Oh yeah? Seems to me he weren't too nice to you back then, either," Z pointed out.

X shrugged. "I reckon he was jes' takin' care a his own."

The men grew quiet, and Maverick didn't ask more questions. Did Jefferson beat his wife, too? Was that why she had died in childbirth?

"Now there was a love story fer ya," Z said to the flames.

"Who? Jefferson and Celeste?" Maverick asked.

"Oh, yeah." Z dug his hands deep in his pockets and pushed his feet straight out in front of him, the orange firelight orange soft on his face. "He met her back East when he come home from 'Nam. Went ta some Percheron Horse Society meeting. Her folks didn't like him none. They was old money, had something else in mind for their daughter 'sides fallin' for a cowpoke from Wyoming."

"Yeah, but you told me them kids had it bad for each other," X interjected.

"They did. Ya see." Z turned to look Maverick in the eye. "Jefferson and me was in 'Nam together. All the time we were fightin' and survivin', he kept tellin' me about how he was gonna raise horses once his time in the Corps was over. When we got home in seventy-one, he gave me this here job. Sure enough, he started with a couple acres of nothing and a pair of bays. Look at this place now."

Zeke Knudsen went up a few notches in Maverick's estimation at the humble declaration that he was a Marine, too.

"But what about Celeste?" Maverick wanted the old guy to stay on track.

"Gawd." Z blew out a long sigh. "She was a purdy girl. Jefferson left her behind on account a her folks threatened to send her off to live with her aunt if'n he kept hanging around. Paris, I think. Heck, I can't remember."

X shook his head very slowly. "Me neither."

Z grumbled, "Well, a course you don't remember. You wasn't even here back then. You's nothing but a whippersnapper to a guy the likes of me."

"Ah huh," X agreed, "but you told me this story a million times, I jes' don't remember all of it sometimes."

"Guys," Maverick interrupted. "It doesn't matter. What happened with Celeste?"

"Why, she jes' showed up here at the ranch one day." Z's eyes lit up remembering. "She done run away from home and took a train out West all by herself. I ain't never seen Jefferson so happy. That boy was dancing on the ceilings the minute she stepped outta the cab. They got married right up there on the porch. Had a big ol' wedding. Everyone in town showed up. Why they kicked up their heels and danced 'til the cows come home that night."

Z settled further back in his chair. "Yep. Them was the good ol' good days. Seemed like everything was going perfect once she got here. Never seen Jefferson happier. Never."

"She looked jes' like Miss China, ya know," X offered. "You seen her picture?"

Maverick shook his head.

"Well, the next time ya decides to fix breakfast fer your lady friend, ya might take a peek at her mama's picture. It's hanging in her living room right where her daddy left it."

Maverick caught the twinkle in X's eye.

"You ain't fooling me," Z teased. "I seen the way you look at Miss China, and I seen the way Miss China looks at you. It's the same way Jefferson used ta look at Celeste, is what it is."

"I think Miss China kinda likes you, son." X poked a gnarly finger into Maverick's shoulder. "Good thing ol' Jefferson ain't 'round no more, or you'd be hightailing it down the road with your britches full of rock salt."

Maverick poked X right back, hoping to change the subject. "Oh, yeah? Well, how did you old ladies come to be called X and Z?"

X sniffed. "You hear that, Z? This whippersnapper done called us ladies."

"Well, we do gossip like old Widow Green and Sister Jones." Z slapped X's leg with a chuckle. "Truth is, we jes' figured if them ce-leb-rit-ees out there in Hollywood could change their names, we could, too."

"Ha. I was hoping maybe folks might think we was rock stars and want our autographs." X puffed up his chest, as if he were someone to be reckoned with.

"Yeah, but they didn't," Z added gloomily. "Guess no one noticed our superhero per-son-as."

Maverick smiled at the old comedians. "But your given names really are Zeke and Xavier?"

"Oh, yeah." Z nodded earnestly. "Them's our real names. I'm Zeke Knudsen. This here's Xavier Albright, jes' like Miss China told ya. She wouldn't a lied."

"Hey." X studied Maverick intently for all of two seconds. "You wanna change your name? We could call you—"

Maverick waved the suggestion off. "No, thanks. I'll stick with the one I've got."

"You sure you ain't related to Kit, though?" X squinted. "Ya kinda look like you got some cowboy blood in ya, I reckon."

"No, sir. Only blood in me is red, white, and blue." Damn. It felt good to remember his patriotic streak, the side of him that made him a Marine.

The flash of pride on X and Z's faces didn't go unnoticed. Z stretched his hand out to Maverick's shoulder. "We's real glad you been helpin' Miss China around here. You've taken a load off her shoulders since you been here. Hope you know that." He looked at Xavier. "You had enough for one night?"

"Nah." X pushed himself up out of his chair and picked up his guitar. "'Fore y'all git going, I want ta show you my horse."

Z lifted his brows at Maverick as X strolled into the bunkhouse. "I didn't know he kept a horse in there, did you?"

He wasn't gone long enough for Maverick to reply. X returned with a gleaming copper statue in his hand, the horse from China's birdbath. His smile threatened to crack his face wide open. "Look it here." He stuck the statue in Maverick's hands. "I fixed it for Miss China, jes' like she asked."

Maverick took the restored figurine, surprised at the piece of artwork in his hand. It wasn't just a horse. The copper had been molded into a fighting stallion, reared on his hind feet with his front hooves striking the air. The copper mane had been twisted into long tendrils behind him to denote action. Its long tail flowed around the feet of the animal, adding support to the base. That X used this for a birdbath took Maverick's breath away. It belonged in an art museum.

He handled the piece carefully. "You did this?"

"Uh huh." X nodded quickly. "I likes ta make purdy things."

Maverick blew out a breath. Here stood a man who spent his days in the fields, either planting, plowing, or harvesting when he should've been in a studio.

"He's got a gift, don't he?" Z asked.

"Yes." Maverick looked up at the childish pride on X's face. "You're a talented man."

He scrunched his shoulders like a little kid. "Nah. I jes' like to play with stuff." X took the statue out of Maverick's hands and walked over to the birdbath. Within a second, the copper stallion was back where it belonged, its wild spirit alive in the glow of the fire. He glanced over his shoulder and asked, "Does it look okay?"

"It looks real good." Maverick nodded to emphasize his meaning. "Real damned good."

"Well, okay then." X yawned and stretched his arms over his head. "I'm going ta bed. Night guys."

"Me, too." Z followed X into the bunkhouse, leaving Maverick alone with Puppy and the cat. And his thoughts.

Chapter Twenty

Maverick threw another couple of scraps of wood on the fire. The scenario of China taking the punishment for her little sister fit her personality to a T. It also fit Leezel. They might have been little girls back then, but little sister Leezel had learned to dodge responsibility at an early age.

He grimaced at the very real way these two women faced life. China, head on; Leezel, not at all. She simply took, and because of Kyrie, China let her.

The notion that Reardon might be at the hospital with Leezel galled Maverick. She would dump Kyrie the first minute she felt overwhelmed. She might claim he couldn't have Kyrie, but Maverick knew better. Leezel was still letting everyone else take her beatings for her, even her five-year-old daughter.

Puppy stretched and groaned in his chair, and Maverick wished someone would call from the hospital and let him know how China was doing. He wanted details. Was she sleeping it off for the night or would she be home—and when? Where was Kyrie? He didn't care so much where Leezel was, but Kyrie should be tucked in bed by now, and someone should be reading her a story.

And China should be, well, she should be in his arms while he explored her very feminine side. He had tasted her lips—now he wanted to savor the rest of her. The light in her eyes when she'd put her hands to his bare chest had only fueled the attraction.

He picked up his guitar and settled on the edge of his chair, his fingers searching out chords on the frets. Holding his Ovation reminded him of better days. He let his fingers remember, too.

The Wild Wolf was peaceful tonight. Plucking at his guitar soothed and he was glad to be there. Heck, he was glad he had been on the hillside with China today, too. The look in her eyes when he'd called Mother still made him smile. She'd thought he was calling his mom instead of the very competent admin assistant he had once worked with, two entirely different women.

His thoughts drifted to his family's farm in Ohio, and Cadence, his mother. *'When Irish Eyes Are Smiling'* came naturally to the instrument in his hand. She had descended from a long line of Irishmen, but if anyone asked, she would proudly declare she was American and that's all there was to it. She was as patriotic to her country as the day was long. While their father, Wade, was more moderate in his political persuasion, it was her steadfast allegiance that inspired her only children to join the Corps.

But the sacrifice proved too great.

Maverick thumped the top of the guitar. The music ceased. His fingers couldn't play what his heart couldn't feel.

When Darrell died in Afghanistan, Cadence couldn't bear the loss. Neither could Maverick. Fortunately, he'd hooked up with two of his closest friends and had a damned good job with The TEAM. Taylor Armstrong and Gabriel Cartwright were with Darrell the day he went down. They knew what happened. That alone brought Maverick what he needed most at the time—a sense of comfort from guys who understood what Hell was really about.

But the ghost of his dead brother lingered. Sometimes he saw it in Taylor's hooded eyes. Sometimes he heard it in Gabe's anxiety attacks, though Gabe would never admit he had PTSD. While the brotherhood of these men was better than any therapy, Maverick needed more.

The Marine Corps Hymn came easily to his fingertips.

From the Halls of Montezuma
To the shores of Tripoli...

Alex Stewart. Hard charger. A good man to work for. USMC to his dress shoes. He had a knack for hiring the best. Some of the guys and gals on The TEAM were still recuperating from their time served. *Like me.* Didn't seem to matter to Alex. He brought them together, gave them tough work to do, and inadvertently transformed them into a family in the process. Sometimes, he pushed too hard, and the sonofabitch demanded one helluva lot, but at the end of most days, Maverick felt like a decent man again. Like he'd done good for his country.

First to fight for right and freedom
And to keep our honor clean...

"It was a decent job," he confided to the sleeping dog beside him. "I liked it."

Puppy opened one bleary eye, groaned and went right back to sleep. The cat didn't bother to do even that. Maverick let his mind wander back to that good job while his fingers strummed the age-old victory hymn. The TEAM was a security business of sorts, its employees all ex-snipers from one service or another. Taylor and Gabe had simply mentioned him to Alex, and Alex hired him, sight unseen.

At first it was the perfect hideout, a last refuge where everyone spoke the same language and understood the spoils of war like others couldn't. Some took bodyguard assignments. Others handled local security issues for diplomats, while others opted for obligations overseas. Most of the time Maverick felt as if he were still in the military, except he made better money, rarely used his weapon and worked for a better man. Uncle Sam had nothing on Alex.

The newest addition to The TEAM proved the last straw.

Landon Truman. Liar. Cheat. Sonofabitch.

He had mis-represented himself to Alex as Maverick's good friend. Taylor and Gabe's, too. Truth was, the bastard had cost Maverick his fiancée, Kimberly. Maverick couldn't tolerate the sight of Truman's lying face one more day. It hurt too much to go home and face his mother. It hurt too much to stay. He hit the road instead.

The memory of that damned Dear John letter came back to him. It was waiting for him when he got back from his team's failed op. The day Darrell died. Maverick had honest to God expected Kim's sweet love to sustain him during the darkest time of his life. Not so.

Kim wrote that she still loved him, but she had found someone else. She hoped they could continue to be friends. *Yeah, right.* Friends with the woman he had promised his heart to? No way in hell.

The letter was tear-stained when he opened it, more so when he finished reading it. Then he shredded it into confetti and threw it into the latrine where it belonged. With all the other shit.

She might as well have sent an anchor and told him to drop dead, because sure enough. Death hurt a helluva lot worse than what his cheating ex had done to him.

Within one week, he accompanied the body of his brother home to Ohio. His baby brother. The annoying youngster who had to have everything his way when they were growing up. The kid who tagged along relentlessly and bugged the hell out of Maverick's friends. The guy who joined the Marines simply because his big brother did. The kid who had everything Maverick ever wanted. A faithful woman. A baby son. Every reason to live. Gone in a flash on the stinking hillside in a land that smelled like an open sewer twenty-four-seven.

Gone.

Just gone.

Maverick focused on his fingertips. This old guitar felt sure and sweet tonight. Heaven opened up and poured the missing words into his heart while he serenaded a mongrel dog and a couple of cats. The love song he'd been struggling with was born.

Baby Brother

They don't make 'em any better.
That's the good Lord's honest truth.
Batman always had his Robin.
Baby Brother, I had you.

We were outlaws. We were firemen.
We were heroes through and through.
Superman had Jimmy Olsen.
Baby Brother, I had you.

Cops and robbers. Cowboys. Indians.
Every bullet we fired true.
We were white knights on wild horses.
Baby Brother, me and you.

Then the day came to be warriors,
To be noble, to be true.
I led proudly and you followed
Like most baby brothers do.

Always lucky. Always daring.
Always brave and bulletproof.
Nothing seemed too hard or dangerous,
Baby Brother, not for you.

Now I sit here and I wonder
'Bout the old red, white, and blue,
'Bout the awful price of freedom,
Baby Brother—about you.

How you charged straight into glory
Never doubting time or place.
Tell me now, my baby brother,
Do you sing Amazing Grace?

Do you shout grand Alleluias?
Maybe, oh, say can you see?
Do you wonder why you followed
Someone wrong and weak like me?

Maverick dropped the melody to his voice and whispered the final tribute to the best friend in his whole life.

You're my hero, Baby Brother.
You're the man I want to be.
I'd give anything to have you back.
I miss you...
Hell, I miss me...

He ended the song with a quiet thump to the face of the guitar. Thinking about Darrell still hurt. It always would. But sitting there under the wide Wyoming sky with a million stars scattered overhead, the hole in his soul didn't seem as deep. He wondered more how his mother was handling the loss.

Maverick swallowed hard and scrubbed a quick hand over his face. Cadence Carson was a strong woman with rock-solid beliefs, but he had left her to grieve alone. He had Taylor and Gabe for company, but who did she talk to when the hole in her heart opened up and swallowed the sunshine out of her day? Who did she cry to? His father? The same sky her only living child was looking at right then and there?

Maverick didn't know, and he wished he did. She needed him, but what'd he do? He deserted her because it hurt too much to face her without his brother at his side.

He set the guitar aside. Yeah. Losing his kid brother would always hurt, but losing Kim? Not so much. He wasn't angry with Landon anymore, either. Heck. He couldn't really blame him for stealing a woman like Kim. If anything, those two cheaters deserved each other. But his mom? She hadn't deserved to lose both of her sons the way she did.

China's new barn stood across the yard like a huge wooden skeleton in the dark. Before long, the neighbors would return to hoist the crossbeams and wrap the frame in rough-sawn cedar. It would make a handsome replacement to the weathered building that stood there before.

He had seen the plans. The horse stalls were designed with individual outside doors, in case there should ever be another fire. The foaling stall was huge. Someone with foresight had included a fold-down shelf on the wall, or maybe it was intended as a bunk. It was long enough. Had to have been China's idea.

The tiniest trickle of relief dripped into his heart.

Not even death had kept China down. Because of her, hope still lived at the Wild Wolf. He could feel it in the air. He could hear it in the chirp of crickets and the gentle murmuring of the finest horses in the world. He should've recognized it for what it was the second he laid eyes on that elfin woman on the broad back of her noble steed. The instant he thought of unicorns and flying horses and glittery fairy wings. China made him think of magic even then, and if anything was magical, it was hope.

Pulling his cell phone from his pants pocket, he took a deep breath. It was later in Ohio, but time didn't matter in magical worlds. The phone only rang once. Cadence Carson must've been waiting to hear from her boy.

"Hi, Mom. Yeah. It's me."

Chapter Twenty-One

Whispered conversation roused China.

You gotta keep yer big mouth shut if... It ain't fair... We gotta make her think... Just two itty bitty pinpricks... I'll try, but I ain't... Two weeks... It'll all be ours.

The voices faded into the mist. She woke with a heart-pounding start to the ugly face of Reardon peering down at her, so near she could smell the stench of cigarettes and decaying teeth on his breath. "You awake?"

Panic choked her. He had gotten too damned close. She shoved backward into her pillow and turned her head. "Get the hell away from me."

"Hey, now." He patted her forearm as if he had a right to touch her, but he didn't step back. "Take it easy, ma'am. Just trying to help. That's all I'm doing."

"You shot me," she hissed. "Get out of my room!"

"Me?" God, he couldn't act worth a lick.

Leezel lifted her butt from the molded plastic chair in the corner and joined her pig of a boyfriend at China's bedside. "You're talking out of your head, Sis. Troy's been with me all day. Just lay down and take it easy."

China shifted her gaze to Leezel, angry enough to knock her sister on her ass for covering for Reardon. *Then you're in on it, too.* "Back off. I'm leaving. Where's Kyrie?"

"Oh no, you're not." Leezel pushed her into the pillow. "And don't you worry about my little girl. She's in real good hands."

China shoved her hands off. "Get the hell out of my way. I said I'm leaving."

Damn. Wearing a hospital gown didn't help her fight or run. The damned IV in her arm wasn't much help, either. She pulled the blanket up to her chin to cover up until these two left. The hole in her hip didn't hurt, but damn it. Reardon was behind what had happened. The fire. The shooting. Everything. She had never been so sure.

Take it easy? Horseshit. It ends today.

China meant to track Sheriff Hammer down the minute she got out of the hospital. Maverick, too. They'd both help her get Kyrie away from Leezel. Leezel could run to Hell with Reardon, but from this day forward, she would do it alone. Kyrie wouldn't be dragged along with her.

Until today, China didn't have enough proof to file for custody of her niece. By hell, proof or not, Kyrie would stay at the Wild Wolf from now on if China had to fight the world. She would sell every one of her horses if needed. Anger climbed up her spine that she hadn't been brave or mad enough to go after child custody of that sweet little girl before.

Well, I'm plenty brave now. Reardon and Leezel can go to hell.

The IV had to go. She pulled the taped needle out of the back of her hand. "I'm only going to ask you one more time. Where's Kyrie?"

Leezel nodded toward the door. "Shit, she's just out sitting with the nurse. Troy, would you go get her so Sis will stop acting like a crazy woman?"

China bit her lip. Trapped and outnumbered, she needed to bide her time. *You haven't begun to see crazy.*

Reardon stepped out of the room and quickly returned with Kyrie's little hand in his big ugly paw. She looked so small and scared. Why was she made to sit outside with the nurse?

She came to the bedside with worry in her big round eyes. "Is you okay?" she asked quietly.

"Come up here." China pulled Kyrie into her side, away from Reardon. She hated that he touched Kyrie at all. Sinking her nose into the little girl's hair, relief flooded her soul for the first time since she had opened her eyes. Her hip was still numb. It wouldn't have mattered if it hurt like a sonofabitch. She wanted Kyrie with her from now on. "Are you okay, baby?"

"Uh huh." Kyrie cupped her hand and whispered into her aunt's ear. "And I helped Unca Mavwick, too."

"Yes, you did. You were a brave girl today."

"I picked purdy fwowers, huh?"

China closed her eyes for a second. "You did real good." Everything would work out. She would call Maverick to come get her, then Sheriff Hammer. Holding her niece helped her think. Life would be simple and good again as soon as she got home.

"Let's go home, Kyrie." China caught the look Reardon shot Leezel. They'd both drawn closer to the bed. By hell, if they wanted a showdown, she would give them one. Her fingers curled. Her shoulders squared. "What's wrong with you two?" *Why the hell are you even here?*

"We was just wondering what the whispering's about. That's all." Reardon settled back in the empty chair by China's bed. "Don't want that little gal of mine bothering you while you're recuperating, do we? You gave us a nasty—"

"It's none of your business what this *little gal* does." China stared them both down. "And she's not yours. What's really going on? Why are you here?"

He lifted one shoulder. "Nuthin'. Just taking care of my family the way I see it."

"Get this through your thick skull, Reardon. I'm not your family and you're not mine. Now, where's Maverick?" She shot a quick glance to her nightstand and counter, wanting to place a call to Z. No phone rested on either. Had Reardon hidden it? Her hackles lifted.

"Now don't you go getting yourself all riled up now—" Leezel started to adjust China's blanket, but China was having none of it. She pushed her sister's hand aside.

"Knock it off. I asked you a question. Where is he? And where's my phone?"

"Why, Sis, he's back at the ranch taking care of your horses. You know how he is." Leezel smoothed the covers anyway. "He's working the same as always."

China pulled Kyrie onto her lap even while she prepared to get out of bed. It hurt, but she needed that little girl out of Reardon's reach. She could call Maverick from the nurse's station. "Get out of my room. I'm getting dressed."

"That might not be a good idea, Sis." The way Leezel kept playing with her blanket irritated China. "They haven't released you yet and—"

"Will you knock it off?" She pushed her sister's hand away again. "I'm leaving. You can either get Reardon out of my room and help, or you can both get out and I'll do it myself."

China caught the subterfuge out of the corner of her eye. He placed a finger to his lips, but dropped his hand when she noticed and left the room. Panic climbed onboard with anger. She and Kyrie needed to run and run fast. Whatever Reardon and Leezel were up to, it wouldn't end well. First, clothes. Then boots. Then Maverick. In that order.

China jerked the blanket off her legs and placed both feet to the floor. Her clothes had to be in the hospital bag setting on the counter.

Kyrie dropped to the floor. "Kin I hewp?"

"Yes, baby. Can you hand me that bag right there?" China pointed at the counter.

A smile brightened Kyrie's angel face. She brought the to China's side.

Dragging her jeans up and over her hip proved difficult with the bandage, but China managed. Little Kyrie stayed at her side and tried to help as much as a five-year-old could. She lined China's boots up next to the bed. China tussled her hair, shoved into her footgear and headed for the door. "Come on. Let's go home."

Kyrie smiled. "Goodie. I is ready to go, too."

They limped down the emergency room corridor with Leezel hovering close behind, but where the hell had Reardon gone? Apprehension slithered up the back of China's neck. The farther away from Leezel and Reardon, the better.

The nurse at the nurses' station looked her up and down when he spotted her. "Miss Wolf. I'm surprised you're up and walking around already. Are you leaving?"

"Yes, I am." She grabbed the edge of the counter for support. Her shaky legs threatened to dump her on her ass, not the best way to prove she meant what she said. "Sign me out of here. I have work to do." *And a lawyer to contact and a man to hug.*

"Well, if you're sure." He laid a single sheet of paper on the counter along with a pen. "Your doctor had already authorized you to leave. Sign and date this line and we'll get you on your way."

China signed without reading the paperwork. "Is Sheriff Hammer still around?"

"I'm afraid he left an hour ago."

"How long have I been here?"

"Three hours. You were sedated when you arrived, but don't worry. The sheriff wants to talk with you, too. Do you want me to call him?"

She thought long and hard for a minute. Hammer was a good man. Hopefully, he had the arson investigation report back from the fire department by now, too. If she had her way, Reardon would go down for arson and attempted murder before the day was done, but she needed to do this in order. For the second time in her life, she would have a real man at her side when hell broke loose. Maverick.

Holy smokes. Leezel had come up too close behind her. Too damned close. With a wheelchair. China clenched Kyrie to her side, needing to keep that baby girl in her possession and safe at all cost.

"Never mind. I'll call him later. May I use your phone?" She ignored the wheelchair bumping the back of your legs.

"You need to sit down, Sis." Leezel clutched China's bicep and—

Sting.

China dropped to the chair. Weak. Dizzy.

"Never mind about that phone call." Leezel told the nurse as she turned the wheelchair from the counter. "My sister's just tired. I'm taking her straight home. Come on, Kyrie. Let's make your Auntie China some chicken soup."

The hospital walls blurred. A bright red exit sign glimmered at the end of a long tunnel. Glass paned doors opened. Somewhere along the line, Kyrie clambered into China's lap, but she couldn't get a grip on her niece. Her fingers didn't work. It took everything just to draw in a breath.

She managed a whine when fresh air hit her face, but then she caught sight of Reardon at the open door of a van. Leering.

"No-o-o," she tried to scream.

Kyrie yelped from somewhere far away. China reached for her, but Reardon had Kyrie under one arm. She squealed. She stretched her little arms out for China, and honest to God, China wanted to save that child, but nothing worked. Her arms had turned to dead weight. She had lost all sensation. Could barely think.

Someone shoved her into the van.

"Git in, boss lady." Leezel folded her legs in next. "Yeah. This is gonna work just fine."

Her snotty voice echoed in China's head.

Just fine. Just fine. Just fine...

Maverick couldn't sleep.

The night dragged on but no word from Leezel or the hospital. He'd seen enough gunshot wounds to know the difference between minor and critical. The round had grazed China, nothing more, and he had applied first aid within minutes. The doctor at the emergency room only needed to clean China's wound, stitch her up, maybe give her a pain pill and release her. She should've been home hours ago.

So where is she?

He waited by the glowing embers of the campfire, paced the yard and walked the gravel road. Still no China.

It was nearly two in the morning when Z scuffled across the gravel in his pajama bottoms and an old tank top. "Miss Leezel jes' called."

"And?"

"She said Miss China had some kinda complication. They're gonna keep her for twenty-four hours' observation."

"A complication?" That surprised Maverick. "Like what?"

Z shrugged. "I don't know. Miss Leezel didn't 'xactly say, and I didn't 'xactly ask, neither. She don't like me much."

"When will she be home? Did Leezel tell you that?"

"Said maybe tomorrow night." Z scuffled back to the bunkhouse. "Maybe the morning after. Miss Leezel moved her into one of them private nursing homes."

"Which one? You get an address?"

Z shrugged. "I asked, but she wouldn't tell me. Miss China will git here when she gits here. G'night, son."

Maverick stifled his anger. The man's lackadaisical attitude aggravated him. Z was the kind of guy who pretty much did as he was told. No more. No less.

Puppy traded his comfortable chair for the ground beneath it. An owl hooted somewhere in the dark. All seemed peaceful, but Maverick couldn't shake the unease slithering up the back of his neck.

Something was dead, damned wrong.

The next day dragged. He called the sheriff's department about the shooter up on the hill, but Hammer wasn't in. He had been called to another sadistic knifing in town. Maverick left a message.

By noon, Hammer still hadn't called, and Maverick ran out of patience. He called Deputy Clark, his gut full of angst. Clark was willing to talk. He had recovered casings and blood at the scene right where Maverick said they would be. What was more, he had a suspect under guard at the hospital—one of Reardon's boys, Vic Cranston. Cranston claimed he had accidentally shot himself in the shoulder while hunting jackrabbits east of the Wild Wolf. With a rifle. A damned difficult weapon to shoot your shoulder with.

Clark had done some detective work. The rifling on the slug pulled out of Cranston matched Maverick's .357 Magnum not Cranston's rifle. Clark promised a thorough investigation, but investigations took time. He urged Maverick to be patient.

Still no sign of China.

Maverick got edgier as the afternoon stretched. He saddled Star and rode back up to the fence line he had repaired the day before. Everything looked good. When he returned home, he pounded a few more nails and finished Puppy's doghouse. By dinnertime, his whole body had transformed into a set of parabolic ears, tuned toward the driveway and hoping for the sound of tires on gravel.

Still no damned car. He couldn't shake the pinch in his gut. *Where the hell is China?*

"You want something ta eat?" Z asked at the bunkhouse door. "X done baked a ham and ya ain't eaten none of it yet."

"No thanks," Maverick answered.

"Yer fixing to hurt his feelings."

Maverick grunted. Z sounded a lot like his mother.

"Come on, son." Z persisted. "Ya can't stop eating jes' cuz Miss China ain't home yet. She'll be here soon enough."

Maverick pulled himself out of the chair and studied the leaden clouds piled in the west. The sun cast its rays in a bright, silvery lining at the edge of purplish black.

The truth was he couldn't eat. His gut clenched so tight he could barely swallow. Pre-battle nerves. A man's body turned into a purging machine. There was no sense putting food through the slippery slide his intestinal tract had become. It would just come back up or sail right on through.

Z squinted at the sky. His nostrils flared. "Rain's comin'. Hope they skedaddle and git Miss China home before it gits here."

Maverick sucked in a lung full of the fragrant air. It smelled like rain and China and Russian Olive trees. Pleasant. Sweet. But he knew better. A storm was coming.

And he was dead, damned tired of waiting.

Chapter Twenty-Two

He strapped on his holster and shrugged into his leather jacket. The ham could wait. A man didn't sit around, not with his woman's life in the balance. The rain commenced before he had the chance to fire up Z's truck. Within seconds, a gray van lumbered up the gravel drive and pulled to a halt at China's front door. *Didn't it figure?*

"Hey guys," Maverick called to X and Z. "They're back."

Maverick secured the brim over his Oakleys and headed toward the van. X and Z followed close on his six. Leezel lifted a newspaper over her head before she dropped off the running board. Reardon rounded the van and opened the side passenger door.

Maverick caught the first tell when Reardon shot a disingenuous smile toward the hired hands instead off flipping them off. A cold chill that had nothing to do with the drizzling rain shivered across Maverick's shoulders.

The second tell double-tapped him straight to the heart.

Reardon activated a hydraulic lift and lowered a wheelchair to the ground. He turned the chair to face Maverick, X and Z, that same sneering smile on his face. "There you go. You're home now. Don't that feel better?"

Maverick's heart dropped.

China. My God. China.

She sat like a zombie in the chair, her hands limp in her lap, her shoulders sagging, and her hair straggly and unbrushed. She still wore the same clothes she had been shot in. A belt held her in the chair. Her bright eyes were dimmed and unseeing. Her cheeks sagged.

Z groaned into his knuckles. "She looks so—"

Dead.

A whimper escaped X. "What 'n tarnation happened?"

"Sure glad you guys are all here. I don't wanna have ta say this twice." Reardon grumbled as the rain matted his straggly hair. The bastard had taken center stage too easily.

Maverick couldn't come up with the word that fit what his eyes were seeing. Betrayal? Farce? All of the above? He gritted his teeth, both hands clenched and needing to strike fast and hard. To save China.

Reardon pulled an umbrella from the van and opened it over her. "Doctor says Miss China suffered a stroke in the emergency room getting stitched up from her little hunting accident." He took over the umbrella, leaving her sitting in the rain.

"Oh my, you poor thing. Let me get that for you, Sis." Leezel leaned over China's shoulder and wiped a line of spittle from her sister's chin, smiling up at Maverick and the guys like someone might want to take a picture of her being decent for once in her life. "She's a little messy now and then. You know how stroke patients are."

Maverick refused to believe what his eyes were telling him. *Not China. No way.*

"Bottom line is, we don't need your help with Leezel's sister. Only with the ranch." Reardon spat to the ground at China's feet. He looked edgy, his shoulders taut, as if ready for a fight. "Just keep doing what you been doing, ya hear? Leezel says the first crop of grass hay's due in. Git it cut and baled. You got any questions?"

Maverick squared his shoulders to face Reardon. "Can't cut wet fields."

Leezel interceded. "Just you never mind. Grass hay don't need cutting 'til the rain quits. You know that. It ain't no problem. Soon as you can cut it is fine."

Zeke raised his hand like a kid in school. He stood with rain running down his weathered face, not even trying to wipe it away. "How 'n tarnation could Miss China suffer a stroke jes' by getting shot in the hip like she did?"

Maverick glanced sideways at him, not sure if those were raindrops or tears leaking out of his eyes. The old guy seemed to be falling apart.

X's head bobbed. "Yeah. They give her the wrong medicine or somethin'?"

"Why yes, Z. Yes, X. That's exactly what happened to my poor sister. They, umm, gave her the wrong anesthetic, jes' like you said." Leezel could've won an Oscar with her *June Cleaver* act. "As a matter of fact, we'll be talking to an attorney first chance we get. Who knows? We might just hafta sue, isn't that right, Troy?"

Sue, my ass. You did this. I know damned well you did. I just can't prove it.

Reardon grunted. Maverick didn't know which of these two held the leash and who wore the collar. He bit his lip and did what he did best. Watched. Waited.

"One more thing." Zeke rubbed the back of his neck, as if he was about to broach a sore subject. "I really hates to ask, this kinda thing being so hard on y'all, but, umm, who's gonna be in charge while Miss China recuperates? I mean, I've got to buy tractor parts and it's payday on Friday and—"

"I am." Reardon stabbed a thumb into his chest. "I'll be signing your paychecks. I'll buy them tractor parts. You got any problems, bring 'em to me from now on, ya hear?"

God, Maverick wanted to go a few rounds with Tough Guy. He shifted his gaze to China. Every piece of him ached to shelter her, to pull her under his arm and wipe the water out of her eyes. Reardon hardly kept the umbrella in place long enough to protect her from the weather. Rain dripped off her chin.

Leezel didn't look too happy with Reardon's answer. She glanced up at her boyfriend. Her nose twitched. She must've thought she was in charge, but damned if she didn't adlib like a pro. Or else, he really was in charge. "Yes, umm, your new *temporary* boss will be my ex—I mean my boyfriend here, Mr. Troy Reardon. He's in charge for now. Y'all know him. Me and Troy's gonna get married real soon, and then we'll both be your bosses. How's that sound?"

Maverick didn't care how the hell it sounded. "Where's Kyrie?"

"Why, she's right here, Mav, ah, excuse me. I mean Maverick." Somehow every word out of her mouth dripped with a twisted, southern belle drawl. "Come here, Kyrie honey. Git out of that van and come see the guys. Hurry up now. It's raining, and we don't got all day. Troy, move that lift outta the way."

Reardon grumbled but moved the hydraulic lift.

A very subdued little girl climbed backwards out of the van all by herself. She dropped to the ground and turned herself around, her eyes wide as she scanned the yard. Maverick removed his glasses, needing to catch her eye, but the second Kyrie spotted China, she ran to the wheelchair. "I is right here, Andy China," she whispered.

The sadness etched on her poor, little face was enough to make a grown man cry, but China never gave any indication that she saw her niece.

Leezel ran up the stairs, beaming like a foolish wife out of a 1950s rerun. She couldn't have looked less authentic if she had batted her eyes and worn a bouffant hairdo. "So here we are. One great big happy family. Let's get outta this rain 'fore we catch our death. Get my sister up here, Troy honey. Come on. Hurry. 'Fore she catches cold."

Reardon's brow lifted. He leveled an evil eye at Maverick and collapsed the umbrella. "Yer in my way. Git back to work." Tough Guy shoved the umbrella at Kyrie. "Take this."

The little tyke clutched its handle with both hands while she stood shivering in the rain.

Reardon tilted the wheelchair back, jostling China while he pushed her through puddles toward the porch. He hadn't considered the difficulty of getting her up those seven steps, though. With a thinly disguised sneer at Leezel, he growled at

Kyrie. "Git yer stupid ass up there with yer mother. Go on. Git outta my way. Move."

She scampered up the stairs, her little butt tucked in behind her, but the umbrella to the mud fell in her haste.

"Kyrie!" Reardon bellowed. "Can't you do a damned thing right? Damn it, Leezel. Get your dumb-assed daugh—"

Maverick ran to intervene. "Let me help." He scooped the sodden umbrella out of the gravel and winked when he handed it back to Kyrie. She didn't look up.

"Now see? What have I been telling you about good ol' Maverick?" Leezel gushed from the cover of the porch roof. "He's a real gentleman and he's as helpful as the day is long, ain't he? He's polite, too."

But Maverick had only offered for Kyrie and China's sake. He lifted the bottom of the wheelchair, sheltering as much of China as he could with the brim of his cap and the curve of his body. His hand brushed her icy cold fingers. The poor woman was drenched. The spark between them didn't crackle to life. She didn't look up with eyes full of sparkling mischief, either. She didn't look up at all.

Her head lolled to the side. A sour medicinal odor wrinkled his nose. Her beautiful hair clung sodden to her skull, as lifeless as her eyes. No punctures marked her hands or arms, though, and he looked. Drugs would've explained her pathetic condition, but by all appearances, China had suffered a stroke just as Leezel said.

Like hell. He knew down to his gut this was all a lie, damn it.

When the back wheels of the chair cleared the steps, Reardon jerked it out of Maverick's grasp. His act of charity was done, but he couldn't let China go. Not like this. Time was short. Too soon she would be out of sight from the world.

He did the only thing he could think to do. He dropped to one knee at China's side and ended the small act of kindness with a melodramatic show that fit the performances on this liars' stage. Only his act was born of desperation instead of deceit.

He cupped China's jaw tenderly in his palm and leaned his forehead into hers. His fingers trembled. He might never see her again. Chances of him being invited inside were slim to none. His voice caught in his throat. "I'll always be at your service, ma'am," he whispered fervently. "Always."

She didn't even blink.

"Why ain't that sweet?" Leezel gushed, the annoying troll.

He froze. Every instinct screamed at him to pick China up, to warm her up and run as fast as he could and as far away from Reardon and Leezel as possible. *Hide her! Save her!*

His gut churned. There was no aspect of this farce that felt even remotely truthful, but what could he do? Until Hammer confirmed Reardon's part in the fire and shooting, the act would go on.

Maverick kept his position until Reardon bumped the wheelchair backward through the front door with another menacing growl. The door closed. A wave of panic hit

Maverick full in the chest. He had never felt so helpless. The woman he cared about was gone.

It was all he could do to stand and walk away. He joined X and Z at the bunkhouse door. Reardon stood at the picture window, the deed done, his arms crossed and a twisted smile on his ugly face. Gloating. The bastard was finally where he wanted to be.

Inside.

Rain kept falling. The horses were up high on the hillside. X and Z ran into town for tractor parts. They spent the rest of the evening in the machine shed getting the two tractors up and running and ready to cut the first crop of hay.

It sat opposite the ranch house, east of the bunkhouse. One end of it held the corncrib, empty at this time of year. The rest of the weather-beaten building housed a variety of farming contraptions: a harrower, a rake, two plows and, for now, two broke tractors. An odd collection of scythes, rubber belts, and other farming implements hung from the ceiling.

Gloom filled the ramshackle building. It mingled with the smell of musty dirt, rain, and oil. And despair. Z's disposition had turned cranky. X was quieter than usual. He fiddled with some small engine at the workbench. Puppy was flat on his back with all fours in the air, asleep as usual.

Maverick had too much time on his hands. He lent a hand where he could, but these two codgers seemed to know what they were doing, so he stayed out of their way and did what he did best. He kept an eye on the house through the open garage door.

Nothing felt right. The hospital would have never released China if she had suffered a stroke in their care, but Maverick was powerless to prove otherwise. All he had were suspicions and a gut feeling that Leezel had betrayed her sister to the devil incarnate, Reardon. She had knowingly brought a predator into the ranch house, and China had become the lamb to the slaughter. Maybe Kyrie, too.

A cold chill clamped the back of his neck. What were they doing in there? Were they caring for China at all or had they shoved her into a closet so they didn't have to look at her? And what about Kyrie? He brushed his hand over his face in frustration. *God. What are they doing?*

"Hey! I'm talking to ya." Z's grumpy voice jolted Maverick back to the repair job at hand. "I need that there wrench. You gonna give it to me or not?"

Maverick grabbed the only wrench nearby and handed it to Z.

"About time. I dun asked ya twice," Z grumbled, cross-legged beneath one of the tractors, grimy, with grease-covered hands. He twisted the wrench and growled at it, but the tool slipped. With a roar, he chucked it halfway across the shed. "Ouch! Guldurned tractor! Dag nab it. Got my thumb!"

X ambled over to where the wrench landed. He picked it up and walked back to where Z sat fuming. Peering under the tractor, he reached in, sunk the wrench onto the stubborn bolt in question, gave it a few quick turns and walked away without a word.

"Why didn't you tell me you was so darn smart?" Z bellowed. He rolled to his feet and dusted the butt of his pants off, wiping his sore thumb on the grease rag hanging out of his back pocket. "Damn it, X. I been working that bolt for hours and you trots in like you was Dale Earnhardt or something. Why didn't you speak up and help me sooner, ya smart alec?"

X shrugged. "Ma always said I had a knack for fixin' them kinda things. All ya had to do was ask. I'd a helped ya."

Z glared at Maverick. "What you looking at? You gotta knack for something, too?"

"He ain't listening. He's watching for Miss China," X supplied the truth before Maverick had a chance to lie.

Z looked out the wide-open doors. "I told ya before, Miss China likes you."

Liking China was no longer the problem. Saving her life was.

"Ya know what ya need to do?" Z wouldn't let up.

"Leave it alone, guys." Maverick waved them off. The solitude of the bunkhouse looked pretty good. "Just drop it."

X had his *I-know-better-than-you* face on, and his hands on his hips. "Me and Z been talking. Look at you. You don't belong here. You're some kinda Army Ranger, ain't ya?"

Maverick gritted his teeth. *Here it comes. Be all you can be. Here we go, off into the wild blue yonder. Be Army strong. He'd heard it all before, and it was crap.*

"Then why don't ya call your Green Beret buddies and do what it is you guys do best?" X pointed a scolding finger at Maverick. The guy might know copper and horses, but he didn't have a clue about soldiers or Marines.

"X is right. What are you, son? Really?" Z asked quietly. "You ain't no cowboy, and you ain't no ranch hand neither. That's for sure."

"You're one a those guys like ol' man Jefferson was, ain't ya?" X quieted down, as if he knew he treaded on thin ice. His brow spiked. "Or maybe you're one of them Navy SEAL guys, the ones no one can see. Are ya?"

"Marine." Maverick provided the correct answer to prevent more wild guesses.

Z stroked his grizzled chin. "I should've known."

X dropped his jaw and stared. "You is? Damn. Really?"

Maverick stared back at his friends, too. They weren't much to look at and they were older than dirt, but he heard what they'd meant to ask. *Why don't you man up?* Yes, he had come out of hiding when China got shot. His training had resurfaced, as if he hadn't buried it after Darrell's death. Doctoring her had come as natural as the rain pouring down, and he helped her because of it. So what was he supposed to do, become *that man* again? That indestructible Corporal Carson who'd charged into Hell and got others killed?

He was lucky up there on the hill with China. That was all. He hit the bastard who had shot her, but it could've just as easily gone bad. He could've gotten her killed. Maybe Kyrie, too.

Liar. His damned conscience pricked him. China wasn't in any danger of dying from that gunshot. She had been grazed, pure and simple, and he'd done nothing but help. He wouldn't ever have lost her like—Darrell.

"But she's had a stroke."

Liar. Just because Leezel said it, didn't make it so. That she said it should've made him think. He was thinking plenty now.

"So?" X asked. "Ya gonna let a little thing like a stroke stop ya from doin' what's right?"

Maverick glared at the ridiculous question. *Well, yeah. It's damn hard to save a woman in a wheelchair who doesn't even know who she is, much less remember who I am.*

"I'm not Rambo," he said quietly.

X about dropped his teeth. His entire face scrunched into one big wrinkle. "Well, duh. Ya think we ain't figured that out?"

"You guys don't get it. I couldn't even save him. What makes you think I can save her?" The telling word came out of his mouth as natural as if he had meant it. *Him. Darrell. My brother, for God's sake!*

Z blinked once. His laser-blue eyes pierced the barricade Maverick had maintained for too long. No Oakleys hindered the view. No brim. Just crystal clarity and the damned, awful truth.

Maverick swallowed past the lump in his throat. "My brother. Darrell. He... I lost him. Helmand Valley. Taliban." *That rat bastard, Mullah Mamood.*

Z pursed his lips and lowered his head. He studied the dirt between his shabby cowboy boots for a spell before he raised his chin and looked Maverick in the eye again. "You're right, son. You ain't Rambo. Rambo's some made-up joke outta Hollywood, but you're for real and you're here." He took a full step into Maverick's comfort zone and stuck a steadying hand to his shoulder. "It takes a helluva man to do what ya done for your country, and I 'spect ya might be sick and tired of the rest of us chicken shits by now. I never served in Iraq and Iran, but I done some time in 'Nam. Ain't none of it easy, is it?"

God, Maverick wanted to look away, but Z's gentle gaze held him fast. It was as if he hadn't seen the older man before.

"This ain't Hollywood, and it sure as hell ain't make-believe, Maverick Carson. This is real-world shit, and Miss China needs ya now more 'n ever. You're the only one can do what needs getting done. Me and X is too old. This one's on you."

Maverick shuddered. It sounded so damned easy.

"I'm gonna tell ya what Jefferson Wolf told me the first day I showed up here on this crazy ranch of his," Z said. "I weren't no good with horses. No good at all, but he says to me, *Zeke. There ain't but one thing ta do when you falls off a horse. You gots to pick yer butt outta the dirt. You gots to cinch yer saddle up. You gots to climb back on that horse and kick ass. There ain't never been a cowboy that couldn't be throwed, but I'm here ta tell ya—there ain't never been a horse that couldn't be rode, neither. 'T all depends on the heart of the cowboy."*

Z took a deep breath and stuck a finger into Maverick's chest. "Son, you got more heart than ol' Jefferson Wolf himself did when he set down stakes and bought his first horse. It's time to pick yer ass up and git back in the saddle, don't ya think?"

"But I'm no cowboy." *And my heart's already wrecked to hell.*

Liar.

X and Z waited.

Maverick swallowed hard, his throat dry as the truth he had been running from caught up with him. His conscience and this old man were right as the rain falling out of the sky. Life wasn't easy by any measure of a good man, but he was made of better stuff. And his heart might be a little wrecked, but he had found the cure for that in sweet China's deep, blue eyes and her love for the Wild Wolf.

He drew a deep breath. The guilt he had carried for the last couple of years had weighed him down for nothing. It was time to let it go. Grief served no good purpose. Not after all these months. Darrell wasn't coming back, and no amount of regret would change the past.

It was time to take chances. To live again. It was also time to drop the good-ol'-boy, I'm-just-a-nobody-passing-through horseshit.

"Ya know what I think?" X was still knee-deep in fantasyland. "I think ya needs some of those ninja guys in them secret stealth helicopters. Ya know, the kind no one can hear? That ways them ninja guys could fast rope down outta the sky to the top of Miss China's roof like I seen 'em do on TV and—"

"What you been drinking?" Z clapped his slightly demented buddy's shoulder. "We need a real plan, not one of yer harebrained ideas."

Maverick winked at Z. "Let him talk. I think he's onto something."

X's eyes widened at that very slim possibility. "Ya do? Well, okie dokie then. So them ninja guys could drop outta the helicopter, only they'd be dressed in black on account a it would be nighttime, and that way no one could see 'em. They could climb real quiet-like into Miss China's room and pick her up real careful, so she wouldn't get hurt no more, and them two scoundrels would never know she was..."

Maverick nodded at X's exuberance, his mind a thousand miles away where an office of highly-trained covert operators could accomplish exactly what X described.

Well, almost.

Chapter Twenty-Three

"Now hold on there. You can't go and do that!"

Maverick came running from the machine shed where he and X were still working on that cantankerous tractor. He had heard the truck pull into the yard, but thought it was a lumber truck bringing the rafters for the new barn. It wasn't. It was a heavy truck all right. The kind that pulled a long horse trailer.

It was early next morning and Reardon was at it again. He had Joker on a lead.

"These horses belong to Miss China," Z argued, his face red with anger. "She's the one who bought 'em, bred 'em, and—"

"Get the hell outta my way, old man." Reardon pushed Z back a few steps, but Z wasn't done arguing. He didn't come up swinging, but his clenched fists told Maverick he wanted to.

"What's going on?" Maverick asked Z.

"He's selling off Miss China's horses, is what's going on." Z stabbed a finger in Reardon's direction. "We gotta stop him."

"No, I ain't selling *Miss China's* horses." Reardon pulled Joker up the ramp. "I'm selling *Miss Leezel's* horses. If yer gonna lie, at least git yer story straight, ya old fart."

"Miss Leezel don't even know the names of these animals," Z declared. "They ain't hers. They're China's. I done told ya that."

"Don't matter what names they got. They're jes' cash on the hoof far as I'm concerned."

Joker ambled obediently up the ramp to the outstretched hand of another rancher, a wiry older gent with a cream-colored Stetson set evenly on his head.

"Z's right." Maverick stepped up to the horse trailer ramp. "Do you have a bill of sale for these animals to prove Leezel owns them?"

"And certificates of veterinary inspection, too," Z added. "Ya can't sell livestock without it."

"That ain't none a your business, *Mr. Carson.* Your's either, Knudsen." Reardon smirked at the rancher as if he was just having a problem with the help. "Hired hands don't get a say in what their boss decides to do with his property."

The rancher tipped the brim of his hat to Maverick, then led Joker out of sight and into the trailer. Maverick glanced at the other Percherons tied to the porch rail. Rowdy, Jinx, and one of the pregnant mares, Sugar, stood in the morning sun, all of them on their way off the Wild Wolf.

Maverick blocked Reardon as he strode down the ramp. "I'm asking you again. Z knows what he's talking about. Do you have a bill of sale? It's a fair question. I'm sure this gentleman wants to know whether he's buying stolen property or not."

The rancher stopped in his tracks and looked impatiently at Reardon.

A dark shadow passed over Tough Guy's face. His lip lifted in a sneer, but he recovered quickly. Reardon cupped one hand to the side of his mouth and did what any reasonable rancher would do when faced with a complicated financial question. "Leezel! Git yer ass out here!"

The staccato clickety-clack of glittery red heels on bare hardwood floors announced her arrival. She opened the screen door and walked onto the porch dressed as always. Barely.

Maverick's heart sank at the brazen way this woman had taken over China's home. Leezel was dressed to party in a slinky, strapless number that matched her footgear and hardly covered her backside. Her nails were the same color as her get-up. Blood red.

"Your pretty boy here's pitching a fit." Reardon jerked a thumb at Maverick. "He wants to know if you got a bill of sale for these nags we're selling. You got one, don't ya?"

Leezel looked from Reardon to Maverick, then back to Reardon. "Not yet I don't. Damn it, Troy. You're gonna git one a them bill-of-sale things when you get paid. Don't you know anything?"

"No, *dear.*" Reardon's voice turned stern. "That ain't the bill of sale I'm talking about."

"Well, for hell's sake, what do you mean then?"

Tough Guy smirked at the rancher. "Excuse me, but I've got to explain things to my little woman. She ain't the smartest when it comes to high finance." He trotted up the porch and leaned into her ear.

She frowned. She shook her head, but she got the message. *If looks could kill.*

"Now we'll see who's buying horses today," Z muttered, but Maverick's heart sank again. The light bulb over Leezel's head had clicked on. Those two were clever. They might not have thought of it first, but they were quick on the uptake.

Southern Belle Leezel turned into the business-savvy rancher without missing another beat. "Oh, *that* bill of sale. Well, a course I've got one of them things from my poor, dear sister 'fore she had her stroke. She signed 'em all over to me for my birthday a while back. Wasn't that nice of her? She always did nice things like that. You just wait a teensy, little minute. I'll get it for you."

Reardon had his chin out again, his lips pursed with his usual arrogance. He swaggered back to the horse trailer where the rancher who thought he had gotten a terrific deal on horseflesh stood patiently waiting. "Why don't we git your horses loaded so you'll be ready to git by the time she comes back?"

The rancher tipped his hat back and crossed his arms over his chest. "Why don't we wait on that bill of sale first?"

Reardon pursed his lips again, not so smug.

Maverick went to the rancher, nodding toward Joker. "Mind if I tell this one goodbye? He's kind of a friend."

"Go ahead." The rancher eyed him suspiciously, but Maverick proceeded into the trailer. Joker might have been a troublemaker, but he was one of China's favorites.

"Hey there. Easy boy." He smoothed a gentling hand over the horse's rump as he stepped alongside the big bay. "Don't worry. Somehow I'm going to get you back. All of you."

The awful thing happening on the Wild Wolf angered Maverick, but there was nothing he could do. No doubt Reardon had told Leezel to create a bogus bill of sale at that very minute to cover their tracks.

"You done in there?"

"Yes, sir." Maverick swatted Joker's rump and turned with an outstretched hand. "May I know your name, sir?"

He gripped Maverick's hand. "Josh Winters. I own the Lazy Susan over in Cheyenne."

"Ex-Marine, Corporal Maverick Carson, sir." With an unexpected burst of pride, he let his identity roll off his tongue for the first time in a couple of years. "Third Battalion. Third Marines. Kilo Company."

Josh Winters grabbed his hand tighter, his eyes glistening. "No kidding? The Three-Three? You wouldn't happen to know my son, would you? Justin Winters?"

"I don't, but I've been out for a while. Where's he deployed?"

"He's not." The rancher wiped his face, overcome by emotion. "He's back in Hawaii for the time being, but he was in the Nawa District over in Afghanistan. Saw a lot of crap. You ever been there?"

"Yes, sir, I have."

Josh Winters's eyes filled with pride. "I'm proud of what you guys are doing for those people, son. If you ever get to Cheyenne, you make damned sure you stop by my house.

Now promise. Justin's mother will be so happy to meet you. She's already adopted every Marine she's run into so, hell, you're already family at my house. All you've got to do is show up. She'll fix a feast that'll put meat on your bones before she'll let you leave."

"Thank you, sir." Maverick heard this father's pride loud and clear.

"You promise me?"

"I will. I promise. Can I ask why you're buying these horses?"

"You bet." Josh Winters nodded at Joker. "These are the best Percherons in the country. I bought a pair off Miss China last year, and I been dying to own a couple more. They're a hobby of mine. At the bargain basement price this guy's giving 'em away, I couldn't say no."

Maverick cringed. China's horses wouldn't last long if Leezel and Reardon weren't asking top dollar.

She reappeared at the front door with a sheet of paper at her fingertips. "Found it," she declared as she minced her way down the stairs and stuck the latest lie under Reardon's nose. "See. Knew I had it all along. Just had to find it. Got them vaccination certificates, too."

Reardon scanned the paper, as if he knew anything about selling horses, then handed it to Josh Winters.

The man looked Reardon in the eye for a long minute after he scanned the documents. He turned back to Maverick. "Sorry, son. It looks like a legitimate bill of sale to me. The health certificate looks authentic, too."

"It ain't!" Z offered one last argument. "It's a dad-gummed lie! Miss China would never sell these animals. No, sir. She's sick, that's all. And these two are making her sicker."

Leezel chuckled. "You ain't nothin' but a crazy old man, Z. Even your name is simple so you don't forget it."

Maverick had no choice. He stepped off the trailer without a backward glance at Joker. The big tease nickered softly from the confines of the trailer.

"I hear you, boy," Maverick muttered to himself. "Trust me. I hear you."

China sat in a daze.

She had always been the strong one, but now she relied on her family. For the first time in years, she was thankful for her younger sister. Leezel took care of her. Well, she tried.

China had fallen once. Slipped right out of her wheelchair and landed on the floor. Couldn't even catch herself when it happened. That big guy, Troy, jerked her by her armpits back onto the chair. It always hurt when he touched her. He didn't like her much, she could tell, but he was stuck with her as much as she was stuck with him.

That's why the belt. It kept her in her place, and if she was in her place, Troy wouldn't have to help her anymore than he wanted. A towel of a pad to sit on would've been nice, though. The bare plastic seat hurt her backside. She tried to find the best position, but without being able to move, her only position became the best position. Blisters wouldn't hurt so much if she kept still.

That's what Leezel said.

China fingered the smooth metal armrests of her shiny chrome world. She spent all of her days and nights in it. It didn't matter that she faced the corner with barely enough space for the footrest. She wasn't going anywhere, and she always liked the old-fashioned wallpaper in this room. Hadn't she?

At least she wasn't in a smelly nursing home with old women stealing her toothbrush and older men stealing her virtue. So China was thankful. Old, losing her mind, and a terrible burden on her poor sister, but thankful.

That's what Leezel said.

Cute little Kyrie came to her once and laid her head in China's lap. She lifted China's hand to the top of her curly hair, almost as if she wanted to be petted. She cried. It broke China's heart to see that baby so sad, but try as she might, she could barely make her stiff fingers muss the girl's curly hair.

Then Troy hollered. Kyrie's sweet face disappeared. And that was that. The little tyke wasn't allowed to come around anymore, and China agreed. She might have hurt her.

That's what Leezel said.

She had been recovering from her stroke for what? A year already? The timeframe didn't feel quite right, but who was she to argue? Some days she couldn't open her eyes. Breathing took more and more effort. It was harder and harder to think. Days and nights blurred together. The stroke had left her weak and listless. Dizzy. Dependent.

Sounds swirled around her like the wind sometimes. Other times, long stretches of silence filled the void in her empty head. Her stomach used to gurgle, but it stopped. China was thankful for that, too. It gave Troy one less thing to be mad about. Nobody liked it when he was mad.

A small blast of cold air from somewhere in the house hit the back of her neck. China shivered. She had gotten old. *Tired and old. Old and tired.*

But something in the draft reminded her of... The outdoors. The sunshine. A hill. That handsome man, the one who said, "I will always be at your service, ma'am."

I wonder what he meant by that.

Chapter Twenty-Four

Kyrie sat alone on the front step.

The only work Reardon had done so far was to take the mama cat and her kittens for a ride to the river. Maverick would've stopped him if he'd known, but he heard about it too late. X was beside himself with grief over the drowning deaths of his cats. Wouldn't eat. Could barely talk without bawling.

After that awful news, Maverick hurried to hide Puppy in the safety of the trees by Gorgeous and China Love's grave. It meant he had another chore every day, but caring for the friendly mutt was a small price to keep a promise to a little girl.

Two more horses stood tied to the front porch railing, China's stallions, Ebony and Aces Wild. They weren't as mild-mannered as the geldings and mares, though. Ebony had struck Reardon's shoulder with a flying hoof when he'd brought them up from the pasture together. That set Aces Wild to dancing and snorting. Reardon got mad and bellowed at Leezel to get off the couch and come help for a change.

Maverick hoped to meet this new owner like he'd met Josh Winters, maybe make another friend and throw another wrench in Reardon's plans. He'd fully expected to be booted off the ranch or a knock-down-drag-out brawl after interfering with the last horse sale, but Reardon was all talk.

Instead of fighting, he'd stuck a finger in Maverick's chest and gotten away with it. "You think I don't know why you're hiding out like you are? You're a child molester. That's what you are. Don't even look my daughter's way from now on, or I'll make sure everyone knows you're a perv. You hear me?" Reardon had himself spun up with his own lies; it wouldn't have taken much to push him over the edge.

For now the stallions were calm, and Reardon had gone inside to nurse his wounds. But China's kids were not the reason Maverick lingered at the Wild Wolf. He glanced sideways at the child on the steps. Kyrie's hair didn't shine. She looked sad all the time, and Maverick wondered again what was going on inside that ranch house. She must have been threatened, too.

So he walked the wire.

He left little prizes for her to find. The risk of getting caught was worth the smile, and Kyrie needed to know he cared. The day before he'd left China's cowboy hat on the wooden swing. This morning it was nothing more than three strands from Star's tail braided into a bracelet just the right size for a little girl's wrist. At the knot, he tied off a silver buckle from a broken halter in the barn. It wouldn't latch. If she couldn't wear it, she would never get caught.

Kyrie had already tucked it in her pants pocket, but never glanced his way.

It wasn't much. Pitiful, really. But until Hammer acted, it was all that Maverick could legally do. China's disappearance worried him to the point he had quit eating. Zeke and Xavier teased him about his new weight-loss program, but he waved it off. The more his body begged for sustenance, the sharper his mind grew.

Late last night, his frustration got the best of him. He called the man he'd walked out on. Alex Stewart. Owner of The TEAM, the elite, covert surveillance company on the East Coast. Toughest man alive. Mover of mountains and killer of bad man the world over. And damned proud of it.

Maverick didn't deserve anything, much less the *package* that was already enroute to him. After a quick rundown of the situation, Alex had released a wealth of resources to his former, *stupid* employee. That he held no recrimination touched Maverick deeply.

"So, they're selling all of her horses?"

"Yes, Boss, all of them. Four went yesterday. Two stallions today."

"Maybe that's just as well. Doesn't sound like China's sister is much of a horsewoman."

Maverick grimaced at the truth, wishing he were in a position to buy China's kids. "She's something else, all right."

"You do know I've still got an empty desk with your name on it," Alex reminded him.

"I might just take you up on that offer." It sounded true when he said it, but honestly, the Wild Wolf had a hold on him, and China's grip was a helluva lot stronger than anyone's on the East Coast.

"Keep in touch. I expect a report on this mess when you're done."

"Will do. Thanks, Boss."

"Kyrie! Git yer ass inside, ya little shit!"

Reardon's stern rebuke jerked Maverick from his mental trip to Virginia. It also added energy to poor little Kyrie's legs. She scrambled into the house, her little butt tucked in tight behind her. Reardon slammed the screen, still cursing her for having been outside without his permission. Poor thing.

The screen door squeaked.

Maverick's head jerked up. He added another job to his chore list. *Oil that damned door.*

He waited until the dead of night.

Until the *package* Alex had sent, a medical helicopter was en route to the high meadow above the Wild Wolf. Everything had to look as if China had simply wandered to the corral and rode away on her favorite horse. That also meant Star had to disappear tonight, too. Alex had better have remembered that very important detail.

After X and Z were snoring as loud as ever, Maverick made his move. Star was his only accomplice, and even he seemed to understand the gravity of the situation. Maverick didn't realize the big horse knew how to walk stealthily, but by hell. He did.

As usual, the front door was unlocked, the screen hinges once again well-oiled and silent. Maverick glanced to the living room at his left. Beer bottles littered the coffee table and floor where Leezel and Reardon must have enjoyed an assortment of late-night snacks, judging by all of the garbage.

The TV filled the room with flashing lights and raucous noise. Both trespassers were sprawled in separate corners of the couch, Reardon with a liquor bottle in his fist, his head tilted back and his mouth opened wide. Wheezing snores assaulted anyone within range.

Leezel cut an equally unimpressive picture with her head back, knees spread. Maverick turned away in disgust. No man in his right mind needed to see that. He didn't go far.

China sat in the opposite room in her wheelchair, facing the corner.

Damn them.

His heart broke as he knelt at her side again. Dressed in an oversized men's T-shirt, her legs were sprawled like some bizarre store mannequin's. Her arms hung over the armrests. The belt at her waist had been left unfastened probably in the hope she would fall and hurt herself.

Damn them to hell.

With one big armful, he slid her out of the chair and onto his knee. She felt thinner. Colder. When he smoothed a hand over her backside to lift her, his fingers met bare flesh. Just the damned T-shirt. That was all she had on. No pants. No underwear.

Rage and frustration boiled over. He glanced sideways at Reardon. *You fucking bastard! I WILL kill you if you've touched her!*

He could've cried right then and there. She, the most beautiful woman in the world, had been reduced to a lifeless ragdoll by those drunken asshats in the other room. God, he ached to wreak hell and damnation on Reardon and Leezel.

But not tonight. He ached for China more.

He lifted to his feet. The minute he did, she laid her head on his chest and breathed out a soft sigh. He held her close for one long moment and let his body transfer heat to hers. "You're going to be okay now," he whispered. "I've got you, and I'm never letting you go again."

She groaned, her face in his shirt, and damn it to hell. For two cents he would pound the living shit out of Reardon for doing this. Instead, Maverick stepped lightly, angling China out the front door without a sound and down the steps to where good ol' Star waited patiently.

Maverick bundled her in the blanket he'd left hanging off the saddle. Very carefully, he placed her into the makeshift brace he'd fashioned on Star's broad back. She'd have to sit sidesaddle, something she would never choose to do under ordinary circumstances, but he needed her upright and belted in. He secured the neck roll to keep her head and neck protected.

Star assumed care of his mistress without so much as a nicker or a shift of his big feet.

But time was running out. Maverick returned to the house and tipped the wheelchair on its side. Leezel and Reardon needed to believe she had crawled away under her own power.

He took one last disgusted look at the degenerates in the other room, and—

Someone very little tugged at his jeans pocket. "Kin I come, too?"

He froze. There at his feet stood a frightened mini-version of China. And there he stood, the *Grinch* who'd just stolen her one and only joy.

The sad eyes of a child about to be left behind blinked up at him. There was no choice. He couldn't just leave her, could he? He did what any knight in shining armor would do. He raised a finger to his lips and bundled Kyrie in another blanket. "Can you hold onto Auntie China for me while I get on Star?" he asked in a whisper as he placed her behind China.

"Uh huh," she whispered back, her head bobbing. "I is a good hewper."

Maverick mounted up and reached both hands around Kyrie and China to the reins. "You are the best helper in the whole world, sweetheart. Now hang on tight. We're going for a ride."

He kissed the top of her head, but noticed the same sour smell in Kyrie's hair as China's. He reined Star toward the driveway. When they were safely out of earshot, Maverick urged the horse into a trot.

Damn Leezel and Reardon to hell.

"Unca Mavwick?" Kyrie's upturned nose and bright little eyes peered up at him from the dark. Star plodded steadily upward while Maverick ensured both of his charges stayed put. It was slow going, but—it was going.

"Yes, Kyrie?"

"Puppy's smiwin'. Kin he come, too?"

Sure enough, that rascal Puppy had broken free of his digs up the hill. He trotted happily behind Star. The crazy mutt did look like he was smiling. Maverick grimaced. His rescue of a single woman was turning into a zoo.

"He is now."

"I missed Puppy. He so cute." She had an adorable lisp to her voice, as if little girls really were made of sugar and spice.

Star kept going. Before long, they arrived at the rendezvous point. A large medical helicopter sat silent on the crest of the grassy hill. Maverick's heart sank. Damn. The chopper was way too small. Kyrie would fit and Puppy too, but not Star.

Taylor Armstrong scrambled out of the waiting helicopter and strolled toward Maverick with a serious smile. "It's about time. Man, you weren't kidding. He's a big horse."

Gabe Cartwright all but fell off the chopper, the klutz. "Hey, bro. We've been waiting a while. Thought maybe you'd gotten waylaid. Where's your lady friend?"

Maverick couldn't have been happier to see his two best buds. They'd literally been through Hell and back with him and every step in between.

"Here's one of them." He handed Kyrie off to Taylor just because he stood closest. "Don't drop her."

"Ah, okay." Taylor accepted the unexpected passenger in surprise. "But I thought you said—"

"Does you yike me?" Kyrie peered fearfully up at Taylor, her little chin a quiver.

"Ah, yeah. Sure. You're cute, kid, but—" Taylor looked down at Kyrie and then to Maverick. "I thought you said—"

"I couldn't leave her behind." Maverick slid off the horse, his hand still on China's side to keep her balanced. "She's small enough. You got room?"

"Sure. No problem." Gabe stood ready to help. "You know us. We've always got room for cute girls." When he winked at Kyrie, she scrunched her shoulders shyly in return.

"Good, because you're taking a dog, too." Maverick nodded to Puppy, who sat at Taylor's feet because he had Kyrie.

Taylor shifted her to his hip. "Man, Maverick. We only brought one chopper. Anything else?"

"Yeah." Maverick dismounted and pulled China gently off Star. "I need a medic. You did bring one like I asked, didn't you?"

Gabe motioned to the man who'd just scrambled out of the chopper door. "Meet Ryan Gibbs. Gibbs, Maverick Carson."

Ryan jogged straight away to Maverick's side with a lightweight gurney under his arm and his medical bag in his hand. "I've got a warm bed inside for Miss Wolf. What can you tell me about her condition?"

"She's been drugged. I don't know with what, but she exhibits all the signs of a stroke, and I don't think she's been given any food or water since she's been home."

When Gabe helped Maverick transition China to the gurney, her head lolled to the side. Her eyes were open. She looked dead.

Maverick sank to his knees beside her. "God. Am I too late?"

Taylor retrieved a heavy-duty flashlight from the chopper. The bright stark light only made her look worse.

Ryan edged Maverick aside and slid a stethoscope under her shirt to the middle of her chest. He listened briefly. "No, but she's damned weak. Let's move her inside and get some fluids into her. Quick."

Together he and Maverick shifted her to a larger bed-like gurney in the chopper. Taylor occupied Kyrie with a couple of surgical gloves he had blown up and turned into animals. He had positioned himself so she couldn't see China.

While they played, Ryan went to work and examined his patient. Maverick assisted in removing her filthy clothes. He covered her with three warmed blankets while Ryan took her vitals, drew several vials of blood, and inserted an IV drip-line into her arm. All the while, he communicated with a doctor or nurse somewhere in the Ethernet in short bursts of medical lingo through the radio pinned to his shoulder.

Anxiety stabbed at Maverick. He couldn't look away. China seemed to be slipping through his fingers.

At last, Ryan huffed and looked up, his eyes serious. "What can you tell me about the gunshot wound in her hip? Why wasn't it treated?"

"It was. I treated her as soon as she was shot. Used an antiseptic clotting agent and sterile packing, too." Maverick raked his hand through his hair, unable to explain why her wound now looked as if he hadn't done a thing.

"Listen. It's gone septic. It's not bandaged and I doubt—"

"But the sheriff took her to the emergency room. I know he did. I was there. I bandaged her. It was clean the last time I saw her. God, it was just a flesh wound."

"Then someone purposely contaminated it. Listen, I'm not arguing. I'm just telling you what I see. I'm not supposed to offer any medical opinions, but you're right. She's been doped. With what, I won't know until we run blood work. She's lucky she's not dead, but she's damned sick. Who drugged her? Do you know what he used?"

Maverick blew out a huge sigh. "Her sister's sonofabitchin' boyfriend. Troy Reardon. And no, I don't know what crap he used."

"How long was she in that guy's care?"

"Three days." Maverick's mouth went dry. *Care, nothing. Three days of hell.*

Ryan stilled as he listened to her heart again. "Prolonged use of any drug means withdrawal, but overuse could cause heart damage. I'm not hearing anything abnormal. All I can do right now is start her on a detox drip." He reached into a nearby cabinet and retrieved another IV bag.

"There's something else." Maverick lowered his voice, not wanting Kyrie to hear. "God, I hope not, but she's been alone in that house for three days with Reardon and—"

"You suspect rape?" Ryan asked, his voice as low. "Got it. I'll make sure the ER docs give her a thorough exam. I won't sugarcoat it. She's in bad shape. She's dehydrated, and I'm only getting a thready pulse. I need to clean her wound and get her on a strong antibiotic, but it's going to be a while before she's conscious."

Maverick bit his lip and nodded. *I'm too late. I should've gotten her out the first day. I knew something was wrong.*

Gabe clapped a hand to his back. "You saved her, man."

No. I didn't. Maverick turned away before his emotions got the best of him, but Gabe wasn't about to let him go. He still gripped Maverick's shoulder and held him in place. "Hey. You've seen guys in worse shape than this. They pulled through. Gals too. We're going to get her to a hospital, and she's going to make it. You want a few minutes before we take off?"

"Yeah." Maverick wiped his eyes. "I do." Here he was telling China goodbye all over again. The hole in his chest where his heart used to be felt incredibly deep and tender. God, did it never stop hurting?

"Hey, Ryan? Can you give us a minute?" Gabe asked.

Ryan took one look at Maverick and stepped back. "You bet, but they've got a trauma team standing by. Make it quick.

We need to lift off in five. No later" He signaled the pilot to start the engine.

Maverick knelt at China's side, his heart breaking. He gathered her cold fingers in his and leaned his forehead to hers. All he could see was the ashen face of the woman he loved. Yes, loved, damn it. He choked. All this time, he had been trying to be tough and invincible. Untouchable. Unreachable. What a waste of time and energy.

He should've picked her an arm full of flowers. Even Kyrie knew how to do that.

He could've spoiled China rotten and helped her more around the ranch.

Hell, he could've married her. Now he might never get the chance to tell her how much she meant to him. How she had saved his life. In locking up his heart, he had locked her out along with everything good. Everything right. There he was, powerless again and unable to stop death from taking China the same as it had taken Darrell.

He placed a soft kiss on her parched lips. "I never told you this, China, but I don't want to live without you. I don't think I can. You've given me another chance." He gathered her sickly body into his arms and buried his face in the crook of her neck, wishing for a way to roll back time.

As tight as he held her, it could never be tight enough. Death seemed to have the upper hand. Maverick sealed his love with his tears, choking on yet another regret. "I love you, baby. I love you so damned hard it's wrecking me. Don't— leave me. God, please don't die."

Ryan's fingers at his shoulder told him it was time. Maverick settled her back against the gurney. He kissed her lips one last time, and he let her go.

Chapter Twenty-Five

"You turn into a damned cowboy or something?" Gabe stood with one arm around the underside of Star's neck as he stroked and patted the horse's long nose. Star stood as calm as ever, soaking it all in. Moonlight shimmered over his broad flanks and withers. Damned horse still looked like something out of a fairytale. A fairytale gone terribly wrong.

Maverick wiped his eyes before he faced his friend. "Something like that. You guys were supposed to bring a bigger chopper."

"We can't take animals on a medical flight, Maverick. You know that."

Gabe's gentle admonition stabbed Maverick. Oh, yeah. He hadn't thought of that. Leave it to Alex to be smarter than him. No wonder he was the boss.

"The boss did you one better, bro. It will be easier on your horse, too." Gabe nodded toward a man standing a ways from the chopper with a big ol' cowboy hat and a horse that Maverick hadn't even noticed until then. "Maverick Carson, meet Ebenezer Carson. He'll take Star with him. The dog, too."

Maverick extended a handshake to the cowboy.

"You wouldn't be related to—"

Maverick shook his head.

"Me neither!" The man had a magnificent handlebar moustache, a shaggy head of hair beneath his ten-gallon hat, and eyes that twinkled with moonbeams. "I hear you've got a horse needs sheltering for a couple weeks. That right, son?"

"I do." Maverick nodded to the Percheron. "His name is Star. He's more like a big kid. I need you to take especially good care of him."

"He belong to that lady in there?" Ebenezer nodded toward the chopper.

"Yes, sir." Maverick stroked Star's very intelligent face. The horse nickered softly and nuzzled his hand. This was another hard goodbye.

"That's Miss China Wolf." The way Ebenezer said her name made Maverick take a second look. The old cowboy looked awestruck.

"Yes, sir. You're right."

"Why you betcha. I'll take real good care of this horse, same as if he were mine. She don't know me from Adam, but I know that lady's world-famous Percherons like I know my own kids. You tell Alex there's no charge for this one. It will be an honor to help this particular lady in distress."

"Alex? How do you know my boss?" Maverick cocked his head at his new friend.

Ebenezer's eyes sparkled with a tender light. "Only that he sure as shootin' knows a thing or two about horses. Yessirree Bob."

"Alex Stewart? Are you sure we're talking about the same man?"

Ebenezer smiled like the cat that ate the canary. "Yer darn tootin'. Who do you think's been buying all of Miss China's horses?"

"But how?" Maverick shot a confused look to Gabe.

He shrugged. "You didn't think the boss would just let you walk away in your greatest hour of need, did you? Shit, Maverick. This is Alex you're talking about. He's been waiting for you to call, you dumbass."

Maverick swallowed hard. He couldn't break down in front of these guys, so he stuffed his emotions away. It didn't work so good.

Gabe pulled him into one of those guy hugs and slapped his back while he growled into his ear. "We've got your back, bro. Always have. Always will. You should damned well know that by now."

Shit. What's a guy supposed to say to that?

Maverick wiped his face, damned glad this elite company of snipers was still willing to claim him. There was nothing better than working with a company of men and women who truly fought the good fight and most times did it alone.

Nothing better in the world.

Maverick made it back to the ranch before sun-up. The rendezvous had taken all night, but he'd had plenty of zero-dark-thirty missions in the past. This was nothing new. He splashed cold water from the horse trough over his head and down his neck because he'd run all the way back to the ranch once Ebenezer took Star.

For the first time in days, he felt hopeful. China and Kyrie were in good hands. Maybe not his, but Taylor's and Gabe's hands would do until he got things finished at the Wild Wolf. And Alex had bought all the horses except the ones Josh Winters had? Sweet.

He waited out back of the bunkhouse at Puppy's now completed and wonderfully pink doghouse. Somewhere along the line, he had decided it needed white trim around the windows. With all his worrying for Kyrie and China, the doghouse had transformed into a damned dollhouse. Kyrie would love it.

"Looks darned purdy if you ask me." Zeke ran a hand lovingly over the edge of the rooftop. "I see ya found a good use for them old shingles. Where you gonna put it?"

"Wherever Kyrie wants it."

That was all it took to get X going. "I hate Reardon. He's a cat murderer, and he's got no business being in Miss China's house, neither."

Z was just as quick on the uptake. "Jefferson Wolf's gotta be turning over in his grave by now."

"Heck, he's probably rolled over a dozen times if he's rolled over once."

"Good thing he didn't live to see this day. Reardon's as dumb as a box of rocks and twice as ugly."

"You got that right. And he's a murderer. He... He drowned all my cats." X swiped a hand over his face, his anguish still raw and Reardon unforgiven. "Miss Leezel shoulda stopped him.

"Hey, guys, now hold on." Maverick thought he needed to offer at least one hopeful word into the playing field, even if it was just a smokescreen. At least until he heard back from Gabe and Taylor. Knowing that China had survived Reardon's hell house would make all the difference. Might even buy Reardon a reprieve. Might not. "We've got to keep our chins up to show China and Kyrie we're here for 'em. They're the important ones, right?"

"I still hate Reardon," X muttered. "That uppity Miss Leezel, too. They's both cat murderers. That's all they is. Good for nuthin' killers."

"And the horses." Maverick reminded them, attempting to stay on track. "We've got to think of what's left of China's horses. Someone's got to care for them. Reardon and Leezel won't."

Z grunted. "Miss Leezel will sell 'em all, every last one of 'em, sure as I'm standing here and spitting chew. She ain't never liked horses, least of all that white one of Miss China's."

Maverick played it cool. X and Z might be angry with him when all was said and done, but he needed their answers to be authentic when it came time to face Reardon and Leezel. Once they woke up from their drunken stupor and discovered China was missing, X and Z needed to act surprised and bewildered.

"Don't worry, guys. Leezel and Reardon aren't stupid."

X rubbed his face. "Why you defending them all a sudden? You like Miss Leezel and her biker stooge, do you?"

"No. Hell no." He shook his head to emphasize his words. "But we've got to hold this place together until Miss China recovers."

But X's choice of words created an odd sensation of cold fingers creeping up Maverick's spine. *Stooge.* If Reardon was the puppet, that made Leezel the puppet master. She certainly had her hand stuck far enough up his ass to make his lips work. Had she sent him to trash China's yard that first night, too? Had she been behind everything from the start?

X scratched his head. "Guess you might be right."

"Ya think she will?" Z peered into Maverick's face. "Recover I mean. You saw her in that wheelchair. Poor thing looked like death warmed over. Ya think she'll ever be the pretty lady we used ta know?"

Maverick had to look away. Z might be an old guy, but he was plenty perceptive. "I think China is stronger than any of us realize." He sent a silent prayer heavenward. *Please, Lord. Help her be stronger than she realizes, too.*

"Okay, then." Z thumped the doghouse roof, as if that was good enough for him. "Guess I'll hook up the cultivator since I can't cut the hay."

"Sure wish ya couldn't cut the cheese neither," X drawled.

Z's left brow lifted at Maverick. "I have gotta teach that guy some manners."

Only after Maverick made a call to Taylor and Gabe could he breathe easy. China's condition was stabilized. She was now on her way to Virginia where Alex had a safe house prepared for her and Kyrie. The weight of the world lifted off Maverick's shoulders. He *would* have that talk with China the first chance he got. He *would* stop being stupid. He *would* tell her he loved her, and she *would* marry him, damn it.

He should've never sat down, though, not as exhausted as he was. But X and Z were off to cut the grass hay in one of the many fields and wouldn't be back until dinner. He stayed behind to keep an eye on Reardon or Leezel. Someone needed to.

He headed for the shade at the far side of the half-finished barn. China had dragged a few wooden lawn chairs there because she liked to watch her horses in the evening. He sat down and rested his boots on the bottom beam of the corral rail. He pulled the brim of his cap down low over his trusty Oakleys and let the cool breeze floating through the Cottonwoods do its thing.

Spring filled the air with the fresh scent of flowers mixed with the fragrance of moist damp earth, newly sawn lumber, and the new mown hay. He dozed off.

It didn't take long before he dreamed that he was riding high with a lovely lady on the broad back of a flying horse named Star. He wrapped his arms around China's slender waist to keep her from falling. He ducked his head into the crook of her neck and savored the smell of her hair in his face. The woman was downright edible, the scent of wild Russian olive blossoms on the wind.

The cool of the dream and the warm curve of her body against his drenched him in peace. Joy spread all the way to his groin, and in his dream, he smiled. Yes. He wanted this woman in every way possible. When the day came to possess her, she would never doubt whom she belonged with. He would claim every inch of her body, and he would take his time doing it. He would brand her with kisses and passion until they were joined as one in all the high heavens and mated for life. Maybe even eternity.

They drifted through galaxies filled with silvery moonlight where Gorgeous and China Love played once more. Damned if Darrell didn't appear out of nowhere, his wife and baby boy in his arms. He waved and Maverick sent a proper USMC salute. All was right with the universe once more. A thousand winged foals raced alongside, and at their center flew a dark-haired woman with smiling blue eyes and flowing ribbons of black hair.

He reached for her.

She came to him and pressed herself into his body. Every inch of him responded to the warmed of her. He gathered her close, wanting nothing more than to kiss her sweet lips and to savor the taste of her—

Foul. Cigarette-flavored. Tongue.

Yuck!

He gagged and jolted out of the dream. Someone was in his arms all right. Someone with red hair. Her bony knees were wedged in tight between the armrest and his hips and her tongue was down his throat.

Leezel. Shit damn!

He choked enough to break her grip on his mouth, then leaned backward to escape her bony clutches. He pushed her shoulders away, but she straddled him, grinding herself into his lap and moaning. He dug his boot heels into the ground and sent the chair flying backward. They tumbled head over heels. If it were anyone else, she would've landed in his arms, but he rolled out from beneath her and shoved her off.

Shit damn and holy hell!

"What's wrong with you?" With a one-handed pushup off the ground, he lifted to his feet and wiped the vile flavor of pure dementia off his lips.

She pushed to her hands and feet, a cat ready to spring into action. Her eyes glittered, and what the hell had she been smoking or sticking up her nose? "That was a lot a fun. Don't ya think?"

Obviously, she hadn't noticed the empty wheelchair or the fact that Kyrie hadn't come down for breakfast, yet. Just as he suspected.

"You don't fool me." She swayed nervously back and forth as if she couldn't hold still—that or she was half King Cobra and thought she could hypnotize him.

"God, woman. Are you crazy?" He spat again and wiped his mouth.

"Come on, cowboy. You know what they say. While the cat's away..." She pulled her shirtsleeve down over her shoulder, her lip stuck out in a pout. "Oh, come on. You've wanted me since the first time you laid eyes on me. You know you did. Go on. Admit it."

He jerked his head toward the ranch. "Get back to your boyfriend."

"Who? Troy?" She wrinkled her nose. "He's no fun anymore. Too bossy. 'Sides, he ain't here."

"Where is he?" Damn, she had a lot of nerve.

She shrugged. "Went to town I guess. Don't really know. Don't much care."

"Sorry." Maverick meant that on so many levels, but her words proved his suspicions. Reardon didn't know that China and Kyrie were missing, either. "Go find your man."

"I'm already with my man." She wiggled her chest at him.

"No. You're not." He turned and spat one more time. "Take off."

"What? Don't you like me?" *So that's where Kyrie got that line.*

He put both hands to his hips and glared at her. Damned if she didn't wiggle from the top of her crazy redhead all the way down to her stupid red shoes. And everything in between.

Aw, shit. He should've known. She liked angry, mean men. She like abuse. Being slapped around, chased around, and maybe doing the slapping and chasing, too. She liked rough sex. That was what excited her, the whole power struggle thing. The Dom/Sub crap he never understood. Their little romp with the chair proved it. The rougher the better.

He calmed down. Getting fired up would only stroke her libido, the last thing he wanted to stroke. He turned and walked away.

She whined and followed. "Oh, come on, Mav. You can't just go."

He let his boots to the talking.

"Mav honey, come on." She resorted to pleading. "Troy ain't gonna be home for a couple hours, maybe longer. We got all kinds a time."

He was nearly to the porch when he heard the threat.

"I'll tell."

He dropped his tired ass on the top step, pulled his ball cap over his eyes and crossed his arms on his knees. "Tell what?"

"That you kissed me." She bee-lined to the steps and stood in front of him. "I'll tell him you had your hands all over me, and you know what? He'll believe every word I say."

Sure he will. Reardon's dumb like that.

Maverick focused on the ground at her feet and counted to ten. As Z might have said, this woman was nine kinds of persistent and ten kinds of disgusting.

"What do ya say, huh? Just one teensy roll in the hay for old time's sake? Troy'll never know. I won't tell him." She placed one high heel-clad foot on the lowest step, her long tanned leg exposed up to her butt.

"I'll do you one better." Maverick edged his cell phone out of his jeans pocket. "How about instead, we show your boyfriend some pictures I found on the web for *old time's sake?"*

He didn't have a single shot of her, but apparently there were some floating around. She backed off quick as lightning, pulled that brazen leg back alongside the other where it belonged.

"How could you...? Where did you...?" She stared him down as if she couldn't decide if he was telling the truth or not.

He tapped the camera app on his phone. "Wanna see?"

"I hate you, Maverick Carson. Y. G. M. M. W. I. G." With a self-righteous huff, she stalked up the stairs beside him.

Whatever the hell that means.

Her heels clicked across the porch. The screen door hissed quietly shut, but the heavy wooden door slammed. Music to his ears. Maverick pushed off the steps and walked away.

Feeling's mutual, lady.

"Where the crap is she then?" Reardon bellowed. He had only been back from town five minutes when the shit hit the fan.

About damned time.

Zeke and Xavier's heads jerked to the porch when Leezel burst out the front door and marched down the steps, her eyes raking the yard from left to right as if she had lost something.

Or someone.

Maverick tucked his brim down good and tight. *Showtime.*

"Hey, you guys!" Leezel ran toward them, but she seemed a might unsteady in her fancy shoes. She wobbled and leaned a little too far to the left to walk straight.

Yep. That's what putting on a good drunk will do for a gal.

"Have you guys seen my little girl?" She asked more politely as she peered toward the corral, her brows lifted.

"No, ma'am. We ain't." Z answered for all of them. "We jes' come in from the field for a rest. Been cutting the south forty. We was wondering where Miss Kyrie wanted her doghouse."

"She doesn't have a dog," Leezel snapped, but the moment she did, she bit her lip and softened her words. "I mean, why, that's very nice, Z, but the last thing my little girl needs is a doghouse. She don't' have a dog. I couldn't possibly let her keep that mangy stray that's been hanging around, and besides, I ain't seen it lately, have you?"

Z shook his head. "Now that ya mention it, I ain't seen it since yer boyfriend got rid a them cats. Have you, X?"

"I ain't neither," X drawled thoughtfully. "I could look around fer it if ya—"

"No! Just stop it already! I'm asking about my little girl, not that mangy mutt. Have ya seen her or not?"

X and Z shut their mouths and shook their heads.

Maverick lifted his head. "I see your old man made it home."

Leezel blinked as if she had just noticed him. She never missed a beat, not like she could have seen his eyes. "Listen. You guys go look for her, and I'll check through the house one more time, and then I'll—"

"I ain't found 'em." Reardon's bellow from inside the house interrupted Leezel's charade. "You found 'em yet?"

"No!" she shrieked back at him. "Keep looking."

"Them?" Z asked, his brows furrowed.

"Oh, you guys know how Troy is. He really means *her*. Have I found *her*? He didn't mean to say *them*. Just Kyrie. I'm only looking for Kyrie. Shit. Who else would I be looking for?" She chuckled nervously, her eyes back at the empty corral again.

Maverick suppressed a smile. Miss Leezel seemed to be having a difficult time playing the doting girlfriend to her very dominant boyfriend with a big mouth. Their house of cards leaned as much as she did. Maverick wanted to be there when it bit the dust, red heels and all.

"Git your fat ass in here then," Reardon hollered again. "Help me look."

"I'm coming!" she screamed, but then she turned very politely to her hired hands, fisted her hands together and smiled as sweetly as iced tea on a hot afternoon. "Would you please excuse me? I need to have a couple words with my, umm, boyfriend."

She performed a semi-decent pivot on the ball of her right foot and marched back into the house. Somehow she'd regained the knack of walking in heels, although she sure looked as if she intended to knock someone's head off if he didn't stop screaming and making her look stupider than she already did.

"Ya know." Z stared at Leezel's twitching backside while she climbed the steps. "She might be a purdy woman if she weren't so dad-gummed mean."

X still scratched his head. "Them two gonna kill each other someday."

"Sure hope so." Z sniffed as the porch door slammed shut behind her. "Hope I'm here when they do."

The shouting match continued indoors the instant Leezel slammed the heavy wooden door. "Don't you dare talk to me like that. You don't own this place yet, Mr. Reardon."

"Don't look like you do neither, you dumb bitch."

"Oh, yeah? Well, it's half mine already, and don't you forget it."

"Not if she got away. It's still half hers, and she's gonna ruin your ass be running to her buddy, Hammer."

Windows slammed. Doors, too. It got harder to hear the verbal fight when the real battle commenced. Someone inside that house was throwing things. A lamp flew out the front window.

"Who got away?" X asked. "Is they talking about Miss Kyrie or Miss China?"

The racket from inside the house stopped and the front door flew open. Miss Leezel marched down the stairs and tramped across the yard in her bare feet all the way to the corral.

Maverick smirked and let her go. *All dressed up and nowhere to go.*

He'd already released what was left of China's kids into the upper pasture. They were halfway up the hill and safely out of sight. Reardon would have to wait until dinnertime to see if any were missing. She had made the trip for nothing.

Leezel stamped her feet at the corral fence. She turned back to Reardon and yelled. "Shit! They're not—" Her gaze settled on X and Z. She snapped her lips shut. Her countenance changed, "I mean, darn it. I mean..." She dropped the act. "Oh, hell. I mean, shit! The damn horses ain't here, and I'm sick of this stupid game."

Reardon launched himself down the steps at her. "This is all your fault, woman. What'd I tell—"

"Shut up." She yanked his arm and hurried him back up the stairs and into the house. When the front door slammed, everything became deadly quiet.

X scratched his head as he stared at China's ranch house. "What in tarnation that was all about?"

"I ain't never seen two folks so mad at each other, have you?" Z asked.

"Did ya hear him?" X was still puzzled. "It kinda sounded like he's looking for two little gals, don't it? I don't get it. Is they looking for Miss Kyrie or not?"

"Sounds like Reardon's been drinking if he thinks Miss Kyrie is twins all a sudden." Z studied the ranch house, his hands on his hips. "They coulda got hold of some bad shine."

Maverick's stomach clenched. He hadn't anticipated how much Kyrie's disappearance would impact these guys. They might not be geniuses, but their hearts were made of pure gold.

"I'm gonna see if poor little Kyrie's hiding around back." X wiped his face with one rough hand. "Gotta find that poor thing. Tarnation. She's jes' a baby."

"I wonder why ain't Leezel out here searching for her?" Z glanced around the yard, his brows furrowed. "You'd think her mama'd be crazy with worry, wouldn't ya? Ya think she would've called Sheriff Hammer and every neighbor within a hundred miles. I don't get it. We need us some help finding that baby."

Maverick followed Z's tender gaze, hating that he contributed to their distress.

"There's wolves in these parts. You might not a known that, but there's bears 'round here, too. Poor little tyke won't last a minute if we don't find her 'fore dark." Z blinked faster as his worry escalated. "I'm taking one of the horses. I've got to find her."

Maverick caved. He couldn't let X and Z conduct a useless search. He clapped a hand on Z's bony shoulder and waved X back to his side. "Guys. I've got something to tell you."

Chapter Twenty-Six

China blinked and opened her eyes. With one deep breath, she sucked in the sweetest, freshest air. Her lungs filled, but her heart stalled. She had opened her eyes to darkness and the sound of hushed voices, but needed one thing and one thing only. *Kyrie.*

Thank God. Her niece lay snuggled at her side, a baby blanket under her chin, sound asleep. China tipped her her face into the child's hair.

She stilled to get her bearings. Traffic noises sounded outside of her room. A TV chattered quietly from somewhere nearby while the sheer curtain panel floated on a light breeze coming through the open window. Glints of sunshine cleared the curtain. It had to be daytime, maybe early afternoon.

"Where am I?" she wondered out loud, surprised her voice sounded hoarse and her throat felt so dry.

The TV stopped chatting. Footsteps approached. A guy pushed open the bedroom door opposite her bed. She blinked to clear her vision. American Indian. Dark, long hair tied behind his head. Gentle features. Black eyes that twinkled. He walked to the end of her bed. "Hello, Miss Wolf. It's good to see you're finally awake."

She nodded, her apprehension increasing the more alert she became. *Where the hell am I?*

"You're safe now."

When was I not safe? She couldn't remember. The last years and months were missing. "Where am I?" she croaked.

"You're in Virginia, ma'am." His voice remained calm and steady.

She blinked at that very surprising news. "Virginia? What? How?"

"You are in a safe house in Old Town Alexandria. Do you remember how you got here?"

"Umm, no." A cold finger of fear spiraled up her spine. How could she not know so much?

More details emerged. An IV line had been taped to the back of her hand. A faint antiseptic lingered scent in the air.

"Sorry. I'm afraid I'm just confusing you. Do you know Maverick Carson?" Despite her escalating unease, the stranger pulled a chair to the side of her bed as if he meant to stay.

She nodded, her heart pounding out a scary beat. "Yes. I know Maverick. Is he... here?"

"No, ma'am. He's still on duty in Wyoming."

"Duty?" She ran a hand through her hair. "Wyoming? But that's where I live."

"Yes. After he removed you and your niece from a dangerous situation, he stayed behind at your ranch to tie up some loose ends. Don't worry. It will all come back to you once the toxin gets out of your system. It just takes time."

"Toxin? What are you talking about?" She snapped her lips shut. Details began filtering back into her mind. Reardon leaning over her. Swearing. His stinking breath. Leezel sticking a needle in her neck. Kyrie crying. Being cold.

"A muscle relaxant. Your sister and her accomplice—"

"Troy Reardon!" China supplied the name with vehemence. She might not know much, but she knew Reardon. Kyrie stirred in her arms, but didn't wake.

"Yes. Mr. Troy Reardon." The kind man lowered his voice.

She was weak, but plenty angry. "What have they done to me?"

"Your sister and her friend kept you sedated with a powerful muscle relaxant called—"

"I'll kill 'em! If he hurt Kyrie, I'll kill him." China came up off the pillow so fast she saw stars. Kyrie's murmur brought her back to her senses. The fact that she nearly blacked out when she lifted her head calmed her down a lot, too.

The young man grinned. "Good. You are feeling better. You'll be on your feet in no time."

"Unca Taylor!" Kyrie stretched awake with a big yawn. She had no more than opened her eyes when she scampered off the bed and climbed onto this strange man's lap. She gave him a big hug, and by the looks of it, he was pleased to see her, too.

China couldn't believe her eyes. Kyrie smiled, as if nothing out of the ordinary had just happened. "Who are you?" she demanded.

"Junior Agent Taylor Armstrong at your service. Sorry. I should've introduced myself earlier."

A lanky man with mahogany hair peered inside the open bedroom door. His face lit up with a genuine smile. "Hey, there. Thought I heard voices back here. Good afternoon." He tipped his head where a ball cap was perched backwards. He doffed it politely. "Nice to see you're awake. Are you hungry yet?"

No, I'm not hungry. I'm out of my mind. What's going on?

China looked up at the ceiling and bit her lip. Tears filled her eyes, but darned if she was going to cry in front of these strangers. They might be handsome and they were kind enough, but she had lost too many days and maybe part of her mind. Her anxiety boiled over. She counted to ten. Then twenty.

"She okay?" the second guy asked quietly. "Did I scare her?"

"I think she's still a little confused. She's only been awake a couple of—"

"Stop talking like I'm not here," she tried to yell, but ended up whining.

China swung both feet to the floor with the best of intentions, if only her brain could've kept up. The minute she was upright, she noticed the hospital gown. Another very intimate thing called a damned catheter. She dashed the tears off her face and came up fighting. "How dare you? Who do you guys think you are?"

Hollering didn't help. It took oxygen she didn't have. Shadows threatened at her peripheral. Gripping the mattress, she drew in a deep breath to steady her nerves. It didn't work, either. She slumped, gasping for air, her legs still hanging off the bed. Tears leaked out of her eyes and ran down the sides of her head. She dashed them away.

Kyrie scrambled back to her side. "Why is you cryin'?" When China didn't answer fast enough, Kyrie burst into one long drawn-out, "Aw-w-w!"

China shut up, because she'd made her niece cry. She tucked Kyrie into her side, needing to hold onto her one and only familiar lifeline.

The second guy stepped out of her room. Taylor tried to help her back to her pillow, but all she could do was hold on tight to her niece and bawl like a damned baby. Poor Taylor looked as bewildered as she felt. He was so careful handling her, but that only embarrassed her more.

Finally, she calmed. She had overreacted, which wasn't her usual forte. She was *not* an emotional, helpless female. She didn't need help—well, not usually. By the time he got her back against the pillows, she was exhausted, and he looked downright stricken.

"I'm sorry," China said, wiping her cheeks with the back of her hand. "I'm not usually like this."

Kyrie scrambled back to sit with him, probably because he was a lot calmer than her hysterical aunt. China bit her lip and wiped her face. That hurt her feelings, too. It was a pretty sad day when Kyrie was scared of her.

The other man returned and talked quietly with Taylor. "Alex is on his way. He's bringing Kelsey."

"Good. I think she needs a woman instead of us."

"Who are you guys?" China asked weakly. "Tell me again. I'm sorry, but damn it. Nothing makes sense."

"Right now we're just two dumb jocks," the friendly guy with mahogany hair said.

His smile seemed so genuine it was hard to stay mad. She swallowed her pride and determined to not cry again.

"I'm sorry if we scared you. I think you've already met Taylor. I'm Junior Agent Cartwright. Call me Gabe. We're Maverick's buddies. He asked us to keep you safe, so that's why you're in Virginia. We've been waiting a couple days for you to wake up."

"A couple days?" The nightmare just kept getting worse, and she hated the tremor in her voice.

He nodded. The man had the kindest green eyes.

"What... happened to me?"

Gabe sat on the bottom corner of the bed. "Maverick suspected you were in serious danger, so he asked us to come get you and your niece. It's no big deal. We do stuff like this all the time. We dropped in by helicopter and airlifted you and your niece out. You spent one night at the hospital in Wyoming, but our boss wanted you here so he could keep an eye on you."

"Where's here?" She peered around the room. It didn't look like any hospital room she had ever seen, not with the comfortable queen-sized bed she was in and the high ceiling overhead.

"Like I said, you're in Virginia. I apologize for the IV and other stuff, but your doctor put you on the detox drip while you were unconscious. Now that you're awake, I'll call her so she can get you unhooked."

China raised her hand to look at the IV line a little closer. "I have a doctor?"

"I'm sorry." Gabe had such kind eyes. "This is probably real confusing, but the important thing is you're safe. Kyrie, too."

Kyrie waved sweetly from Taylor's lap. "Is you feewin' bedder now, Andy China?"

China nodded, glad her niece wasn't upset anymore. "Yes, I'm okay. How are you?"

"I bedder, too. Unca Taywer is nice to me."

Taylor smiled. "And Kyrie is a happy little girl now that her Auntie China is awake, huh?"

"I is!" The way her eyes sparkled when she crowed calmed China. "And I gonna marry Unca Gabe. You too!"

Gabe's face flushed at Kyrie's cheerful news. "We've been, umm, bonding while you've been asleep. My wife's expecting a little girl in a couple months. I hope she turns out like Kyrie. She's a cutie."

"And Unca Awex buyed me a fwing." Kyrie scrambled off Taylor's lap and back to China's bedside, her eyes wide with wonder. "You wanna see it? Come on! We kin pway."

Gabe tussled the top of Kyrie's head. "She means a swing. How about we let Auntie China rest a little longer, young lady? She needs her nap just like you."

"Aw, I guess." Kyrie looked up at him with a cute pout before she scrambled back to her *Uncle* Taylor's lap. "But I don't gotta take a nap, do I?"

"Nope. You're a good girl. You already took your nap today, remember?"

Kyrie's chatter with Gabe seemed natural. China calmed even more. "Sounds like my niece has a lot of uncles."

"The bottom line is your sister wants the Wild Wolf Ranch, ma'am. She's been drugging you since you were shot last week," Taylor said somberly.

"Drugging me? Last week? But she told me... I thought..." She shook her head to clear the mental fog. *What day is it anyway?*

"She probably told you a lot of things." Gabe reached for her hand, and China let him hold it. "But I do have to ask one question. Did you sell your horses to your sister?"

China searched those green eyes, wondering why on earth he would ask such a ridiculous question. "No. Leezel doesn't like animals. I'd never... Where are my horses?"

Gabe waffled. "Listen, you haven't eaten for at least six days and you're weak. Wouldn't you like a decent meal before we overload you with more information?"

"No. I want to know where my horses are." China sat up straight. "You know, don't you?"

Taylor sighed. "Your sister sold them."

"She sold them? All of them? God. Why?"

"She's clearing inventory. Good horses bring fast cash."

China's hand sprang to her mouth. *God, no.* "She's not selling them to the butcher, is she?"

"No, nothing like that. I really think you should eat first, ma'am," Gabe intervened again. "We can talk more about this when you're stronger."

"No, I can't. I need to know now. " China shook her head, her eyes fixed on Taylor. "What else?"

He looked uncomfortable, but he continued. "She's listed the ranch with a real estate agent."

Her resolve flagged. Leezel meant to kill the Wild Wolf, too.

Gabe kept trying. "Listen. I made chicken and wild rice soup just this morning. It's not bad. It will go real easy on your stomach."

At last, Taylor followed Gabe's lead. "You really should eat before you make yourself sick again. I made yeast rolls. They're not as good as my wife's, but they'll do." He looked so sad. "I'm sorry."

"We never got along, but... Holy smokes. She must really hate me," China whispered, more to herself than anyone else. Her world had just dropped out from under her.

Gabe squeezed her hand. "We'll talk more after you've eaten. It's not all bad news. I promise."

China couldn't reply. Leezel had not only been drugging her, she had starved her. The enormity of what her sister had intentionally done was more than China could bear. She lifted her arm to cover her eyes. Everything was gone, and her heart with it. Her horses. Her father's ranch. How could Leezel be so cruel? It took a minute before she could face these men again.

Taylor whispered, "Come on, Kyrie. Let's bring your aunt some of that fudge we made."

"Yeah." Again, Kyrie sounded so genuinely happy as she traipsed out the door with her new friend. Gabe took advantage of the quiet moment to bring China some tissues and a damp washcloth.

She blew her nose and wiped her face. "You guys are too kind. Thank you."

"We're just brothers, that's all." He straightened her blanket and pulled a chair close to the bedside. "Nothing to worry about—just let us know what you need. We're here to protect and serve."

"You're... his brother?" He didn't look anything like Maverick.

"In a lot of ways, he's closer to me than my real brothers. We served together overseas."

"So, you guys are Taylor and Gabe, and I've been drugged for a week?"

"Actually three days, ma'am." He smiled when he answered. "Maverick said he was pretty sure they drugged you the same day they got you from the hospital."

It seemed a lot longer. Leezel had told her years, and she had believed her. Leezel had told her she was old and dying. China shook her head. She'd believed everything. Lies. All lies.

"Do you remember being in the emergency room?"

China shoved her hand into her hair and tried to think. She had no recollection of being in a hospital, nor anything since the shooting.

Gabe gently persisted. "Tell me the last thing you remember."

"I was... I mean Maverick and I were riding horses." Which horses? Why couldn't she remember which horses?

"Yes. Maverick said you were shot while checking the fence for your cattle."

"Oh, yeah. I have cattle. I mean, I had cattle. Has she sold them, too?"

Gabe shook his head. "I really don't know about that."

A memory filtered back, piece by piece. Kyrie rode with Maverick. It was sunny and warm. She closed her eyes as the picture of him straight and tall in the saddle solidified in her mind. Her cowboy. Her man. Now she remembered. "He rode Star. I rode Ebony."

Gabe's eyes brightened. "And?"

"And someone cut my fence again. The minute I jumped off Ebony, I got shot and—"

The memory of Maverick's hands on her hip and the heated look in his eyes jolted her. His hands. Warm and tender. His handsome face. Gentle. Endearing. His body. Protective of her. Wanting her.

Warmth crept up her neck and blossomed across her cheeks. She wanted him, too. His chest. That muscular body. The sizzling kiss. She reined in her very tumultuous thoughts, but too late. She had to be ten shades of crimson. "Where is he? Is he okay?" she asked to get her mind back on track.

"Maverick is one of the best. You already know that, don't you?"

"I know he's a good man, but he never said anything about a team. I heard you talking before. Who are Alex and Kelsey?"

"Alex is Maverick's boss—at least, he was until Maverick up and quit last year. Kelsey is Alex's wife. You'll like her. Everyone does." Gabe accepted the course correction like a gentleman.

Taylor returned with a tray of food while Kyrie proudly strutted beside him with a small plate of fudge. Judging by the smudge on her lips, she had sampled the fare.

"What do you have there?" Gabe asked.

"Chocowat," she mumbled proudly, and China's heart ached for the kindness these strangers had shown her niece.

Gabe situated China so she could eat, but holding the soupspoon was beyond her capability. Without asking, he placed a napkin under her chin and fed her. Embarrassment for her weakened condition kicked her pride back into gear, but the soup tasted heavenly. She just wished she could stop crying.

"Hey now," Gabe chided her softly as he handed her more fresh tissues. "You keep those two spigots turned on and you'll never get off your IV."

"I'm sorry. I don't know what's gotten into me."

Taylor smiled from the chair where he bounced Kyrie on his knee. "It's okay. We both know how you feel. It's nice to wake up and find out you're still alive, huh?"

China nodded. Alive was a very good feeling.

Just then the door opened and a man with piercing blue eyes peered cautiously into the room. A pretty woman with long dark hair peeked in beside him.

"This our girl?" he asked quietly.

Gabe nodded. "Miss China Wolf, Alex Stewart. He's the man responsible for bringing you east."

"Now hold on." Alex smiled as he and his wife came to stand at her bedside. "I only supplied the means. You blame Maverick for everything else. It's a pleasure to finally meet you, Miss Wolf. How are you feeling?"

"I... I don't know what to say." She reached to shake his hand, emotional as hell all over again, damn it.

"No need to say anything. You've had a rough couple of days." Alex covered her hand with both of his, but he didn't release her. "Sounds like you've kept my agent busy out there in Wyoming. He was one of my best before he got it in his head he had to leave."

"Why'd he do that?"

Alex squeezed her hand very carefully. "Guess he needed to find you."

Gabe moved the soup bowl just in time. The tears hit her hard. She pulled her hands out of Alex's grip and covered her face. She needed Maverick. He knew how to hold her together, because yes. She was lost and found and so damned in love with that moody guy who didn't know he was a cowboy.

"For heck's sakes, Boss." Gabe reached around Alex with another hand full of tissues. He stuffed them in China's fingers. "You had to go and say something like that. Sheesh. We just got her settled down."

Gabe's cussing only made it harder for China to compose herself. All she seemed good for was plugging her face with more tissues and sobbing like a baby. Alex still stood over her. Neither Gabe nor Taylor moved. If anything, they'd closed ranks around her bed. She knew it all the way to her soul. She was safe. Kyrie, too.

Alex pulled the brown-haired woman to his side, as if she could somehow rescue him. "This is my wife, Kelsey. Watch out. She's a crier, too."

China would've giggled if she had the strength. Maverick's handsome boss seemed panicked. Kelsey lowered to the edge of the bed and snagged one of China's hands, her pretty eyes already blinking back tears. "I came to keep you company, honey."

China couldn't answer, the lump in her throat too big. The stroke was a lie. She wasn't the old woman Leezel had said. She would be herself again. Everyday she would get stronger, and soon she would go home. She wasn't ready to die.

No. She was China Wolf, the owner of the Wild Wolf Ranch and the breeder of the finest Percherons in the whole damned country. Not only would she live, but she would kick Leezel's ass and get her horses back, too. Every damned one of them. And the next time she saw Maverick, she meant to knock him down and kiss the hell out of him.

Chapter Twenty-Seven

He watched his back. X's and Z's, too.

There was bound to be trouble once Leezel and Reardon stopped screaming and put their heads together. Nothing happened until dinnertime when, right on schedule, Leezel made another trip to the pasture. The few horses left had already strolled home for the night. Maverick counted them to be sure they were all there. It wasn't hard. Eight was a pretty lonely number.

"Evening, ma'am." He tipped his hat to her from where he stood inside the corral with China's kids. They used to scare him. Now being with them felt more like being at recess with a bunch of rowdy youngsters. But there were so few. He missed Star most of all.

"Can I help you with anything?" he offered.

"You're too late," she snapped. "I'm not interested in playing with you anymore. Get the rest of these nags up to the house. Got a buyer."

"Even the pregnant mares?" Her news sucked the air out of him. Sunshine, Cookie, Minnie, Misty, and Frost were close to foaling. Travel would be hard on them, but hell on any foal dropped inside a moving horse trailer where its mama might not be able to reach it. Where she might step on it.

"Yes. All of 'em."

"Tonight?" He had to ask. "Someone's coming tonight?"

"What'd I say? You got a problem with that?"

He ran a hand over Sunshine's wide belly. What was Alex thinking? Did he even know he had bought pregnant mares that were ready to drop?

"A foal won't stand a chance in a horse hauler, ma'am."

"You think I care?"

"No, ma'am."

That pushed her over the edge. "And what's that supposed to mean, *Mav*?" she asked sarcastically. "You don't think I care or you think I'm mean?"

"I think you used to care," he said simply.

She closed her mouth. A different look passed over her face, like a glimmer of sunshine trying to break through the dark clouds of a thunderstorm before an F-5 tornado. She almost—*almost*—resembled China for a split second. It didn't last. The light faded. She focused on counting again.

"Well, you think wrong. Damn it to hell. Why don't you just tell me which one of these stupid nags is missing? I figure you already know."

"Star." Maverick admitted. "He hasn't come in from the field yet."

"Shit," she cussed under her breath before she looked him square in the eye. "So where is he?"

"Probably still up in the quakies. It's peaceful there."

Maverick felt her gaze on him. She might be a poor sister and a worse mother, but Leezel was no dummy.

"You don't think maybe someone might a stole him?"

"Don't rightly know, ma'am." He strolled from horse to horse, patting a gentle face here and a wide rump there. "Strange things have been going on lately." *Like you and Reardon.*

The silence stretched until Leezel grunted. "Ya know what I think, cowboy?"

He shook his head, still avoiding eye contact.

"Dammit! Would you look at me when I'm talking to you?"

He did.

They stood with the metal corral fence between them, still not enough distance as far as he was concerned. Her malevolent gaze raked him up and down. Everything about her emphasized how hard and mean she had become, from the wrinkles around her lips to the black eyeliner smudged around her eyes. She was and would always be a predator.

"I think you know a whole lot more 'n what you're saying, Mav honey," she purred. "Well, I got news for you. There's more 'n one way to skin a cat."

"One thing's fer sure." Z slapped his old hat against his knee. "I was lookin fer a job when I got this one."

X nodded sagely. The three hired hands made a sorry sight as they watched the final horse trailer pull away. Every last one of China's beautiful Percheron kids was sold and gone—even the regal stallion, Hex.

Reardon and Leezel had scurried back into the ranch house the moment the dirty deal was done. They hadn't even waited to seal the transaction with polite handshakes, just snatched the check out of the driver's hand and hightailed it inside like a couple of rats with a wedge of cheese.

Maverick sighed as the big rigs disappeared. His fears about foals being born during transit vanished the moment he saw the luxury horse haulers that Alex sent. He had the money to make things happen. He spared no expense.

The three spacious trailers came equipped with temperature-controlled stalls and a veterinarian. It made loading this batch of four-legged friends a joy. The sooner they got away from the ranch, the better. Even Hex rode in the luxury of a separate rig, alone but spoiled nonetheless.

"You guys know anyone around here who's hiring?" Maverick asked his two old friends.

"Nope." X shoved a hand over his head, completely derailing the comb-over he usually maintained. Long strands of hair hung off his scalp like the ribbons of an unwanted present. All of a sudden he had transformed into a lost kid.

"Ain't no one gonna hire us." Z kicked at the gravel road. "Guess I might call my sister over in Colorado. See how she's doing."

"She got a ranch?" X asked hopefully. "Any cats?"

Z snorted. "She's got a poodle. Prissy little lapdog named Rocky. Damned thing passes gas like a warthog."

"Guess we's too old." X seemed rooted to the spot, still watching the dusty road where the trailer had disappeared.

Their plight stabbed Maverick. This was their home. When the Wild Wolf died, everything and everyone would die with it. "You got somewhere to go, X?"

"Nope. I only ever worked for Miss China, but now..." He let the unfinished thought hang.

Maverick looked away, afraid X would start bawling.

"When you leaving?" Z turned, his eyes just as sad as X's.

"Now." That wasn't what Z or X wanted to hear, but he had no reason to stay. His new life waited for him on the East Coast, and he was anxious to join China and Kyrie.

He couldn't wait for Sheriff Hammer to act on his suspicions anymore. Even though he had talked to Deputy Clark just hours earlier, nothing happened. The sheriff's office seemed rooted in indecision, as if every shred of evidence had to be indisputable before Leezel and Reardon would be arrested for kidnapping and attempted murder.

The hospital had confirmed she'd been drugged and starved. Hammer had Maverick's testimony of China's deplorable condition when he had rescued her. It should've been enough.

Maverick flat didn't understand until Deputy Clark confided that the latest string of grisly murders in his little town had Hammer thinking about retirement. Clark had contacted Hammer's superior with his concerns. They promised action. Yeah, right. It didn't matter anymore. Maverick intended to wipe the dust of this town off his ball cap as soon as he could.

"Ya could at least help us drink the rest a that beer I bought." X interrupted Maverick's dark thoughts. "Then we could take off in the morning together, kinda like we was the Three Musketeers or something."

Maverick hesitated.

"I hates to leave it fer them two bloodsuckers." X nodded toward the house.

Z shrugged. "It don't matter, Maverick. There ain't no reason for ya to hang around here no more. Ya did what needed getting' done. We's real grateful for that. Come on, X. Let him go. I reckon we got some packin' to do."

An old Marine motto nagged at the back of Maverick's mind, something about *never leaving a man behind*. He blew out a big sigh and stowed his Oakleys in his shirt pocket. "Any turkey sandwiches left?"

Z's eyes lit up. "No, but I got some leftover ham. I can slap some sandwiches together faster 'n a horse can swish a hornet off its butt."

X's crooked smile spread across his face. "Let me git you a couple long-necked bottles. I been keepin' 'em cold jes' for you."

Maverick grinned and slapped his dusty ball cap on his thigh. Yeah. He was gonna miss these guys.

"You should a seen your face!" X laughed so hard that tears dripped off his jaw.

"'Tweren't funny." Z didn't crack even the hint of a smile as he stared at the campfire. "I honestly thought that little bugger liked me. I thought we was friends. Honest, I did."

X howled louder, holding his stomach with both hands. "Stop. Stop," he gasped between peals of laughter. "You're killing me."

Maverick leaned back in one of the lawn chairs by the bunkhouse. It was good to be able to eat again. The ham sandwiches were gone, most of the beer, and the story of how gruff old Zeke had nursed a baby critter back to life was funnier than hell.

"Named him Chip," he muttered pensively, his face awash in the orange glow of the flames. "'Cause he was a chip... munk."

His deadpan explanation elicited another howl from X. He jumped out of his chair, roaring and barely able to breathe. He circled the fire pit, wiping his eyes and shaking his head.

"Yep," Z drawled, extra slow and somber, his poker face intact. "That was the day I knew I had ta let 'im go. Hardest thing I ever done."

"And you had... you had..." X pointed at Z, gasping to spit out the punch line. "You had a guldurned chipmunk stuck ta the end a yer nose!"

Maverick took another hit of his beer and chuckled, but Z did not.

"'Tweren't funny," he said as calm as before. "He mighta bit me, but I still miss that little fella once in a while. Yessirree, Bob."

Maverick downed the last swig. Sitting around the campfire with these two old codgers turned out to be the perfect way to end their friendship. Reardon and Leezel hadn't made a peep since the trucks and trailers rumbled away. He had finally heard back from Deputy Clark. The man told him to be patient. A warrant was in the works and would most likely be served first thing in the morning. Maverick was welcome to stay and watch, but neither he, X nor Z were under suspicion, so it wasn't necessary.

First thing in the morning, they'd be gone and this place would be a memory.

Maverick smiled in relief at the knowledge of where China's horses were. He meant to buy every last one of them back. He had checked with Alex. China's chances of a full recovery were one hundred percent. Things were looking up.

"What ya smiling about?" Z caught Maverick red-handed.

X turned at that question, his eyes searching Maverick's face again. "You got something else ya wanna share with us, Mr. Carson?"

What the hell? These guys deserved the truth. Maverick glanced at the darkened house, needing to be sure Reardon couldn't hear him. He doffed his ball cap and dropped it beside his chair. "I know who bought Miss China's horses."

"Ya do?" X sounded incredulous. "Who?"

"A guy back East," Maverick whispered.

"He wouldn't be the same guy who sent that helicopter to rescue Miss China, would he?"

Maverick nodded. "One and the same."

"Why'd ya ever quit working fer him?" Z asked bluntly. "Seems ta me you gotta helluva good man for a boss."

Maverick nodded. "You're right. I do."

"That boss a yers reminds me a Miss China." X settled in his chair again and just like that, the mood turned somber. He eyed Maverick as he popped another beer top. "I got somethin' for ya 'fore ya leave."

That raised Maverick's brows. "You do? Me?"

X ambled into the bunkhouse and returned with an old shoebox. He dropped it at Maverick's feet with a *thunk* and resumed his seat.

"When did you have time to go shopping?" Maverick asked as he looked at the box.

X didn't answer, just rocked back and forth in his chair, so Maverick removed the lid.

"What'd he give ya? A rock?" Z asked teasingly.

It was a rock, all right. An oblong rock the size of a shoe with a single word etched in the middle of it then filled with gold paint. *Frend.*

"You made this?"

X nodded quickly, his lips pursed tight and his eyes aglow. "Yep. Made it jes' fer you."

Z peeked inside the box. "Well, I'll be. Looks like the one ya made jes' fer me."

"Yep. I only ever made two on account a I only ever had two friends. Oh. Never mind that; I only made three. Miss

China's my bestest friend. I made her one, too, a long time ago."

Maverick brushed a hand over his chin. It might have been the beer or maybe because he had said too many goodbyes in the last week, but a single tear hit the dirt next to the shoebox. "This is damn nice, Xavier," he said hoarsely.

Without guile, his friend replied, "Yeah. I know."

Z cleared his throat. "Well, I ain't got nothing ta give ya, son, and it's high time fer us old guys to be gittin' to bed, but it's been a pleasure." He reached for Maverick's hand. "When you git to where yer gittin', make sure you give Miss China my best, will ya? And give that little Missy Kyrie a hug for me too, ya hear?"

"Yes, sir, I will." Maverick gripped the older guy's hand, a big knot stuck in his throat. "The pleasure's been all mine, Mr. Knudsen. I won't forget you."

"Aw, pshaw. I'd a liked ta told her myself, but I'm telling you now. Miss China was the best boss I ever got ta work for, even better 'n her daddy, ol' Jefferson."

"Yep," X said softly. "She gave me a chance when no one else thought I was worth much or worth keepin', not even my ol' man. She reeled me in an' never once thought a throwing me back."

"And you marry that little gal, ya hear me?" Z released Maverick's hand to wipe his eye. "Now git."

Chapter Twenty-Eight

The stench of body odor woke him. Smelled like something had died right under his nose. He needed fresh air, but got rushed instead. The floorboards of the bunkhouse creaked beneath what sounded like a crowd of tramping boots. Fists came out of nowhere in the dark, hammered his cheek and jaw. Bound him tight before he could warn the others.

Z grunted from his bunk. X never made a sound.

"You got him?"

Reardon. The jerks holding Maverick had to be his biker club.

"Weren't no problem at all," one of them boasted. "Like wrestling bitches, jes' not so much fun afterwards."

Maverick couldn't see a thing. Someone gagged him. Another blindfolded him. Rough hands jerked him off the bunk and pushed him face-first to the floor. They tied his hands behind his back with what hurt like baling twine, pulled him to his feet by his elbows and shoved him into a wooden chair.

"Good and tight, boys."

Reardon's boys made it tight all right. Twine circled Maverick's legs, his upper torso, too. In no time at all he was immobilized and bound to the chair. Blood or sweat trickled down the side of his face. He'd been punched. His eyebrow stung. His lips.

"Me and old Mav here got some business to take care of, don't we, buddy?" Reardon chuckled. "Might as well do that old fart, too."

Maverick listened while Z growled back at his captors, no doubt manhandled and restrained, as well. It didn't make any difference what Z tried, though. Maverick figured he, X, and Z were outnumbered six to one, maybe more.

He focused intently to get his bearings before the situation got more out of hand. The bunkhouse wasn't any bigger than six bunks, a rickety table, and a corner full of appliances called the kitchen. He had to be seated near the table, which meant he was also near the only door. It faced the ranch house. The sound of boots scraping the doorstep told him the exit was to his right.

Someone dragged something heavy toward him. Z groaned again. The poor old guy had to be in the same fix. A chair thumped across the floorboards to Maverick as a gruff voice snarled, "Here's the old man. They're all yours."

Okay. I'm facing Z. Where's X?

Another chair scraped at Maverick's right. Reardon sat down on it with a growl. "Jes' the way I like 'em. It's time. Git her ass down here."

Maverick strained to detect every nuance and noise he could. *Get who? Leezel? Did Reardon mean to drag her down here, too? Was he angry with her? Or was she part of this? At least he couldn't get at China or Kyrie, thank God.*

Boots thumped out the door and crunched away.

"You got some explaining to do, *Mav*." Reardon tapped Maverick's knee with a hard object.

Gun barrel? Knife handle? Maverick couldn't tell. He could only guess what might happen next and try to remain calm enough to live through it.

"Ya think I oughta shave this old geezer while we got him trussed up like a Thanksgiving turkey?" a guy with a mean edge to his voice asked from Z's direction.

"Go ahead. Might loosen his tongue," Reardon replied.

Maverick cocked his head. By the sounds of it, Z resisted what was being done to him. Knives in play always meant trouble, especially if Reardon's boys really were shaving him. Maverick clenched his biceps and fists to test the restraints, needing to help his friend. No wiggle room at all. Just the sharp cut of damned strong twine on his wrists.

The struggle ceased. A chair thumped back to the floor. "There. That'll teach 'im."

Maverick stilled. He had no way to know if Z was still alive. The old guy didn't make another sound. *Damn it to hell! If they killed him...*

More boots on gravel signaled the biker's return. Lighter footsteps accompanied it. He could picture them as clear as day. Six-inch heels. Red. He held his breath, mindful of the whole *woman scorned* thing. As if things weren't already bad enough, Leezel had arrived. *Shit.*

"Pull up a seat, good lookin'," Reardon offered cheerfully.

Leezel took a seat opposite Reardon, directly at Maverick's left. Instantly her hand was on the inside of his thigh, pinching a line up to his crotch, as if she knew him intimately enough to do that. "I like 'em better like this—all tied up and no way to get away from me."

Maverick swallowed hard. Damn. Reardon wasn't mad at her. No. She just hadn't needed to make her appearance until playtime got serious. *Shit.*

"Yeah. I knew you'd like 'em this way." Reardon chuckled. "You always was a kinky little thing, but I only got the two. Where's crazy Dick?"

"You mean X," Leezel purred. "And I never told you he had a crazy dick. I jes' said it was a teeny little thing, kinda like one of them pencil erasers."

Reardon guffawed while Maverick absorbed that info bite. So, Leezel had some kind of a history with Xavier. Couldn't have ended well. No wonder the poor guy was socially awkward.

She ran a hand alongside Maverick's head and over his mouth. "Kinda hard to talk with this though." She pushed the gag under his chin. "There you go, Mav honey. Now you can breathe. Is that better?"

Still blindfolded, he sucked in a deep breath and prepared for the worst.

"Knock it off, woman. They ain't toys to be played with. They's rats in a trap. That's all."

"Are you sure I can't play with 'em?" Leezel continued stroking Maverick's cheek. "I coulda had me a whole lot of fun with this one."

Maverick leaned away from her wandering fingers. She kept rubbing the cut over his eye.

"Ewww. Damn it, Troy. He's bleeding. You didn't tell me you had a go at him."

"Ya don't think they'd be sitting here if I just asked 'em pretty please, do ya?"

"What... do you want?" Maverick finally got a word in edgewise. He couldn't see yet, but he knew enough. With Reardon on his right, Leezel at his left, and Z out cold in front of him, he was in a bad way. *But where the hell is X?*

"Shut up!" Reardon punched Maverick's jaw, knocking his head sharply toward the left.

A swell of dizziness roared through him. Leezel's concern squealed nearby, but he couldn't make out any words through the ringing in his ears. He shook it off and dropped his chin to his chest to steady himself and catch his breath. Blood filled his mouth. He swallowed it, rather than let Reardon know he had been hurt.

Reardon slapped Maverick's cheeks and face again. "Come on, princess. Don't go passing out just 'cause I hit yer purdy face. We got a long night ahead of us. The party's jes' starting."

"Damn it, Troy. Don't hit him if you still need answers. He ain't no good to us dead."

"He ain't no good to us if you keep playing with him, neither. You keep handling his junk like that and I ain't gonna wait for no answers."

Maverick lifted his head to avoid more face slapping. *God, help me. I'm stuck between two psychos.*

Reardon scraped his chair close enough that Maverick could smell the chew on his breath. "Let's try this again. I only got one question for you anyway, so make it easy on yerself. Where you hiding your girlfriend and the brat?"

Good to know. Z was alive, but where was X?

Leezel's fingers edged up the inside of Maverick's thigh again, drawing closer to his zipper. "Yeah, where are they, Mav? You can tell me," she coaxed while she traced her fingernails along the seam of his jeans. "Where'd Sis and my kid go? You're the only one smart enough to have done something like that. Where'd you hide 'em?"

"They're gone."

"That ain't good enough!" Reardon's fist came down hard on Maverick's knee and now he knew what that other object was. The blade nicked his neck at the same instant. Reardon had a knife. "You got to do better than that, pretty boy. Gone where? Spit."

"Back East." Maverick gasped for enough air to speak. "Virginia."

"Shit, what'd I tell ya? He ain't gonna tell us nuthin'." Reardon shoved Maverick's chair backwards, crushing his arms behind him as he hit the floor. Pain wrenched through his mashed hands and shoulders, but the blow to his head sent a wave of nausea up from his gut. He choked it down, wishing like hell he could see.

Leezel's voice sounded eerily calm overhead. "You might be right. Why don't you work that old guy over a few rounds first? Maverick likes him. Use that new blade I got you. Maybe my boy will be ready to talk then."

Someone's boots hit the floorboards.

"Z... doesn't know anything." Maverick writhed against his restraints. "I did it. It's my fault. Leave him."

"I know I'm gonna enjoy whipping yer ass when I git outta here!" They must have removed Z's gag and he had come up fighting again.

Maverick grimaced at his plucky friend's rage, glad to hear it despite what would happen next. Someone punched and slapped the old fellow. He grunted and groaned.

"God! Let him be!" Maverick yelled, but the beating didn't stop until Z was once again silent.

Reardon kicked Maverick's chair legs. "Your friend ain't saying much. You ready to talk or do we need to open him up and see what makes him tick?"

"I already told you." Maverick bucked against the chair and floor. "Z didn't know anything about it. I did it. China and Kyrie are safe in Virginia where you can't reach them."

"Oh, come on, Mav honey." Leezel knelt beside him and asked in her most syrupy voice, "How could you get them all the way to Virginia? That's what, a dozen states away? What'd you do? Sprout wings and fly them there?"

"Alex Stewart." He blew out a big breath as he struggled to talk. "The man I work for. He helped me get them out of here."

"You believe that?" Reardon asked Leezel. "'Cause it still sounds like he's lying. Looks like it's time for a little game of cut-n-bleed. Let me get the boys and we'll git started."

"No. I don't like that game." Leezel's left hand was once again on Maverick's thigh, her fingers roaming upward. "It's messy. 'Sides, sometimes you cut 'em too deep. I can't play with 'em if they bleed out too fast."

Not unless you know someone who's just plain mean with a knife. Sheriff Hammer's warning came back to Maverick. These two had killed before. They were the ones who'd knifed those men. What'd he say? Cut their balls off and their eyeballs out? Shit. Maverick's throat went dry. It was gonna be a damned long night.

Leezel had her hands on his crotch again and her fingers in his hair. Having sex with men while they bled slowly to death was a whole new low. He'd heard about animals like her before. They scared the hell out of him. For the first time since all that crap went down in Afghanistan, fear shuddered through him. Damn.

She pushed the blindfold off, and Maverick blinked into the face of a coldblooded killer. Her face split with an odd smile, the kind with no joy to back it up. She stared through extra-thick eyelashes and enough eye shadow to give Dracula a run for his money. Her lips were painted the same color as her shoes. And that slinky dress. Damned if Leezel Wolf wasn't dressed to kill.

With an intentionally long, slow lick of her lips, she dipped down to his ear. "You're shaking, Mav," she whispered. "I kinda like it when a big, strong guy like you starts shaking and sweating. Makes me all wet inside. I'll bet you want to play now, don't you?"

"What'd you say to him?" Reardon demanded. "What's he telling you?"

Leezel breathed out a big sigh. "Oh, nothing. Maybe you oughta give me a few minutes alone with—"

"Enough!" Reardon jerked her off her feet. "You had your chance to loosen his tongue; now it's my turn."

"All right. All right. Hell, Troy. Don't get yerself all worked up." She sidled up to Reardon, her hands all over his chest and up his neck. "You know I love you, don't you?"

He bent one elbow around her neck and jerked her into his face. Maverick looked away at the wet kiss. God. Reardon had to be twenty years older than Leezel. Twenty years of damned tough riding that had made him uglier than sin.

When he released her, she glanced down at the man at her feet. "I do kinda like the chair and rope thing you did though. Look at him. Mav can't fight back with his arms trapped behind his back like they are. Makes him look all sorts a weak and helpless for a change, don't it?"

"He don't look so tough, that's for sure." Reardon kicked him in the side.

Maverick gasped as the shockwave reverberated through his whole body. He forced himself to focus. His head pounded and he would be unconscious before long, if Reardon didn't kill him first. He had to make his last few seconds count.

"Him laying there on his back like that makes me feel all sorts a powerful and, I don't know, kinda hot. You know what I mean, Troy?" She gave Reardon an eyeful with one of her chest jiggles. "I mean, here I am standing over a damned fine piece of male meat. I could do anything to this drifter that I wanted, couldn't I? Who'd care? Who'd even know? He ain't nobody."

Reardon grabbed her up tight against him, his breath ragged and angry. He clenched the cheeks of her ass with his fingernails. "What'd I tell you? You better knock it off, woman."

"Why a course, Troy honey." She knew how to pour it on thick and sweet. "Think about it, though. You and me could be having us a good time while we make him watch. You wanna get kinky with me?"

Reardon face lit up. "'S why I love you, little girl. You're as sick as they come."

She clutched his head and planted another disgusting, wet kiss on his ugly mouth. Reardon moaned, and Maverick closed his eyes, sickened that he might be forced to watch something as ugly as Reardon screwing Leezel while he bled out at their feet.

"Hey, chief," one of Reardon's boys called through the open bunkhouse door. "We got trouble. Spike says Hammer's headed this way."

About damned time!

Leezel separated herself from Reardon's mouth, her fingers still fluttering on his chest. "Troy, honey. Hurry. I heard talk Hammer's been asking lots of questions at the hospital, too. If Mav ain't gonna talk, burn him. Catch X 'fore he gets away. He ain't smart enough to git too far."

"Then let's get the hell outta here." Reardon dragged her out the door behind him. "Come on, guys. My old lady says light 'em up. The ranch house, too. Let's give Hammer a real warm welcome."

God! Where the hell is X?

Maverick stopped worrying when the smell of gasoline reached his nose. Reardon guffawed at the door over something one of his biker buddies said. A roar went up outside the bunkhouse. Reardon's voice rose above the noise. "It'll go up in a sheet of flames, jes' like the barn did. Don't need to waste the gas—"

Another round of raucous laughter drowned out Reardon's last words.

"Wait!" Leezel's voice rose above the enthusiastic howls. "Don't light the match yet. Just one more teensy, little thing I gotta do before you guys have your fun. Okay?"

"Damn it, woman," Reardon growled. "You drive me crazy with all yer games. Git it done before I burn yer ass, too."

"Well, okay, sweet thing. If you say so." She giggled at the doorway, looking over her shoulder. "Be right back."

Reardon's slapped her ass so hard she nearly tripped off her heels. "And that dress better not be hiked up to yer tits when you're done if you know what's good for you."

Another shudder ripped up Maverick's back. He sucked in a deep breath and sent his heart flying to China's across the miles. *I love you, baby. Know that.*

Leezel dropped to her knees beside him.

A guy had no choice but to look at her boobs, shoved in his face like they were. He swallowed hard and faced the crazy bitch, hoping against hope she had an ounce of China's kindness buried somewhere under that stupid dress.

No way in hell. Dark, black eyes stared down at him. Not a hint of goodness showed through the void between her lashes. Goodness had no chance against the evil in her soul.

"I jes' can't resist you, Mav honey." She leaned into him and took his head in both of her hands. This was no loving caress. She dug all eight fingernails into his scalp, her thumbnails beneath his cheekbone. She meant to draw blood, her eyes wide and full of nothing but animal lust. She licked her lips. "I gotta do this 'fore you're roasted, cuz you know. I don't like fried chicken."

"Untie me. Get us outta—"

"Oh no, I can't let you go. I only came for this." She covered his mouth with hers, and pushed her tongue past his bloodied lips. Deepening the assault, she moaned like this was in some way a moment of passion.

Nose to nose, he stared into her bright eyes, bright with an emotion he had never seen this close and personal before. Leezel was stone, cold insane. She meant to kill him and she meant to laugh when she did it. Maverick prepared mentally to die with some semblance of honor and dignity.

Leezel giggled. She ended the violation of his mouth with her teeth clamped on his lower lip as if this was an exciting part of the game. Then she made it worse. She hiked that damned dress up over her bare ass and straddled him.

He growled, wishing she would get the hell off of him and do without the torture he knew was coming his way, if not from her then surely when Reardon caught her in the act.

She ground her core against his zipper and growled, too. The damned lunatic grinned—just before she bit through his lower lip.

Muscle crunched. Flesh tore. He couldn't struggle or pull away. It was all he could do to hold still and not scream in her mouth. His eyes watered. Every muscle shook at the assault. *Enough already!*

She bit harder. And harder. When she let go and leaned back, his blood dripped from her lips. Leezel closed her eyes with a throaty moan. "Mmm, yum. You taste real good, Mav."

"You're insane."

She dabbed the blood on her chin with the tips of her fingers. Each bloodied digit went into her mouth one at a time, her eyes closed and a stupid look on her face. "Hmm. Yes. You could say I'm certifiable."

He squeezed his eyes shut. "God, get me the hell out of here!"

"Sh-h-h-h-h. Quiet now. You don't want Troy back in here, do you?" She pushed slowly back to her feet, still sucking her fingers and thumbs after she pulled her dress down and covered herself. "Y. G. M. M. W. I. G. I can promise you that."

"I'm what?" Damn her and her asinine word games. He'd never asked what she meant last time and he wasn't sure he cared now.

Leezel blew a kiss down at him. "You're gonna miss me when I'm gone, Mav honey. That's all it means. Soon as you start burning. You know you will. You'll smell that hot body of yours on fire, and you'll wish you'd loved me."

"Never. I love China." Leezel needed to get that through her thick skull. "Never you."

The demonic woman in front of him seemed to grow taller with rage, her eyes more deadly. The kinky seductress was gone. Only the bloodthirsty murderess remained. "I got news for you, cowboy. It don't matter what you say. By the time Sis hears about this little barbeque, I'll be gone, and you won't be nothing but ash and cinders. She'll never know if you loved her or not, will she?"

Leezel slammed the bunkhouse door so hard the windows rattled behind her.

Maverick sank back against the floor, shaking with pain and adrenaline, the blood from his torn lip pouring down his neck. He swallowed hard and summoned his woman into his mind. Anchoring her deep in his heart, he breathed, "You're wrong, bitch. China already knows."

Chapter Twenty-Nine

"What's wrong?" Kelsey asked.

China sat fidgeting at the edge of her bed. "Has anyone heard from Maverick yet?"

"He's called every morning." Kelsey came to her side. "He knows you're doing better, but he doesn't know you're awake yet. Do you want to call and tell him?"

"Yes, please." China pushed a hand through her hair. Maybe talking with Maverick would calm the butterflies in her stomach.

"Here." Kelsey dialed the number on her cell phone and came to sit on the edge of her bed. "It's ringing. He'll be happy to hear from you."

China held the phone to her ear. Wyoming was two hours earlier. Shivers of excitement tingled down her arms. She couldn't wait to hear his voice, but the phone just rang. Her hopes dashed, she handed the phone back.

"He's not answering?" Kelsey's brows furrowed. She checked the number. "That's odd. He said he would keep it with him at all times."

Unease skated over China's shoulders. "I have a bad feeling. Something's wrong."

"We'll try him again in a few minutes. Do you want to sit on the porch while we wait? It's a nice night."

But China's mind had flown to Wyoming. Maverick would be in the bunkhouse by now, tired from another hard day's work. The man had probably finished the barn. Single-handedly. That was the kind of work ethic he had. Those back muscles would be sore. He might need a massage. Maybe a hot shower which he wouldn't be taking alone. Heat pooled in the pit of her stomach at the other things he might need.

"China?" Kelsey still waited for an answer.

"Umm, what? The porch. Yes, that would be nice."

"Before we go, there's something I need to tell you."

Oh, oh. What now?

"I didn't want to say anything with the guys around, but you need to know that Maverick was worried that you might have been, umm—" Kelsey stalled, biting her lip. "He was afraid that while you were out of it that maybe your sister's boyfriend might have, umm..."

"That bastard Reardon wouldn't," China hissed. "Maverick was afraid I'd been assaulted while I was unconscious? Is that what you're trying to tell me?"

Kelsey nodded quickly. "But you weren't. Dr. Jenkins gave you a thorough physical. You're clean. There was none."

China's heart stopped. In her wildest fears of Reardon, she had never suspected—that. Tears brimmed all over again. Her entire body cringed at the thought of him touching her. *Holy smokes. He could've done anything he wanted with me. To me. I never would have known.*

Kelsey wrapped her arm around China's shoulders and drew her in tight. "I'm sorry. You've been through so much, honey, but when he rescued you, you were in nothing but a ratty T-shirt. You were dehydrated and dirty. He just wanted you taken care of in all possible ways."

"No, that's okay." China choked on a sob, trying like hell to catch her balance again. Leezel's and Reardon's actions appalled her at every turn. "Did Dr. Jenkins check Kyrie?"

"Do you think she should?"

"Yes. Maybe. I just don't know anymore."

"Let's talk with Kyrie first, okay? She's old enough. She'll tell you if he's ever touched her inappropriately."

China nodded. Kelsey had a calming way about her, but—*so help me God. If he laid one finger on Kyrie, I'll kill him.*

"Let's think positive," Kelsey urged as she helped China into the wheelchair. "Alex has a saying. Don't borrow trouble. It'll show up soon enough."

China wanted to believe, but trouble had been showing up pretty damned regularly in Wyoming the past few weeks.

She had showered earlier and changed into casual active-wear instead of her open-backed hospital gown. Dr. Jenkins had already visited, removed the IV and catheter and pronounced her not exactly well, but doing much better considering all she had been through. The good doctor prescribed rest, but China was disgusted being sick and weak. She needed to be with her kids again. And Maverick.

"Holy smokes," she muttered as Kelsey helped her transfer to the wheelchair. "I feel like an old woman."

"I know what you mean. I'm not a big fan of wheelchairs myself." Kelsey wheeled China past the open bedroom where Kyrie lay sound asleep, and into the living room where Gabe snored lightly from the couch. A basketball game droned on the big screen.

Taylor sat engrossed at the desk, the muted light from a laptop computer shining on his face. He looked up in surprise when the women appeared just above his monitor. He shut the laptop. "You two are up late. What's up?"

"China can't sleep so we're headed for the porch for a midnight chat. Want to join us?"

"Sure." Taylor scrambled to hold the door while Kelsey maneuvered the chair outside. "Feel like sitting in something besides that wheelchair for a change? I could help you into the swing."

"Please." China rose unsteadily to her feet while Taylor eased one arm around her waist and lifted her up from the chair. She transferred to the wooden porch swing with a great feeling of accomplishment, but an unexplainable bad feeling still niggled at the back of her memory. "I don't know why, but I don't ever want to sit in that thing again."

"You had bedsores when you got here," Kelsey told her gently. "They probably left you sitting in the wheelchair until Maverick came for you."

"You ladies need something to drink?" Taylor offered. "I've got lemonade, beer, bottled water and—"

"I'd die for a beer." China embarrassed herself when she blurted it right out. "Join me?"

"You bet. I think you can have one beer with your meds. How about you, Kelsey?"

"Sure. It's late enough." Kelsey turned with a sheepish smile to China. "Alex says I'm a lightweight when it comes to beer. It puts me to sleep."

Taylor returned with three ice-cold bottles and glasses. He pulled another chair near to the swing and sat opposite them. After he twisted the bottle tops off, he handed the ladies their drinks, his dark eyes probing from Kelsey to China. "Did I miss anything?"

"Just girl talk," Kelsey said.

China couldn't look him in the eye. She took a bottle, and an extra-long swallow, afraid that her teary eyes would give her away. Taylor didn't need a weeping woman on his hands again.

She should be happy. At least, happier. The fenced yard of what Gabe and Taylor called the safe house looked like any other on the street, except for the brand new swing set in the front lawn. Another agent, Mark Houston, had dropped by earlier with his two little girls, JayJay and Faith. Kyrie played to her heart's content with her new girlfriends and pitched a fuss when they had to leave. It made China smile to hear the high stakes bargaining of a five-year-old when her newly adopted Uncle Taylor bribed her to come indoors for bedtime.

"Uh uh. I ain't gonna. I don't wanna," she had answered from her swing, her head tipped back and her legs extended as she flew for the first time in her life. "I yikes ta swing."

"Oh, yes. You have to come in, little girl. It's time for a story."

"But I don't wanna story. I is pwaying."

"Not even from your very own storybook?"

"No. I wanna pway." She had leaned so far back that her hair swept the grass beneath the swing. "Come pway wiff me."

"Well, I guess I'll have to eat the chocolate chip cookies Aunt Kelsey made all by myself then."

"Huh?"

"Hey. Did you know Uncle Gabe bought chocolate milk for a special little girl?"

"Me?"

Kyrie's stubbornness crumbled. That hit the spot too, just knowing her niece acted like a normal five-year-old for a change. Everywhere she turned, the little gal had an adoring uncle who spoiled her rotten.

Yes, China should be a lot happier. But she wasn't. Her new reality included a psychotic sister who meant to destroy all China held dear.

"It's fairly warm tonight." Kelsey poured a small portion of her beer into a glass and daintily sipped through the froth. She was so refined and genteel, China's exact opposite.

"So why can't you sleep, Miss Wolf?" Taylor eyed her intently. "Are you feeling okay?"

"You've got to stop calling me that. It's so formal. China, please." She smoothed the condensation off the long neck of her bottle, her mind a couple thousand miles away. "I can't shake this edgy feeling."

Taylor planted his bottle on his knee and studied her with that same probing look. He was the ultimate tall, dark, and handsome Hollywood stereotype, only with a serious streak that rarely allowed a smile. She estimated him to be the same age as Maverick, maybe mid to late-twenties. Like her. In the dim porch light, he sat relaxed yet still alert, his shoulders back but his eyes constantly searching their surroundings. "What kind of edgy feeling? Explain it to me. Is it like nausea? Do you feel like you're going to pass out?"

"No, it's different. It's more like... have you ever been in a tornado?"

He shook his head. "Can't say that I have."

She looked to the darkening western sky. "Maybe I'm just anxious because I want to be home."

"That stands to reason," Kelsey offered. "You've been through a lot."

Taylor leaned forward, still probing. "Maybe someone is trying to tell you something. My grandfather believes our feelings of unease are messages sent to us from our ancestors." Taylor's voice turned reverent. "We must learn to listen when they speak."

"How do I do that?" China rubbed the shiver of his words off her arms. "I feel like something evil is coming for me." *Or Maverick.*

Taylor's dark eyes pierced hers. "In the old times, my ancestors used medicinal plants to achieve an altered state where they believed our ancestors could communicate with them. But that isn't our way anymore. My wife has taught me how to use relaxation instead. I would be pleased to show you a technique I've learned if you aren't too tired."

China nodded. "Show me."

He set his beer to the floor near the leg of his chair and dropped to one knee at her feet. "May I hold your hands?"

She nodded. She trusted this gentle Native American, simply because Maverick did.

Taylor accepted her hands into his, her fingers nestled into his palms and his thumbs firmly fastened over the tops of her hands. "China Wolf. You are named after a fearless hunter, as am I. Fearless hunters stand apart from the world. We don't choose to follow the flocks of deer and sheep, and because we don't, our path isn't easy. We walk lonely roads. We climb higher mountains. We soar above and beyond the crowd."

She peered into the depths of his dark eyes. Something about them reminded her of Maverick. It wasn't the color though. Maverick's were lighter brown, like coffee. Taylor's were nearly black. It wasn't the angles of his handsome face or the light coppery tone of his skin, either. He and Maverick shared a quality she couldn't yet pin down, but it glowed deep in the recesses of his pupils. Like an ember that could flame to life at any moment. Like a hurt that lingered, unhealed and unforgotten.

"If you allow me, I'll take you on a journey." Taylor took another deep breath. "Before we begin, you must open your mind to the universe. Close your eyes and see that all things are for your good. Know that all blessings are poured out upon you. Believe that all creation was created for you and you alone."

She closed her eyes and pictured the great night sky of Wyoming, full of stars, galaxies and a crescent moon. With the Milky Way sprinkled high above her, she stood alone in the universe, yet not alone at the same time. The vast night sky swirled around her. Crisp mountain air feathered her cheek with kisses. Dew settled lightly on her face. A hoot owl hooted from the nearby pines. All the elements of her rugged mountain home were very much with her.

"Give up all your fears and worries, China." Taylor gripped her hands tighter. "Give up all of your strength, from the power resting at the crown of your head to the energy stored in the soles of your feet. Release it. Let it go. Relax."

She clenched his hands in return and took a deep, cleansing breath.

"All, China Wolf," he commanded. "Every last stress. Everything you feel and more."

She took another deep breath and slowly released it, trying to do as he ordered, but the more she tried, the harder he gripped her hands and the tighter her muscles contracted.

From out of the dark Wyoming sky in her mind, a herd of magnificent Percherons galloped toward her. Dust lifted around them from their journey, but not a sound did they make. Not a nicker, grunt or footfall. *Ghosts.* The thought popped into her mind. These magnificent creatures were the ancestors of her horses. Her dreams. Her family.

"All of it, China Wolf." Taylor's voice turned hoarse. He gripped her hands tighter still.

He squeezed so hard she didn't think she could stand it much longer. Biting her lip in one last effort to relax, she envisioned a shooting star, flung across the Wyoming heavens in an arc of light.

Just as the image of the star faded in her mind, Taylor released her hands. A sensation of warmth prickled up from her bare toes all the way to her scalp. Her body relaxed like it had never relaxed before. Her shoulders, biceps, abs, and every other muscle down to her feet rippled as the edgy feeling diminished. Every tightened muscle let go of the angst she didn't know she had been holding.

The cool Virginian air smelled sweeter. She leaned back into the swing, needing the support of its wooden slats. Maverick's handsome face came easily to mind, his eyes glistening from the depths of humility. His reticent smile, the one he had given her that day on the hill when he had asked if she trusted him. He spoke to her again. "I love you, China Wolf. Know that."

She heard his voice as surely as if he had been standing in front of her. *I do.*

China opened her eyes to Taylor still kneeling at her feet, his dark eyes fierce and kind. She had seen that look before, up high on a Wyoming hillside when the man who loved her had shielded her from a sniper's bullet. In her yard when that same man backed down a vicious biker gang. That morning when he wept in Star's neck.

A knowing look lighted Taylor's face, a sign of recognition from one kindred spirit to another. "You saw him, didn't you?"

She nodded, finally content, her body relaxed. "I did."

"He spoke to you."

The unease she had felt earlier returned with a vengeance. China knew then what quality these two warriors shared.

They'd both seen death, and Maverick was seeing it again. Now.

She jumped to her feet. "He's in pain. Maverick's in trouble. Help him, Taylor. You have to help him!"

Chapter Thirty

Reardon was right.

The bunkhouse went up in a sheet of flame. The front window shattered inward, probably because one of the bikers threw something through it. Maverick coughed and tried like hell to see Z through the smoke. He had seconds before the whole place went up. He had to save his friend.

With a puff of white smoke, a ribbon of fire materialized along the lower edge of the front wall. Flames already engulfed the tinder dry roof overhead. Melting shingles dripped tentacles of fiery hot tar to the floor. So far he had been spared, but it wouldn't take long before one drip of tar would hit him or the roof would collapse. He had minutes to live. Seconds maybe.

And he was still tied tightly to the chair.

He thrashed his body back and forth until the chair turned on its side and took him with it. At last he caught sight of Z sagging in the other chair, his head to his chest, still gagged and blindfolded. Heat blistered Maverick's arms and hands from the spreading flames on the floor, but there was no other way. With jaws clenched tight and a gut full of old-fashioned USMC bullheadedness, he shoved his hands into the flames behind him. It hurt. He shuddered and endured the red-hot tongues devouring his skin. At last, the twine gave way. *Holy hell.*

He strained against the final shred of it imbedded in his blistered skin until it snapped. Free at last. Kind of. Nanoseconds counted now.

He dragged himself and the chair to the kitchen counter, jerked the cabinet drawer open, and felt around until his fingers skimmed a steak knife. He cut the twine off his legs and rolled to his feet. *I have got to get Z out of here!*

But the man was unconscious deadweight. Maverick hurried, his heart climbing out of his chest. He cut Z free and dragged him to the rear bunkhouse wall. To the back window. It would be tough, but there was no other way out.

The roof groaned. Foul-smelling, acrid smoke billowed down from the rafters. Tongues of flame materialized and vanished, only to reappear as clumps of tar melted and dripped.

Time was gone.

Maverick kept going. He eased Z to the back wall, then used his elbow to break the window. Choking from the bitter fumes, he grabbed his leather jacket and covered the jagged windowpane. The rafters groaned. So did Maverick, every last muscle on fire with the need to *get the hell out of there!*

He grunted Z over the ledge and shoved him outside. The roof sagged then—Whoosh! It collapsed and pulled the rafters with it. Just in time. Maverick dove into the night, shielding his face with his arms. He rolled to his back and landed beside Z. For a second, he just lay there and stared at the stars overhead, gulping in fresh air and damned surprised to be alive.

Breathing hurt. Hell, everything hurt. Z moaned beside him, his face bloodied and battered, no thanks to Reardon's goons. But alive.

No time to rest. Maverick grunted up from the ground and dragged Zeke toward the encroaching shrubbery and quakies behind the machine shed. He would've made it, but like the asshat that he was, Reardon rounded the burning bunkhouse with his zipper undone. The moron chose the only corner of the structure not engulfed in flames to pee on.

With his hand in his pants, he caught sight of Maverick. "Boys! Git back here! He's getting away!"

A roar went up, but Reardon was already in pursuit.

Leezel cleared the corner of the bunkhouse, shrieking, "Kill him! Burn him!"

Out of sheer dumb luck, Maverick dropped Z in time to land a solid right to Reardon's left jaw. Not good enough. The biker hadn't just had the crap beat out of him. His hands weren't burned and blistered. He didn't wobble, much less go down. Instead, he hauled back and delivered a suffocating punch dead center to Maverick's chest.

Maverick dropped to his butt, fighting for air.

BOOM! A gunshot shattered the night.

Maverick froze, waiting for the round with his name to release him from this hellish nightmare. *Almost* thankful the pain would be over. *Almost* glad he would get to see Darrell again. Almost just wasn't good enough, damn it. Seeing Darrell meant not seeing China. Ever again.

The bullet never came. He wasn't hit. All bikers had stopped dead in their tracks, though. All except Reardon. The bastard bobbed like a prizefighter, daring Maverick to get on his feet again. Dumb move or not, Maverick did.

Reardon zeroed in on him, this time with a roundhouse kick that sent him sprawling.

Shit. Maverick dropped face down in the dirt, still gasping for air, spitting blood and bone-weary as hell. His head pounded like a mother. Shadows danced around him in orange-tinted double vision. Out of all the smoke and carnage, trotted the snowy-white ghost of Gorgeous. Time seemed to move in slow motion with the swirl of her mane and tail.

The gentle beast that had claimed his heart the moment she had laid eyes on him came to him now. He rolled to his back, on his way out of this life for certain if he was seeing ghosts. She curled one front leg into a bow and dipped her long face into his chest.

There was no sudden burst of power. No magic shield. She hadn't brought anything but the certainty they'd known each other in some different lifetime. Just as he lifted his blood-smeared fingers to touch her velvety nose, her death screams rang in his ears again. The lovely vision evaporated.

He was back in Reardon's version of Hell.

Maverick rolled to his hands and knees. He was hurt. He might be dying, but he had one thing to do before he died. *Make Reardon pay for killing Gorgeous and her baby.*

Reardon feinted close and danced back, a shitty grin on his face. The bastard honestly considered this fight won and over. *No way.*

Maverick staggered to his feet, his tortured vision providing multiple opponents instead of one. Reardon might just be right. *They's rats in the trap is all.* As if to prove his point, he closed in for the kill.

But the memory of Gorgeous persevered. Maverick straight-armed Reardon and landed a solid right. He got in a lucky left. *Take that, you sonofabitch.*

Reardon dropped to one knee, shook the blood off his lip and looked twice at his nearly-dead opponent. He jumped to his feet and charged. "You're going down!"

After a half-dozen more body blows, Maverick kissed the dirt again. He couldn't understand why Reardon's buddies hadn't already kicked the shit out of him. They were still out there, but they held back. They watched. *Why?*

He lifted his heavy, battered head and squinted into the dark. Who else was out there? Who was so powerful they were able to keep Death and the chicken shit *Kings and Kreepers* at bay?

Kyrie's sad blue eyes peered out of the smoky darkness. *Does you yike me?*

Maverick blinked hard. Her sweet eyes vanished. Only the truth remained. *God yes, I like you, Kyrie. Actually, I love you, sweetheart.*

He shook his head to clear his vision and gathered what was left of his strength. Maverick staggered to his feet. One last time. No child should have to live in fear. Reardon shouldn't have hurt her. He had to—HAD TO—pay.

Reardon dodged in between Maverick's weak attempts to protect his face with his upraised fists. He landed a double tap to Maverick's chin. One to his solar plexus. Chest. Chest. Chest.

Somehow in the midst of the pummeling, Maverick landed a blow. Reardon's chin lifted skyward. Left him stunned and reeling. His split lip bled.

Unfortunately, the impact had a rebound effect. Maverick dropped to his butt, surprised that even when he had won, he lost. *Shit. I'm not gonna win this.*

Out of the fog in his throbbing head, between the jackhammering beats of his heart, China's smile reached out to him. His elfin princess. The woman who'd shown him that life was still good after incredible loss. That life was worth living.

Her black hair blended with Star's mane in the wind of their uphill charge, both flying in the wild Wyoming sky, happy and carefree. *Then.*

The last time he'd seen her, she'd been near death. Reardon and Leezel did that. They'd hurt everyone and everything he loved. They'd meant to kill China.

Never again.

With his last ounce of strength and more courage than brains, Maverick swayed to his feet for what would very likely be the last time. A guy doesn't get this many last chances.

He could barely see through the sweat and blood coursing down his face, but one thing was sure. He would go down fighting for the woman he loved. He squared his shoulders and posted his feet while dancing, dumbass Reardon closed in for the kill.

"Say your prayers, dirt bag." Tough Guy spat to the side and charged, his right fist jabbing while his left covered his chin.

Maverick caught him under that supposedly protected chin, and for once, Maverick didn't fall down.

Reardon's head jerked back. Surprise glinted along with the reflection of the fire in his dark eyes, but he didn't go down, either.

Maverick took a step forward and miraculously dodged Reardon's left hook. He took another step into his enemy's comfort zone. He lashed out in a lightning strike that knocked Reardon's head back again. And again. Maverick stayed on his feet this time, too. *Now who's dancing, punk?*

Reardon recovered, but worry lines furrowed his brow. He charged, his lips twisted with fury.

Maverick cocked back with his fisted hammer.

In that incredibly long instant between fist and face, time paused. Z whispered, *Miss China needs ya, son. You're the only one can do what needs getting done.*

Maverick glanced past Reardon's shoulder to where Z lay on the ground. Still out cold. He hadn't said a word. Couldn't have if he wanted to. Didn't really need to. Maverick caught the message on the blistering wind.

There ain't but one thing ta do when you fall off a horse. You gots to pick yer butt outta the dirt. You gots to cinch yer saddle up. You gots to climb back on that horse and kick ass.

Maverick sucked in a deep breath of hellfire and righteous rage. Blood flooded the chambers of his heart with enough oxygen to get the job done.

The power of a damned good man rippled down his spine. Then another, because you know what? *Marine's don't fucking quit!* USMC Corporal Maverick Carson—the real Maverick Carson—showed up for the fight. He had brought his second wind, too.

Maverick raised his head just a little higher. He thumbed his nose and shifted his weight. Planted his feet. The end had come. He might die at the hands of Reardon's bullyboys when the fight was over, but by heaven and all that was holy, Reardon would go down first.

Right on cue, Reardon's lip lifted into a sneer.

Maverick charged. He landed a one-two punch that felt damned good when it connected with Reardon's ugly jaw. It felt so good Maverick did it again. And again.

Something in Reardon's ugly face crunched. His skull bounced backward. An arc of spit and blood went flying. A tooth. Tough Guy stopped dead in his tracks. Bewilderment glazed his eyes. He dropped his guard.

Maverick offered no quarter. He pressed forward with a lightning volley to Reardon's midsection. Three, four, five times Maverick hit, and he hit him hard.

Reardon never even lifted his hands to protect his face. When the volley ended, he sagged to his knees. Drool dripped off his lip. Enlightenment had arrived.

Anger propelled Maverick forward for the final blow.

Red and blue flashing lights colored Reardon's surprised face as Maverick hit him one last sonofabitchin' time. The police had finally arrived.

Tough Guy dropped like a ton of shit and—*whoosh!* The finale. The bunkhouse walls caved in with a resounding crash of cinders and sparks. The fight was over.

Maverick fell to his hands and knees in the middle of a flaming fireworks show. Spitting blood. Drenched in smoke and sweat. Nothing left to give. Righteous anger could only stoke a man's strength for so long before reality stepped into the ring and announced the real winner. He bowed his head and waited. If the police weren't quick enough, Reardon's biker buddies would kick him to death.

With a garbled prayer to the wind, he bowed his face to the dirt. *God. Tell China I love her. Let her be sure. Let her be happy.*

But nothing happened. He peered up through his mauled eyelids. Several sheriff cruiser were parked haphazardly throughout the yard. A swarm of police had the bikers on the ground. All of them. *God. Miracles do still happen.*

But damned if it wasn't X standing across the yard waving like a little kid in his overalls, with nothing but pride in his eyes—and ol' man Wolf's lever-action Henry rifle on his hip. He gave Maverick a face-splitting grin and a thumbs-up.

So. It was X all along. He was the one who had held Reardon's pack of bloodthirsty bikers at bay. With as much of a smile as he could muster, Maverick offered the hero of the night, his best bud, X, a quick two-fingered salute.

"Xavier. My man. Hey," he muttered hoarsely.

The war was won. Maverick eased his cheek to the ground and collapsed.

Chapter Thirty-One

"Is he okay?" China asked. "Have you heard?"

Taylor held one finger up, his cell phone tight to his ear. "Yes, Boss. Understood. I'll tell her."

She could hardly wait for him to pocket his phone. "Well?"

"He's good. He's got a few things to tie up before he'll be back in town."

"But I had the strongest impression that he was dying. Is he okay?"

Taylor huffed. "He is now. Reardon burned the bunkhouse last night, but everyone got out alive."

China ground her teeth. *I knew it.* "My sister's a murderer," she whispered the words out loud for the first time. "So is Reardon."

Kelsey ducked her head into China's and hugged her tight. "We can't choose our family, and even when we can, sometimes we still make mistakes. Sometimes we marry them."

After a restless night of waiting for Alex to call, they sat together on the porch watching Kyrie with Kelsey's ten-month-old daughter, Lexie. Big girl Kyrie hovered over her newest girlfriend. Lexie wasn't walking much yet, but every time she tried to stand, Kyrie picked her up by her armpits to help her.

"But she had everything. Leezel was always prettier and smarter than me. She could've done anything with her life."

"Sounds like she made her choice." Kelsey blew out a big sigh. "That's the biggest lesson I've learned. When I think I'm the only one with problems, I look at Alex and the men and women he leads. They've all suffered in one way or the other, but they're all going strong."

Taylor nodded and excused himself.

China had grown close to Kelsey in the short time they'd been together. Today, like two old girlfriends, they'd gone clothes shopping. China finally felt normal in denim jeans and a button-up blouse. She had bought new boots, but wore the simple penny loafers she'd also selected.

"But then someone special comes along and makes everything you've suffered worthwhile, huh?"

China caught her friend's smile. "You mean Maverick, don't you?"

"Who else?"

"He did kind of drop out of the sky." China remembered the day of the slide. "I didn't think he would stay. He was always looking down the road like he had somewhere else to be. Like he wanted to leave."

"What changed?"

"I don't know. It just seemed he was always there when I needed him. He helped me when Star got caught in the slide, then he showed up in the middle of Reardon's biker club ransacking my yard. Then the fire. I would've lost all my horses if he hadn't been there. Maybe more."

"He's been busy," Kelsey replied somberly.

Now it was China's turn to be quiet. She used to feel bad for her sister. As angry as Leezel could make her, China always hoped she would change, that maybe she'd see the light of her selfish ways and decide to be a real mother. Instead, Leezel had chosen booze, drugs, sex, and crazy over her beautiful baby girl. The new boots she'd bought reminded her of the work ahead, kicking Leezel's ass out of Kyrie's life once and for all.

"Alex is here." Kelsey interrupted China's dark thoughts as a black pick-up rumbled up to the curb. Kelsey all but flew off the porch to welcome him. He grabbed her and lifted her over his head as if she were a child. China had only to look at the light on his ruggedly handsome face to recognize true love. This man had it bad for his wife.

China couldn't help but like him. Alex Stewart had a heart as big as the Wyoming sky. He had literally opened his wallet without a second thought of being repaid, and even now kept her and Kyrie under his protective care.

He kissed Kelsey and set her back to her feet. The minute he spied Lexie, his face lit with a grin. He picked her up and tossed her into the air. Lexie giggled as she fell into his arms, not alarmed at all. Alex blew a raspberry into her neck before he launched her again.

Kyrie stood watching Lexie sail up and fall down, her little fingers clenched. She beamed and wiggled her little backside when the baby fell laughing into her father's arms a second time. Excitement got the best of her. "Me too! Me too!"

Alex handed Lexie off to Kelsey with a big smile and lifted Kyrie into his arms. He positioned one hand under her backside, the other under her arm. "Are you ready for a ride to the moon?" he teased.

"Uh huh," she answered quickly, but China saw the flash of worry crease her brow before Alex launched her. Up she went. China's heart leapt to her throat, but Kyrie giggled as he caught the happiest little girl on the planet.

China's eyes brimmed over. The happy scene played havoc with her tender heart. Poor Kyrie craved male attention. She had latched onto Taylor and Gabe the same as she had with Maverick. Now Alex. It almost hurt to watch. All that child wanted was a father. A good father.

"One more time?" Alex asked once she was safe in his hands again.

"Yeah!" She bounced on his arm, so he swung her a little higher this time, and she fell giggling even more. When he set her on her feet, she ran to the porch and buried her out-of-breath body against China. "I gonna marry Unca Awex," she whispered, her little heart pumping hard.

China couldn't help but chuckle while she gathered Kyrie onto the swing beside her. "You can't marry every man you meet."

"Uh huh. I kin, too." Kyrie glanced shyly at her newest beau. "He nice 'n he cute."

Kyrie had a little girl's crush on Alex. Well, good for her. Alex seemed like a good man to have a crush on. Of course there was also Taylor, Gabe, and Maverick, and heaven forbid any other guy who showed up while Kyrie was in the marrying phase of childhood.

Taylor and Gabe joined the group on the porch while Kelsey and Alex climbed the stairs with Lexie. He plopped Lexie into Kyrie's lap and immediately she hugged the baby, her blue eyes shining up at her new beau.

"Hang on tight, okay?" he told her. "Lexie's not a big girl like you. She might fall."

China had to chuckle. Kyrie sat there with both arms around Lexie and all her favorite guys standing with her, so enamored she couldn't speak. All she could do was scrunch her shoulders. Not for a second did she take her eyes off Alex.

"How's work?" Alex asked his agents.

"Best job you ever gave me, Boss." Gabe pulled up the nearby bench and made himself comfortable, his arm extended along the back of it. "You staying for dinner? Taylor made enchiladas."

"Chicken?" Alex asked with interest.

"You bet. With sour cream and green chilies."

Alex's blue eyes scrolled over China before he answered. "Not tonight. Thought I'd show Miss Wolf something besides the city, maybe take her out to the Shenandoah."

A look passed between the men. Taylor scratched his jaw. "Everything went as planned?"

"Couldn't be better. The deal is signed, sealed, and delivered." Alex tapped Kyrie on her upturned nose with his index finger and she blushed.

"That happened fast," Gabe said.

China didn't have a clue what they were talking about. She enjoyed watching her niece. Kyrie positively glowed with all this male attention.

Alex shrugged indifferently. "You guys are invited to join us if you're not too busy."

Gabe and Taylor high-fived each other like a couple of teenage boys out of school for the summer. "Never too busy for you, Boss."

"Good. We'll take the Escalade."

China watched the easy camaraderie of these ex-military men. They'd all been to war, they'd all seen too much, but right then they looked like three boys with a secret.

Kelsey's arm around her shoulder reminded China she was part of this happy family, too.

"Do you get the feeling they're not telling us everything?" China asked quietly.

Kelsey beamed. "Welcome to my world."

The trip to the Shenandoah was filled with beautiful scenery and better conversation. Kelsey and Alex chatted in the front seat like the two old married folks they were. China sat between Gabe and Taylor in the middle seat while Kyrie's booster seat and Lexie's car seat had been placed in the rear. In no time at all, both little girls were sound asleep while the adults talked.

Taylor and Gabe played off each other as tour guides, filling China in on the Civil War sites in the area. One minute she was listening to the heroic anecdotes of Gettysburg, and the next, the strategy behind Bull Run.

At last Alex pulled off the freeway and proceeded along a frontage road bordered by a green pasture lined with a white post fence. They drove for a few miles before he turned onto a winding gravel driveway.

China felt a prickle of anticipation when he parked the Escalade in front of a spacious colonial home, complete with four stately columns along the front of the house. Magnolia trees bordered the drive. Cherry trees and redbuds in blossom added all shades of pinks and reds to the landscape.

An old-fashioned horse trough and hitch were stationed near the front door. No doubt about it. A horseman lived here. She liked the place.

Gabe took her hand and helped her out of the vehicle. For a moment all she could do was stand and absorb the beauty. A red cardinal flitted by, another splash of color on an already resplendent canvas of vibrant spring hues. She turned in a full circle and breathed deeply. "This is almost as pretty as Wyoming."

Kelsey agreed. "It's awesome, isn't it?"

"Well, don't just stand there." Alex had already unbuckled the little girls from their back seats. Kyrie ran to Taylor who immediately picked her up. "Let's go see who's home."

Alex and Kelsey led the way through a circular arbor to the east of the home that dropped them into a spacious backyard. A long whitewashed stable and fence ran the width of the yard to the east. What made it better was the quiet equine conversation beyond the whitewashed fence. Whoever lived her owned horses.

The peaceful sound caught China short. Her heart ached for the four-legged friends she had lost to Leezel's greed and the fire. A tear threatened her, but holy smokes. China chose to focus on rebuilding her life instead of crying for what was lost.

Kyrie giggled in Taylor's arms, and that was enough for China. Her niece was safe. That was all that really mattered. Jefferson Wolf would understand.

Alex looked around in dismay. "I thought he said five o'clock."

China asked, "Who?"

He pointed behind her with mischief in his blue eyes. "Him."

She turned. A tall handsome *him* walked toward her from the stable. Dark glasses in place. Ball cap, the brim pulled low. Scruffy cheeks and chin. No hint of a smile. A black button-up shirt set off smartly by a gray vest. Black jeans. Sexy damned swagger.

Her heart jumped to her throat. *Maverick?*

Kyrie scrambled out of Taylor's arms and ran to him with a shriek. Maverick caught her mid-stride, his gaze still fixed on China while he returned Kyrie's joyful hug and kisses.

"You is here!" she squealed.

Gabe placed a steadying hand to China's waist. She couldn't move she shook so hard. In a few long-legged strides, he was there. Gabe stepped aside with Kyrie. Maverick peeled his dark glasses off his nose and folded them into his pocket. Very gently, he cupped China's face in his bandaged hands, his breathing heavy and her heart on fire. "Thank God, you're alive," he choked.

She started to cry, her hands on his biceps. "You saved me and Kyrie and... and..."

He wrapped her in his arms with a groan, his face buried in the crook of her neck and his palm between her shoulder blades, pulling her in tight.

She anchored her fingertips to his shoulders and took a deep breath of wind and horses and—*him*. "I love you so much." She let the words come. She had been thinking them for too long. They needed to be spoken. She tipped his cap off his head, needing to see his eyes.

The angst was gone. Unshed tears glistened on his lashes. Forehead to forehead with her, he said what she needed to hear, his voice deep and low. "I love you, China Wolf. God, I love you so damned hard."

He couldn't have reached into the core of her soul and offered anything better. The feelings she had suppressed for this quiet hero swarmed up from her toes like a hive of happy, buzzing honeybees. She melted into him, her lips pressed to his. They clung to each other.

At last he released her, but kept her encircled in his arms. "The last time I saw you, I thought you were dead." His voice cracked. "I was so afraid I'd lost you. That I'd messed up. That I'd never have the chance to tell you what you meant to me."

She peered up at him and saw the details she had missed. The bruises on his cheeks and stitches on his lower lip. Butterfly bandages curled over one brow. She cupped his cheek, filled with the need to keep her hands on him. "What happened?"

"Reardon." He smoothed a gentling hand through her hair, tangling his fingers in her tresses and tugging lightly. "I'm okay now, but I think I still owe you that—more."

She blushed. Every nerve ending fired recalling his promise on the hillside and her state of undress. That same steamy haze darkened his eyes now. His heavy breathing matched hers. She lifted to her toes and circled one hand to the back of his neck to kiss those sore-looking lips, but he pulled back just enough to bring her to her senses.

"How about we save that real welcome home kiss for when we're alone? I have plans for you."

China glanced around, embarrassed. Everyone stood waiting and watching. Kelsey's eyes sparkled. His quick thinking kept his shirt buttoned and his pants zipped. *For now.*

Little Kyrie grinned from ear to ear from Uncle Gabe's arms. She clapped and pointed. "I gonna marry Unca Mavwick, too!"

Everyone laughed, but China. She peered into Maverick's dark, sexy eyes. "My sister?"

He shook his head. "No one knows where she is right now."

"But Reardon is—"

"In jail. Sheriff Hammer wanted to retire, but he's real busy now. Every one of Reardon's biker buddies has been charged with attempted murder, arson, and other crimes. This wasn't their first crime. Reardon and your sister were behind those knifings in the area. I'll have to tell you all about it, maybe after we're done getting reacquainted." He smiled one of those rare Carson smiles, the kind that poured honey into her soul and heat between her legs. He never looked sexier.

China touched the tip of her index finger to the ragged mark on his lower lip. "She bit you?"

He shrugged it off. "Yeah, well, I am irresistible."

"But you're mine," she blurted. *All mine and I'll fight the world for you.*

A spark of sadness flashed deep in those wells of coffee brown. "Do you have any idea how long I've waited to hear those words from the right woman?" His voice had tightened. So did his grip. He lifted the back of his hand to his brow, his eyes squeezed tight against his tears. He tugged his dark glasses over his eyes. "Shit. I hate this. You're breaking my heart. I don't deserve you. Your love. None of this."

She could have cried, he looked so genuinely tormented. She cupped his chin and turned his mouth to hers. "You're all I need, Maverick. I love you more than I've ever loved anyone. Let me in. Stop walking. Stay. Please stay with me."

He nodded, the cords in his neck tight. "I will. I promise." He planted a chaste kiss on her forehead. The feel of those poor stitched lips on her mouth meant everything. She closed her eyes and breathed, "Amen."

"I didn't drive all the way out here to watch you two mug each other." Kelsey's husband had a very bossy streak. "Are you two going to stand around all day?" He pointed behind her yet again. The sound of footfalls got her attention. Horse footfalls. A lot of them.

She turned in Maverick's arms. "My horses! How did you...? How could you...?"

"I didn't." Maverick nodded to Alex. "He did."

"I'm sorry. I'm afraid I've played a mean trick on you." Alex walked into the crowd of gentle animals, patting a broad shoulder there and a friendly nose here. "I would've told you that I had your kids sooner, China, but I wasn't sure the last four would make it in time. Josh Winters made it here this afternoon with Joker and his buddies. We're still missing Star, but he's in Wyoming with Eb. So's your dog."

"You bought my horses? All this time, you've had them? You... saved them? You've got Puppy, too?" China's voice caught. Her eyes filled again. There was no way to repay this amazing man for all he had done to help her. No way. Not if she lived to be one hundred. Her gratitude welled up and ran out of her eyes. "I don't know what to say," she squeaked. Yes, squeaked. Between the warmth of Maverick's hard body at her side and the tender glow in Alex's gaze, she was coming undone. She needed her own dark glasses, damn it.

Too late. Her tears fell despite her best efforts. She buried her face in Maverick's chest. He wasn't the only one whose heart was breaking with joy and gratitude.

Alex didn't help. "This is what families do, China. We take care of each other. It's as simple as that. Where there's a will, there's a way."

She traded Maverick's arms for Alex's, her heart filled to overflowing. He wasn't even related to her. They didn't share a single bloodline, but he had rescued all that was dear to her, and he had done it before he'd even met her. Unbelievable.

"Thank you, Mr. Stewart," she said fervently. "I'm speechless. I'm…" Words failed. "Thank you. Thank you so much."

"Alex," he corrected, his voice a little on the gravelly side. "It was my pleasure, China."

Gabe coughed. Taylor already straddled Jinx. He looked like a natural, but Gabe? Earthbound and his brows furrowed. He called out to Maverick, "Hey, I've got a little problem with this horse."

"What's that?" Maverick asked, his chin once again tucked into China's neck, his arms around her and her back to his front.

"He's, umm, standing on my foot."

Chapter Thirty-Two

Kyrie had her first sleepover—ever.

Thank God the Stewarts volunteered to take her for the night. As much as he loved Kyrie, Maverick couldn't wait to be alone with China even though it meant a long drive back to the safe house. He cussed himself for not planning better.

Gabe and Taylor didn't hang around, either. Gabe said something about taking his wife, Shelby, out for a much-needed date night. Taylor just disappeared. Before he knew it, Maverick was alone with China with nothing to do. *Yeah, right.*

The minute the front door closed behind Alex, Kelsey, and Kyrie, Maverick peeled the tape and gauze off his fingers, never breaking eye contact with China's. "I'm ready now."

"For what?" she asked innocently, a definite catch in her throat.

She knew damned well what. He raised her knuckles to his lips. "For more."

The words were barely out of his mouth when he crashed into her and fastened her to the wall by the front door. His ribs were damned sore and his hands tender from the burns, but the fire in his heart needed quenching. Right damned now.

He sliced one hand through the buttons on her shirt. It hit the floor while he covered her neck and shoulders with kisses. Goosebumps sprang to life on her skin. He nipped. He suckled. She shivered.

The snaps on his western shirt popped as her hands smoothed over his chest and moved downward. His vest slipped off his shoulders. "I've wanted to do this since..."

He finished her thought with a mouthful of China. "That day in the barn."

"Yes-s-s," she hissed.

The fire racing through her body jumped circuits, entering his at the same time. All of her little noises urged him on. He unsnapped and unzipped the rest of her clothes, right down to her underwear. "Glad you're not wearing boots." Although a naked woman in cowboy boots did have a certain erotic appeal. He hardened at the notion, crazy as it was.

"Me, too." She wrapped her arms around his neck.

Clutching the cheeks of her backside, he lifted her off her feet and angled their way down the hall to the first available bedroom. Dang. A twin bed and stuffed animals. Not quite what he had in mind. Impatience stoked his fire. "Help me out here. Where am I going?"

She giggled deliciously in the crook of his neck, her fingers trailing sparks with every languid touch down his back and up his neck. "Last door at the end of the hall."

He strode to the darkened room and tossed her to the bed before he turned and locked the door. There would be no interruptions. Not tonight. It had been too long since he trusted a woman the way he trusted China. With his heart and soul. His life.

God, she looked sexy sitting in the middle of the bed in nothing but a white lacy bra and boy shorts, her hands on her knees and her eyes aglow. Irresistible with desire. Black tangles cascaded over her arms.

"You're overdressed," she murmured.

"That's your problem."

It took her two seconds to bounce off the bed. She made quick work of his boots and socks. His belt and jeans. His boxers. He couldn't stop watching her at work. This woman was on a mission. She knew zippers and buckles, but the curve of her ass while she worked him over? Sweetest sight ever.

His pulse throbbed. By the time she tossed his boxers over her shoulder and smiled up at him, he was down to his skin and breathing heavy. "Your lead," he said, his voice hoarse with desire.

She backed him to the mattress, pushed him flat to his back and climbed on top, and damn. No wonder Ebony danced with this delightful woman mounted on his back. The heat from her core commanded every male cell in Maverick's body.

Time to ride.

The safe house fell away. There were no noisy robins chirping their evening song through the open window. No

Northern Virginia sunset. The world could've come to a screeching stop for all he cared. Nothing and no one existed but this amazing woman peering down at him through a veil of silky black tendrils. She'd become his world. His everything.

Her hands roamed his chest even though she wore nothing but her bra and panties. Her gaze swept over his chest and down his abdomen, then back again. She licked her lips, the same appraising light in her eyes as when she had handled her stallions.

The comparison added high-octane racing fuel to the already out-of-control twitch in his blood. Yeah. He was ready to be anything she wanted. *Stallion. Tiger. Bunny rabbit. You name it.*

He took charge. The clasp to her bra offered no resistance. Soon his hands filled with the warm softness of her delightfully plump breasts, her girls, so much happier out of those pretty lace restraints. His thumbs had no problem pebbling her nipples. Maverick groaned, needing a mouthful of her creamy tasting skin. He had found heaven on earth with a spike of some serious lust.

She shook her head, brushing his chest with that curtain of shimmering silk. Igniting nerve-endings. Stoking his need. God, he wanted to be wrapped up warm and wet inside of her. Her arms were still holding her over him, her elbows still cocked, but then. So was he. Cocked and ready to command or be commanded.

C'mon. Let's ride, damn it.

He smoothed his hands down her arms to her ribcage and from there to her hips. He pulled her close, his chin lifted and his lips poised for action and—

"Stop."

He groaned. "You've got to be kidding." *Stop? Now?*

"I wasn't sure." The awe in her voice struck him as adorable. Kind of annoying given the fiery ache in his groin, but adorable. He played along.

"Weren't sure of what?" She had better get sure if she knew what was good for her. It had literally been too damned long since he had been with a woman. All this foreplay was killing him, because damn it, China Wolf was the right woman. The only woman. My woman!

Her hands smoothed over his chest and downward. Her face lit with wonder. "I thought I dreamed this."

He groaned at the treasures in his hands and licked his lips, barely able to wait for the conversation to end so he could start tasting those perfect rosebuds under the pads of his thumbs. His burned fingers really ought to hurt more than they did, but nothing registered except the light in her eyes and his mission ahead: claiming every last part of China.

"What? You've never seen a man undressed before?" he growled.

"But you're... you're beautiful." There was that awe thing in her tone again.

Enough. He rolled her over, one arm cradling her head while he eased his body between her legs. He nibbled and sucked a path from the tip of her chin down between her breasts. "Guys aren't beautiful," he murmured before he closed his eyes and sucked in one perfectly peaked nipple.

She moaned and arched her back, offering more. He took it, inhaling the clean scent of her skin and hair. The wildfire called passion flared. His control slipped away at the taste of honey on his tongue.

"Handsome then," she whispered hoarsely.

"You know what I dreamed?" he breathed, blowing on her freshly kissed skin. With goosebumps lifting on her breasts, he kissed a moist trail up her neck to her ear, breathing heavy as he went.

She cringed. Ah, China's neck was ticklish. Good to know. He nestled his nose and mouth into that ticklish neck good and tight.

"What?" she asked, her voice tight and needy, just how he wanted the rest of her to be.

"Of you," he breathed.

She whimpered, her arms hugging his head to her, and conversation was over. They melted together in the fiery heat of too much anticipation. He took her lips, savoring the taste of honey and mystery, the puzzle of an amazingly strong woman who wanted him in her life. He deepened the kiss, pouring his ragged soul and his battered heart into the promise of a lifetime.

Never again would he roam. His walk was over. Everything began and ended—with China.

She arched at his touch, and he touched plenty. He stroked. He petted. He pinned her hands over her head and ravaged every inch of the warm, giving body beneath him until she squirmed with desire. And pleasing her became everything. His life. His final mission.

The energy sparking off her skin filled him with heat. He sank his mouth to her breasts, aching to hear her groan for more, that blessed *'more'* which he fully intended to give to her for the rest of her days.

Her body responded to his every touch. Pebbling. Dampening. The scent of her arousal intoxicated every last male receptor in his body and he was drunk on her.

She tried to be careful of his bumps and bruises. He tried to be careful of hers, but the need for each other took on a passionate life of its own. He released her hands and settled against her core. She scraped her fingernails over his shoulders and down his back, adding another shot of nitrous to ordnance already primed to blow.

He stopped to catch a breath, consumed with his need for her lovely body. So beautiful. Her skin, soft as silk, as luscious as sweet cream.

Sexy dark blue eyes peered up at him wearing nothing but love. Her lashes fanned her flushed cheeks. She huffed at him the way Gorgeous had once huffed into his chest. He had to know. He had to ask, if only to feel her body quicken around his. "Am I allowed to breed?"

She answered with ten fingernails dug into the cheeks of his ass and her body opened wide.

Good answer.

They crashed together, two separate fires that consumed each other in one glorious blinding light. Both offered precisely what the other needed without delay. She arched upward, accepting all of his body and all of his heart. *And more.*

The heavens burst with stars. He kissed her lips as they sank to earth together, needing every breath of hers. Every murmur of contentment. They lay together in silence, their hearts beating in sync. She felt good in his hands: soft, warm, and still panting against the chest she seemed so enamored with. She smiled. He could feel her smile all the way to his toes.

He lowered his mouth to her lips and kissed her long and hard. The moment she stirred against him, he wanted her all over again. Every last inch, taste and nibble.

"How are you feeling?" He had to make sure she was up for more athletics. There was still the shower, the coffee table, and the porch swing if they were brave enough. He had plans for this little lady.

The steamy look in her eyes answered for her.

Nothing in the world could keep Miss China Wolf down. But tonight, and in all the best ways possible—he meant to give her his best shot.

She woke in a cocoon of manly arms and legs with heated breath in the back of her neck. She shivered. Maverick snored softly. Their night together had been filled with hard sex, slow sex, enlightening conversation, and what else? More sex.

No wonder he was still asleep. This man wrapped around her knew a few tricks she hadn't expected. Chocolate syrup? Who would've thought? It surely added a different flavor sensation.

And who would've thought she would wake up wanting more after their marathon night together? The sensation of his naked body against hers under the sheets, primed for action, was irresistible. She wondered how long this man would stay asleep if she moved just a little to the right and pushed backwards, just a tiny bit.

He shifted in his sleep, his hips bumping her backside. The contact elicited a spark of pleasure deep inside. She held her breath, waiting for him to say something. When a soft snore reached her ears, she grinned like a naughty little girl. She should let the poor man sleep. He was exhausted. She knew it. But every part of her craved his, and his best parts seemed to be craving hers at the moment.

She angled her body to accommodate his position, just a little bit more to the right. If she was very careful, he would never know and—

A soft hiss breathed out of him. She glanced over her shoulder to make sure she hadn't disturbed him too much.

Two dark heated eyes pierced hers with desire.

Oh, oh. The beast had awakened. What would he do with her now?

Shivers of anticipation danced up her spine, the spine he now breathed on with full knowledge and need. He gathered her hair into a ponytail and scrolled his gaze down her back to her bare ass. The darkest, sexiest eyes filled with lust.

She smiled apologetically, or as close as she could come to it, her veins throbbing with need. The next thing she knew, his palm was flat between her shoulder blades, pushing the top of her forward while he circled her waist and pulled her lower half tightly into his. Right where she wanted to be. Apparently, Maverick was a morning person, too.

He hadn't said a word, not like he had to. He seemed to know what to do with her ass tucked into his body like it was. He planted a row of kisses. One big hand cupped her breast. He pinched her nipple, adding an element of surprise to her libido that right then and there had a mind of its own.

She growled unexpectedly at the new sensation of pain and pleasure. He pushed forward. She shoved backward and... and...

Every muscle clenched around him. Wanting him. Needing him in ways she had never needed another. Loving him. He set a steady rhythm that reached parts of her that had remained untouched before. With every stroke in, he created an appetite and a craving until her entire body clenched around his, needing every last inch.

With a final thrust, he buried his face in the nape of her neck and pushed her over the edge of pleasure. The tightening sensation of her softness around his steel brought a tear to her eye.

She wanted him. Only him. There could never be another who served her so diligently or as thoroughly as this drifter named Maverick. Who worked at her side in silence and respect. With whom she wanted to mingle breaths and days and hearts.

The warmth of his body encompassed her. China closed her eyes and pulled his arms tighter around her, content to serve him all the days of her life.

Chapter Thirty-Three

Team picnic. Duffy's Swim-N-Slide. 5PM. Swim trunks optional. Maverick glanced at the text message on his phone. "Looks like you're invited to meet everyone."

The phone rang. He checked the caller ID and hit speakerphone so China could listen. They were tangled together on the porch swing enjoying the late morning sun and each other. "Good morning, Kyrie."

"Unca Mavwick!" Her happy voice bubbled over the line. "Unca Awex says I hafta call you an axe if I kin go fwimmin'."

"Are you going swimming with Uncle Alex and Aunt Kelsey?" Maverick couldn't keep the smile off his face. China, either. This little girl sounded so happy.

"Uh huh, and Unca Gabe and Andy Gracie is coming, too. He buyed me a dragon!"

Maverick listened while Kyrie dropped the phone and Alex came on the line. "Guess she's off to play with her dragon."

"A dragon, huh?"

"Yeah. The TEAM is picnicking at Duffy's Swim-N-Slide. Just wanted you kids to know. It's Lexie's first time swimming."

Maverick studied China's happy face. "Probably Kyrie's, too."

China chimed in. "But Kyrie doesn't have a swimsuit."

"She does now." Alex sighed in the way of a good husband with a wife who knew how to use plastic. "Kelsey took care of that. Join us if you can."

"We'll be there," Maverick said. "Anything I should bring?"

"Swimsuits and sunscreen. I've got the rest covered." Alex hung up in his usual brusque way.

China's eyes were still fixed on Maverick's. They'd spent an incredible night together, and, even though a picnic sounded fun, he hated ending this private time with China.

"Are you hungry?" he asked quietly. He had never known a woman who tasted so good, from the curl of her ears to the tip of her nose, her chin and all the way down to her toes. He had tasted them and everything in between, but as hungry as he was for her, they needed real food, too.

She smacked her lips, that smoldering heat in her eyes again. "I could eat."

He grinned, loving the double meaning and the sexy smile on her face. "If you do that one more time, we'll never get out of here." He placed her on her feet and stood with her, resisting the urge to throw her over his shoulder and haul her back inside. "Alex always puts on a big spread. We'll get plenty to eat there. Let's get going."

"Sounds like fun, but Maverick. He's already done so much. How can I ever repay him?"

"Let him spoil you and Kyrie."

"But I—"

Maverick pressed the pad of his index finger to her lips. "You might as well get used to it. Alex makes good money, but I'm here to tell you. He doesn't have a stingy bone in his body when it comes to his agents. The man's a genius the way he pours good money into his business. Hell, into his TEAM, too. We're all overpaid. He covers our health benefits one hundred percent. Believe me. If you think you can repay Alex, you're wrong. The guy makes too damned much and gives plenty of it away."

"But I have to do something," she insisted. "This doesn't feel right."

Maverick shrugged. "I don't know what to tell you. Maybe find a way to pay it forward. Come on. Let's go meet the rest of the TEAM." Maverick locked the safe house door, and led China to the vehicle that Taylor and Gabe had left parked at the curb. He pressed the keypad to unlock the SUV, then hit the ignition button.

"Wow." China climbed in next to him and fastened her seat belt. "High tech."

"I guess." Maverick fastened his own seat belt before he turned to China. The normalcy of her riding shotgun struck him. There she sat with a look of contentment on her face, and not a single worry line anywhere.

"You're such a beautiful woman," he murmured, his thumb brushing her cheek.

"If you keep doing that..."

"You're right." He shifted the vehicle into drive and merged into traffic with a big smile that felt almost natural. It had been a long time since he woke to a really good day.

"So tell me why you left The TEAM."

He sighed. "Long story."

"But it's one I'd like to know."

He hooked into the freeway headed south and drove for a few minutes before he could continue. China didn't push. Her hand on his arm comforted instead of nagged. "My kid brother joined the Marines. He did it because I did. Darrell. He looked up to me. Heck, I couldn't do anything wrong in his eyes."

They drove in silence. That she didn't probe helped the rest of the story pour out. "Guess we were a couple starstruck guys on our way to save the world. He became a scout sniper like me. Somehow, we both ended up on the same mission. Big mistake."

The traffic flew by as the day came back to him. It was a purple task force of Marines, Army Rangers and Navy SEALs, their mission to apprehend a known Taliban warlord, Mullah Mamood. They'd entered the valley with a force of Afghani friendlies. By morning they were inside the village, a stinking conglomeration of mud brick huts, rickety goat corrals, smoky fire pits and mangy dogs. Reconnaissance proved faulty. A force of more than one hundred insurgents were waiting. By the end of the failed operation, Maverick pounded down ground fire to cover an excruciating retreat that cost nearly half the team of special operators.

"The thing was, we all knew it was a suicide mission going in." Maverick steeled his eyes on the road, shielding her from the particulars. He might tell her eventually. He might not. "We knew once we got in, we'd be fighting tooth and nail to get out. Guess we thought we were invincible."

Her hand on his forearm gripped tighter and he was done talking.

"You lost your brother." She said it so he wouldn't have to, which was good because all he could do was nod at that point.

They drove in silence for miles. Once again, the very act of not speaking was exactly what he needed as the pain that was Darrell's death sucked the joy out of the morning.

"Anyway." He blew out a big breath. "Got my very own Dear John letter when I got back. Then the bastard that my ex dumped me for showed up in Virginia where I worked, and I..." He couldn't finish. He had quit, plain and simple. Grew weary with being politically correct, of drinking too much to numb the pain, and damned sick of looking that liar, Landon Truman, in the eye every day and pretending he didn't want to break his neck.

"You started walking."

He nodded. Yeah. It seemed the only solution at the time. Walk and never look back. But in leaving, he had deserted his mother and the best friends who no kidding cared about him. Alex for one. Taylor, Gabe, and every other agent on The TEAM. Even sweet Kelsey.

He hadn't realized until then how much family he had. The phone call home confirmed that. After his mother had cried, she had chewed him out, told him he was wrong and cried again. So had he.

"I'm glad you stopped in Wyoming." China's quiet truth pulled him back to the road.

"So I've got a question for you."

"Shoot. Whatcha need to know? My story is your story." She couldn't have said anything better.

"Tell me about Xavier Allbright. What's Leezel got to do with him?"

"Oh, that." China blew out a deep breath. "I've never understood my sister. Umm, it's like this. X is older than us. He worked at Shorty's Saloon when we were in high school. You've probably noticed he struggles with language and communication most times, but he's really quite smart. Anyway..."

She blew out another sigh. "Leezel set him up. Said one of her friends had a crush on him and wanted to go dancing. Poor X fell for it. He got all dressed up in his best shirt and bolo. Even bought a brand new pair of cowboy boots instead of wearing his usual pair from Goodwill. Only, his date was a Longhorn bull dressed up in a stupid dress and a straw hat. Leezel made sure everyone in town knew about it, including Reardon and his boys. The *Kings and Kreepers* were all there. A lot of other idiots, too. By the time I heard about it, it was too late."

Maverick let her talk.

"The thing is that X didn't get it. He just stood there laughing along with everyone else and looking for the date Leezel promised him. It took me a couple minutes to convince him there was no girl, but then Leezel made it worse. She handed him a box all wrapped in pretty paper and tied up with a big red bow. I swear I've never seen a full-grown man get so excited. He couldn't wait to get the wrapping off. Only..." China tucked her hair behind her ear. "Damn it, Maverick. She'd gift-wrapped his cat, only it was dead. She claimed she found it run over by a car and that she only gave it to him because she knew how much it meant, but damn her. Knowing her, she probably killed it herself. Poor Xavier pulled that cat out of the box like it was still alive. He started petting it. It took him a minute to figure out what was really going on, then he took off running and wailing."

"The guy's got a big heart."

"He does, but Leezel and her so-called friends roared like it was all a great big joke. The poor guy ran all the way back to his room above Shorty's Saloon with that poor, dead cat. I finally caught up to him, but damn her. He sat there on his doorstep, hugging that cat and crying his eyes out. Broke my heart."

"So you gave him a job."

"No. I gave him a home, Maverick. I gave him a safe place and told him he could keep every damned stray cat that showed up in my barn. Xavier's been with me ever since. He's a damned good man is what he is. X wouldn't hurt a flea. Wish I could say that about Leezel."

"He's a keeper," Maverick said quietly, a plan for rescuing X and Z percolating at the back of his mind. "You need to know that Reardon rounded up all the cats around your place and dumped them in the river. I'm not sure Kyrie knows."

"He didn't," she hissed, her hands clenched on her lap. "Kyrie's kitties, too? Damn him and Leezel. Why are they so mean? X never hurt anyone, and cats keep the snakes and mice population down. Everyone knows that."

Maverick covered her fisted hands with his palm. He pulled into the water park, found the nearest parking stall and stopped the vehicle. China slid over the console and nestled into his lap. Damned if this woman didn't hold every last piece of his heart in her hands.

He kissed her with the very ends of his soul, the tendrils of it that had been searching for her for years. She had seen her own share of heartache, yet there she was, filling the void in his chest with serenity and kindness and—her. A man couldn't get any luckier.

"You know what I just realized?" she whispered.

"Huh?"

"We don't have swim suits."

"They sell them here."

"You'll have to help me pick one."

A salacious glimmer shifted over his handsome face. He lifted one eyebrow. "I'm thinking purple."

"Wh-e-e-e-e-e!"

She heard Kyrie before she saw her. Coming down the children's waterslide in yet another handsome man's arms and with a big grin on her face, Kyrie had never looked happier.

China scanned the crowded swimming area. Maverick had selected a one-piece swimsuit for her. Purple. What else? It not only fit perfectly, but he had added a fringed, open-weave cover-up to shield her from the sun, flip-flops and a trendy pair of sunglasses. Oakleys. Of course.

One look in the full-length mirror, and China almost didn't recognize the starlet staring back at her. She had actually primped and posed for a couple of minutes while Maverick watched. He grinned like a little boy. What woman wouldn't pose with her sexy man drooling over her? He had even pushed his Oakleys to the top of his head and winked, the flirt.

She selected his swim trunks, black with a purple lightning bolt on the cuff. Combined with his black TEAM polo, he cut a fine sight, too. But man, there were a lot of Chippendale-types standing and talking with Alex and Taylor, who were nothing to sneeze at themselves.

Taylor waved Maverick and her over to their gazebo where a plethora of food covered the picnic table, but China was content to just stand and take in the pleasant male scenery for a long, make that *extra-long*, moment.

What was it with the men Alex hired? Were they all bodybuilders and male models? Standing there with her hand as a visor over her eyes, she could make out two very handsome guys, one dark-haired and the other dark-skinned, both built like weightlifters. They weren't the huge bruiser types on wrestling shows, but they were definitely broad-chested, thick-necked, narrow-hipped, and hot-damned good looking. Sexier than hell.

All wore swimming trunks and open shirts—not like that concealed enough bare skin. Or muscled chests. Or tanned legs and rock-solid calves. Biceps. Six pack abs.

She fanned herself with her new matching purple sunhat. Alex, Gabe, and Taylor were no slouches, either. Every last one of those half-dressed male bodies was worth taking a minute—or ten—to appreciate. She knew good bloodlines and these guys all had it.

Kelsey waved Maverick and her over to where she sat with a group of pretty women. Kelsey introduced Libby, the blonde, Judy, the redhead, Mei and Gracie, both with long, straight black hair, and another blonde with a pixie cut, Shelby.

"That's Ember and Rory Dennison." Kelsey pointed to a handsome couple sharing an over-sized chaise lounge. "Hey Ember! Hey Rory! Look who finally made it."

They waved back. Other agents and their wives tended to their children in the kiddie pool. All sported sunglasses and beach apparel. Some wore straw hats. With the fragrance of suntan lotion heavy in the air and the drift of chlorine from the pool, the day felt more like summer than spring.

"Look. She's over there." Maverick pointed at Kyrie climbing onto a huge green dragon in the kiddie pool.

"Who's she with?"

"That's Harley. His wife is Judy, the redhead holding twin boys, the one sitting on the other side of Libby."

China's head spun. She would never remember all of these names.

"'Bout time. Everyone's been waiting for you." Gabe appeared behind them, a dark-haired, wiggling toddler under his arm. He grabbed Maverick in a solid handshake while he rolled the little boy onto his back for a horseback ride. For the first time, China noticed the prosthetic foot joined to the middle of Gabe's left lower leg. She blinked. She would never have guessed he was handicapped.

"High-dive competition in ten, bro."

Maverick waved him off. "Not going to happen. Not today."

"Oh, come on." Gabe's eyes lit up. "What's the chance you'd lose your trunks again?"

That caught China's attention. "You did what?"

"Yeah." Maverick beamed down at her. "Lost 'em last year when I hit the water after a high dive."

"But..." Gabe jabbed Maverick's shoulder and China knew there was more to the story.

"Yeah, but then some *smart ass* took off with 'em." For the first time since she had met him, Maverick sounded like one of the boys instead of a way-too-serious man carrying the weight of the world.

Gabe poked him again. "Come on, old man. Suck it up and tie a knot in it. You're going down. In nine. Bank on it."

Maverick pulled China into his side and waved him off again.

"I'd a stole 'em too," she whispered, her cheek to his chest.

"And I wouldn't have minded," he whispered back. "Come on. Let's go meet the rest of the guys." He smacked Gabe's shoulder. "Later, bro."

"You've got that right," Gabe taunted, a big, shitty grin on his face and his index finger pointed at the high dive. "In T-minus eight and counting."

Chapter Thirty-Four

In short order, China found herself introduced to more agents, their wives, and children. In the midst of the pleasant mayhem, she scanned the group for her niece. "Maverick. Do you see Kyrie?"

"I've got her." The tall, lanky guy that Maverick had introduced as Harley, joined the group with a smiling little girl sitting on his shoulders. "You're raising a fish. Did you know that?"

"I fwimmed! I fwimmed! I pinched my nose and I took a big breff and fwimmed!" Kyrie crowed with enthusiasm. She had probably added every single one of these handsome men to her list of potential marriage partners by then, too.

"Good to see you again." Alex extended his hand in welcome. His open beach shirt with black palms printed over an orange and yellow sunset drew China's eyes to a firmly corded abdomen. Tanned. Tight. Just plain sexy. No wonder Kelsey smiled a lot. This guy was built.

"It's good to be seen instead of viewed," China replied. "You put a nice picnic together."

"It's not much." Alex shrugged her compliment off. "Thought you might like to meet the gang. This seemed a good way to get you two out of the house."

"Don't let him kid you." Maverick nodded toward the picnic tables spread with rotisserie chicken, grilled steaks, corn-on-the-cob, baked-potatoes, watermelon, and *you-name-it*. "When the boss throws a party, we eat like kings."

Kyrie ran pell-mell into China so she scooped the wet little girl into her arms. "Are you done swimming?"

"Uh huh. I been pwayin' all day." Kyrie leaned against China with a tired sigh. "I missed you, Andy China."

Alex huffed. "I don't see how she had time to miss anyone. That's the busiest little gal I've ever seen. She asked me bright and early this morning if she could be Lexie's big sister."

"She loves children," China explained. "How'd she sleep last night?"

"Like a rock." Kelsey joined the group with a tray of lemonade and beers all around. "She and Lexie were sound asleep by the time we got home. It was a very quiet slumber party."

"Until she woke up this morning," Alex said as he snagged a long-necked bottle. "I hope you don't mind, but I gave Kyrie one of Lexie's blankets. I think she was missing you this morning."

China smoothed a hand over Kyrie's cheek. "You've got a new blankie, huh?"

Kyrie nodded matter-of-factly. "Lexie has yots of 'em, but I onwy got one."

China kissed her niece's forehead. "You're tired."

"Uh huh. I is." Kyrie agreed quietly.

"She's a doll." Kelsey stroked the little girl's hair. "She looks so much like you, China."

"Good looks must run in your family the way they run in mine." Harley had both of his boys in his arms, a big cheesy grin on his face. "What's the word, Boss?"

"The word is no sign yet." Alex nodded at China and she knew he meant Leezel. "Mother is on it."

That reminded China. "Okay. You guys have to tell me who this Mother person is. I thought Maverick was calling his mom when he called her the day I got shot."

Alex rolled his eyes. "Oh, God no."

"She's the computer genius who works for The TEAM," Maverick explained. A grin tweaked the corners of his mouth. "You shoulda seen the look on your face that day."

"I'll bet." China chuckled. "Here I'm shot, and you pull a phone out of the air and all of a sudden you're talking with your mother."

"She should be here pretty soon," Kelsey offered.

"In the meantime." Maverick snagged Kyrie who by now was on her way to sleep. "Let's get something to eat while the getting's good."

"Oh, no you don't." Gabe was back. "The high tower competition. Now, bro."

Alex grunted. "Who took it last year?"

Maverick smacked Gabe's back. "Old Cartwright, of course."

That sparked China's attention. Apparently an artificial foot didn't slow this man down. She looked up at the tower. "How tall is that thing?"

"Ten meters," Harley responded with raised brows. "Kinda high if you ask me."

"Thirty-three feet," Maverick translated. "It's the same height they use for Olympic diving."

"That explains why no one's up there right now, huh?" she asked. "Do you guys do this every year?"

"I guess." Maverick looked at China.

"You shouldn't," China murmured. "You're still hurt. And your hands are burned."

The corners of his mouth crinkled upward. He winked. "Are you telling me to stay here where it's safe?"

She ran a fingertip over his still healing lips. Somehow *safe* did not fit Maverick. "No. Do what you need to. I'm just telling you I'll kick your ass if you hurt yourself."

A grin cracked his face. He ducked his face into her hair. "Will you doctor me?" he whispered salaciously.

"Oh, hell, yeah," she breathed. "With chocolate sauce. Whipped cream. And me."

The lust in his eyes swallowed the simmering color of brown coffee. His hand slid under the swim-cover to the small of her back. Two nosy fingers dipped inside her swimsuit.

"People are watching," she warned, her blood on fire for more than just those two fingers.

Maverick removed his hand and dropped a quick peck to the tip of her nose. "One other thing. If I dive, you have to judge."

China would've said no, but Kelsey and the other wives had a row of chairs lined up facing the tower. Maverick waited until she sat down. He transferred a sleeping Kyrie and gave her a quick kiss before he took off with the guys. "I won't be long," he murmured. "Then we'll play doctor."

"Okay, so how do we judge?" China looked at her new friends to get her mind off of that handsome, half-naked man strolling away from her and his latest sexy come-on.

Kelsey shrugged. "We just pick the pluckiest and go from there."

Mei giggled. "It's more a testosterone contest than anything else. The guys climb all the way up there, show off their physiques, and hopefully, no one chickens out."

"Look at how serious they are." Libby pointed to the tower. Sure enough, every member of The TEAM looked pretty focused right now. The higher they went up the ladder, the more serious they became. "I've been on that platform. It's one of the highest around."

"Libby used to swim competitively in high school," Kelsey explained.

"Oh, look." Judy pointed. She tried to get her two little baby boys to look up at Harley at the edge of the diving board. "Look at Daddy. He's going first."

Harley stood with his toes curled over the edge of the board, flexed his knees once as if he were ready to jump, and suddenly, he was falling. With just one foot planted, he waved his arms. The women gave one huge gasp. He cupped his hands to his mouth and shouted something to them, but his words went unheard. He jumped back a step and walked away from the edge.

"Darn him." Judy blew out a huge breath. "He does that to scare me. I could just smack him sometimes."

Libby's dark-haired husband, Mark, stepped up next. He also flexed his knees, but he didn't goof around like Harley. Instead, he followed through with a forward dive and a full somersault. China watched him surface in the pool and swim to the side. He lounged against the edge, wiping the water off his face, but he also shot a look to Libby and a big smile. She gave a big sigh of relief.

Once again it was Harley's turn. "I hope he's careful, darn him," Judy murmured.

"He looks like a natural athlete," China offered.

"Oh, he is." Judy's eyes were fixed to the diving tower. "He's a runner. He hits every marathon he can when he isn't out of the country."

"Does he travel a lot?"

Every wife's head swiveled to face her. Their brows lifted as if she had sprouted three eyes.

Kelsey rescued her. "Yes. All of these men travel internationally for their country. Sometimes the work they do can be dangerous."

"Oh?" China hadn't thought of the danger. She knew Maverick was in excellent physical condition and that he was an expert with the pistol he carried, but she hadn't connected all those dots, yet.

"You don't know what The TEAM does, do you?" Libby asked.

"Umm, no." China looked at the serious gazes focused on her. These wives weren't just women at a picnic. She sensed something else, more of a feeling of solidarity, as if they were more than just girlfriends who liked to hang out together. "I thought they were like ambassadors or bodyguards. Stuff like that."

Libby's serious blue eyes betrayed the seriousness of their husband's jobs. "They run black ops, China. They might handle bodyguard duties once in a while, but most of the time, they're involved in dangerous operations, and sometimes things go wrong. Mark still can't use the pinkie finger on his right hand. He was on an op in Mexico. It's a small thing considering how bad it could've been."

China stopped breathing. *Considering how bad it could've been?*

"Sometimes they do get hurt," Kelsey confirmed, "and things go wrong. Alex only hires the best and he pushes them too hard."

"And sometimes they take too many risks." Libby's cobalt blue eyes sparked with worry. She shook her head. "I'm sorry. Don't listen to me, China. I'm tired. That's all. Mark just got home from Nepal. It's been a long month."

Kelsey patted Libby's arm. "No. You're right. Mark's been in the line of fire too many times."

"That's the problem. That's who these guys are. Even if Alex hadn't hired Mark, he would still be doing something just as dangerous for someone else. At least Alex is good to him."

"Alex isn't taking on as many dangerous contracts anymore."

"I know." Libby sighed. "And I'm glad he promoted Mark to a senior position. That helps. At least he wasn't in danger in Nepal."

"Oh, look. There he goes," Mei interrupted.

All eyes fixed on the tower. Harley put both arms forward and dived off the platform, arms and legs flailing. At the halfway point, he pitched downward and executed a perfect ninety-degree angle into the pool.

Judy's sigh of relief was hard to miss.

Again all eyes looked upward. Alex stood at the edge. Now it was Kelsey's turn to hold her breath. Without any hesitation, he executed a jackknife, and pierced the water at a precise angle.

"See?" Libby said. "He's safe and sound."

Kelsey visibly relaxed while Libby rubbed big circles over her back. She nodded, but her eyes betrayed her. By then, Harley joined the ladies. "Did you hear what I said up there?" he asked while he brushed the water out of his hair and all over Judy and his boys.

She shook her head. "It's too noisy down here. I couldn't hear a word. Stop dripping on me. What did you say?"

He clamped his wet arms around her neck, gave another shake of his wet hair and leaned into her ear. "Just that I love you, woman. That perfect dive was all for you."

"Aw. Sit with me. These boys are heavy."

"You bet." He slid into the lounge chair with one arm around her shoulders, the other around one of his sons. That simple act caught China's attention. She saw the tender look on Judy's face as her very wet husband planted another, slurpy kiss on her lips. Yeah, he might annoy her, but there was a lot of love in her eyes while she wiped the drips away.

The women's conversation changed with Harley's arrival, and as more of the men joined their wives on the lawn chairs, but now China wondered. Maverick had never really explained what The TEAM did. She had assumed it was more or less a security business, what with the safe house and her two very military-like escorts, but now she needed to know the rest of the story.

Everyone watched the remaining contestants. Rory, Connor, Zack, and David each executed dives with either a twist or a somersault. The audience clapped. China couldn't help but notice the relief on each wife's face when her man was finally safely in the pool.

Her own anxiety ratcheted up. The worry over this friendly competition must be what these women lived with every day of their lives. While China felt as if she had been watching the best display of half-naked men she had ever witnessed, her half-naked man had yet to take the jump. After their late-night sexing, he had to be tired.

Finally, only Maverick and Gabe remained. They walked to the edge of the platform, looked down and stepped back. An audience of interested onlookers gathered on the edge of the pool to watch. They chanted, "Jump. Jump. Jump."

Once again, Maverick and Gabe looked over the edge.

Alex shielded his eyes with his hand and peered upward. "What are those two up to?"

Shelby, Gabe's wife, stood, her clenched fingers to her lips as she watched her husband. China knew how she felt.

The suspense was getting to her, too. This competition seemed like no big deal until it was Maverick's turn, but he had two good feet. What was Gabe thinking?

"There they go." Harley pointed upwards.

Gabe and Maverick pressed into handstands at the lip of the platform. In doing so, they faced away from the water. Their bodies lean, taut, tan, and damn it. China couldn't catch her breath.

They balanced like two pillars, their legs straight and their toes pointed at the sky. It took a lot of upper body strength to pull off that stance, but then they held their position.

"Are they still talking?" Harley asked in disbelief.

Only when Kyrie grumbled in her sleep did China realize she gripped her niece too tight.

"Any second now and..." Harley drew out his words while Maverick and Gabe lingered at the edge. Chatting. While doing handstands.

China cringed. *Just do it. Dive. Be safe. For me.*

At last. Lift-off. They tipped backward from the platform, executed double-somersaults and hit the water within seconds of each other. The audience roared, but China only had eyes for one handsome face. Maverick bobbed to the surface, with a sputter and a big cheesy grin. She blew out the breath she hadn't realized she had been holding.

Maverick shot her a devil-may-care grin and wiped the water off his face and hair. He never looked handsomer. Well, except for last night in bed. And this morning in the shower. But damned. This guy lived to take dangerous chances.

Shelby let out a small cry of relief. Her eyes pooled with tears, which she promptly brushed away. "I don't know why I worry. Gabe's smart, but I still hate it when he does this kind of stuff. He scares me."

"Me, too." China turned to face the women. "Men. Can't live with 'em and—"

"Can't live without 'em." Kelsey, Libby, Mei, and Ember took the words out of her mouth.

The men roared their approval when the best dive applause went to Harley. He was as surprised as they were. "Moi?" he asked with a definite swagger and a big cheesy grin.

"Yes, you. Harley won because..." Kelsey held her hands up for attention. "Difficulty and risk aside, he was the only one of all you men who came straight to his wife after the dive and told her he loved her."

"Aw, shucks." Gabe rolled his eyes. "The ladies are right. Dang, I missed my chance." He turned straight away to Shelby, grabbed her in a dramatic dip and planted a big wet kiss on her surprised face. It would've been funny, but she started to cry and the kiss developed into something much more serious.

"Good call, Judge Kelsey!" Zack shouted as he headed for his wife, Mei.

Everyone clapped. Gabe settled down with Shelby in his lap, and Maverick with China. "Did I scare you with that jump?" he asked as he nuzzled her neck.

"Not until I saw Shelby's reaction." China nodded at Gabe and Shelby. It looked like Shelby was doing better with whatever he was telling her.

"Shell suffers from anxiety." Maverick hugged China close. "Gabe should've known better. He should've taken her up the tower with him. She would've been okay with him diving once she saw for herself how skilled he is. The man's got massive upper body strength. He's a pro."

"He takes a lot of risks for a man with one foot."

A frown creased Maverick's forehead. "One what? Oh, yeah. That. I guess he does. He lost his foot during that same op I told you about."

She stilled. That day in Helmand Valley had been damned costly.

Maverick pulled her to her feet. "Come on. Let's eat."

China stopped him with a hand to his arm. "Not until I know exactly what it is you guys do."

"I'll be very glad to show you what I do." He scanned the group around them before he returned a heated gaze to her. "Later might be better, though. I mean, umm, there are a lot of people around, but if you insist..."

"No. Really." She adjusted sleeping Kyrie on her lap as her face turned ten shades of red at his sexy insinuation. "The work you do is dangerous, isn't it? I want to know what I'm getting myself into."

He stopped the tease right then and there. Pulling a chair opposite China, he sat, his knees touching hers and his hands on her thighs. "What you're getting yourself into?"

"Yes." China met his eyes. Time stood still. She knew his friends were close by, that husbands were chatting with wives and children were being fed. That people were listening. His friends. His team.

Daily life was out there somewhere, but right now, it was just Maverick and her. Every fingertip of his on her bare thighs touched off a tiny firestorm in her belly. He had power over her that he didn't realize but she needed to know where that power would lead.

"If I go back to work for Alex..." Maverick took a deep breath, "then yes. There will be dangerous assignments and I will carry a weapon twenty-four-seven. If necessary, I'll use deadly force to complete my mission, hopefully, not often. My work will be similar to what I did while I was in the service."

"What did you do?"

"I was a scout sniper, China. A damned good one." He studied her intently. "I protected other Marines who needed cover. I neutralized the bad guys who meant to kill our men and women. I protected our boots on the ground, and I was damn proud to do it. I saved lives, China, and I'd do it again if needed."

Wow. The earnestness with which he proclaimed his patriotism and love for his fellow Marines all but bowled her over. "You're like my father. He was a Marine, too. In Vietnam."

"I figured as much. That was his jacket you gave me." Maverick took her hand and kissed the first knuckle. "So,

Miss China Wolf, just exactly what are you getting yourself into?"

"Umm." Her throat went dry. He hadn't so much as blinked, and he was way too serious. She knew she had that deer-in-the-headlights look. Her heart fluttered. "I just wanted to know."

"We'll discuss this more later." He tapped her knee and stood. "Come on. Let's eat."

And just like that, he was done talking. He closed up and turned away from her to the picnic table. He lowered his Oakleys. All that was missing was the brim on his ball cap to hide behind.

The wall between them was still there. Only now it felt like he had just activated a force field, too.

Chapter Thirty-Five

"First of all." China reached to Maverick's expressionless face and removed his dark glasses along with his cap. "I need to see your eyes when we talk."

The drive back to the safe house had been quiet. They'd already put Kyrie to bed. The poor little thing was sunburned and exhausted from her first day of swimming.

He smirked, and China worried maybe this might be their first fight. Finally in love for the first time in her life and already a lover's quarrel. Well good. She was head over heels in love with this fierce warrior. She trusted him, but she needed a few things out in the open.

He blinked those gorgeous dark browns, and she stifled an overwhelming urge to kiss him. He must've read her mind, only he didn't falter like she had. In one quick move, she was in his arms and his lips were on her mouth. Every touch of his hands, every taste of his tongue melted her concerns away.

Suddenly, he released her and dropped to his knees. She expected to be tossed over his shoulder and carried off for another night of sexual bliss, but there were those baby browns again, shining up at her with nothing but love. Her heart stalled.

"You asked what you're getting yourself into? I couldn't do this in front of everyone at the pool today." He bit his lip. Could he get any more handsome? Here he was still in his swim trunks and his TEAM polo, kneeling like a—

Her jaw dropped. *Oh. My. God.*

"This is what you're getting yourself into, China Wolf." His thumb and index finger pinched a ring between them. "I know we've got a lot of talking to do, but I meant what I said. Will you marry me? Will you spend the rest of your life loving me, because I sure as hell don't want to live another day without you?"

Now she was the one doing all the blinking. *What? Marriage? Me?*

"I know you've still got a lot of questions to ask and I promise to answer every last one."

His gaze never left hers. She saw the glittering stone between them, but the light in his eyes shone brighter. Worry creased his forehead.

"And I know I've made mistakes. I'm not an easy man to live with. I can be downright moody. Sometimes I'm an ass."

There he knelt, baring his soul, rambling and confessing. In all the things they'd been through during the past few weeks, she had never seen him like this. Maverick kept biting his lip. Her hero was scared.

"I'll do whatever you want. I just want you to be happy, and God, I love you with all my heart." Tears glistened at the corners of his eyes.

She sank to the floor with him, her fingers at the sides of his head. There was no way on earth she could resist this gentle man on his knees and pouring his heart out. "Oh, yes."

He crushed her in a smothering hug and a kiss that left her breathless.

"Damn it. Can't believe I'm doing this." He wiped his face with the back of his hand and she pulled back to see him better. Tears still welled up in his eyes. "Look what you've done to me. I'm a damned bawl-gut."

She wiped the moisture off his cheek. "I know what I plan to do to you. As long as we're in this together, I can handle whatever line of work you need to do. I trust you."

That put a smile back in his eye. With a gentle tug off the floor, she was once more in his arms and on her way to the bedroom.

Could life get any better? He still held the most beautiful woman in the world in his arms, she'd said yes, and a gentle breeze wafted through the open bedroom door—

Wait. Why is a breeze blowing through the damned door?

He bolted upright. "China?" He nudged the sleeping beauty on his chest.

She stretched, her lips tracing a line up his neck as she awakened slowly and sensually. "Hmm. You taste good."

"Did you get up during the night or something?"

"Uh uh." Her hands roamed over his stomach, headed downward. "I was pretty happy where I landed."

He grabbed her wrist to halt her wandering fingers. "Listen to me. Is Kyrie up already? Do you know where she is?"

China pushed her hair out of her face as she rolled off of him. "I don't think so. Why?"

"Because I shut the bedroom door last night. I didn't lock it because of Kyrie, but—"

"Kyrie?" China scrambled off the bed, wrapping her robe around her as she ran. "Kyrie!"

Maverick tossed the sheet aside and followed, but the panic in her voice scared him.

"Maverick!"

He already knew.

Kyrie was gone.

The police were there in record time. Alex was faster. "Where is it?"

Maverick handed him the note Leezel had left on Kyrie's pillow.

You want her? Come get her. WWB. YGMMWIG, XOXO. MCO.

"What the hell is this? Some kind of crap code?" Alex asked, his ire up.

Maverick shook his head. "Not sure. We can't figure it out. Not yet."

China was beside herself with worry. She paced the length of the safe house hallway over and over, circling the home looking for her niece, but the girl was gone.

More disturbing was the knowledge that Leezel had opened their bedroom door and seen them sleeping together, if that was all she had seen. What would the sight of China lying in Maverick's arms push her to do to her daughter? He couldn't bear to think of it.

"Mother tracked her to the airport," Alex said.

"Reagan?"

"Dulles. She's got her on airport surveillance leaving the terminal and flagging a cab. No suitcase."

"When?"

"Yesterday. One PM."

"While we were at the picnic?"

Alex nodded somberly. "The cab dropped her at a hotel in Crystal City. That particular hotel has metro access. She boarded the blue line late yesterday afternoon and—"

"Mother lost her." Maverick grimaced. China groaned and stepped away. "We'll find her, China. I promise."

"How?" The flash in her eyes stabbed him.

"Because it's what we do," Alex said calmly. "It's too early to panic. Your sister's crazy note proves it."

A forest green Yukon rolled up to the curb. Taylor and Gabe had arrived. One look at her face and Taylor went straight to China. She flung herself into Taylor's arms. "She's gone! And my sister has her! Taylor, she's gone!"

Taylor's dark eyes pierced Maverick's over the top of China's head. Maverick took a disbelieving step back. Here stood the woman of his heart seeking comfort in another man's arms? Again? Exactly what Kim had done with Landon Truman, the bastard.

Anger flickered inside his soul. Kim's face flashed to mind while China unraveled inside Taylor's arms. What the hell? Was Taylor just another liar like Landon? Worse, was China Kimberly all over again?

"Leezel will kill her. I know she will!" China poured her heart out while Maverick stood there like a sonofabitchin' third wheel, his heart pounding in his chest and everyone else witness to yet another betrayal.

"Remember what I told you the night you couldn't sleep?" Taylor's eyes held fast to Maverick while he spoke to China.

Maverick didn't know what the hell Taylor meant. Was he talking to him or China?

She calmed. "Yes. I remember."

"You knew something was wrong that night too, didn't you?" Taylor asked. "You knew Maverick was in trouble, remember?"

"Reardon tried to kill him that night."

The intensity in Taylor's eyes drew Maverick in. "And?"

China whimpered. "And you told me to close my eyes. You said all blessings are mine."

"Open your mind, China." Taylor's soft command startled Maverick. "What did you see?"

"Maverick." She sobbed. "I saw... him. I saw my... Maverick."

"What did he tell you?"

China turned to Maverick. "That he loves me." She rushed from Taylor to bury herself in Maverick's chest.

He huffed out a snort of relief. He gulped his foolish panic attack down. His woman. China. Was. Not. Kim.

The enlightenment came swiftly. Maybe it was the influence of Taylor's words, maybe not. Maybe it was just the shock of seeing China with another man. Whatever. The moment she was back in his arms, Maverick knew what those letters meant.

He and Alex blurted it at the same time. "She's at the Woodrow Wilson Bridge!"

"And MCO could mean Maverick Carson Only," Gabe offered quickly. "Just saying."

"And XOXO is Leezel being a drama queen." China looked up at Maverick. "She's always wanted you, you know that. I don't know about the YGMMWIG, though."

"You're Going to Miss Me When I'm Gone." Maverick supplied the missing cipher. "Those were her last words to me before she burned the bunkhouse. She's got Kyrie at the Woodrow Wilson Bridge and she means to end everything today. That's not far from here."

Mark Houston and Rory Dennison let themselves in the front door. Mark nodded toward the curb. "The police are here."

"Tell 'em they're welcome to join us, but we're leaving." Alex already had his keys in his hand. "Taylor. Stay here with the police. You know where we'll be."

Maverick and China hurried past the surprised officers with Alex in the lead. Maverick secured China in the seat behind Alex while he rode shotgun. In seconds, they were on their way with Gabe, Mark, and Rory following close behind in another TEAM vehicle.

"What does she want?" China cried. "Maverick, what does she want? To hurt me? Well, she's done it. God, this will kill me."

Maverick reached over the back seat for her hand. "We're going to get her, I promise."

"But why the bridge?"

"I think it would be best if you stay in the car once we get there, China," Alex said.

"No." She clutched Maverick's hand tighter. "I have to be there. Maybe she'll listen to me."

Maverick knew better. Leezel didn't take her daughter to the bridge because she wanted to talk. No. She wanted China to suffer. Him, too.

Taylor's voice came over the vehicle's Bluetooth phone. "Boss. Coast Guard Station Washington has a boat in the river. DC Metro police are on site. Maryland highway patrol, too."

"Is Miss Wolf in sight?"

"Negative. Several pedestrians are on the bridge. None with a small child and none matching Leezel Wolf's description."

"What if we're too early?" China asked. "What if we're already too late? What if—"

"China, stop it." Maverick squeezed her fingers tightly as Alex turned the vehicle onto the bridge. "We are getting Kyrie back. Trust me. Okay?"

She stared, taken aback by his harsh tone, and Maverick felt like an ass. Kyrie was everything to China, but her falling apart wouldn't help the situation. He needed her focused and thinking positive.

"Boss." Taylor's disembodied voice sounded in the car again. "North side. Just heard from police dispatch. Cab dropped off a woman in a red trench coat with a child matching Kyrie's description."

"Copy that," Alex replied. "Where?"

"North side. Dead center. Ah, Boss?"

"What?" Alex snapped.

"Don't lose that little girl."

"Not gonna happen," Alex replied in a gentler tone. "Keep the porch light on."

And there she was. Leezel had Kyrie in her arms on the north side of the bridge. Alex drove to the center of the east bound lanes and pulled his vehicle as far to the left shoulder as possible before he set the emergency lights. He turned to China. "You will stay in the car."

"No, I won't! Let me go. Leezel will kill her." She already had the door open and one foot to the ground, twisting her hand to get out of Maverick's hold.

Maverick gripped her fingers tighter, needing her to stay with Alex. A span of maybe ten to fifteen feet divided the east and west bound lanes. The cold Potomac lay below. There was no way to make a U-turn, no way to get to the other side of the bridge without jumping the spans. Or die trying.

Only when Alex exited the vehicle and intercepted China did Maverick let go of her hand. "You got her, Boss?"

"Go!" Alex ordered. "Get the girl!"

"My baby!" China screamed, fighting Alex with all she had. "Let me go."

Maverick didn't have time to make sure Alex had a good hold on China before he ran. With a flying leap, he cleared the concrete barrier and the open span. Adrenaline propelled him.

Traffic screeched to a halt just as he landed solid in the left lane of astonished westbound drivers. Horns honked. Some idiot cussed. But Maverick kept going.

He dodged the first two lanes of west bound traffic. More horns blared. Other drivers cursed his lineage. He kept going. Leezel had already spotted him, but she had spotted the rest of The TEAM, too. Maverick didn't have a clue what they were doing behind him. No doubt setting up their rifles and preparing to take a kill shot if it came to that.

God, just shoot her, Gabe. Blow her head off. Send her back to hell where she belongs. Now, before she hurts that little girl.

The smell of the river filled the air. Gulls hovered and screeched overhead. A Potomac River charter boat slipped above the waves on its way to National Harbor while Maverick dodged the last four lanes between him and Leezel.

Finally, he cleared the concrete barrier between the traffic and the walkway.

Leezel had backed up to the metal barrier at the edge of the bridge with her daughter clutched on her hip. Poor Kyrie's frightened face paled against the fiery red of Leezel's coat. The little tyke still wore the pink pajamas Kelsey had bought her. Tears streamed down her wind-chapped cheeks. She reached for him. "Unca Mavwick!"

Leezel grabbed her daughter's head, her mouth in Kyrie's ear. Maverick couldn't hear the words, but he saw the impact. Kyrie bit her lip and cried, but she didn't make another sound. Neither did she break eye contact with him.

"See you got my message, *Mav.*" Leezel looked amazingly good for a psychotic killer, all dressed in red again right down to those damned sequined heels. Her dark mascara wasn't smudged, but the edge to her voice gave her away.

"What's this about, Leezel? What do you want?"

"I just want my little girl here." Leezel planted her scarlet lips against the side of Kyrie's tear-drenched face, her eyes fixed on him. "That's all."

He took one step toward her, but she edged away. She nodded her chin toward the other agents across the bridge. "Call your friends off. Do it."

"Why are we out here? There are better places to talk." He took another step.

Her eyes sparked with anger. "So now you wanna talk, huh? I don't think so. Do as I said. Call 'em off."

His gaze shifted to Kyrie. Frightened blue eyes stabbed him.

"Now!" Leezel shook her daughter like a ragdoll. "I'm done playing. Tell 'em all to back off or she goes swimming." Kyrie whimpered, but Leezel only shook her harder. "Shut up!"

Maverick glanced over his shoulder to where Alex and China stood on the opposite side of the span. The Maryland state police had joined them. Two officers were in position and ready to fire. A news helicopter hovered overhead. Traffic had come to a standstill. Gabe wasn't in sight, but Mark and Rory were set up and poised to shoot, too.

Maverick had no choice. He signaled them all to stand down.

Chapter Thirty-Six

Leezel seemed to calm, but her eyes were still fixed on the scene behind him. "You sure run with some good-lookin' hunks. Them your friends?"

"Yes." Maverick took a step closer, but that only incited Leezel to shift Kyrie's little backside onto the cold metal guardrail. The little girl's eyes widened at the river far below. Instinctively she arched forward, trying desperately to lean away from the edge. "Mommy!"

"No!" Maverick reached for Kyrie, but Leezel laughed, tipping the child farther backward.

"Stay where you are. One more step and I drop her."

Kyrie jerked forward. "Mommy! I fawin'!"

"Don't do it!" His heart lurched to his throat. He reached his palms forward without advancing. "God, Leezel. What do you want? Money? I can get you whatever you want. Let me have Kyrie, and I swear, you can have whatever you want. I can make you rich."

Leezel shook her head. "That's not how this is gonna go down. You oughta know that by now. 'Sides, money isn't everything, is it? Sure didn't work out too well for Troy."

"Then what do you want? Kyrie's your daughter, Leezel. For God's sake, she's just a baby." He counted the distance between him and Leezel. Eight feet. Maybe nine. If she dropped Kyrie, he could clear the rail in two seconds flat and hit the water in time to save the baby. He knew he could—if the fall didn't kill them.

Leezel let go of one of Kyrie's hands, immediately throwing the poor girl off-balance again. Her curly hair swung in the breeze. "Unca Mavwick!" she screamed, her free arm flailing to grab her mother.

Leezel let her slip over the rail until Kyrie hung to it by her knees. Only Leezel's hand at her wrist kept the frantic girl from slipping over. She flailed at empty air. "Unca Mavwick! I fawing! I fawing! Hewp me!"

"God! Leezel! Stop it!" Maverick screamed, too. "Let me have her! What do you want, damn it?"

"You're gonna make me do this, aren't you?"

Her eerie calmness angered him. His fists stayed clenched and useless at his side. He debated charging her, knocking her out of the way to save Kyrie.

Right on cue Leezel did something he hadn't expected. She swung one high-heeled foot over the four-foot high railing and straddled it, still gripping Kyrie's wrist.

The girl assumed her mother meant to save her. She latched onto Leezel's coat sleeve with her free hand. Leezel scraped the child's fingers off. "Get off! Don't touch me again!"

Kyrie lurched backwards. "Mommy! I scared! Mommy!"

"Kyrie!" Maverick's heart all but stopped. He focused on the baby. She had to believe with all of her heart that he would save her. That he couldn't fail. "Hang on, baby. Look at me, honey. I'm coming for you."

"No, you're not." Leezel's snide bark cut him off. "You won't catch my baby because I won't let you. She's going to fall, and then she's—"

"No!" Maverick roared, crazy with desperation, his eyes glued to Kyrie's. "I'm coming for you. I promise, baby. I won't—"

"Don't you hear me? You. Can't. Help. Her! I'll drop her and you get to watch her fall like everyone else!"

Kyrie's sad eyes pierced him through the metal guardrails. For that split second, it was just Kyrie and Maverick. He sent her his unspoken promise. *Don't listen to her. I'll save you. Trust me. Believe me. Hold on.*

Leezel tipped her head back and laughed. "God, I've waited for this day for a long time. Free! I'll finally be free!"

Maverick couldn't tear his eyes off the girl. Time was running out, but worse, she would fall no matter what happened now. Leezel didn't want anything but the pain she would cause the two people who loved Kyrie. He planned accordingly, his mind made up.

There is no try. Only do. Well, he would do.

Stupid Leezel balanced on the rail, straddling it with one leg on each side but neither secured. If only she had wedged one of those spiky heels or her foot between the vertical rails, she would've been more stable, but no. This had nothing to do with safety. She teetered back and forth as if it were a fun game, using Kyrie's weight and feeble knee grip on the slippery rail as her only source of fulcrum support.

Her gaze shifted to the other side of the bridge again. "I see my sister over there with your friend, that handsome guy. Who is he?"

Maverick was speechless. He couldn't take his eyes off Kyrie. Her long hair dangled in the breeze. The little girl was having trouble breathing through her fear. She gasped, hiccupped and choked while her arm stroked the air for something—anything!—to grab hold of.

"Mav! Listen to me." Leezel jerked Kyrie's arm up enough to terrorize the child. "I asked who is he?"

"Alex!" Pure adrenaline shot up his spine. "My boss. God, stop it!"

"He the guy who helped you steal my baby?"

"He's the man who helped me rescue Kyrie and China."

"Huh." Leezel's voice took on a detached tone. She stared across the highway where Alex stood with China. Maverick edged closer, hoping for a handhold on that baby, but Leezel's eyes zeroed back to him. "What the hell line of work are you in anyway, cowboy? Male strippers?"

"We're ex-military, Leezel. Most of us were Marines. Some soldiers. Some of us served in Afghanistan together." He hoped something he said might get through to her hard heart.

"I seen you last night, ya know. You and Sis looked all sorts of cozy in bed together. I coulda killed you both."

Maverick ran a desperate hand over his head. So. She had seen them. There wasn't much he could do about that. God, he had never felt so helpless.

"You think your boss would kiss me?" Leezel nodded her chin toward Alex again.

"Is that what this is all about?" Maverick took a step toward Leezel. "God, I'll kiss you right here and now. Just don't drop her, Leezel. Please, don't do this."

"Come kiss me then." She lowered her voice to a breathy, seductive tone. She wiggled.

He went to her, intent on grabbing Kyrie before her demented mother changed her mind. He was nearly there when—

"Oops." Leezel let go of her daughter.

"No!" China's panicked shriek pierced the morning breeze.

Kyrie fell, both hands clutching nothing but air, and Maverick flew, his arms outstretched to catch the impossible pass of a lifetime. There was no way she would fall without him.

Leezel lunged at him, but in that single second of lunacy, she lost her balance. She fell.

He expected nothing but air, but grabbed the railing just in time. There she was. Poor little Kyrie. Clinging by her fingertips to the concrete ledge beneath the railing he was damned near hanging over. Terrified blue eyes lanced his.

"Wait, wait, wait! I'm coming, baby. Hang on." He climbed over the rail, gripping a vertical post for support and stretching every last muscle to rescue Kyrie. The ledge wasn't wide enough to accommodate the width of his boots. He crouched as low as he could. Still no good. "Don't fall, Kyrie."

God, please don't fall. It will kill China if we lose you. Hell, it will kill me.

He couldn't get to her! In order to reach him, she would have to let go of the ledge, but the poor thing was too little to take the chance. Her eyes rolled wild with fright. "Unca Mavwick! Huwwy. Save me."

"Almost got you, baby," he said, but *sonofabitch! I can't reach her!*

"Maverick, grab my hand! Now! I'm falling to, you know," Leezel ordered.

Only then did he notice her hanging by her elbows and both hands to the same concrete ledge as her daughter, her eyes just as frightened. Her demand just as desperate. She reached five long, red fingernails toward him, but the simple movement threatened her hold. She replaced her hand to the ledge, for a minute stable, but with her feet swinging back and forth. Her grip slipped. "Don't just stand there, you asshole. Pull me up."

Maverick chose Kyrie instead. He slipped out of his boots and let them fall. He extended every muscle to reach her until he was barely holding onto the railing by his fingertips.

Just a little more. Just half an inch more, and—

Kyrie's right hand slipped completely off the ledge. She couldn't grab hold of his fingers anymore if she tried. "Unca Mavwick," she said quietly.

He willed her, the wind, and everything in the sonofabitchin' universe to keep her from letting go, but he also saw the look in her eyes. Even a five-year-old knows when she's going to die. "I'm right here, baby. Don't let go. I'm not going to let you fall. Hang on."

She cried softly. "I reawwy scared."

God, me, too. "Don't look down. Look at me. Don't let—"

"Mav! For hell's sake, I'm falling, too," Leezel snarled.

He didn't even look at her. Only Kyrie. A gust of wind from the Potomac below had lifted her little body up and her chances were gone. Maverick released the vertical rail, for a second suspended like Kyrie. If she was falling, he was going with her.

The wind pushed her toward him, but not close enough. He leaned into the air and grabbed hold of her flailing hand. With one fell swoop, he pulled her in tight and clasped her snug into his chest. She would not fall alone into the cold dark waters below.

"Hang onto me, baby. I've got you now," he whispered; content to die because she would live. He vowed it with every fiber of his heart. It was only seventy feet. He might not survive the fall, but she would. The wind whipped her black hair into his face, but he had her, damn it. He closed his eyes and let the wind take him. Kyrie would live, and China would be happy again. Only—

BAM!

A vicious jerk halted his forward momentum. *Shit.* It damned near pulled his head off.

"You crazy sonofabitch," Alex cursed in his ear.

Instead of falling, Maverick found himself suspended by two sets of grappling hooks latched to his belt and back pockets. The human kind of grappling hooks. The kind with hairy knuckles. The kinds attached to the strong arms of ex-Marines. His brothers.

Alex and Gabe dragged him and Kyrie back over the rail, scraping his back and butt as his feet flailed for solid ground. He held her in a suffocating grip, his hands in her hair and hanging on tight. She sobbed her heart out, but damn it. She was safe. And so, by hell, was he.

"Got you, buddy," Gabe ground out, panting a blue streak while he pushed Maverick to the ground and held him there. "You kids aren't going anywhere. Not without me. Damn you, Carson. Do not EVER try a stupid stunt like that again! You hear me?"

Gabe sounded a lot like a drill sergeant, only scared. Maverick could have laughed if he hadn't been just as scared as his buddy. He blew out a huge breath while adrenaline turned his insides to pure crap. Kyrie clung to him like a little spider monkey, her nails dug into the skin at his neck and her face buried in his shirt. She shook as much as he did, but damn it to hell. Staring up at the blue sky was one helluva lot better view than looking down at the gray Potomac.

"Maverick!" Leezel shrieked.

Gabe eased the crying child out of Maverick's grip. "Come on, baby. Let's take you to see Andy China."

Maverick pushed up from the ground. His legs were weak as hell and shaky, but rescuing Leezel would be easier. She was stronger and had a better grip on the ledge. When he peered over the guard rail, the wind toyed with her, but she was still resting on her forearms. Plus, her red heels had fallen. She was barefoot, better able to scramble up once he had a hold of her. Her red coat still flapped in the breeze like a damned declaration of her stupidity, though.

Alex gripped his arm and belt.

"You got me, Boss?" he asked before he did anything stupid.

"Now you ask?" Alex muttered sarcastically. "Just don't fall. I hate swimming in the Potomac, and if I have to dive in after you, I might drown you myself."

Enough said.

Maverick proceeded with his second rescue of the day. He reached for China's sister. "Grab hold. Come on. It's your turn. You can do it. Let's go home and have a tall one," he coaxed to give her incentive.

She didn't answer, and for a second, he thought she was just plain scared. He sure as hell was. He hadn't noticed the distance to the river until now. Seventy feet was a helluva long drop.

A Coast Guard cruiser waited nearby, all hands on deck.

"Come on," he ordered again, his fingers almost in reach of those fake fingernails. "I'll save you. Don't worry. I won't let you fall."

With a lurch, she grabbed hold of his wrist with one hand, her other arm still supporting her weight on the ledge. And God, she was killing him. He hadn't re-bandaged his burned hands or wrists after making love with China. He hadn't even felt the pain when he rescued Kyrie, but now? Leezel's grip was skinning him alive.

"Good." He encouraged her, despite the slimy sensation that she had pulled the skin off his wrist and hand. He gritted his teeth and clamped down on his lip. *Almost there.* "Real good. Don't let go," he growled, "you hear? Lift one knee onto the ledge, and you're home free. Alex and I'll haul you up."

It was an easy enough feat. She wasn't a big woman, and he had a solid grip on her. She had a solid grip, too. It was the best hold possible. No way could she fall.

The look on her face startled him. Her panicked eyes had gone vacant. The light gone. "You think *you've* got *me*?"

"I do," he answered, bewildered she would ask. "Of course I've got you. Up you go. Keep trying. Get one knee on the ledge. Hurry. Let's go home."

The morning sun glinted off her brassy short hair. She shook her head. Instead of hoisting herself onto the ledge, instead of trying to help herself—she let go.

"What the hell?" Maverick lunged forward to adjust to the sudden shift of dead weight at the end of his arm.

Alex grunted while Leezel dangled. She swung out over the river, her bare feet kicking in the breeze, and her free hand loose at her side.

"Damn it!" Maverick dug his fingernails into her wrist, struggling for a better grip. "I've still got you. We can do this. Take my hand again! Come on. You can do it." He let go of the railing and reached for her, but the hollow, blank shadow in her gaze chilled him to the bone.

"You really do love her, don't you?" she asked, her tone as empty as her eyes.

Maverick didn't answer, just kept on holding on. Leezel would *not* die. Not like this. Not today.

She lifted her other arm upward and like a fool he reached for her, but—

Shit! A flash of silver sliced his forearm. Bright red blood spurted down his wrist and over the fingers gripping her. "Leezel! Damn it! What'd you do that for?"

With a crooked sneer, she reached up and cut him again.

He refused to let her go. With all his might, he clenched his bloody fingers tighter, trying desperately to hook into her hand muscle and bones—anything!—to keep her from falling.

From out of nowhere, Rory joined him on the same narrow ledge, but there was no way he could reach her, either. Time was running out.

The blood provided a warm, slick lubrication that defied traction. Maverick growled for all he was worth, sure as hell not going to let this woman die on his watch. Crazy or not, she was family. Whatever mental illness she had, he could get help for her.

"You were supposed to love me," she said, the breeze spinning her back and forth, her coat furled behind her like a cape.

"Don't do this," Maverick begged. "Please. I can still save you. Try, damn it!"

"But I left you a note."

"What?" He didn't understand. Then, oh yeah. The stupid note. "You're right, Leezel. I'm going to miss you when you're gone. I get it now. All of us will miss you."

"No, you won't. No one will. Not my sister. Not my daughter. Not even me." She winked once, her eyes dead and flat. She jerked her arm and dead weight won. She slipped through his bloody fingers and Leezel Wolf fell.

"No!" Maverick lunged after her, but all he could do was watch her drop, the red coat cocooned around her like a death shroud. With barely a splash, she hit the Potomac. Leezel sank below the choppy waves without a struggle.

"God! No!" The image of her falling burned into his memory. Her eyes. Her last words—a curse he would never forget.

Strong hands dragged him over the railing. He dropped to his knees. Adrenaline hummed in his ears along with Leezel's poisonous promise. *You're gonna miss me when I'm gone.*

"I could have saved you!" he cried, his nose to the concrete and bile creeping up his throat. "Why, Leezel? Why?"

Alex thumped his shoulder hard. Rory, too.

But the concrete never answered.

China and Kyrie barreled into him, both clutching his neck while he tried to zero his soul and heart on what truly mattered. While he tried to save himself from all that despair again.

All he could see was Leezel, the bright reflection of the sun off the river at her back. The flutter of red around her as she fell. The knowledge that she had chosen poorly. There at the end, he saw the truth. She was just like him. Running scared. Beyond reach or rescue, but still afraid to die.

I could've saved you. Why didn't you let me?

"Maverick," China cried, but there was no comfort to be had. She and Kyrie gripped him in a stranglehold, but he could barely think.

He wrapped his arms around them. Kyrie sobbed under his chin, and finally he heard the sad, soft lament of the women in his life. They loved him and he let their love reach into his heart. He let it wash over him and through him. He let it save him.

He sunk his face into their hair and he took a tortured breath. China's lips caressed his forehead, and he let her magic into his soul. His heart. There would be no more long walks across country to escape this grief. No more running away from the hard knocks of life. This time, he let the darkness go before it choked the goodness.

He chose life.

Chapter Thirty-Seven

The construction paper picture propped up on the bale of hay caught him by surprise.

The biggest crayon person in the cowboy hat was obviously China. Any dumb jock could see that. Her hair consisted of one continuous black strand that draped from her toes over her head and down the other side of her stick body. The bright blue eyes were a giveaway, too.

Maverick smiled to himself. He had to be the second-largest figure, because that stick person had a black baseball cap on its head and dark glasses with the stems hanging in the air next to the head where the ears might have been. If the artist had thought to draw ears.

But the remaining two figures made him grin. For sure the black-haired, little stick girl in the pink crayon dress was Kyrie, but he could only guess which of his friends with red and brown curly hair had been drawn holding her hand. The little girl's finger sported a black line with bright yellow rays extending from it like sparkles. All the figures' faces were filled with red lips and big smiles.

Happy Fathrs Day was written proudly across the top in lovely five-year-old penmanship. He had come to the barn to muck stalls and instead he'd gotten the gift of a lifetime. His first Father's Day gift.

He pushed back his ball cap and dropped to the nearest bale of hay just to get a grip. Kyrie had easily resorted to calling China *Mommy* after they'd sat her down and explained that from now on, they were her new mommy and daddy. For whatever reason, calling Maverick *Daddy* didn't come as easy. She attempted it a few times, but always resorted back to *Mavwick*. It didn't matter. It would happen in due time.

He listened to the gentle sounds of Percherons in the back pasture. Good ol' Star hung his head over the lower half of the birthing stall door, still keeping track of the newest arrival at Wild Wolf East. The big fellow seemed more like a faithful dog than a horse. Whenever Maverick was out in the field or with the herd for any reason, the horse was sure to follow. He nickered as he stood watch.

Crystal Love had come into the world in the wee hours of the morning. Even now her proud mama, Sunshine, kept careful guard. She was a nervous mare and this was her first foal, but Crystal Love was already nursing and rambunctious. Maverick had been there when the other mares dropped their foals, but when this particular little miss made her debut, he embarrassed himself and bawled like a baby. Despite her bay coloring, she had reminded him of another foal and another time. Another life.

This barn held a magic all its own. This was where he hid out at times, hugged his Ovation to his chest and sang to his brother. He lifted it out of its case and let the latest remembrance roll out of his heart. He'd finally gotten the song right. Darrell had to be listening. Maybe smiling down from heaven at the latest love song Maverick had written to his kid brother.

Heroes

Little boys turn into heroes in imaginary ways,
Fighting Indians and cowboys. Desperados. Jesse James.
You were always right beside me when we'd ride out on the
range,
When we'd hear the thunder coming, we were braver than
the rain.

We'd sing one one-thousand, two one-thousand,
Three one-thousand, four;
Lightning crashing all around us,
Two brave heroes off to war.
Wyatt Earp and all his brothers,
They had nothing on us,
Let the thunder do its damnedest,
We were braver than the storm.

Little boys turn into men one day, no battle left undone,
Fighting real no-kidding monsters. Keeping evil on the run.
Full of righteous wrath and honor. Invincibility!
We were brave. We were courageous being all that we could
be.

Now I look into the sky at night, a new tempest on its way,
I can hear the thunder coming. Another war. Another day.
But I hear your proud 'Oo-rah' 'longside the Warriors on
high!
You were never one for running. I finally know why.

I sing one one-thousand, two one-thousand,
Three one-thousand, four;
I'm so damned proud of you, brother,
Still hell bent on heaven's war.
Give 'em hell where e'er you find 'em,
'S why there's lightning in the sky.
You're still brave, you're still courageous and truly Semper Fi.
Let the thunder do its damnedest...
It can't drown out Semper Fi.

God, it felt good to remember Darrell with stars in his eyes again. Fighting the good fight. Living his dream. Saving decent folks from evil men. Maverick strummed a few more chords, resigned to live the life he had been given instead of wishing it were different. Darrell surely understood. A man can't ask for more than to die doing what he loved.

"Semper Fi, baby brother," he whispered. "Give 'em hell for me, too."

The barn door creaked open.

"Is you in here?" Kyrie peeked into the dark barn tucked away in the northeast corner of the Shenandoah Valley.

"Over here." He waved her on in and set his guitar aside.

She bounded onto his lap like a little kangaroo with Puppy fast on her heels. Planting a noisy kiss on his cheek, she said, "Happy Fader's Day! Why is you cryin'?"

He wiped his face. "Just got some dust in my eyes, that's all."

She snuggled under his chin. "Do you yike my pitcher?"

"Yes, I do. You're quite the artist."

She scrunched her shoulders, suddenly shy. Her speech pathologist had made some progress with her, but Kyrie still struggled with her old habits, and he didn't correct her. She would get there in her own good time. For now, she needed a stable life and all the assurance he and China could offer.

"I drawed it by mysewf."

"It's the best picture anyone ever made for me." He kissed the top of her curly head.

Her nightmares over the incident at the bridge were fewer and farther between. His, too. The memory of Leezel's flat dead eyes still haunted him, but he had accepted there was nothing more he could've done.

China and he talked long into the night sometimes, both coming to the conclusion they weren't responsible for their siblings decisions. Leezel had made her choices the same way Darrell had made his. They were both the youngest in the family and both hell bent on their particular missions in life. Darrell's just happened to be a helluva lot more honorable.

In her crazy state of mind, Leezel intended her death to hurt the people who loved her. The sad truth was that it did, for a while. Once they'd buried her alongside Jefferson, Celeste, and her baby sister in far off Wyoming, the grief turned into peace. She was finally home, and she could never hurt anyone again. Even herself.

The proof that life had gotten better at the Wild Wolf was Kyrie. With her mother laid to rest and her sperm-donor father behind bars, she had turned into a happy girl who liked nothing more than to go to princess parties with her girlfriend, Lexie. Of course, there were other agents' daughters to play with, too—JayJay and Faith Houston; LiLi, Song, and Miki Lennox: Jamie Maher; or Chai Yenn Tao. That was one definite plus to living and working in Virginia. Maverick's work family became Kyrie's extended family. Her social life expanded exponentially.

It didn't hurt when Reardon readily relinquished his parental rights. Maverick and China had already seen their lawyer and a judge. Kyrie finally had a real mother and a real father. Maybe not by blood, but by something a helluva lot better. By heart.

"What's this?" Maverick pointed at the black mark with yellow sparkles on the little girl stick figure's finger.

"You know. It's a wing. Umm, I mean a r-r-ring." She blushed with a wiggle in his arms, enunciating that difficult letter *R*.

"A ring?" he teased. "And just who did you marry this time?"

"Unca Gabe."

"Oh, my little Kyrie." He kissed her forehead. "Who are you going to marry next?"

She beamed. "I wike him."

"Who don't you like?"

"Ebryone," she said as coyly as ever. He knew what she meant.

"Where's your mother?"

"Right here." China stepped through the rear barn door leading Star. "This guy needs to leave Sunshine alone for awhile. I'm putting him in his stall. You miss me?"

"Always." Truer words were never spoken. "Come here, Mrs. Carson."

She settled Star into his stable, peeled her gloves off and joined Maverick and Kyrie on his bale of hay. Her eyes glowed at the sight of his present. "Ah. I see you found it. Kyrie could hardly wait to give it to you."

He couldn't speak without getting emotional, so he smoothed the picture against his knee to keep her from seeing his watery eyes. This one little hand-drawn piece of artwork meant more than he could've guessed. He finally had all he had ever wanted—a happy life and a family to call his own. Funny. With China it seemed like so much more.

She leaned back to pull a box out from behind the bales of hay. "For you," she said as she placed it in his hands.

Kyrie wiggled out of the way, her blue eyes lit with excitement. "Open it."

He grunted. He already had what he wanted. Didn't need anything else to make him happy.

"Go on. Open it," Kyrie urged again, her fingers clenching and unclenching to *hewp*.

He slid the lid off and grunted again. A Stetson. Brown. Teardrop crease with a braided leather band.

Maverick doffed his ball cap and peered into it at the two faces still smiling back at him after all these miles. Both in cammies. Both surprised as hell they'd come together in the middle of godawful Afghanistan. Two brothers in arms. Two sons of their mother's heart.

Darrell and me.

Only Darrell wasn't the one who had gotten lost. Not by a long shot. It was big brother Maverick who'd forgotten how to live. Who'd forgotten how to put the past behind him. Who'd forgotten how to get back into the saddle. Damned good advice from a crusty, old cowboy named Zeke.

Maverick hung his well-travelled cap on a nail sticking out of the nearby post. He was lucky it escaped the fire back at Wild Wolf West, but its days were done. Finally.

With a deep breath, he lifted the Stetson out of its container and tugged it over his head. Damned thing fit like a glove.

"Does you wike it?" Kyrie asked, her fingers folded under her chin and her brows lifted high with excitement. "Umm," she fidgeted, blinking because she knew she hadn't spoken correctly. "I mean do – you – like – it?"

He hugged her into his side. "I knew what you meant, sweetheart, and yes, I do like it. I like it a lot." He kissed her forehead. "In fact, young lady, I love it so much I'm going to keep my very first Father's Day present inside of it. Would that be okay with you?"

She clapped her hands, her eyes full of stars. "I hewped Mommy pick it out," but then she scrunched her nose and said extra-carefully, "That's a funny pah-lace to keep a pwes, umm, a pr-r-res-s-sent."

Her striving so hard to speak properly touched his heart. This little girl. Now his daughter. Every time he picked her up to ride on his shoulder he recalled the day he had nearly lost her, and he thanked God for the miracle that he didn't. Kyrie deserved a chance at life.

He folded the Maverick Carson family picture once and then again before he removed his Stetson and tucked it inside. The tables had turned. Darrell didn't need his big brother worrying over him anymore. He was already home, safe and sound. Now it was China and Kyrie's turn.

"Why don't you see if you can find those new kittens?" he asked his darling daughter. "I think I saw their mama with them before."

That was all the encouragement that Kyrie needed. She slid off the bale of hay and scampered away with a drawn out, "He-r-r-re kitty, kitty."

China leaned against his arm, her index finger under his chin, gently angling his face toward hers. "I figured it was time you had a new hat, cowboy. You've worn your old one out."

Maverick gathered her in tight against him. "I'm not a cowboy."

She tipped the Stetson back an inch or two. "Yes, you are. I hate to admit it, but Leezel was right. You are a cowboy. You might not say much, but when you talk, people listen. You're fearless and brave and, oh yeah, you're a softie."

Maverick shrugged. He didn't know if it was Leezel dying the way she did, or the total commitment of this sweet woman at his side, but he had turned into a pantywaist crybaby over the past couple of months. He had so much to be thankful for. And he was, but for some reason that tough, old heart in his chest had been tenderized beyond his control.

Maverick ran the back of his hand over his eyes, fighting for composure. Everywhere he looked was contentment and peace, even at work. No one said a thing when he showed up at the office. Alex didn't even blink. Taylor nodded as if he'd only been gone a day. Gabe grinned. And that was that.

China didn't buy her horses back from Alex, either. After the bunkhouse burned and Reardon and his gang were arrested, Sheriff Hammer located the cashier's checks on a desk inside the partially burned ranch house. Alex groused about not getting to keep the horses that he had bought fair and square, but even that was nonsense. China's kiss on his cheek mellowed him right out.

Another shining speck of karma had followed Maverick home. Gabe couldn't wait to share the news. It seemed while Maverick traipsed about the countryside, Junior Agent Landon Truman, the liar who'd ruined Maverick's engagement to his cheating fiancée, Kim, came up against the granite wall who'd built The TEAM.

Alex.

It seemed Landon *neglected* to mention the single civilian injury he had caused during a risky op inside the Republic of Chile. Big mistake.

Everyone knew Alex's hard line on collateral damage, but covering it up? *Bigger* mistake. After a butt chewing most of Alexandria had to have heard, Alex handed Landon his walking papers and told him to get his ass out of there.

Whether out of loyalty or sheer stupidity, Junior Agent Lisa Channing, the woman Landon had cheated with while he was married to Kim, quit The TEAM and followed him out the door. Guess Lisa had to learn the hard way. Once a cheater, always a cheater. Good riddance.

Despite Leezel's curse, life at Wild Wolf East was damned good. The birth of Crystal Love proved it. It didn't hurt when Kyrie bounced into Maverick and China's bed early in the morning just because she was glad to see them, either.

He wiped his eyes, damn it. Not able to get a grip.

"X and Z are flying in today." China leaned into his shoulder, her hand gentle on his chest. She eased a couple fingers between two snaps on his western shirt, and he was glad for the touch of her fingertips on his bare chest. China could calm him like no other woman on earth. Just waking up next to her every morning centered him for the day. Playing with her delicious body before breakfast didn't hurt, either.

"Good." He blew out a big sigh to get his emotions under control. Gabe and Shelby would pick the two hired hands up from the airport. Maverick was thankful for that, too. He would probably break down in front of his friends the moment they arrived, and those two old geezers didn't need to see that.

"They're going to love the new bunkhouse you built for them."

He nodded. They'd better. He installed air conditioning, a huge big-screen television and a sauna for Z's arthritis. Plus, he stocked the fridge with beer, fresh turkey sandwiches for their first meal and enough food to last a month. *What's not to love?*

Two oblong stones with similar etchings now graced the front entry of the stately colonial in Shenandoah. Both declared *Frend* to all who entered. China's birdbath with the copper stallion stood in a flowerbed of bee balm and rosemary between the stones. Xavier Allbright would be tickled to death to see his artwork displayed. Between him and Kyrie, every stray kitten in the neighborhood would be well snuggled and cared for. Cat Haven at Wild Wolf East was open for business, alive and well.

China wrapped her arms around Maverick's neck and pulled him into her lips. "Are you ever going to play something on that old guitar for me?"

He nodded. "Sure. What would you like to hear?"

"One of those songs you've been working on. I like the one you were just singing. The one for Darrell."

"You heard me?"

"Of course. You have a strong, deep voice. I'm always listening to you." She pressed a kiss on his cheek. "You know what I think you need?" she muttered suggestively against his mouth before she nibbled on his lower lip. "S. E. X."

He nodded. Yes. Sex with China was certainly at the top of his to-do list every day. Spending quiet time with her cured most of his problems. He pulled her tight, content to feel her feminine curves tucked against him, and an entirely different kind of a love song coming to life in the back of his mind. One about walking and Wyoming and falling in love with his reason to live. Yes. It was past time.

The smell of this woman's shampoo filled his nostrils with a hint of lavender and his heart with peace. A man could get used to this. He took a deep breath of hay and horse and his wife and let the quiet of the barn work its magic.

Kyrie bee-lined to the edge of the foaling stall where a tiny orange kitten had crawled out from a pile of loose hay. She scooped it up and pressed it under her chin. "Daddy! Look what I found!"

That did it. Maverick choked. He was surrounded by pretty girls. His pretty girls.

There was no stopping the tears now.

THE END

Sneak Preview of CASSIDY

Book 10
In the Company of Snipers

She woke. Face down. Palms to the floor. Too weak to lift her head.

With one eye swollen shut and blood in her nose, Junior Agent Cassidy Dancer's blurry view was limited to a murky stretch of damp, wooden planks. The vibrations beneath her aching body soothed as much as they worried. Her last coherent memory consisted of—stars.

Where am I?

The floor moved, that was why the vibrations. It creaked. It rattled. It smelled.

She groaned. *I'm in the back of a truck? Why?*

A glimmer of light reflected off something on the floor, blinding her one good eye. Her brain struggled to explain, at last providing the disgusting answer. Her nose twitched to confirm.

Oh, shit. I'm in a horse trailer. In a puddle. It's not water. Ewww.

She willed her body to roll out of the mess she had been dragged or thrown into. Not going to happen. The command center in her brain no longer controlled her limbs. The well-muscled biceps that could pump quick sets of push-ups on a good day failed her. Even her eyes felt crossed and unfocused, not the sharp vision of a highly trained covert agent at all. Not her finest moment.

Never one to cry or whine, she cursed her agent in charge instead. "Damn you, Rourke."

Her voice sounded too weak for the tough woman she was. The mission would have to wait. The filthy mess beneath her head galled her last nerve. The thought and feel of animal waste in her hair, on her cheek and seeping up into her ear, the coppery taste of her own blood, the sickening odor—

Argh! Too much! She squeezed her eyes tight and promised, *I will not throw up. I will not throw up.*

Wrong. She threw up. Now the mess was worse. Summoning every last shred of willpower, she borrowed Rourke's drill sergeant method of motivation. *Damn you, Dancer. Get your ass up and move. Don't just take it, you wuss. Do something about it.*

She couldn't. Just plain damned could not. Every muscle in her finely toned body had turned to lead. Still, she couldn't lie there one more minute, either.

Where there's a will, there's a way, right?

And Cassidy Dancer was very willful, right?

And everyone on The TEAM knew that, right?

For some deep, dark reason she didn't understand, cussing always helped during desperate times. "Son of a bitch," she ground out, her teeth clenched. Summoning every last vestige of her very hard-headed spirit, she...

Flopped over.

Damn. Never had doing so little reaped so much agony. Pain ratcheted down her neck all the way to her toes. A whimper escaped between her clenched jaws. Tears filled her eyes and dripped down the sides of that hard head, but she was out of the puddle. Hers and Mister Ed's.

What little air she could breathe in through her one open nostril still smelled as bad. Her heart hammered like a run away locomotive, but damn it. Nothing kept Cassidy Dancer down.

Something nearby shifted with the change in direction of the truck. First, to the left. Then, to the right. Not her. She kept her palms to the floor. For the moment, she had the mobility of concrete and intended to keep it that way.

Calming her wretched nausea took precedence until the trailer jerked to an abrupt stop. Its rear gate clanked, screeched, and fell to the ground, filling her box of a world with blinding sunlight. The floor moved as someone climbed aboard. Heavy footsteps shuffled toward her, stopping within inches of her nose. She kept her wits and feigned the smarts of a corpse.

"She alive?" a man asked.

Another male voice from the rear of the trailer grunted in reply.

Two men. Easy. I can take 'em.

"Git her outta here," the shuffler ordered. The grunter grunted again. Hands gripped her ankles, dragging her across the floor. Her resolved faltered. *Damn. Maybe, I can't take 'em. Yet.*

"Let's git her inside 'fore Jerusha and the kids see her," Shuffler muttered.

One pair of hard hands under her armpits and another pair at her ankles made the transfer. They didn't lift her high enough, though. They dragged her, as if she were too heavy. Her butt bumped along on the ground. Odd.

Out of the light and into the dark she went. The barn door banged shut. She expected to be dropped and discarded, but Shuffler and Grunter dragged her farther into the dark. When they finally stopped, they took extra care that her boots were side by side. Things went from really bad to a thousand times worse.

"Make 'em tight. He likes the belts extra snug," Shuffler ordered.

Her heartbeat kicked into overdrive. *Belts?*

Cracking her one good eyelid, she spared a quick look at her predicament. Lines of sunshine streaked between the wooden planks of the barn walls. A shadow danced across the light. Dust hung in the air. She had been laid on a slab of rough sawn timber, a board Shuffler and Grunter were crouched over her while they fastened a series of belts around her ankles, thighs, hips. Plain leather belts like the kind Dr. Frankenstein used when he created his monster. The kind a victim couldn't wiggle out of while...

Oh, shit. Her thousand-times-worse scenario had just nose-dived to damned scary. She gulped as another very real scenario emerged in the recesses of this very dark place where no one could hear her argue, cuss, or scream. *Torture.*

Thunder erupted in her chest.

"That oughta do it." Shuffler lifted to his feet. "She won't be going anywhere."

She closed her eye. The sound of Shuffler's and Grunter's footsteps receding brought instant relief. At least they didn't intend to torture her right away. She still had time. Cassidy blinked both eyes open, despite resistance from the swollen one. She needed all of her faculties, every last one of them.

Escape! Get up. Move!

Her mental commands had no effect.

Okay, I get it. Rest first. Breathe. Strategize. Then escape the hell out of here.

The fragrance of freshly baled alfalfa settled over her as the morning's miscalculation came back to mind. She had thought she was so smart, even smarter than Senior Agent Rourke O'Neill. He'd told her to stay put, but did she? No, she saw an opportunity and she took it.

Her hard-charging mindset usually paid off in dividends. Covert surveillance rewarded risk takers and fast thinkers. Not this time. The shovel she had been hit with brought enlightenment she'd literally not seen coming.

But really? How could she have known two Melissas belonged to this deranged cult? How bizarre that both Melissas were recently widowed and independently wealthy? How freaking coincidental they were both blond, that they looked alike?

Rourke's previous warning filled her mind. *One of these days, your bullheaded ways are going to get you in trouble, Butch.* How many times had she heard that before? Like a gazillion? The smart ass. Butch Cassidy, Rourke's nickname for the outlaw he claimed she was, the rebel who thought she knew everything.

Cassidy tried to recall her smart remark back at him, no doubt her usual, '*Yeah, whatever.*' But damn. Here she was bloodied, strapped to a board, and lucky the wrong Melissa used on her hadn't knocked her head off. Rourke might have been right.

She stretched her index finger, beckoning the door. Neither had a chance in hell of meeting. At this rate, neither did she nor her senior agent. Squeezing her eyes tightly shut, Cassidy sent a mental order to the only one in the world who could rescue her sorry butt.

Get me the hell outta here, Rourke!

Thank you for reading Maverick!

Be sure to check out the rest of the guys and gals of Irish Winters' series: *In the Company of Snipers*

Other Irish Winters' books:

King of Hearts, Deuces Wild Series, *#1*

Joker Joker, Deuces Wild Series, *#2*

Smoke, Hearts and Ashes Series, *#1*

Ash, Hearts and Ashes Series, *#2*

Coming soon!

Seth, In the Company of Snipers, *#17*

One-Eyed Jack, Deuces Wild Series, *#3*

YOU are the key to this book's success!

Please tell other readers why you liked Maverick and China's story by leaving an honest review at the retail site where you purchased it.
Recommend it to your friends. Lend it.
Most of all, enjoy it!

The best way to keep up with my new releases, giveaways, and actionable intel is to sign up for my spam-free newsletter at IrishWinters.com.

About the Author

Irish Winters is an award winning, Amazon best-selling author who, when she isn't writing, dabbles in poetry, grandchildren, and rarely (as in extremely rarely) the kitchen. More prone to be outdoors than in, she grew up the quintessential tomboy on a dairy farm in rural Wisconsin, spent her teenage years in the Pacific Northwest, but calls the Wasatch Mountains of Northern Utah home. For now.

She believes in making every day count for something, and follows the wise admonition of her mother to, "Look out the window and see something!"

Connect with Irish!
On Facebook: https://www.facebook.com/author.irishwinters
On Twitter: https://twitter.com/irishwinters1
Or at www. IrishWinters.com

www.ingramcontent.com/pod-product-compliance
Lightning Source LLC
Chambersburg PA
CBHW030354200726
48286CB00014B/1355